MANGA SHAKESPEARE®

THE MERCHANT OF VENICE

ADAPTED BY
RICHARD APPIGNANESI

ILLUSTRATED BY
FAYE YONG

Amulet Books, New York

PUBLISHER'S NOTE: This is a work of fiction. Names, characters, places, and incidents are either the product of the author's imagination or are used fictitiously, and any resemblance to actual persons, living or dead, business establishments, events, or locales is entirely coincidental.

Cataloging-in-Publication Data has been applied for and may be obtained from the Library of Congress.

ISBN: 978-0-8109-9717-2

Originally published in the U.K. by SelfMadeHero
(www.selfmadehero.com)

Illustrator: Faye Yong
Text Adaptor: Richard Appignanesi
Designer: Andy Huckle
Textual Consultant: Nick de Somogyi
Publisher: Emma Hayley

Printed and bound in China
10 9 8 7 6 5 4 3 2 1

ABRAMS
THE ART OF BOOKS SINCE 1949
115 West 18th Street
New York, NY 10011
www.abramsbooks.com

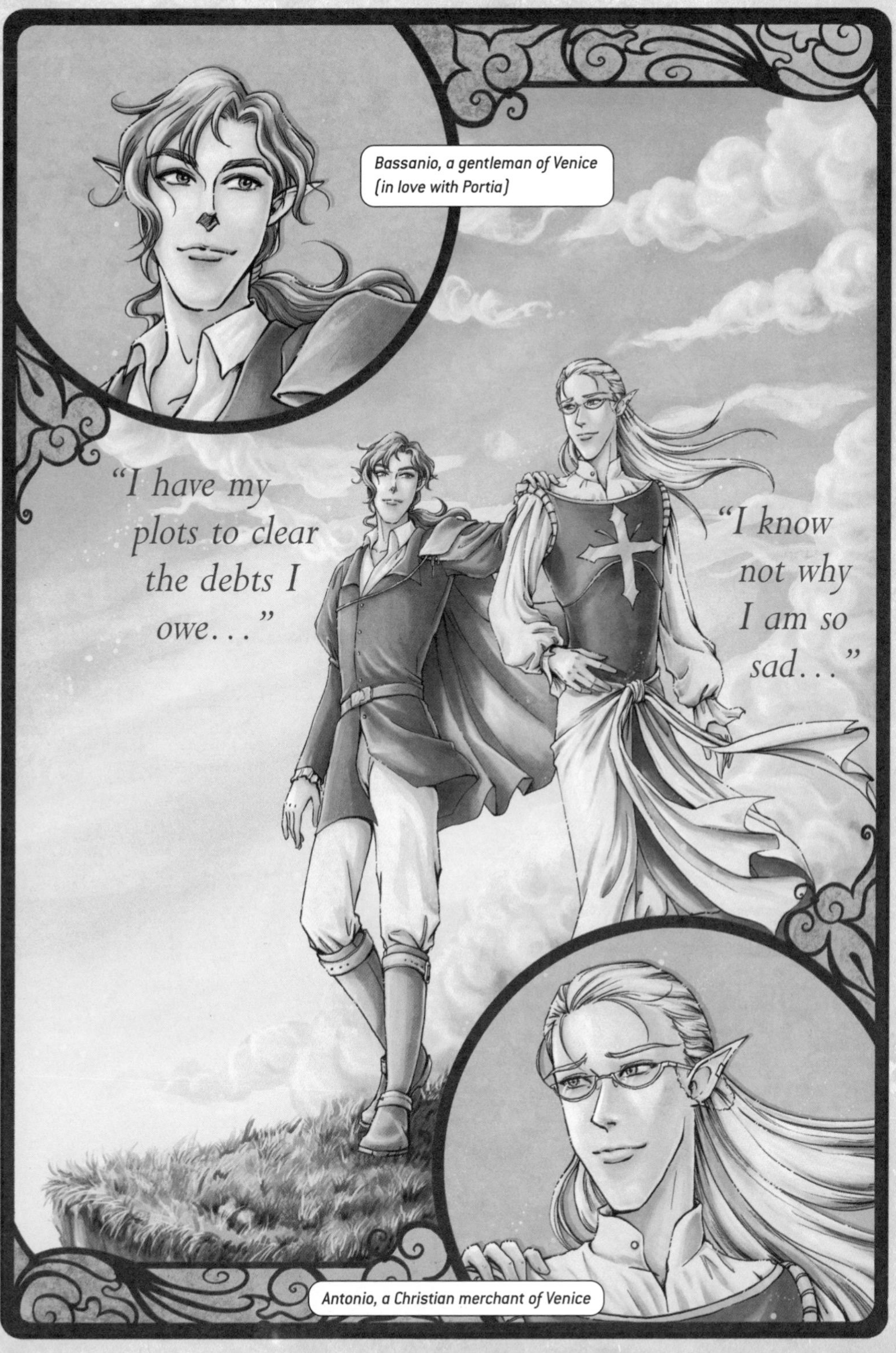
Bassanio, a gentleman of Venice (in love with Portia)
"I have my plots to clear the debts I owe…"
"I know not why I am so sad…"
Antonio, a Christian merchant of Venice

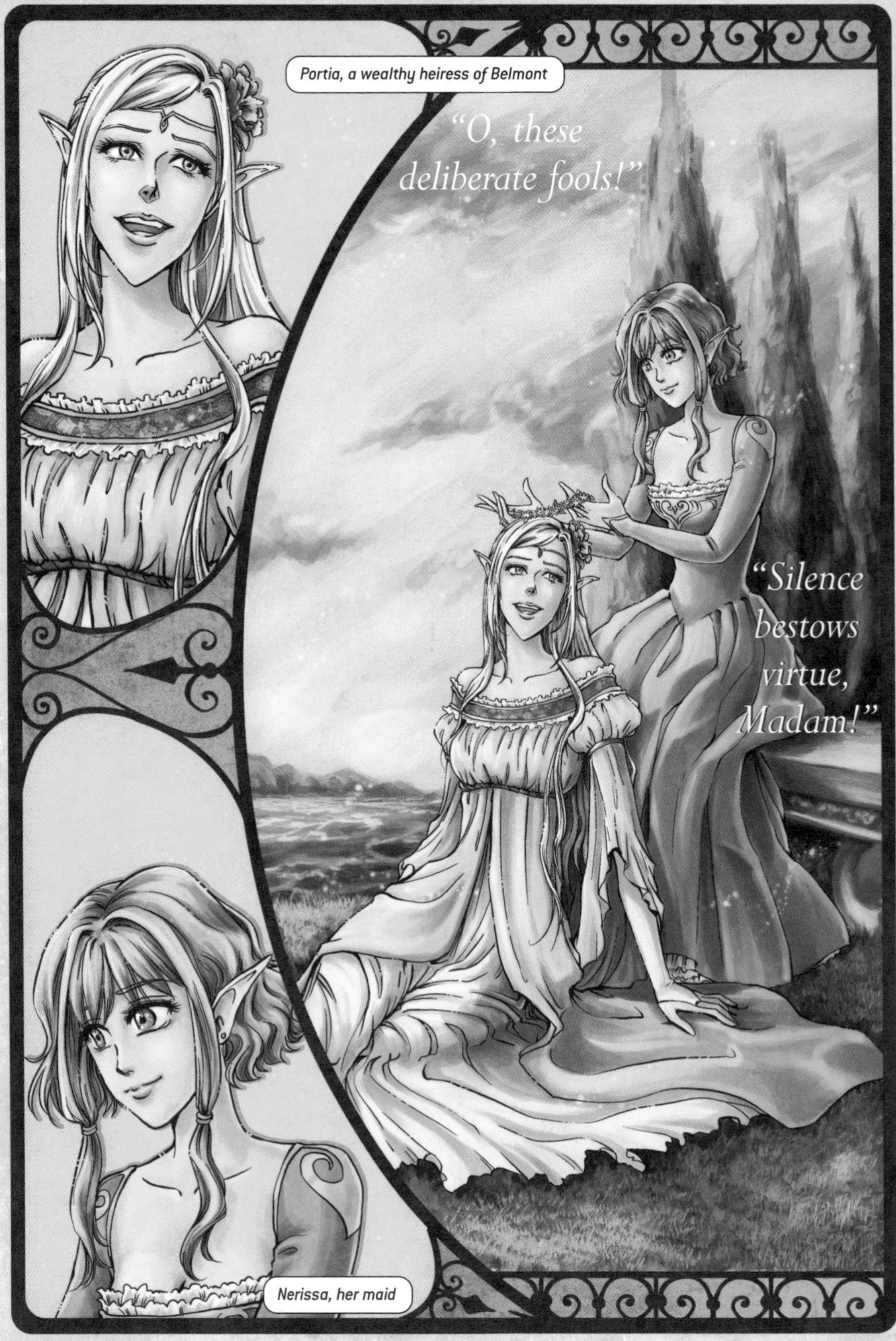
Portia, a wealthy heiress of Belmont
Nerissa, her maid
"O, these deliberate fools!"
"Silence bestows virtue, Madam!"

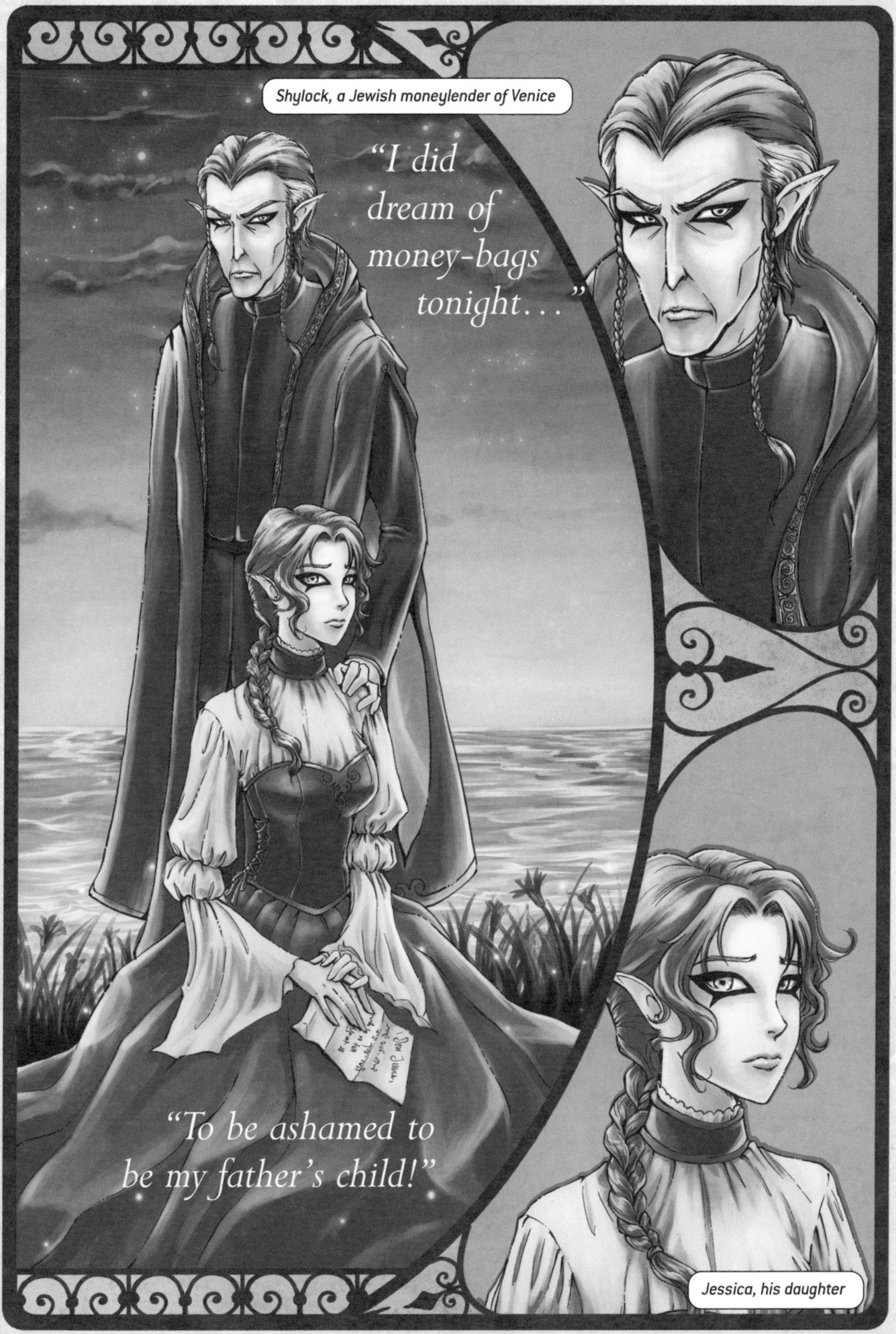
Shylock, a Jewish moneylender of Venice
"I did dream of money-bags tonight. . ."
"To be ashamed to be my father's child!"
Jessica, his daughter

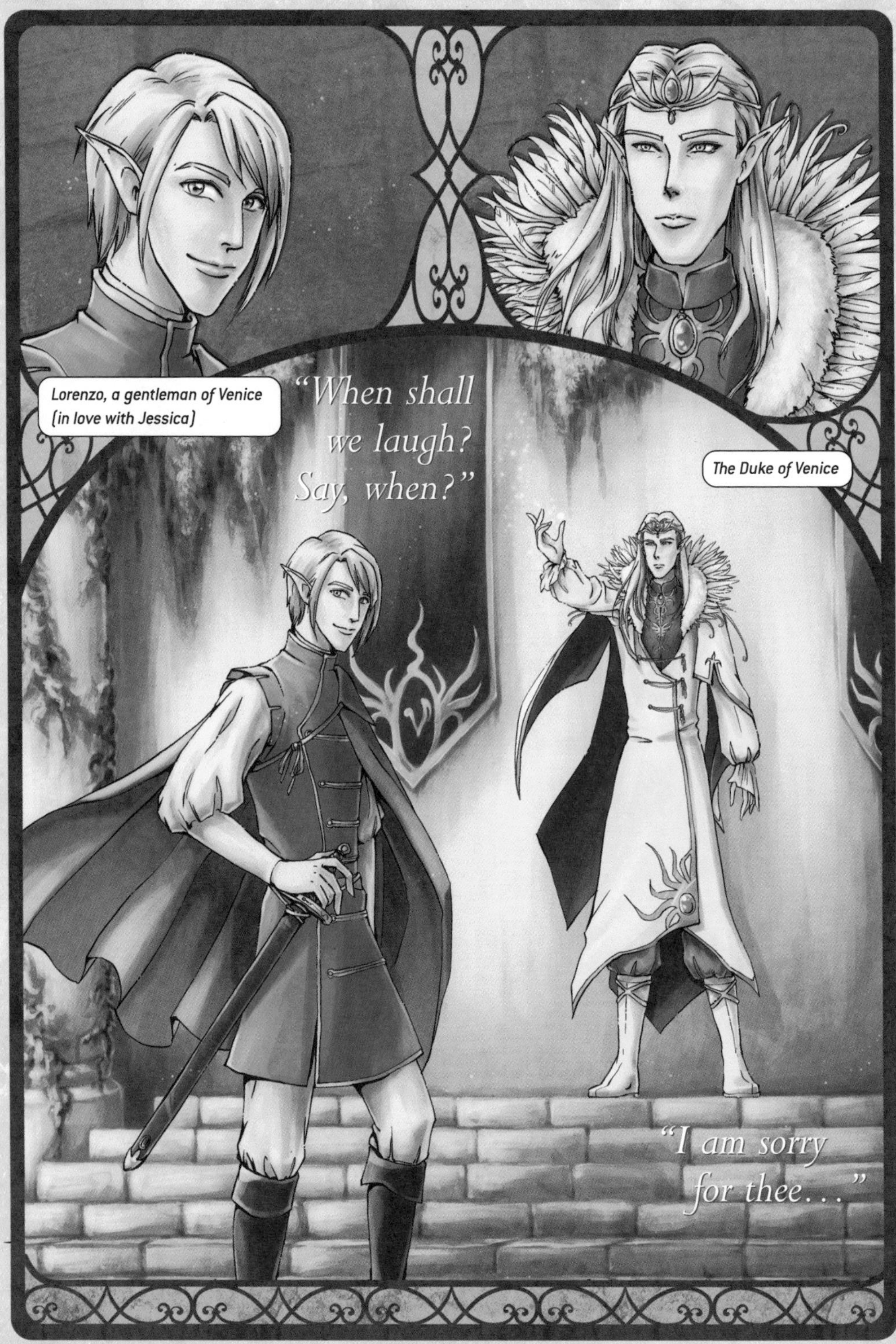
Lorenzo, a gentleman of Venice
(in love with Jessica)
"When shall we laugh? Say, when?"
The Duke of Venice
"I am sorry for thee…"

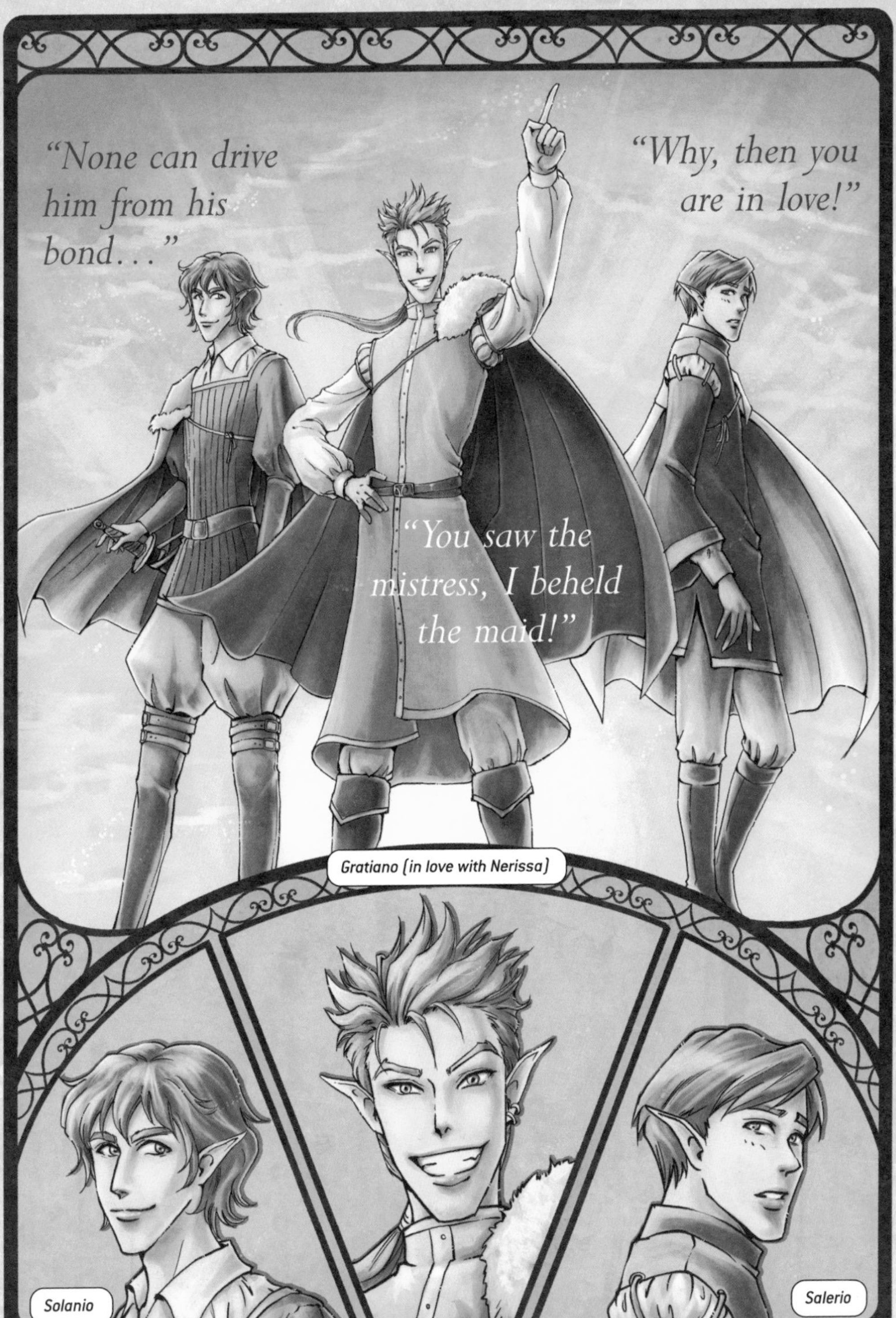
"None can drive him from his bond…"
"Why, then you are in love!"
"You saw the mistress, I beheld the maid!"
Gratiano (in love with Nerissa)
Solanio
Salerio

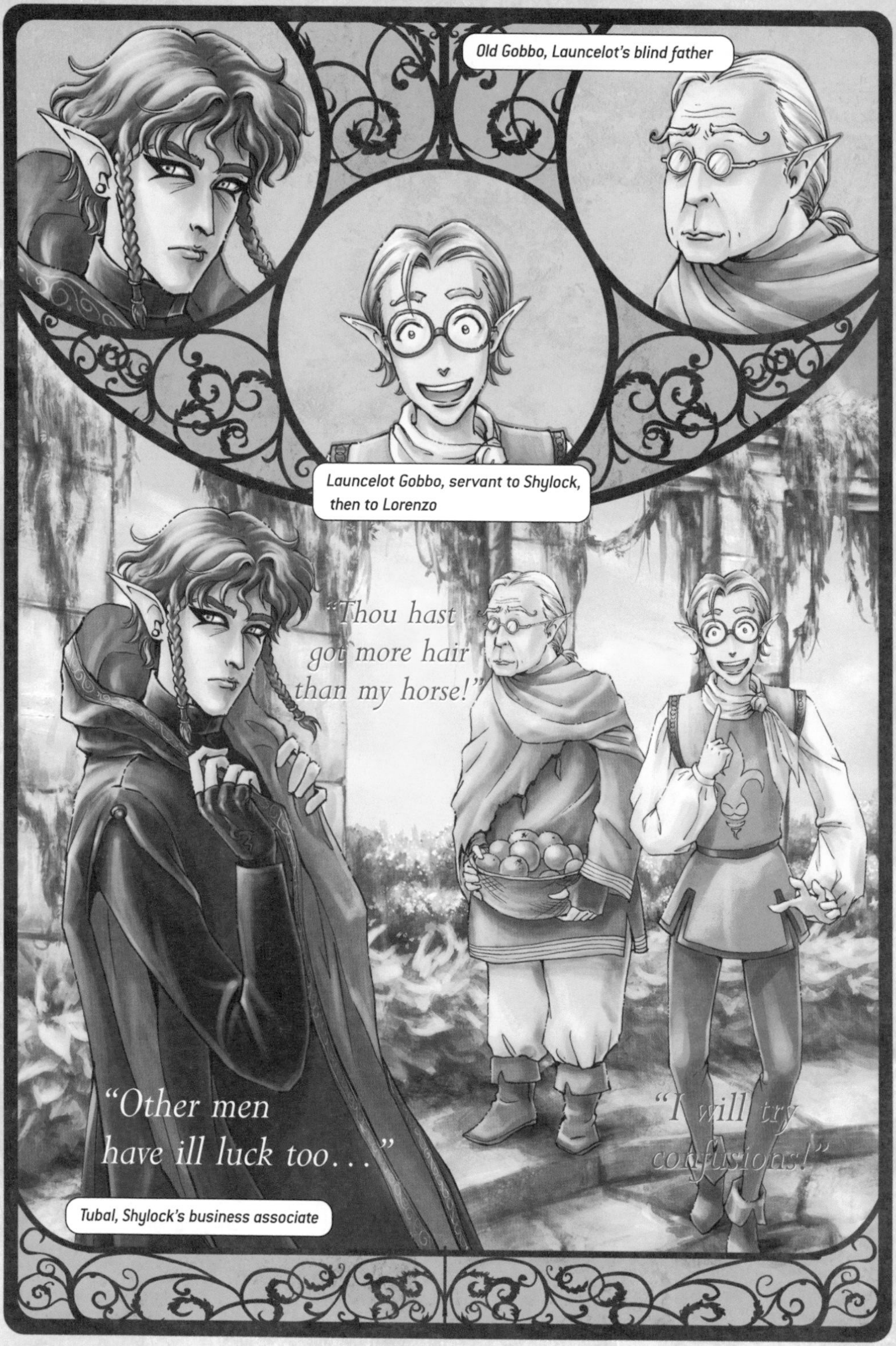

Old Gobbo, Launcelot's blind father
Launcelot Gobbo, servant to Shylock, then to Lorenzo
"Thou hast got more hair than my horse!"
"Other men have ill luck too. . ."
"I will try confusions!"
Tubal, Shylock's business associate

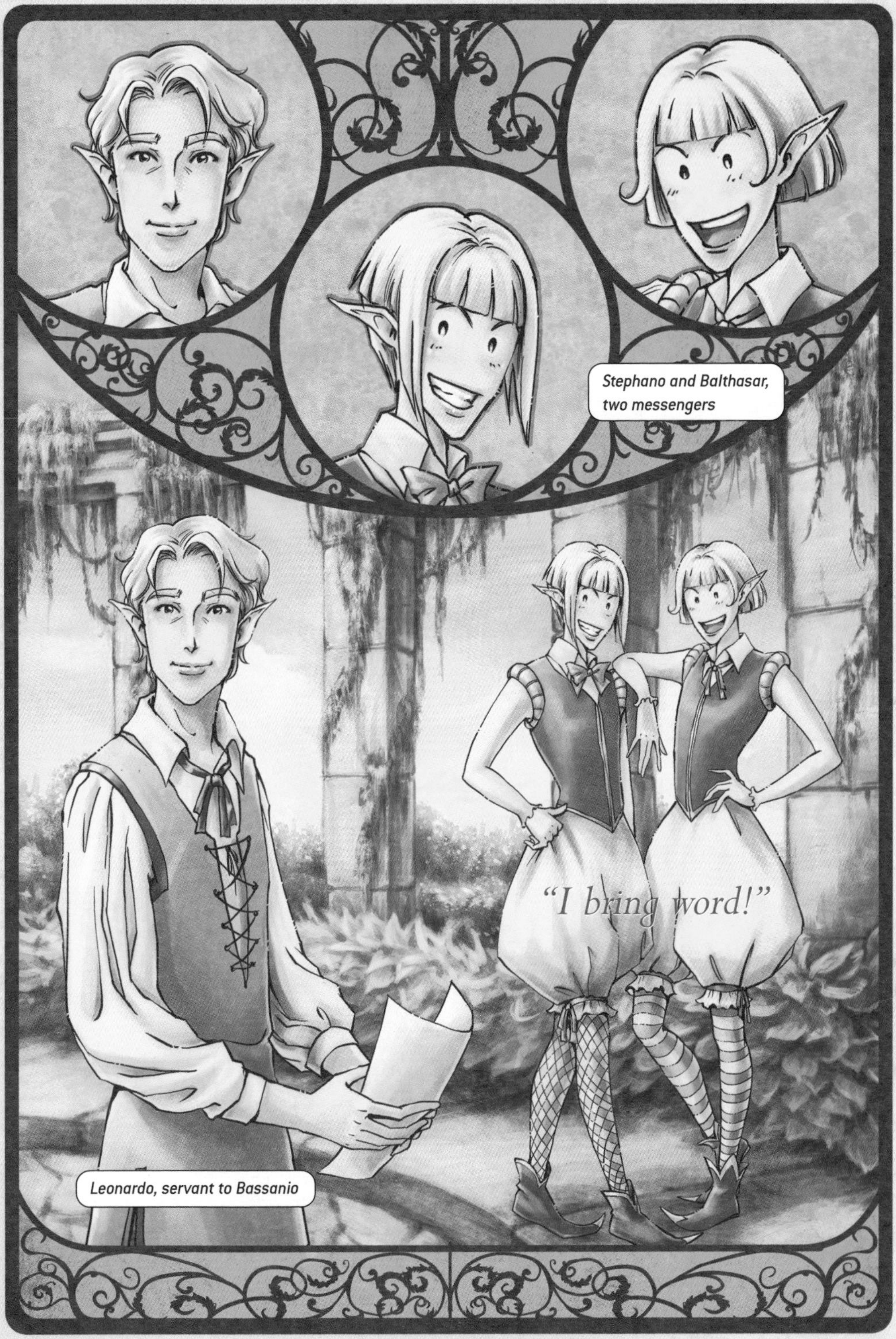
Stephano and Balthasar, two messengers
"I bring word!"
Leonardo, servant to Bassanio

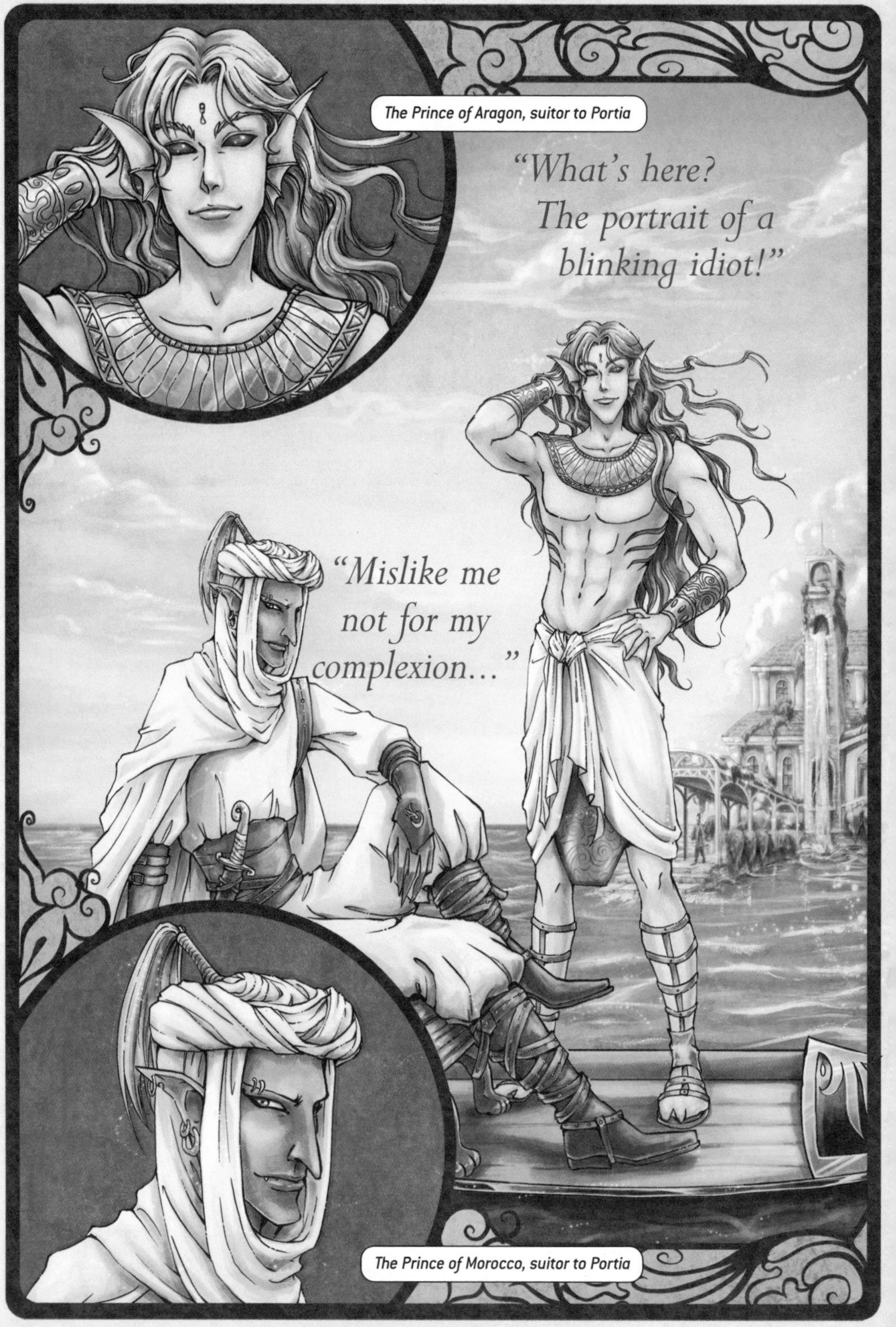
The Prince of Aragon, suitor to Portia
"What's here? The portrait of a blinking idiot!"
"Mislike me not for my complexion..."
The Prince of Morocco, suitor to Portia

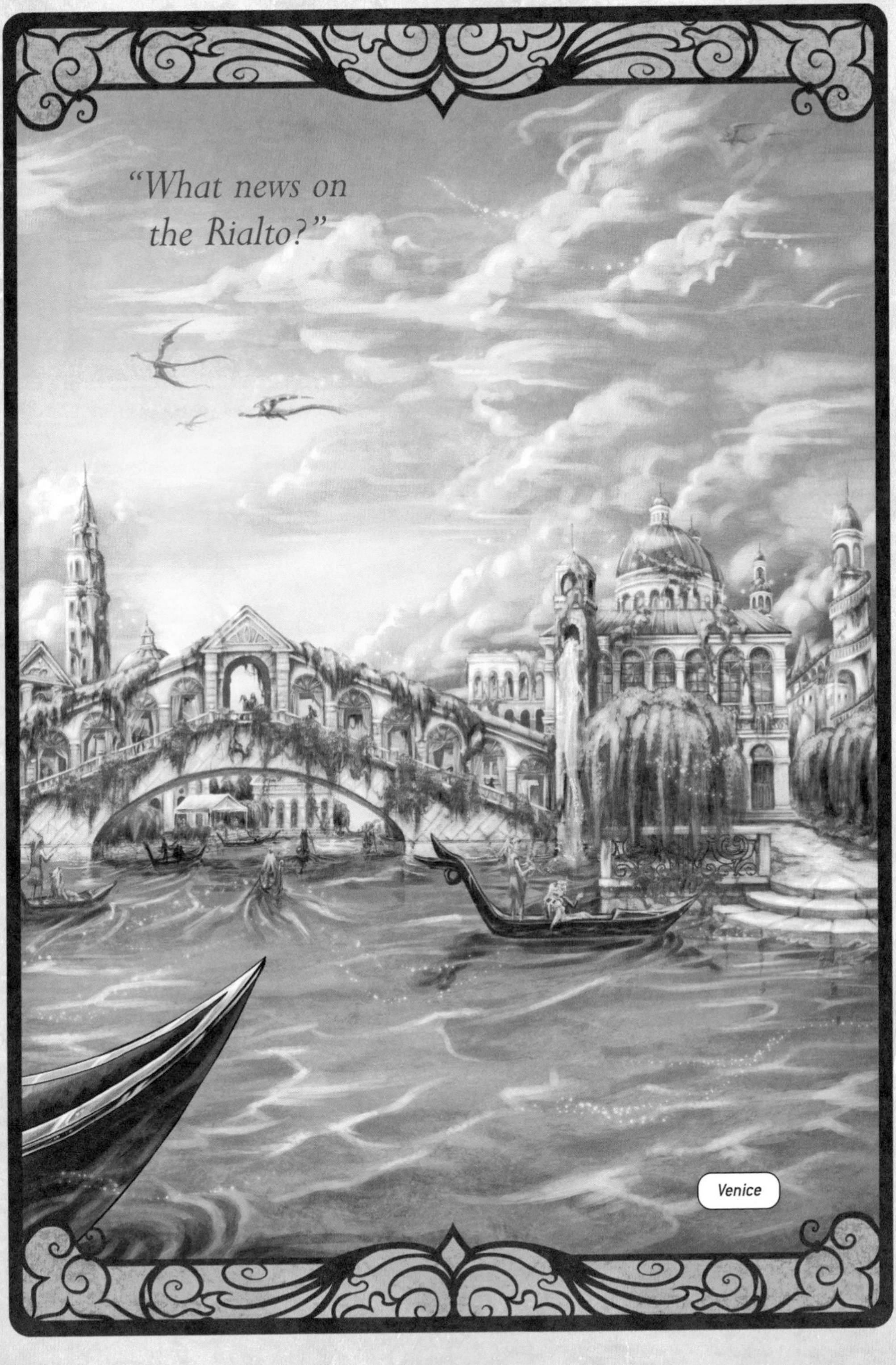
"What news on the Rialto?"
Venice

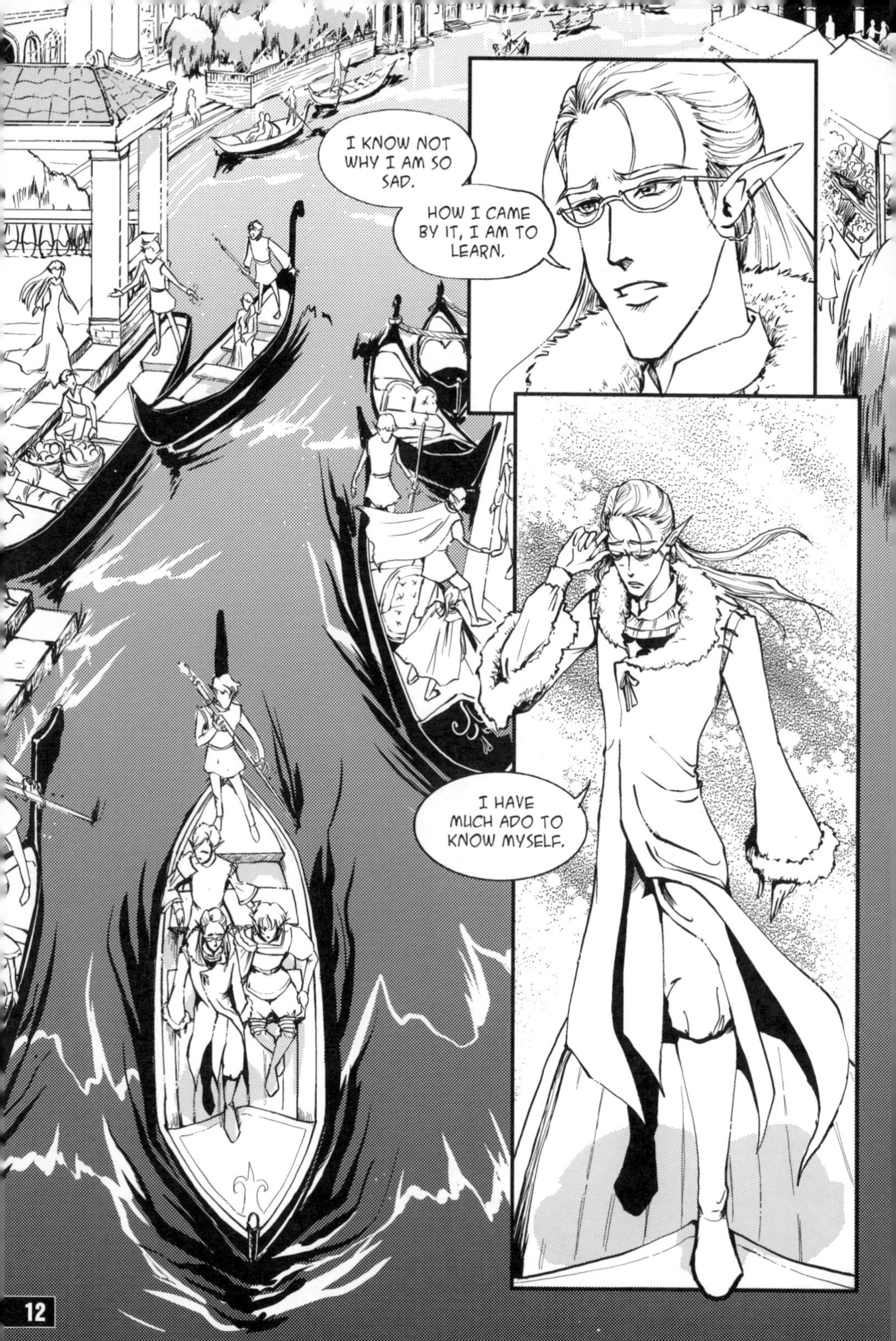
I KNOW NOT WHY I AM SO SAD.
HOW I CAME BY IT, I AM TO LEARN.
I HAVE MUCH ADO TO KNOW MYSELF.

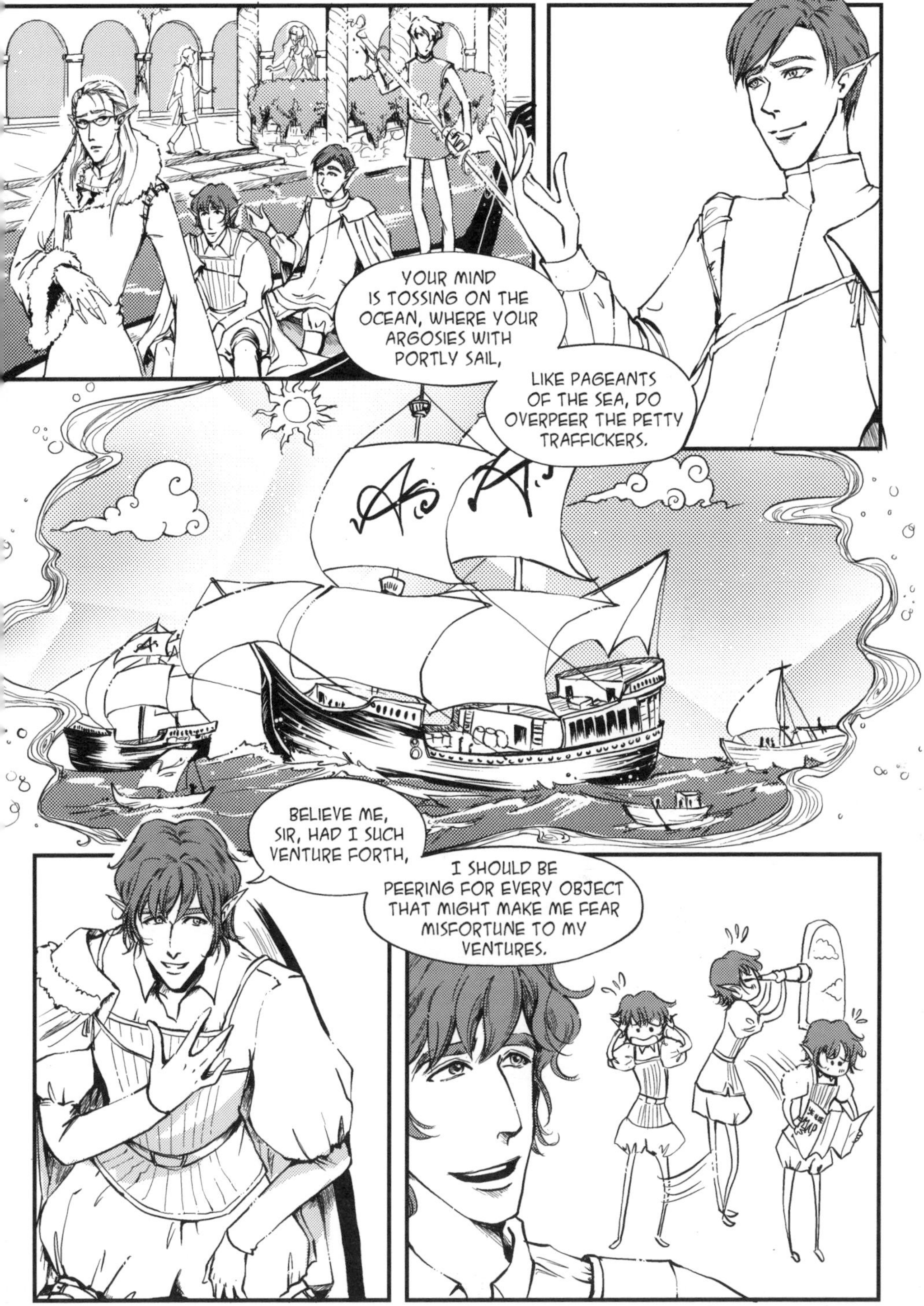
YOUR MIND IS TOSSING ON THE OCEAN, WHERE YOUR ARGOSIES WITH PORTLY SAIL,
LIKE PAGEANTS OF THE SEA, DO OVERPEER THE PETTY TRAFFICKERS.
BELIEVE ME, SIR, HAD I SUCH VENTURE FORTH,
I SHOULD BE PEERING FOR EVERY OBJECT THAT MIGHT MAKE ME FEAR MISFORTUNE TO MY VENTURES.

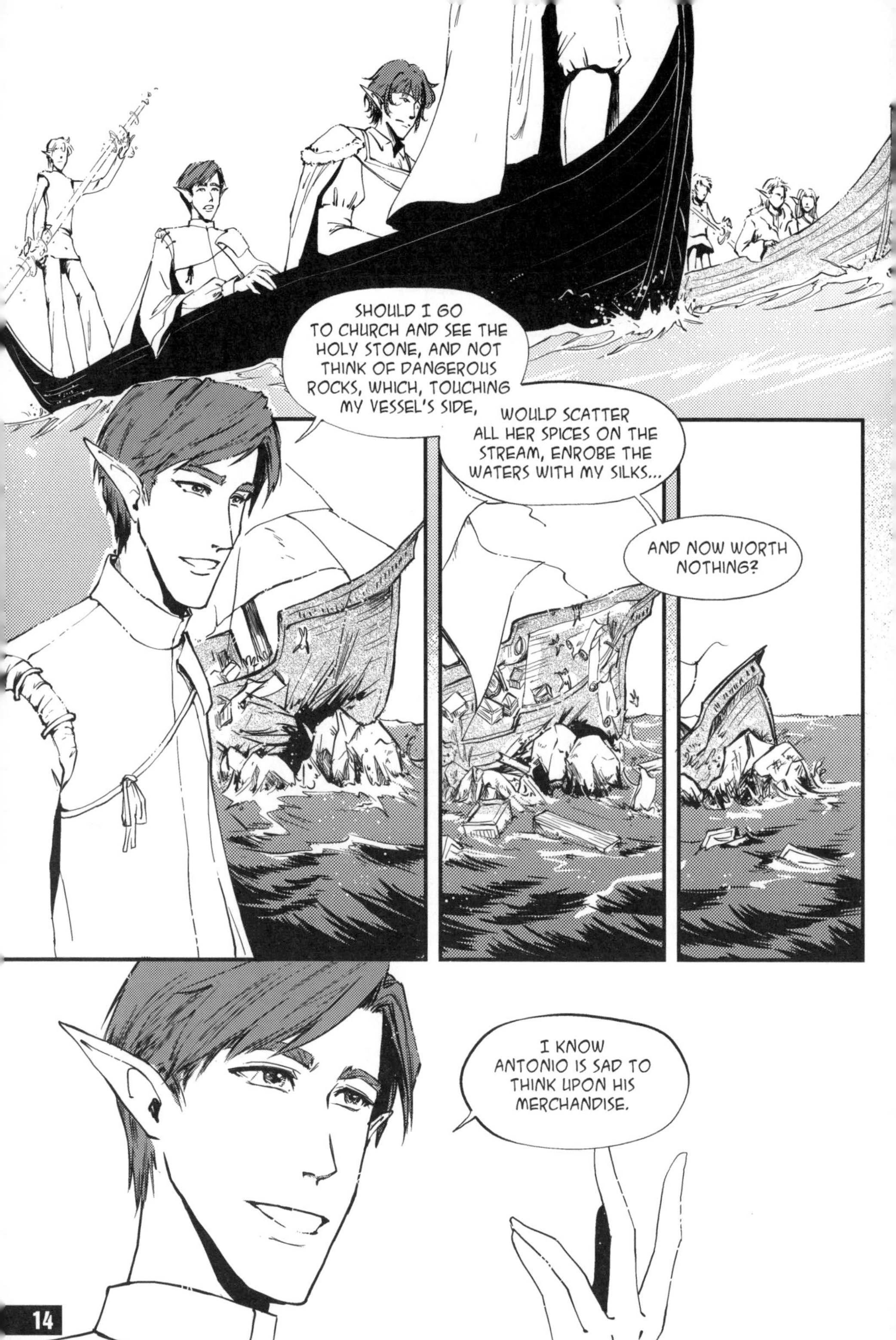
SHOULD I GO TO CHURCH AND SEE THE HOLY STONE, AND NOT THINK OF DANGEROUS ROCKS, WHICH, TOUCHING MY VESSEL'S SIDE,
WOULD SCATTER ALL HER SPICES ON THE STREAM, ENROBE THE WATERS WITH MY SILKS...
AND NOW WORTH NOTHING?
I KNOW ANTONIO IS SAD TO THINK UPON HIS MERCHANDISE.

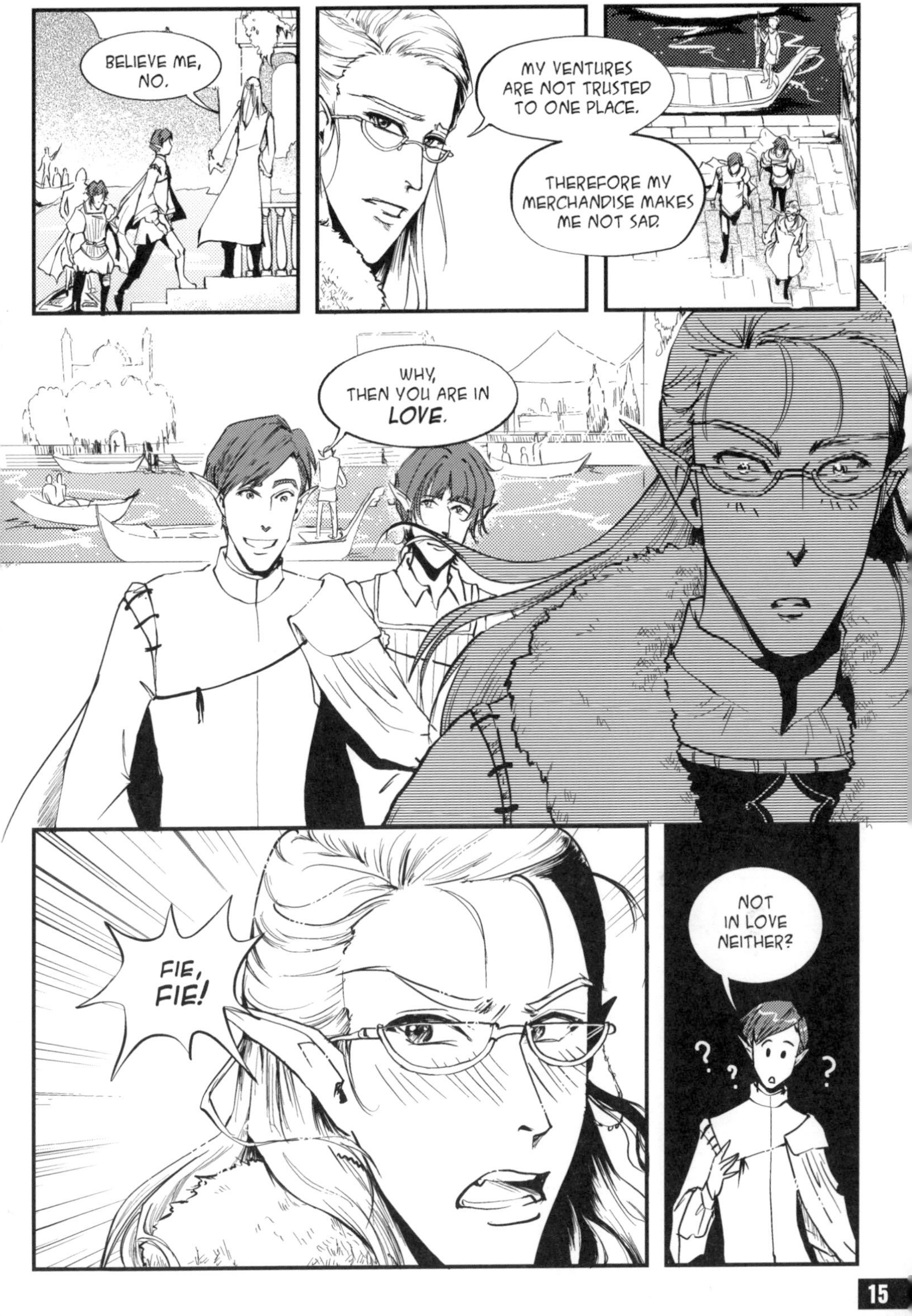
BELIEVE ME,
NO.
MY VENTURES ARE NOT TRUSTED TO ONE PLACE.
THEREFORE MY MERCHANDISE MAKES ME NOT SAD.
WHY, THEN YOU ARE IN LOVE.
FIE, FIE!
NOT IN LOVE NEITHER?
? ? ?

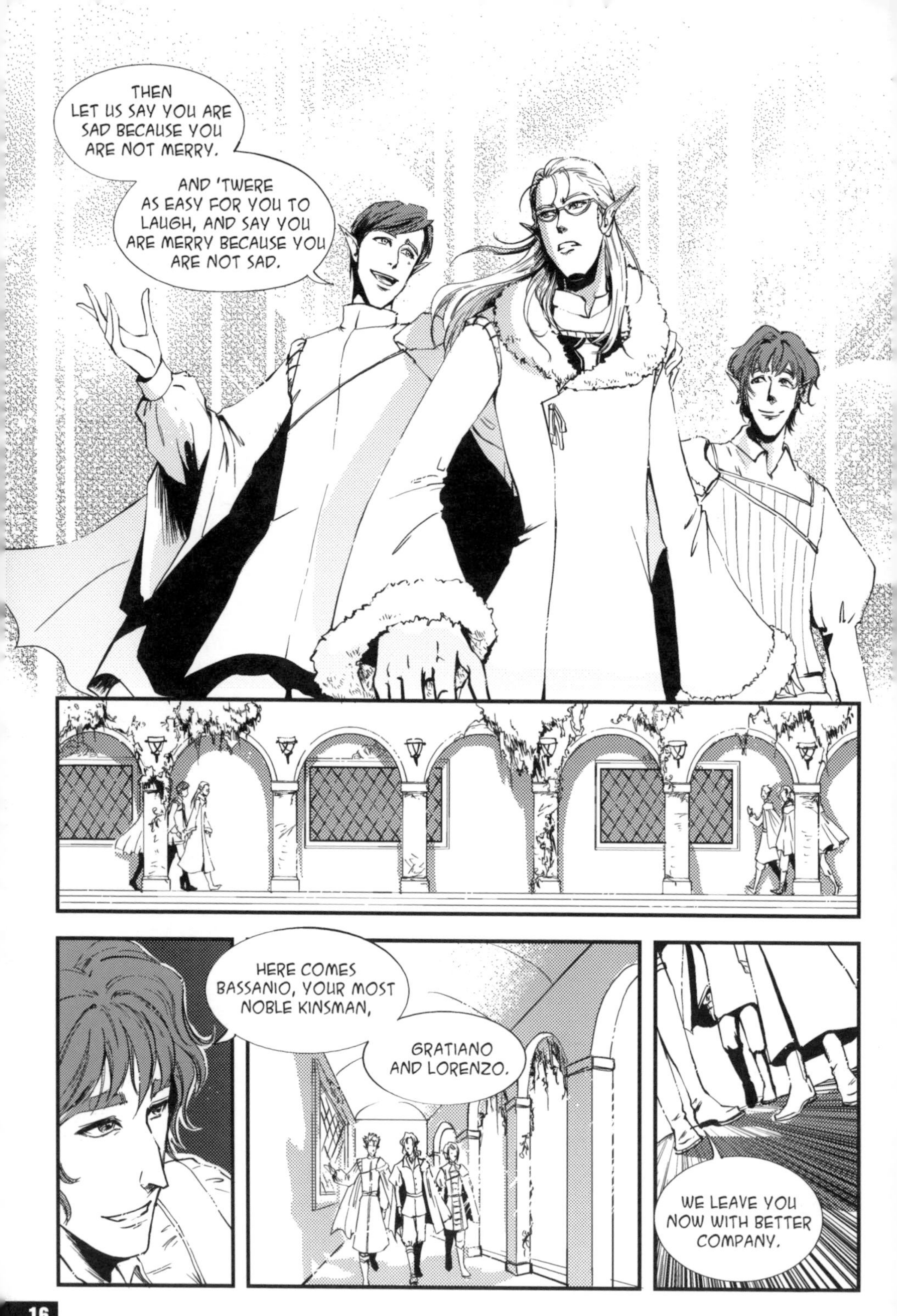
THEN LET US SAY YOU ARE SAD BECAUSE YOU ARE NOT MERRY.
AND 'TWERE AS EASY FOR YOU TO LAUGH, AND SAY YOU ARE MERRY BECAUSE YOU ARE NOT SAD.
HERE COMES BASSANIO, YOUR MOST NOBLE KINSMAN,
GRATIANO AND LORENZO.
WE LEAVE YOU NOW WITH BETTER COMPANY.

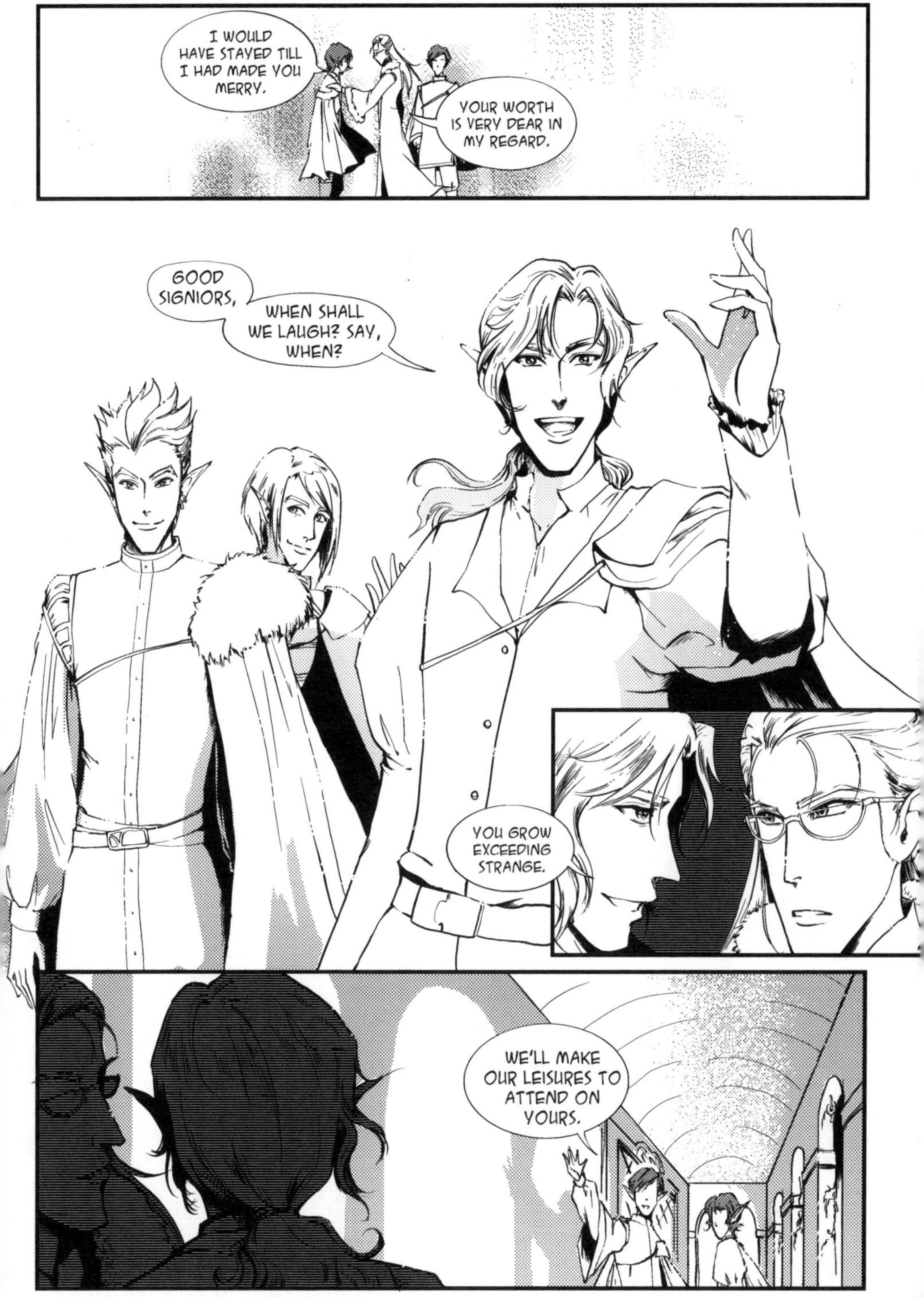
I WOULD HAVE STAYED TILL I HAD MADE YOU MERRY.
YOUR WORTH IS VERY DEAR IN MY REGARD.
GOOD SIGNIORS,
WHEN SHALL WE LAUGH? SAY, WHEN?
YOU GROW EXCEEDING STRANGE.
WE'LL MAKE OUR LEISURES TO ATTEND ON YOURS.

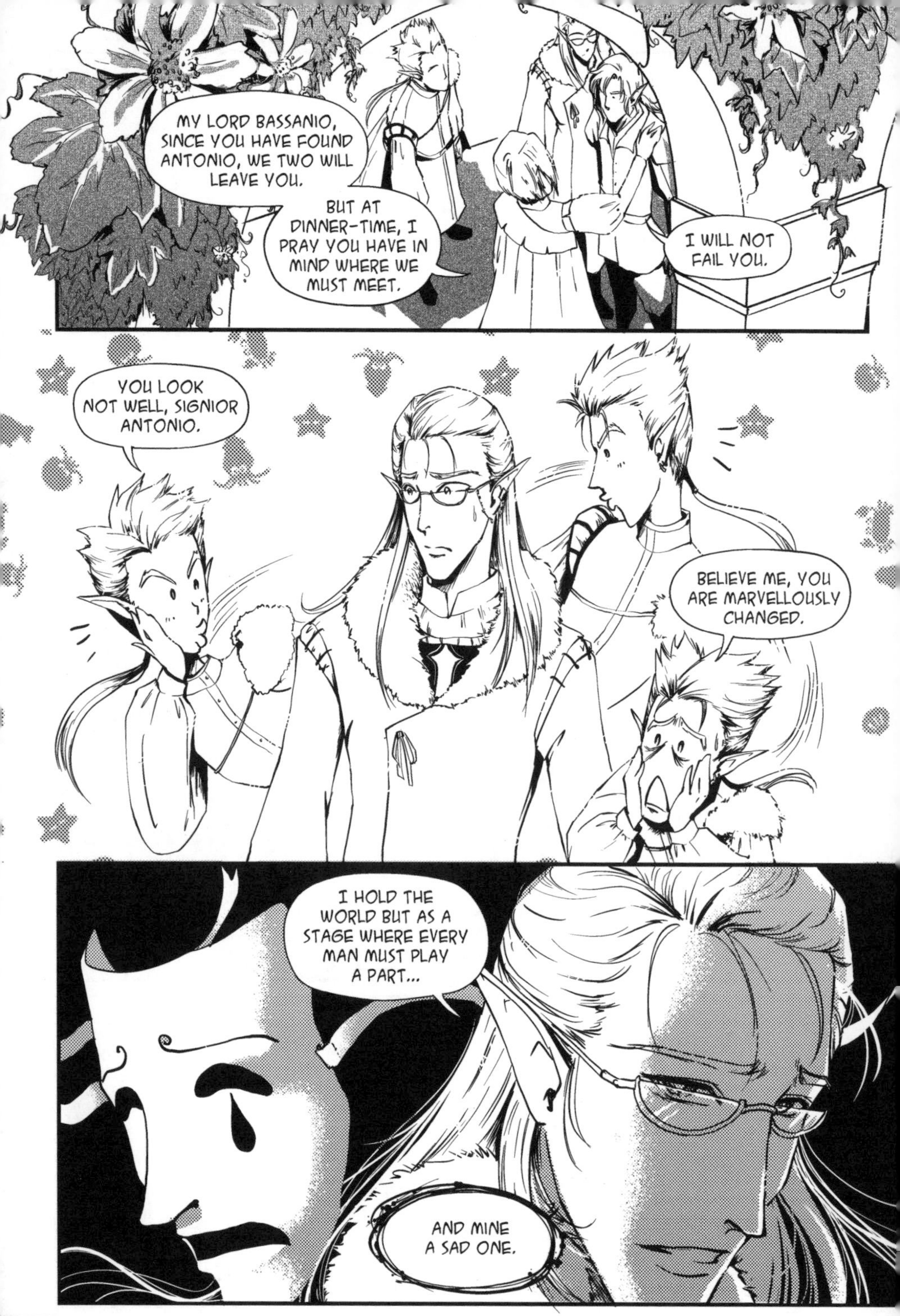
MY LORD BASSANIO, SINCE YOU HAVE FOUND ANTONIO, WE TWO WILL LEAVE YOU.
BUT AT DINNER-TIME, I PRAY YOU HAVE IN MIND WHERE WE MUST MEET.
I WILL NOT FAIL YOU.
YOU LOOK NOT WELL, SIGNIOR ANTONIO.
BELIEVE ME, YOU ARE MARVELLOUSLY CHANGED.
I HOLD THE WORLD BUT AS A STAGE WHERE EVERY MAN MUST PLAY A PART...
AND MINE A SAD ONE.

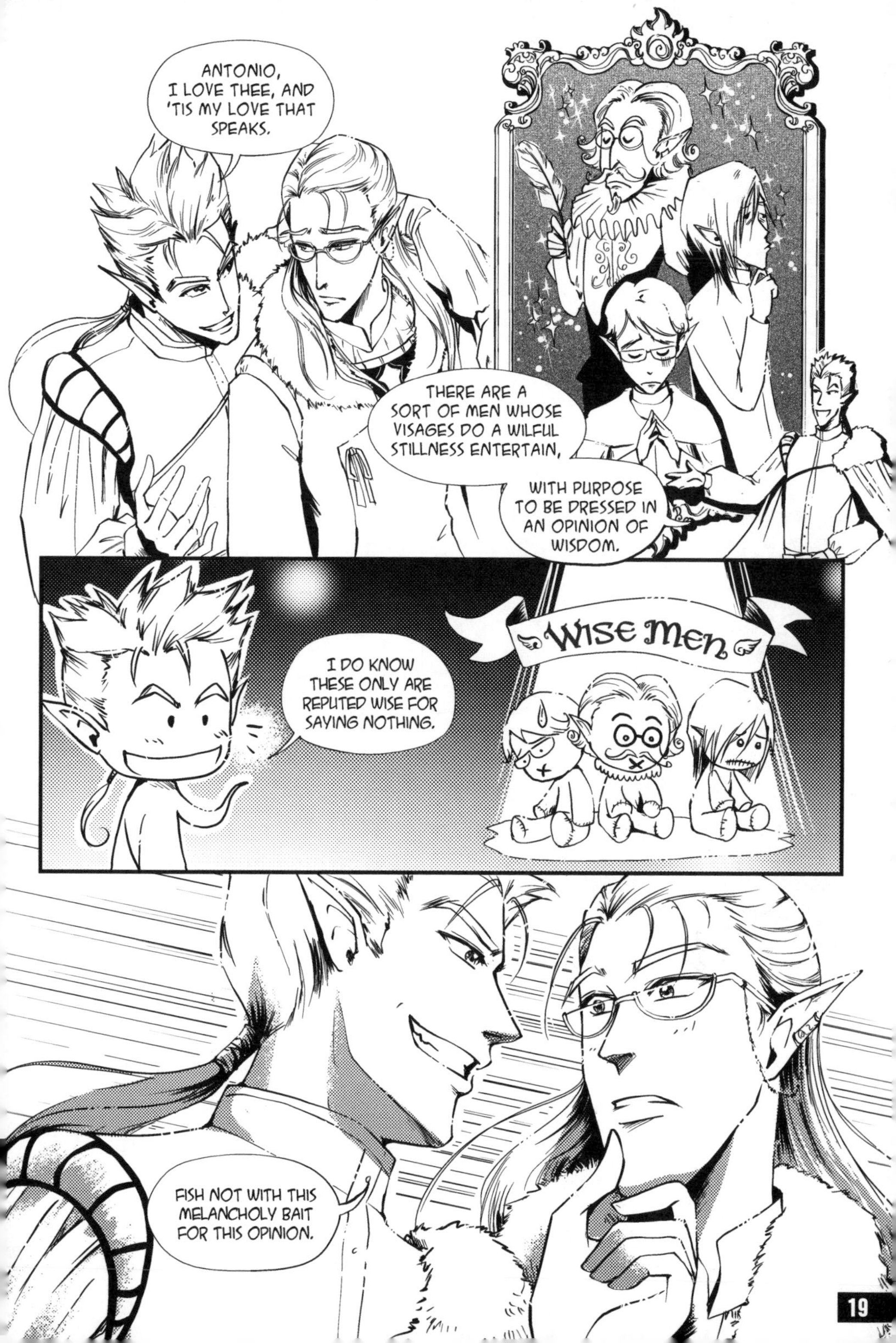
ANTONIO, I LOVE THEE, AND 'TIS MY LOVE THAT SPEAKS.
THERE ARE A SORT OF MEN WHOSE VISAGES DO A WILFUL STILLNESS ENTERTAIN,
WITH PURPOSE TO BE DRESSED IN AN OPINION OF WISDOM.
I DO KNOW THESE ONLY ARE REPUTED WISE FOR SAYING NOTHING.
WISE MEN
FISH NOT WITH THIS MELANCHOLY BAIT FOR THIS OPINION.

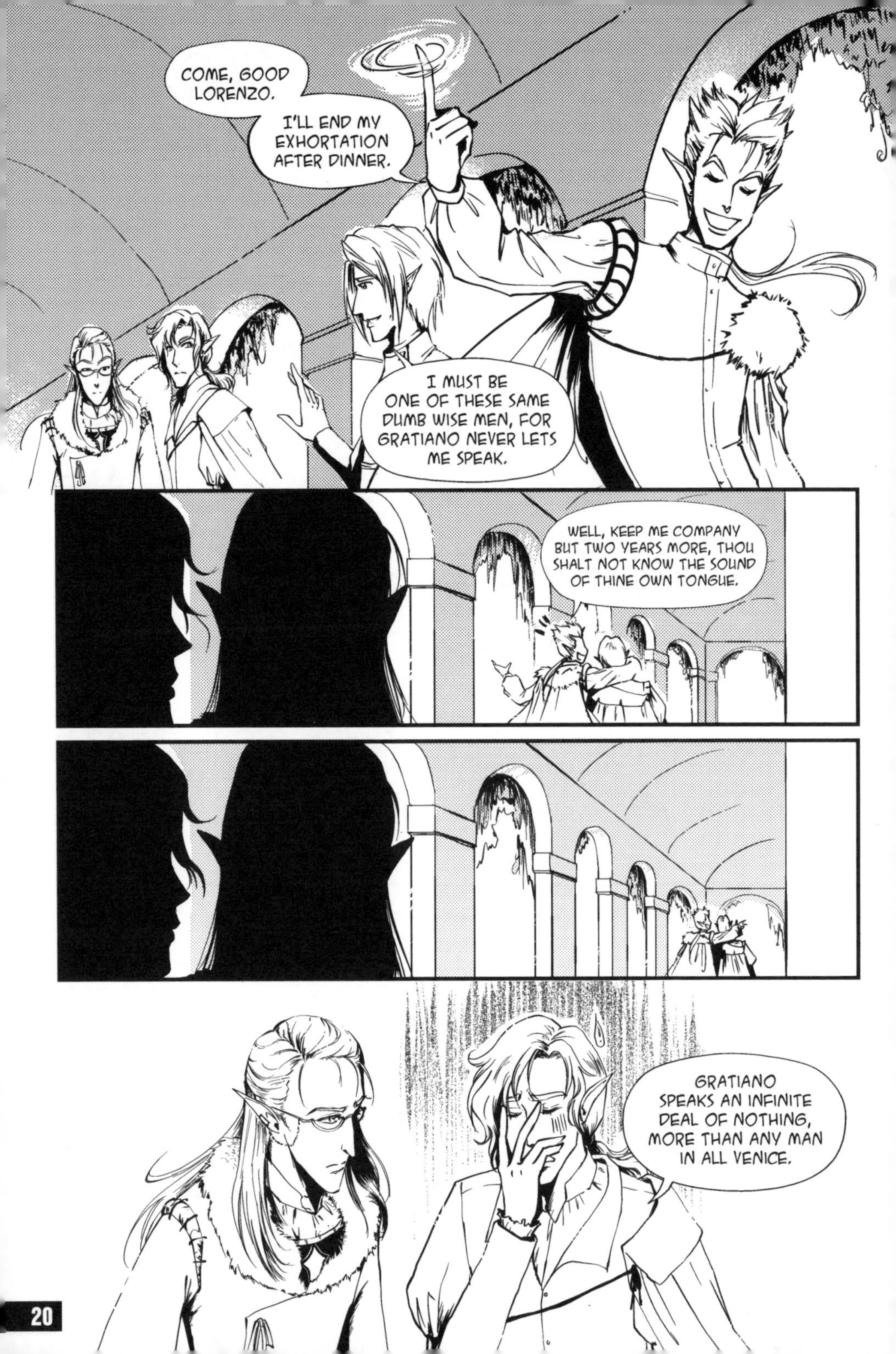
COME, GOOD LORENZO.
I'LL END MY EXHORTATION AFTER DINNER.
I MUST BE ONE OF THESE SAME DUMB WISE MEN, FOR GRATIANO NEVER LETS ME SPEAK.
WELL, KEEP ME COMPANY BUT TWO YEARS MORE, THOU SHALT NOT KNOW THE SOUND OF THINE OWN TONGUE.
GRATIANO SPEAKS AN INFINITE DEAL OF NOTHING, MORE THAN ANY MAN IN ALL VENICE.

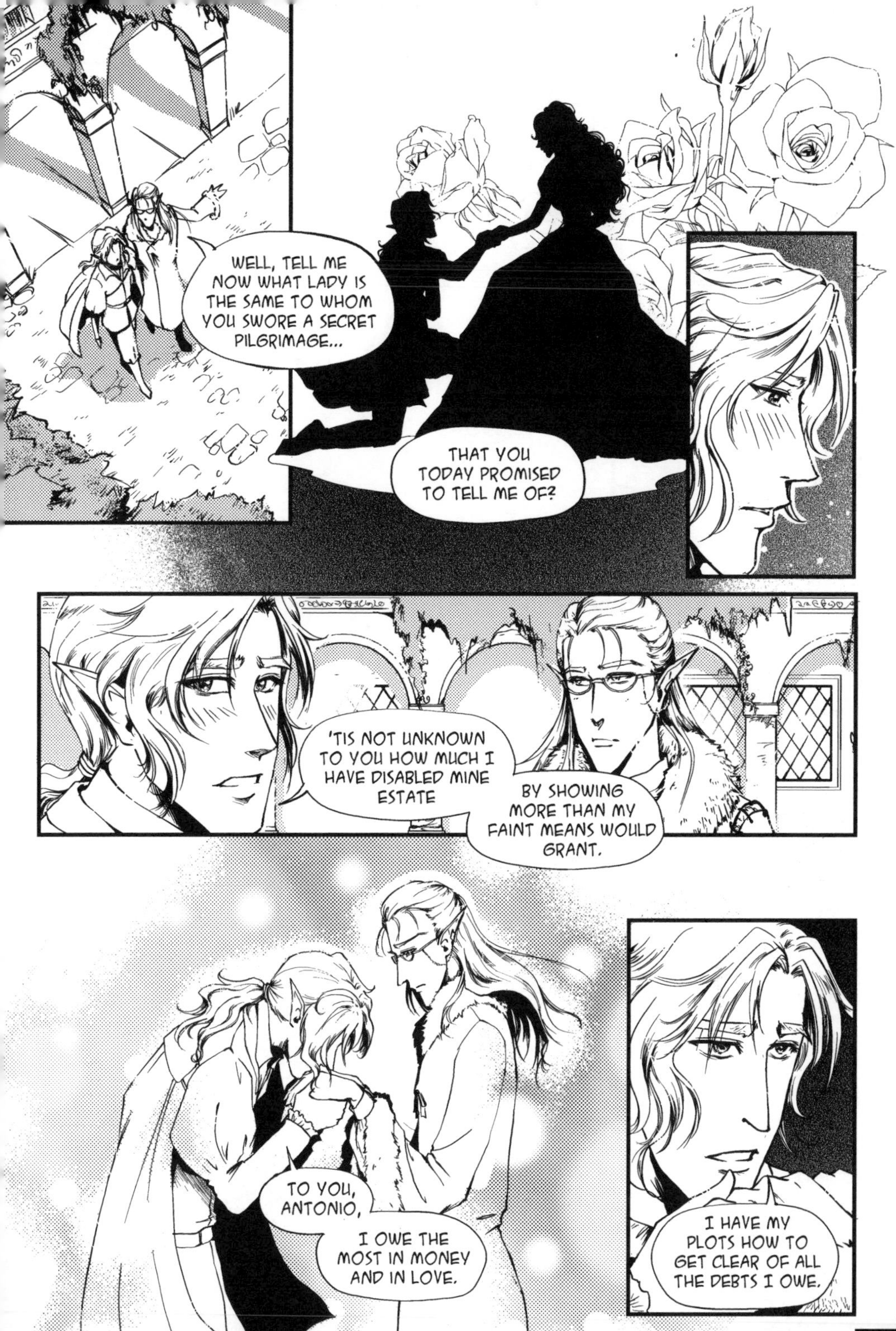
WELL, TELL ME NOW WHAT LADY IS THE SAME TO WHOM YOU SWORE A SECRET PILGRIMAGE...
THAT YOU TODAY PROMISED TO TELL ME OF?
'TIS NOT UNKNOWN TO YOU HOW MUCH I HAVE DISABLED MINE ESTATE
BY SHOWING MORE THAN MY FAINT MEANS WOULD GRANT.
TO YOU, ANTONIO,
I OWE THE MOST IN MONEY AND IN LOVE.
I HAVE MY PLOTS HOW TO GET CLEAR OF ALL THE DEBTS I OWE.

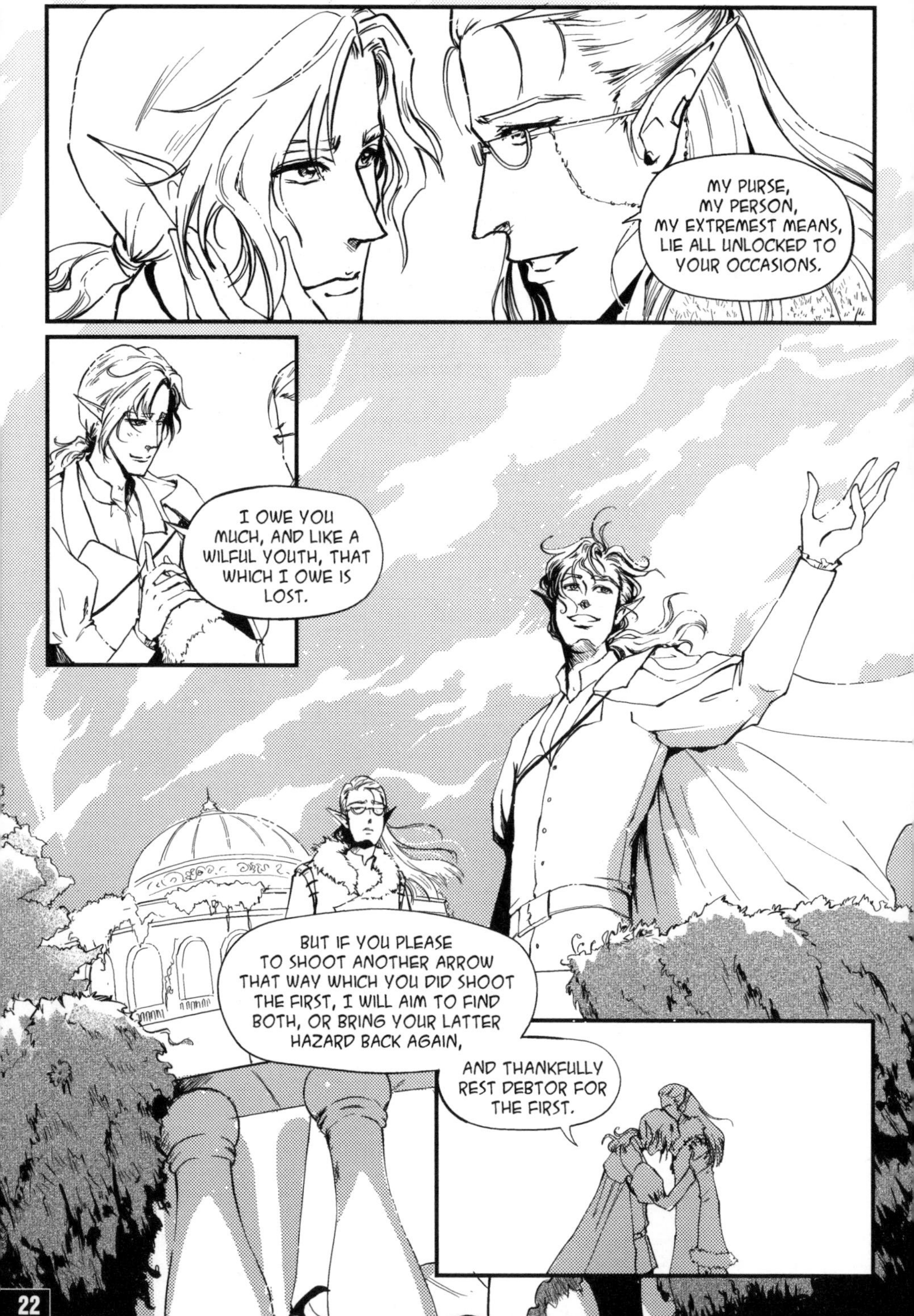
MY PURSE, MY PERSON, MY EXTREMEST MEANS, LIE ALL UNLOCKED TO YOUR OCCASIONS.
I OWE YOU MUCH, AND LIKE A WILFUL YOUTH, THAT WHICH I OWE IS LOST.
BUT IF YOU PLEASE TO SHOOT ANOTHER ARROW THAT WAY WHICH YOU DID SHOOT THE FIRST, I WILL AIM TO FIND BOTH, OR BRING YOUR LATTER HAZARD BACK AGAIN,
AND THANKFULLY REST DEBTOR FOR THE FIRST.

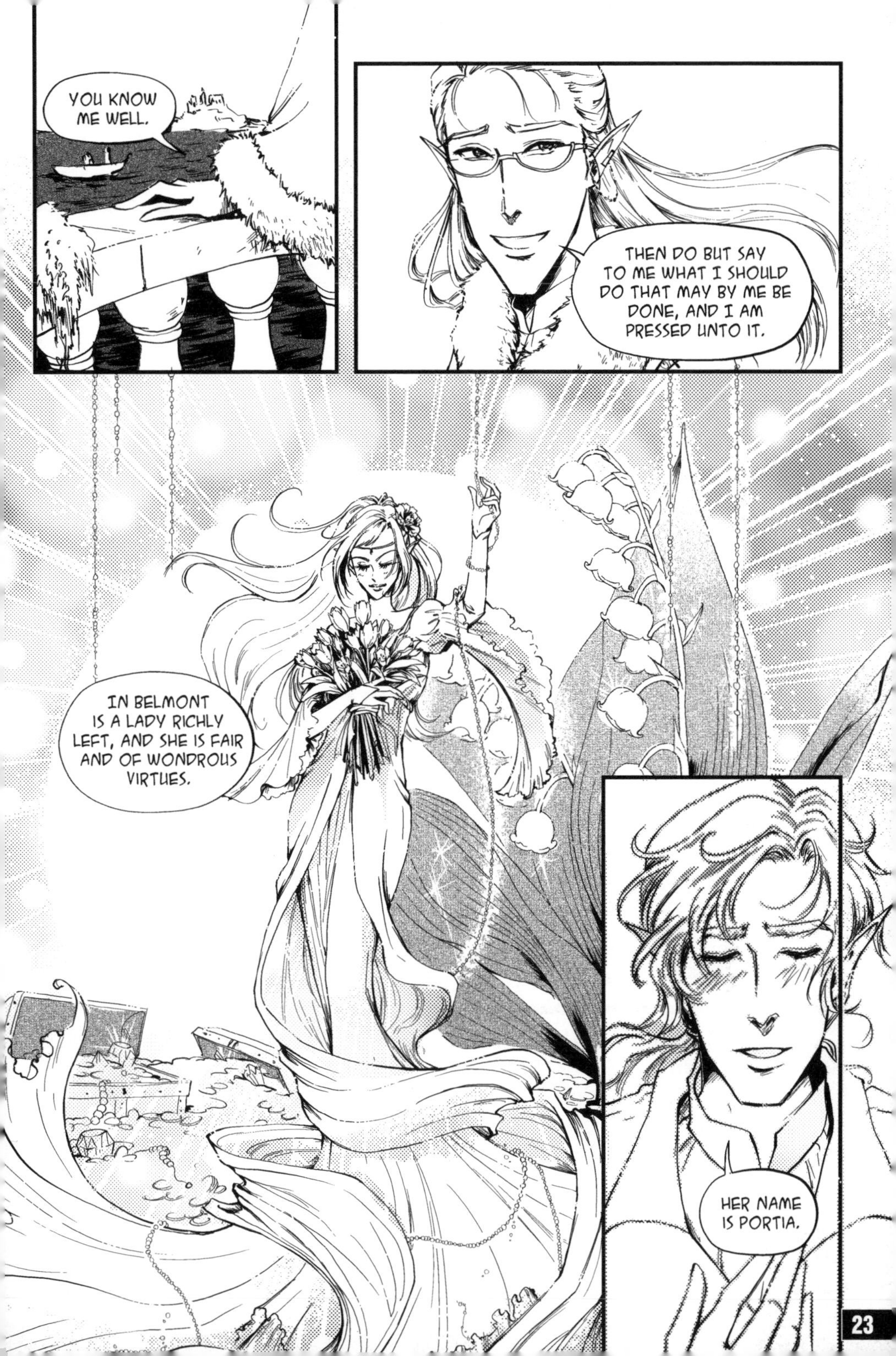
YOU KNOW ME WELL.
THEN DO BUT SAY TO ME WHAT I SHOULD DO THAT MAY BY ME BE DONE, AND I AM PRESSED UNTO IT.
IN BELMONT IS A LADY RICHLY LEFT, AND SHE IS FAIR AND OF WONDROUS VIRTUES.
HER NAME IS PORTIA.

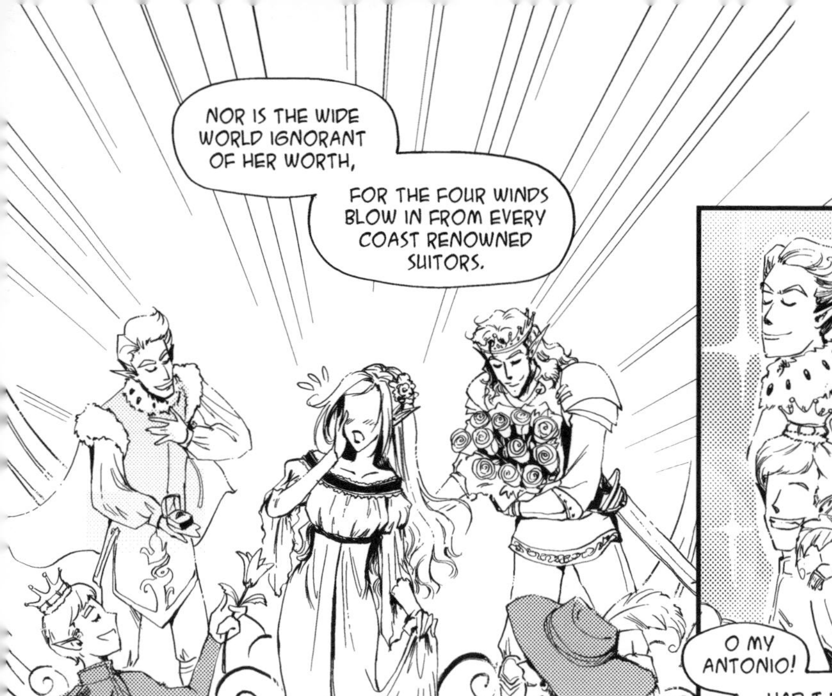
NOR IS THE WIDE WORLD IGNORANT OF HER WORTH,
FOR THE FOUR WINDS BLOW IN FROM EVERY COAST RENOWNED SUITORS.
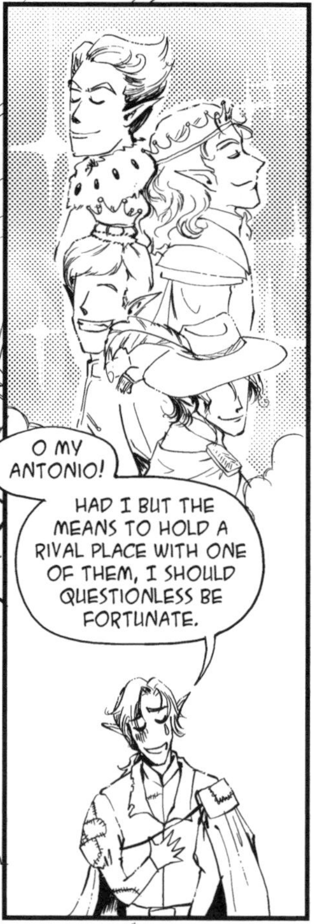
O MY ANTONIO!
HAD I BUT THE MEANS TO HOLD A RIVAL PLACE WITH ONE OF THEM, I SHOULD QUESTIONLESS BE FORTUNATE.
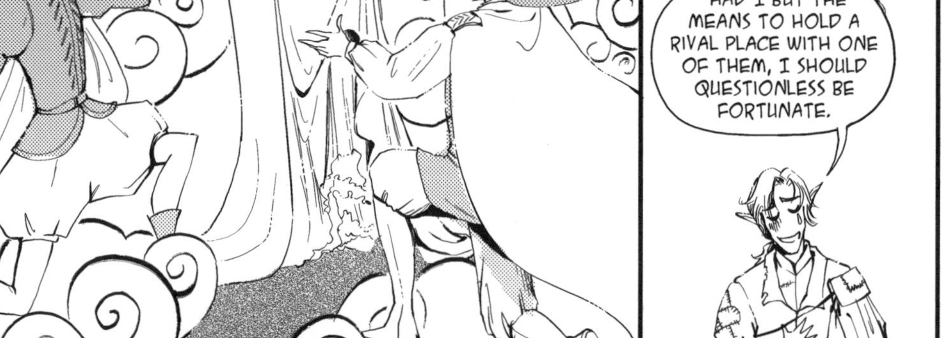
THOU KNOW'ST THAT ALL MY FORTUNES ARE AT SEA.
NEITHER HAVE I MONEY NOR COMMODITY TO RAISE A PRESENT SUM.

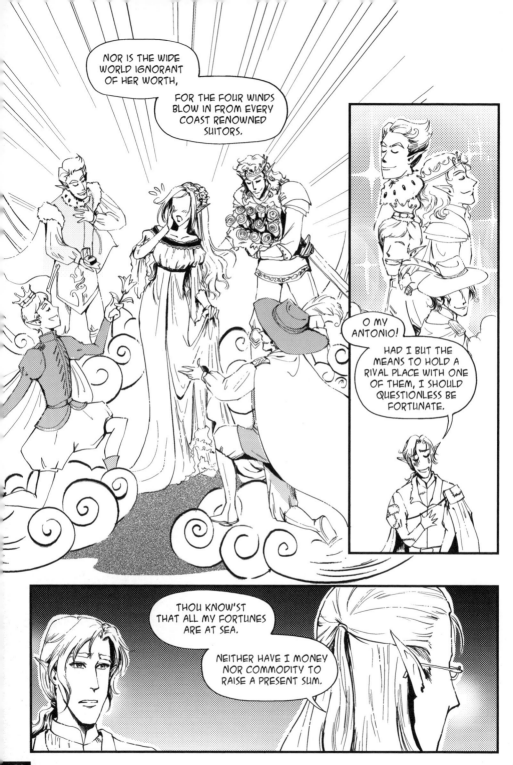

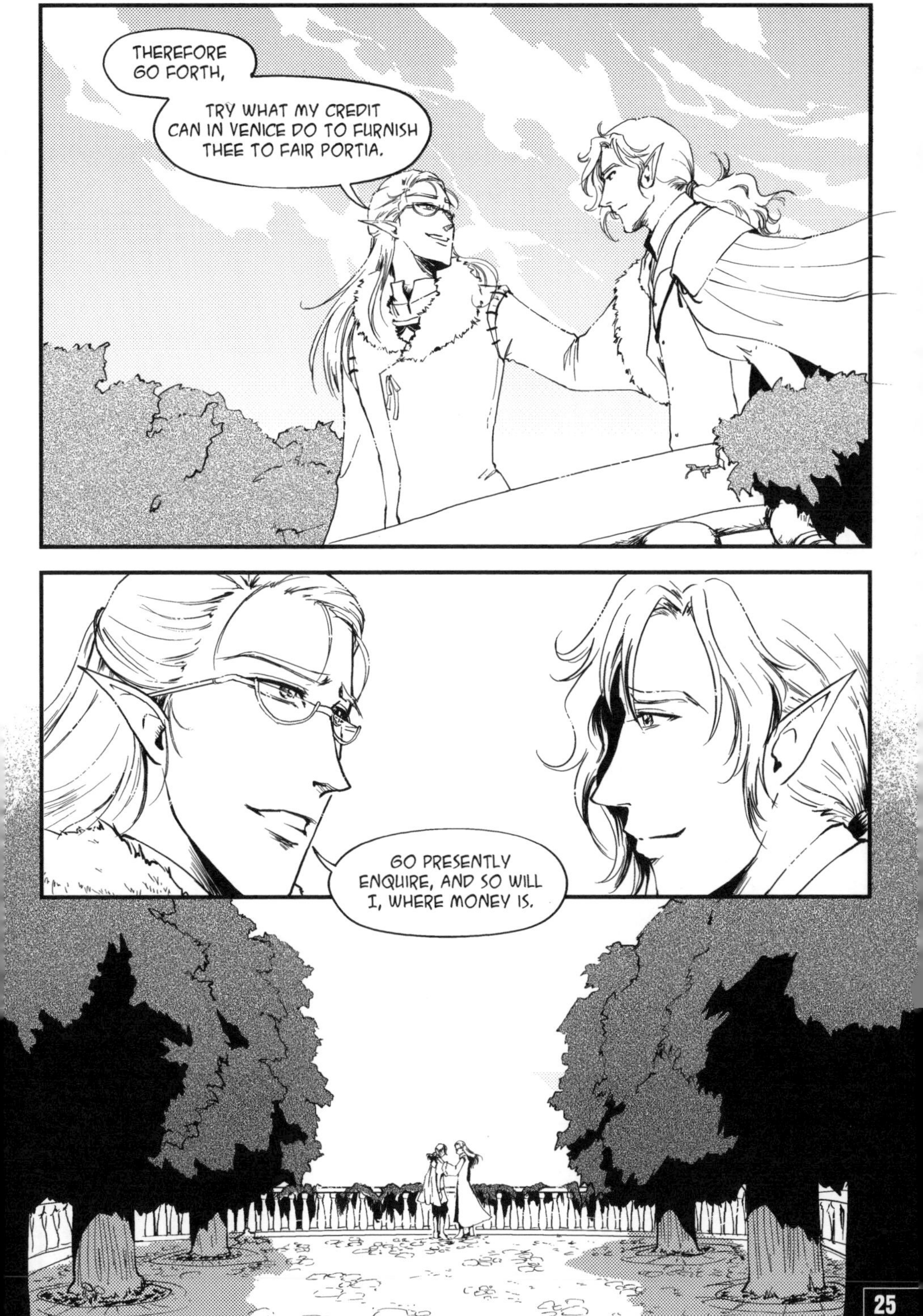
THEREFORE GO FORTH,
TRY WHAT MY CREDIT CAN IN VENICE DO TO FURNISH THEE TO FAIR PORTIA.
GO PRESENTLY ENQUIRE, AND SO WILL I, WHERE MONEY IS.

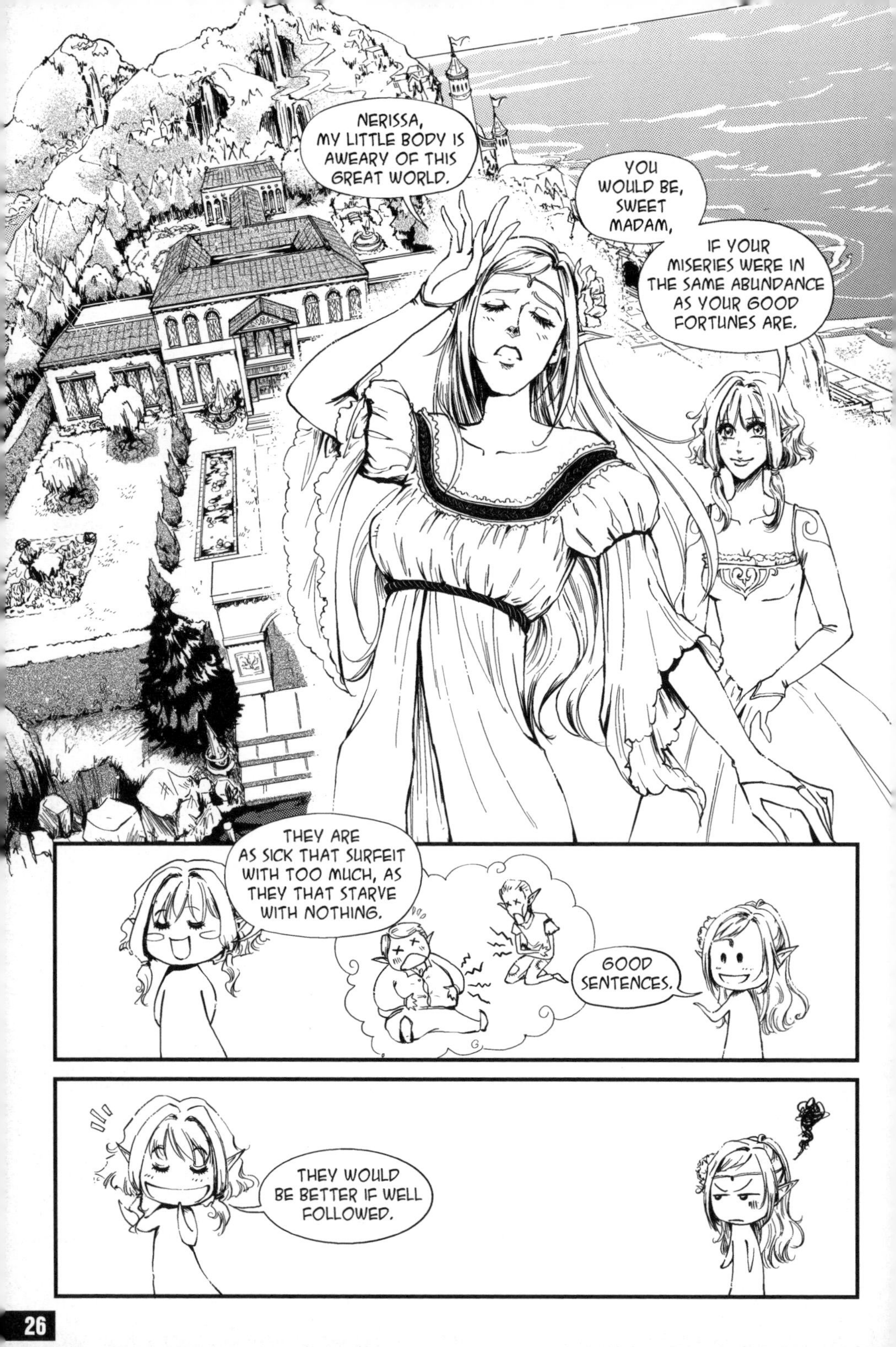
NERISSA, MY LITTLE BODY IS AWEARY OF THIS GREAT WORLD.
YOU WOULD BE, SWEET MADAM,
IF YOUR MISERIES WERE IN THE SAME ABUNDANCE AS YOUR GOOD FORTUNES ARE.
THEY ARE AS SICK THAT SURFEIT WITH TOO MUCH, AS THEY THAT STARVE WITH NOTHING.
GOOD SENTENCES.
THEY WOULD BE BETTER IF WELL FOLLOWED.

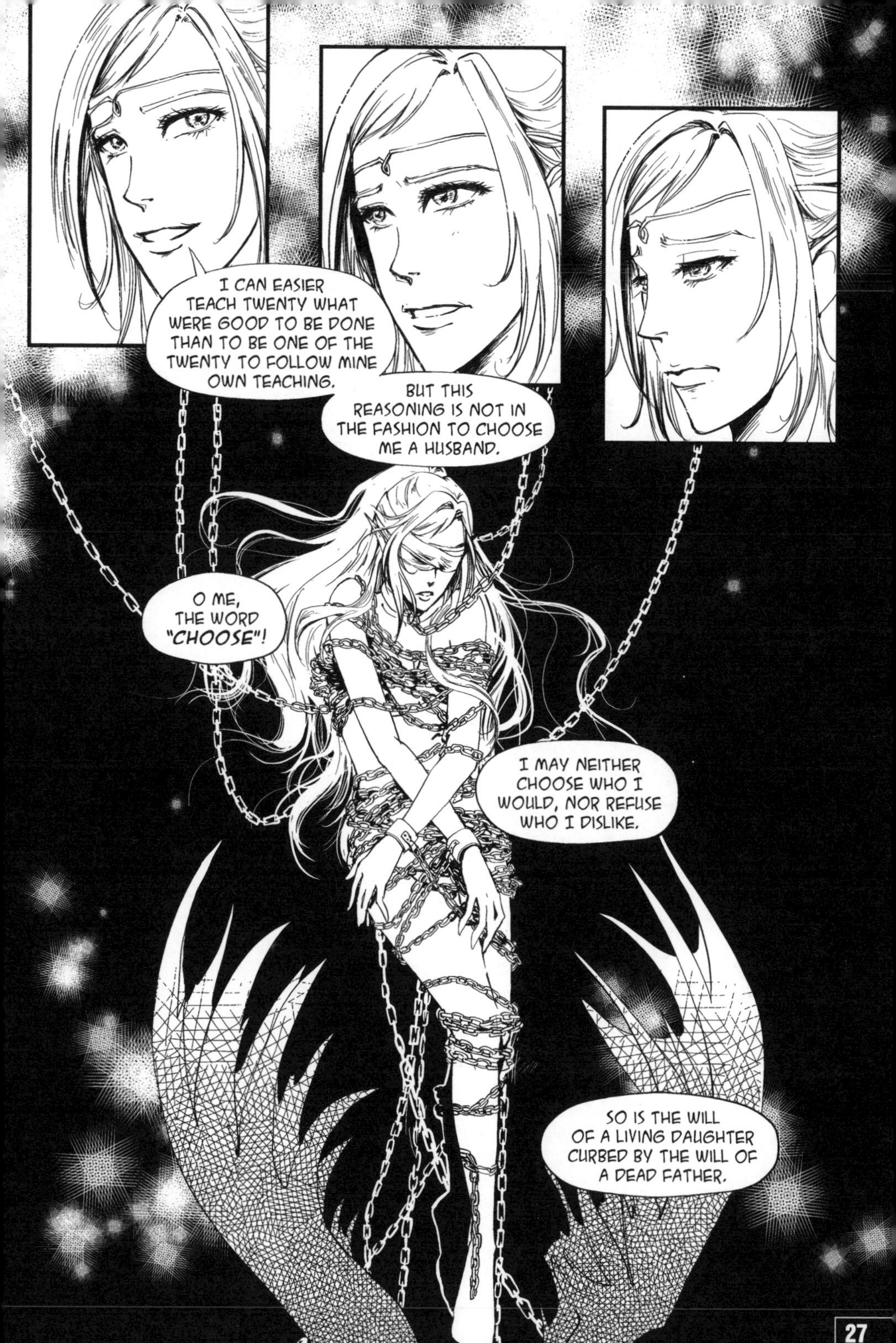
I CAN EASIER TEACH TWENTY WHAT WERE GOOD TO BE DONE THAN TO BE ONE OF THE TWENTY TO FOLLOW MINE OWN TEACHING.
BUT THIS REASONING IS NOT IN THE FASHION TO CHOOSE ME A HUSBAND.
O ME, THE WORD "CHOOSE"!
I MAY NEITHER CHOOSE WHO I WOULD, NOR REFUSE WHO I DISLIKE.
SO IS THE WILL OF A LIVING DAUGHTER CURBED BY THE WILL OF A DEAD FATHER.

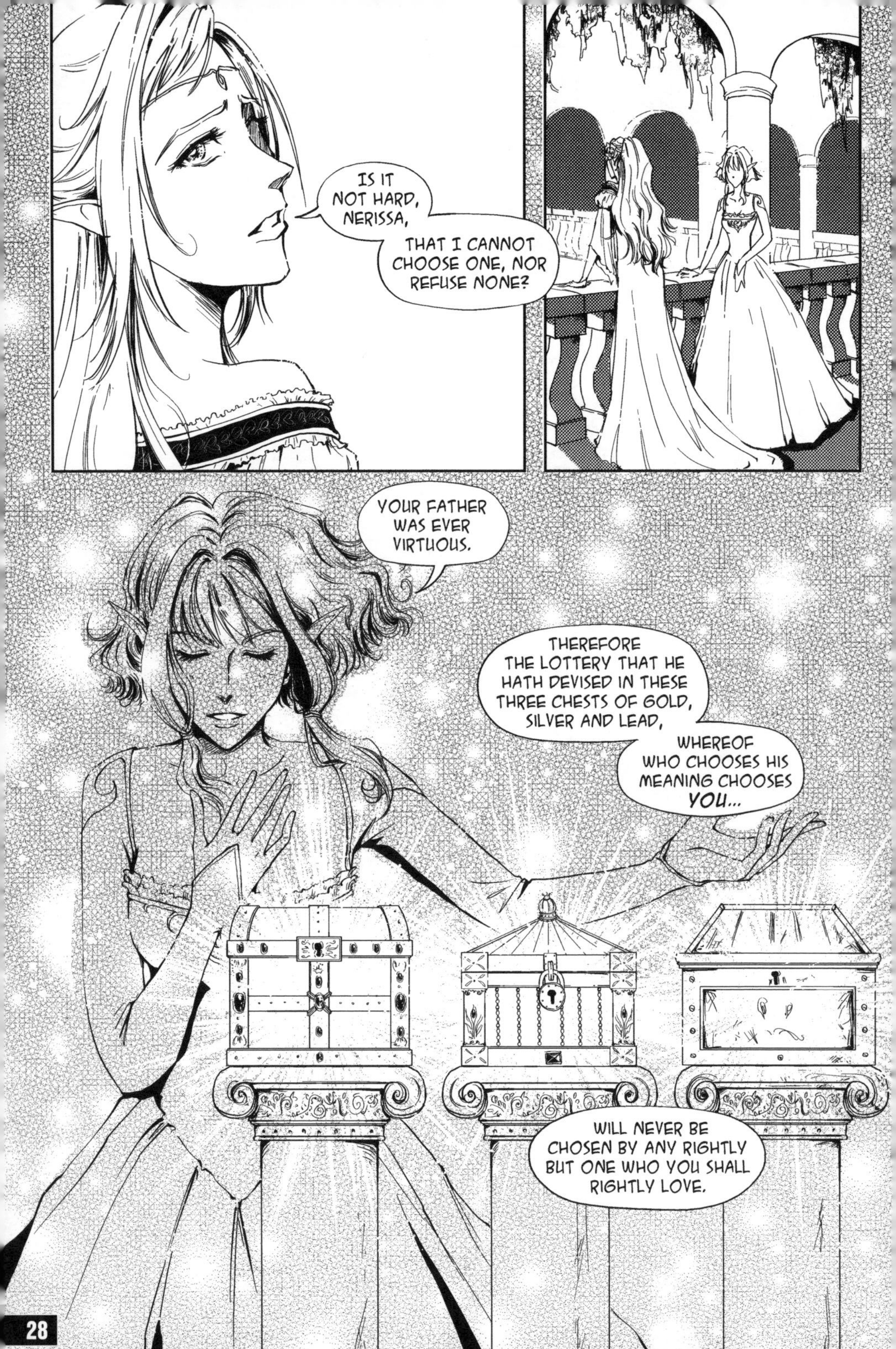
IS IT NOT HARD, NERISSA,
THAT I CANNOT CHOOSE ONE, NOR REFUSE NONE?
YOUR FATHER WAS EVER VIRTUOUS.
THEREFORE THE LOTTERY THAT HE HATH DEVISED IN THESE THREE CHESTS OF GOLD, SILVER AND LEAD,
WHEREOF WHO CHOOSES HIS MEANING CHOOSES YOU...
WILL NEVER BE CHOSEN BY ANY RIGHTLY BUT ONE WHO YOU SHALL RIGHTLY LOVE.

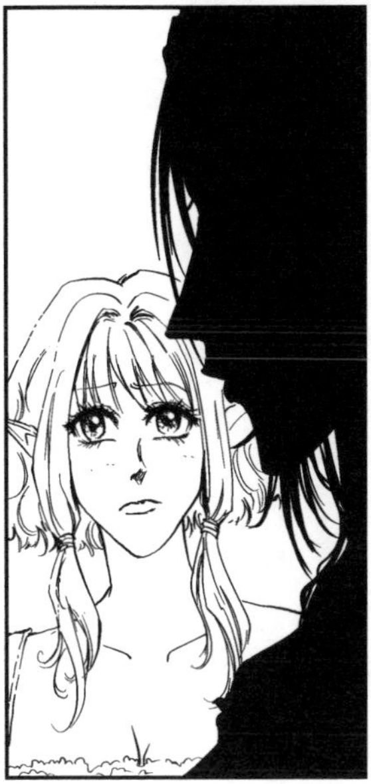

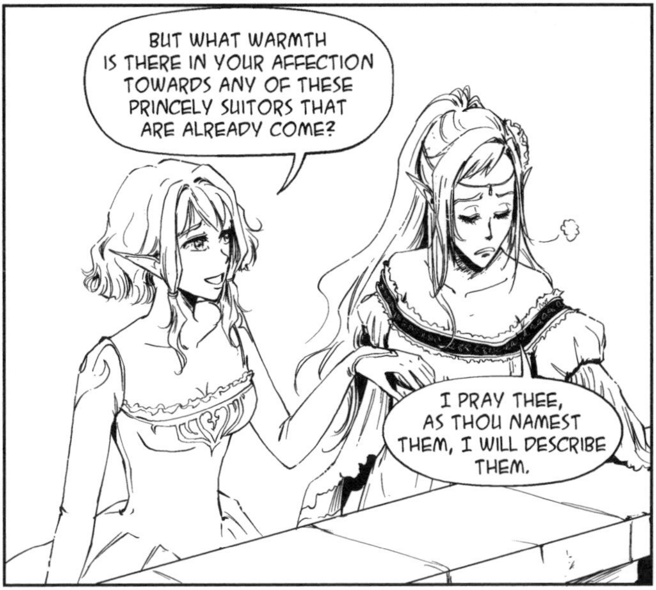
BUT WHAT WARMTH IS THERE IN YOUR AFFECTION TOWARDS ANY OF THESE PRINCELY SUITORS THAT ARE ALREADY COME?
I PRAY THEE, AS THOU NAMEST THEM, I WILL DESCRIBE THEM.

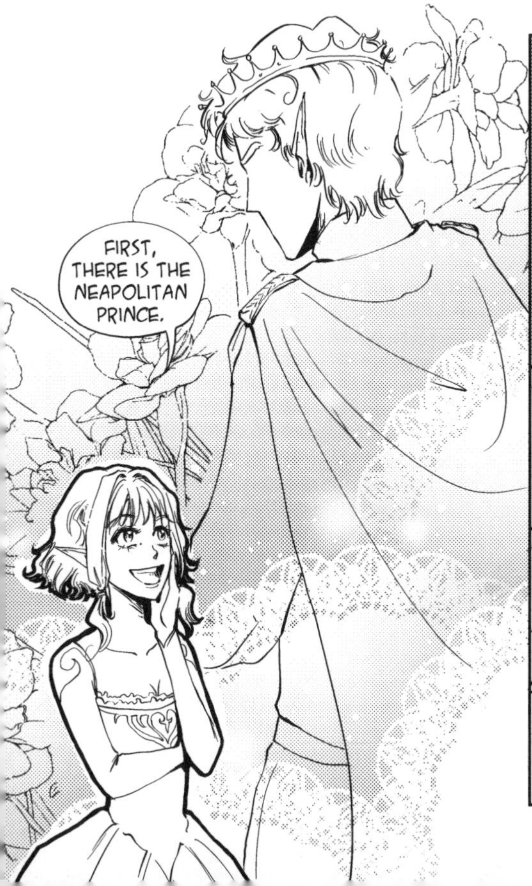
FIRST, THERE IS THE NEAPOLITAN PRINCE.

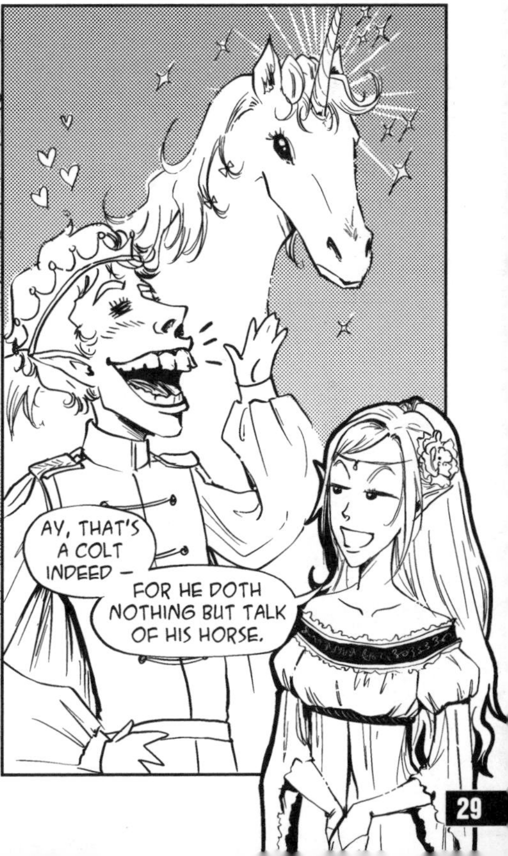
AY, THAT'S A COLT INDEED —
FOR HE DOTH NOTHING BUT TALK OF HIS HORSE.

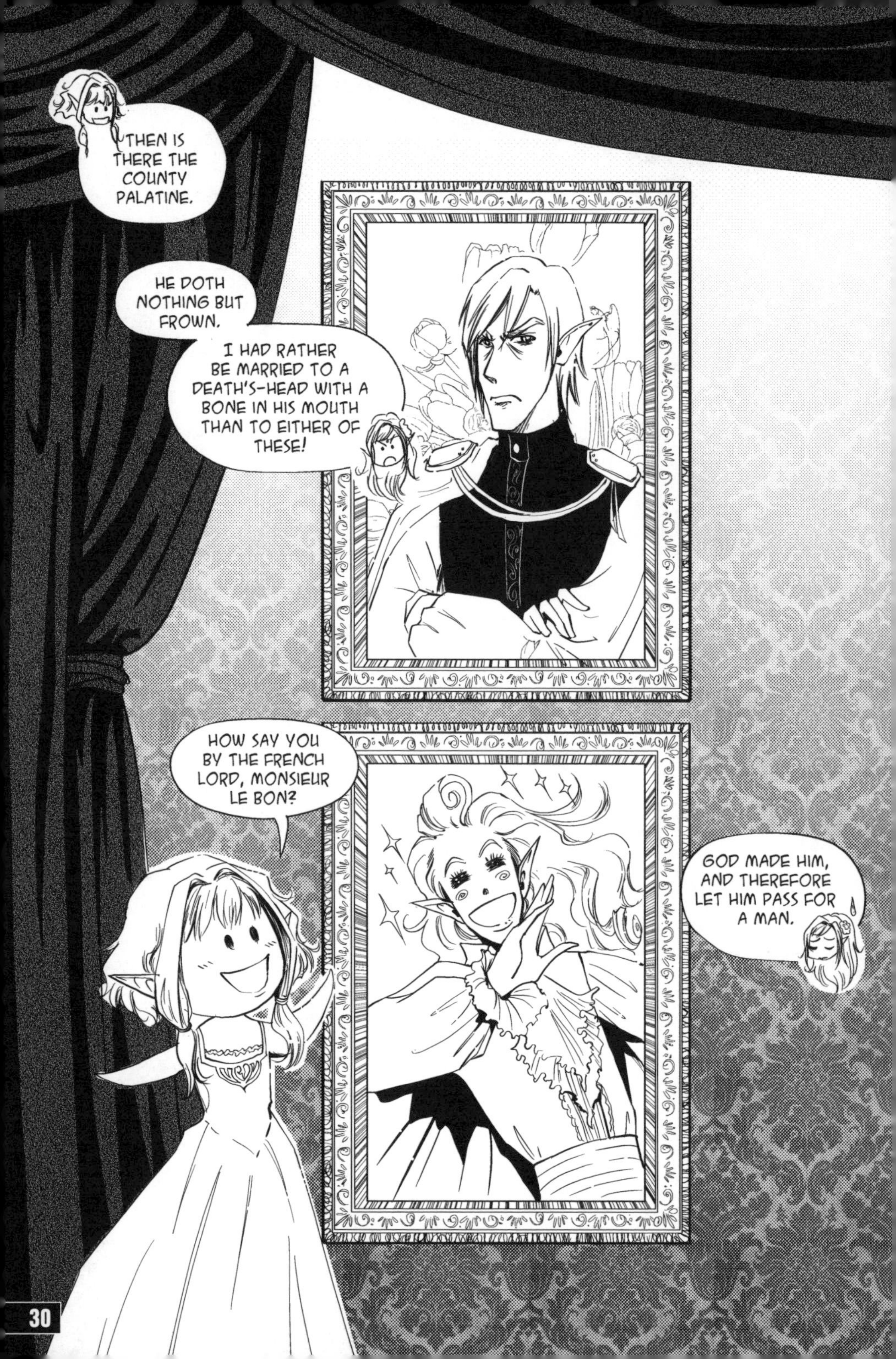
THEN IS THERE THE COUNTY PALATINE.
HE DOTH NOTHING BUT FROWN.
I HAD RATHER BE MARRIED TO A DEATH'S-HEAD WITH A BONE IN HIS MOUTH THAN TO EITHER OF THESE!
HOW SAY YOU BY THE FRENCH LORD, MONSIEUR LE BON?
GOD MADE HIM, AND THEREFORE LET HIM PASS FOR A MAN.

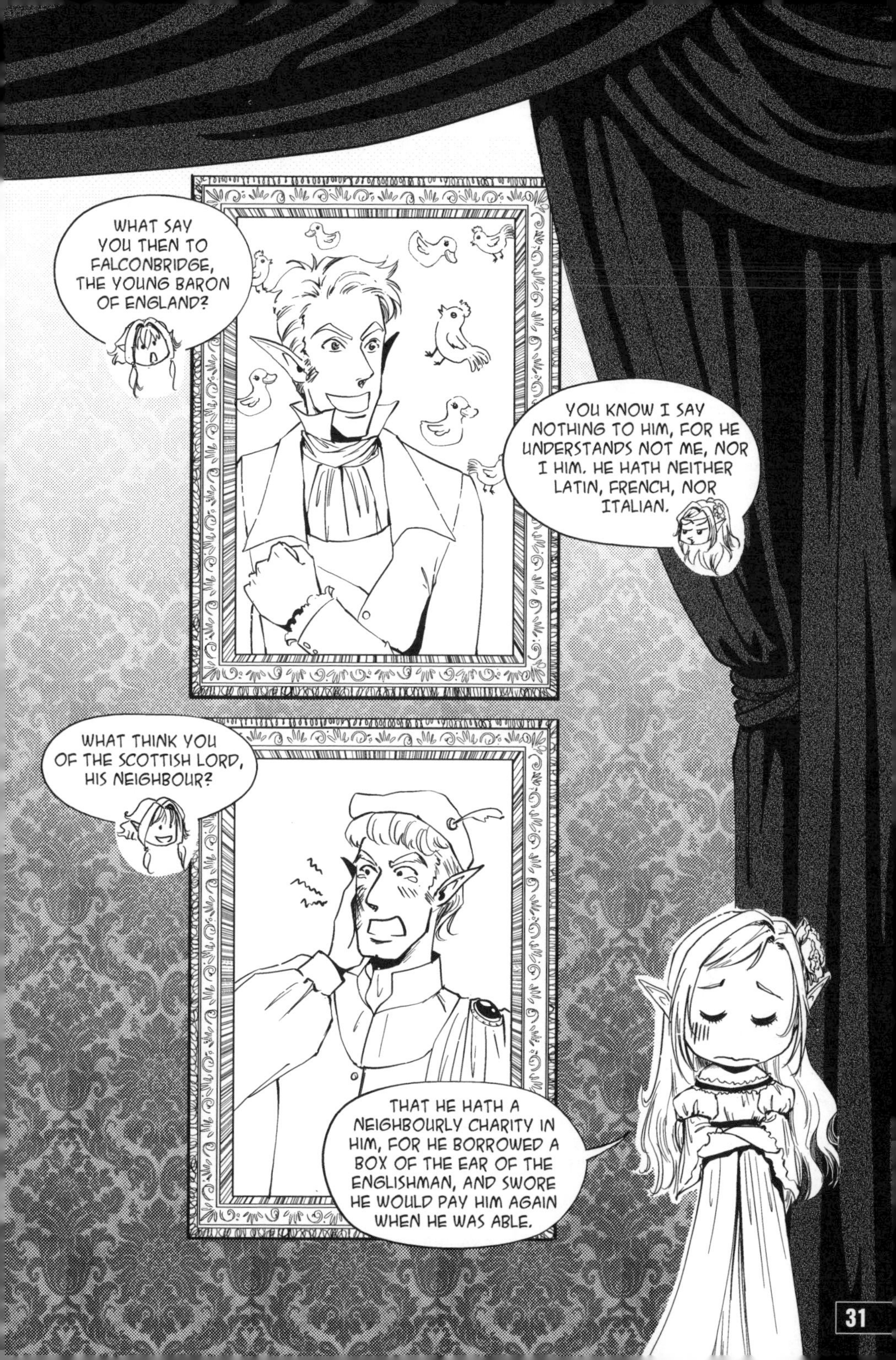
WHAT SAY YOU THEN TO FALCONBRIDGE, THE YOUNG BARON OF ENGLAND?
YOU KNOW I SAY NOTHING TO HIM, FOR HE UNDERSTANDS NOT ME, NOR I HIM. HE HATH NEITHER LATIN, FRENCH, NOR ITALIAN.
WHAT THINK YOU OF THE SCOTTISH LORD, HIS NEIGHBOUR?
THAT HE HATH A NEIGHBOURLY CHARITY IN HIM, FOR HE BORROWED A BOX OF THE EAR OF THE ENGLISHMAN, AND SWORE HE WOULD PAY HIM AGAIN WHEN HE WAS ABLE.

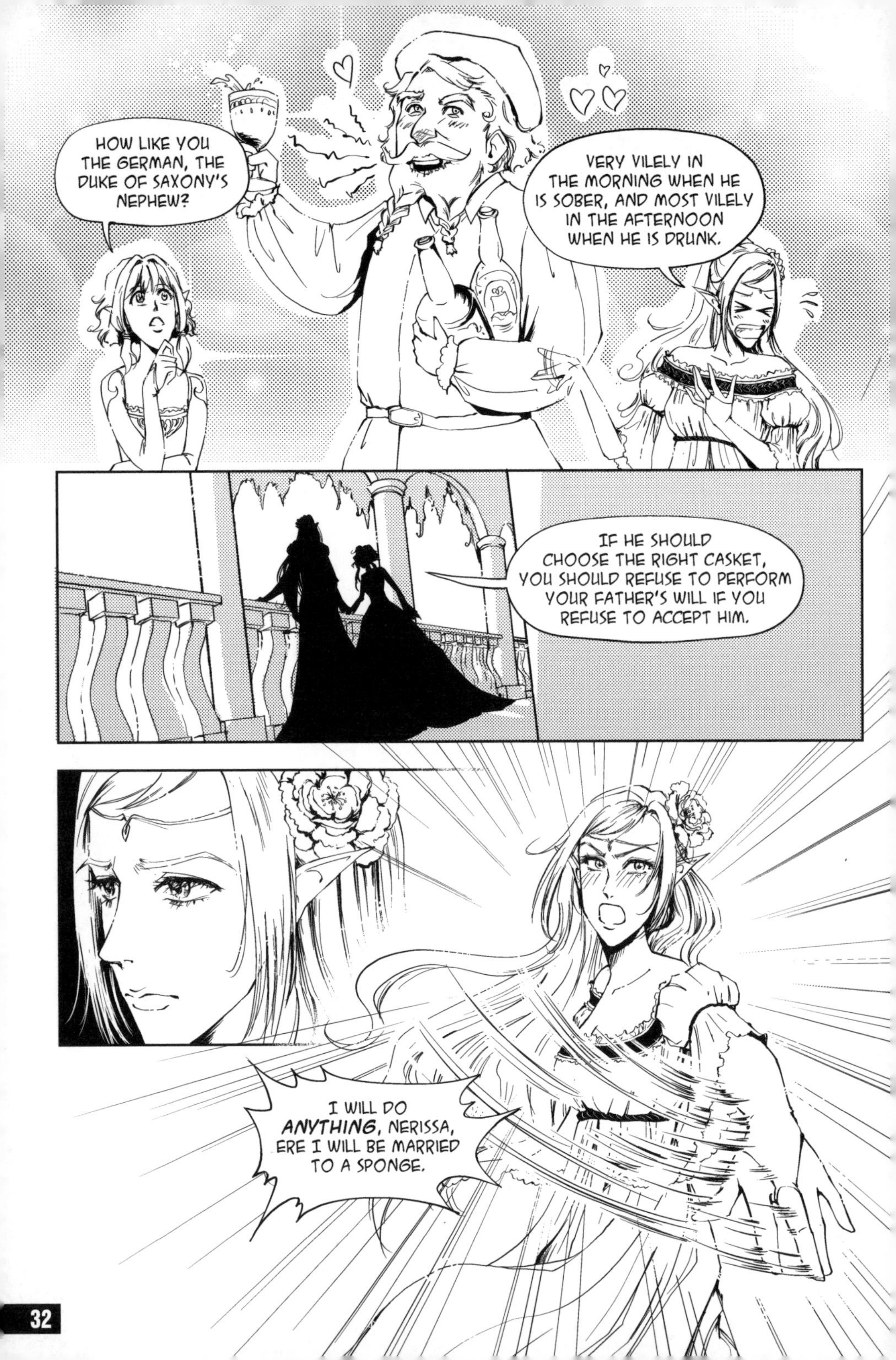
HOW LIKE YOU THE GERMAN, THE DUKE OF SAXONY'S NEPHEW?
VERY VILELY IN THE MORNING WHEN HE IS SOBER, AND MOST VILELY IN THE AFTERNOON WHEN HE IS DRUNK.
IF HE SHOULD CHOOSE THE RIGHT CASKET, YOU SHOULD REFUSE TO PERFORM YOUR FATHER'S WILL IF YOU REFUSE TO ACCEPT HIM.
I WILL DO *ANYTHING*, NERISSA, ERE I WILL BE MARRIED TO A SPONGE.

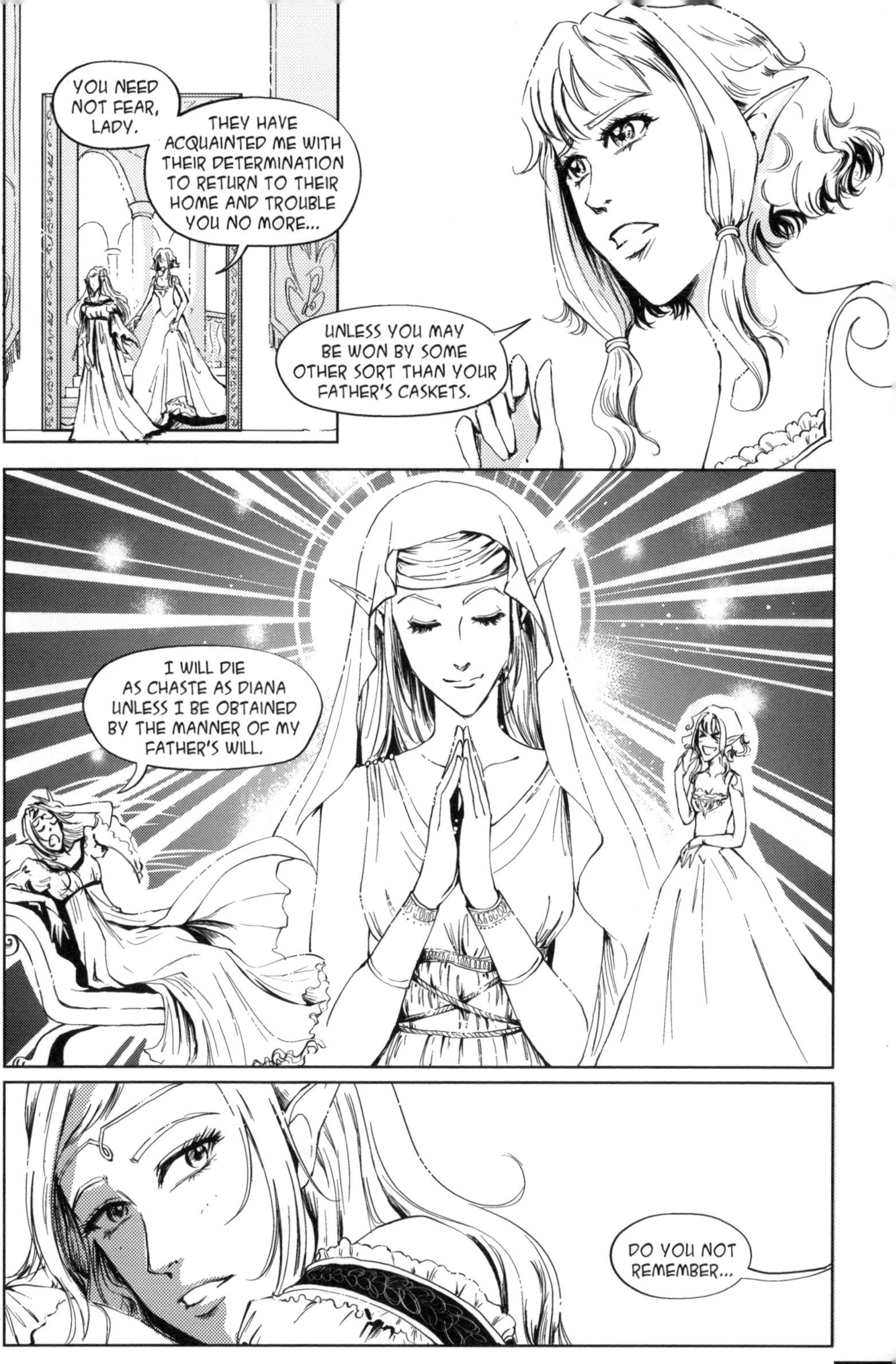

YOU NEED NOT FEAR, LADY.
THEY HAVE ACQUAINTED ME WITH THEIR DETERMINATION TO RETURN TO THEIR HOME AND TROUBLE YOU NO MORE...
UNLESS YOU MAY BE WON BY SOME OTHER SORT THAN YOUR FATHER'S CASKETS.
I WILL DIE AS CHASTE AS DIANA UNLESS I BE OBTAINED BY THE MANNER OF MY FATHER'S WILL.
DO YOU NOT REMEMBER...

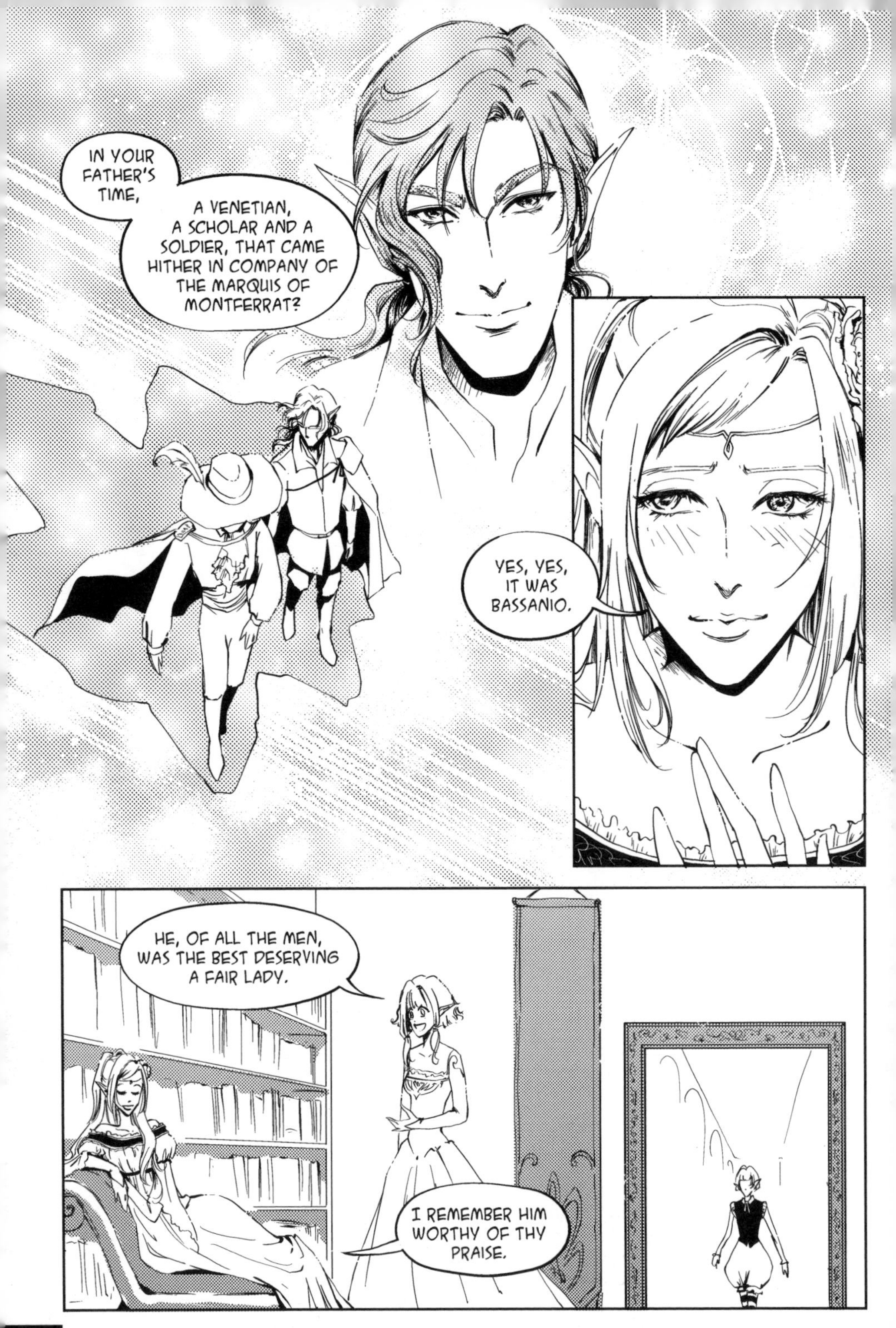
IN YOUR FATHER'S TIME,
A VENETIAN, A SCHOLAR AND A SOLDIER, THAT CAME HITHER IN COMPANY OF THE MARQUIS OF MONTFERRAT?
YES, YES, IT WAS BASSANIO.
HE, OF ALL THE MEN, WAS THE BEST DESERVING A FAIR LADY.
I REMEMBER HIM WORTHY OF THY PRAISE.

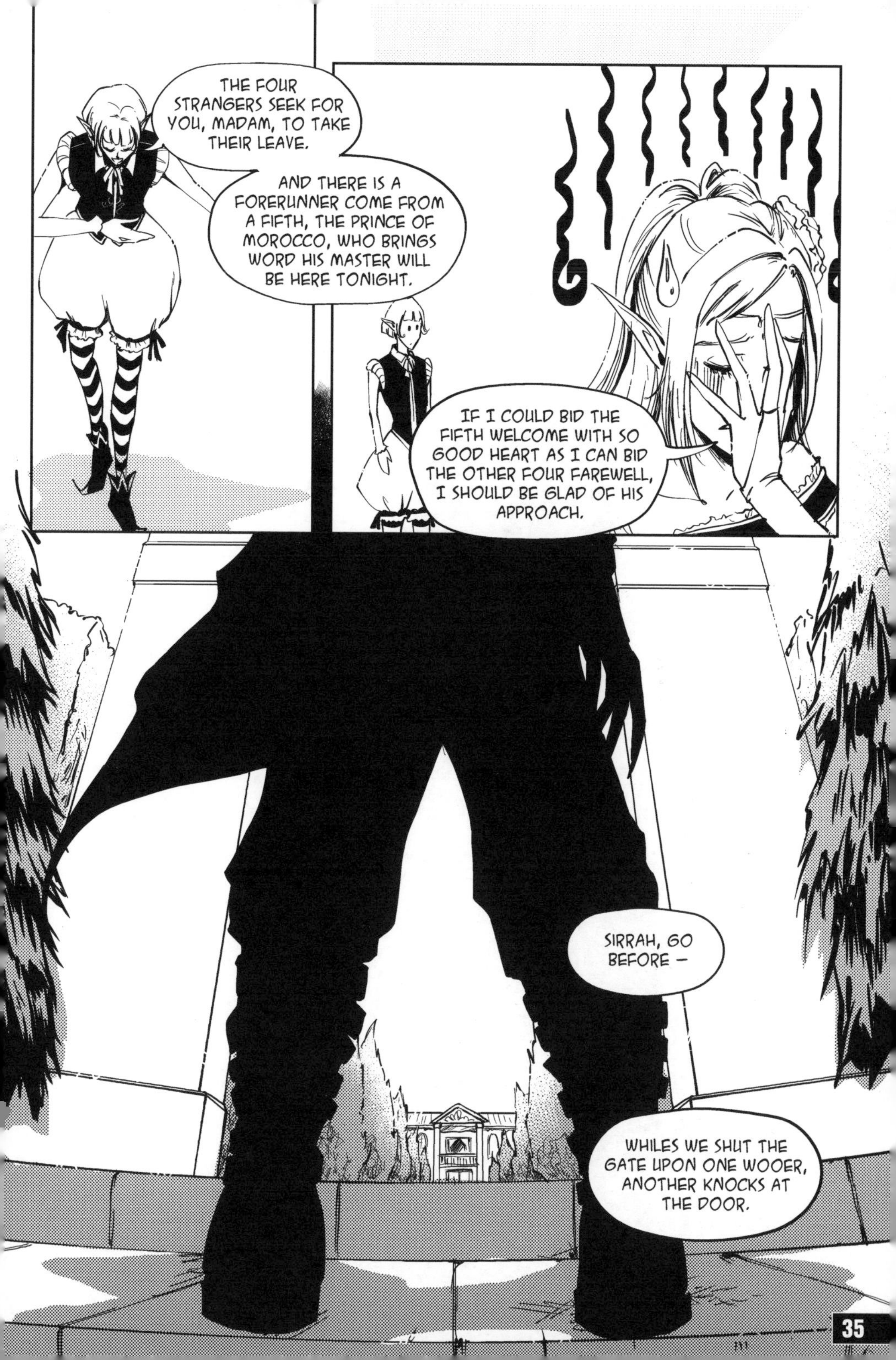
THE FOUR STRANGERS SEEK FOR YOU, MADAM, TO TAKE THEIR LEAVE.
AND THERE IS A FORERUNNER COME FROM A FIFTH, THE PRINCE OF MOROCCO, WHO BRINGS WORD HIS MASTER WILL BE HERE TONIGHT.
IF I COULD BID THE FIFTH WELCOME WITH SO GOOD HEART AS I CAN BID THE OTHER FOUR FAREWELL, I SHOULD BE GLAD OF HIS APPROACH.
SIRRAH, GO BEFORE –
WHILES WE SHUT THE GATE UPON ONE WOOER, ANOTHER KNOCKS AT THE DOOR.

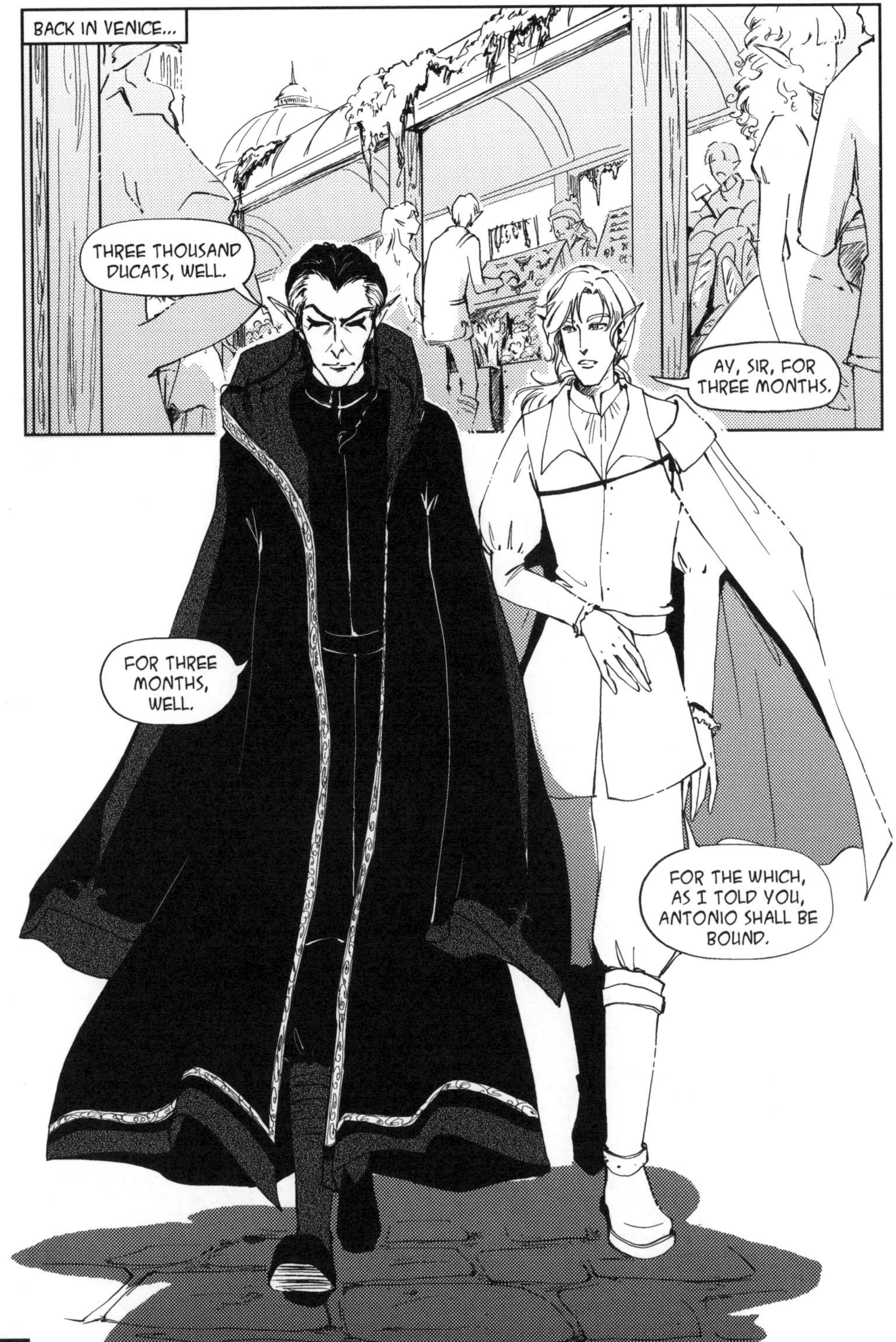
BACK IN VENICE...
THREE THOUSAND DUCATS, WELL.
AY, SIR, FOR THREE MONTHS.
FOR THREE MONTHS, WELL.
FOR THE WHICH, AS I TOLD YOU, ANTONIO SHALL BE BOUND.

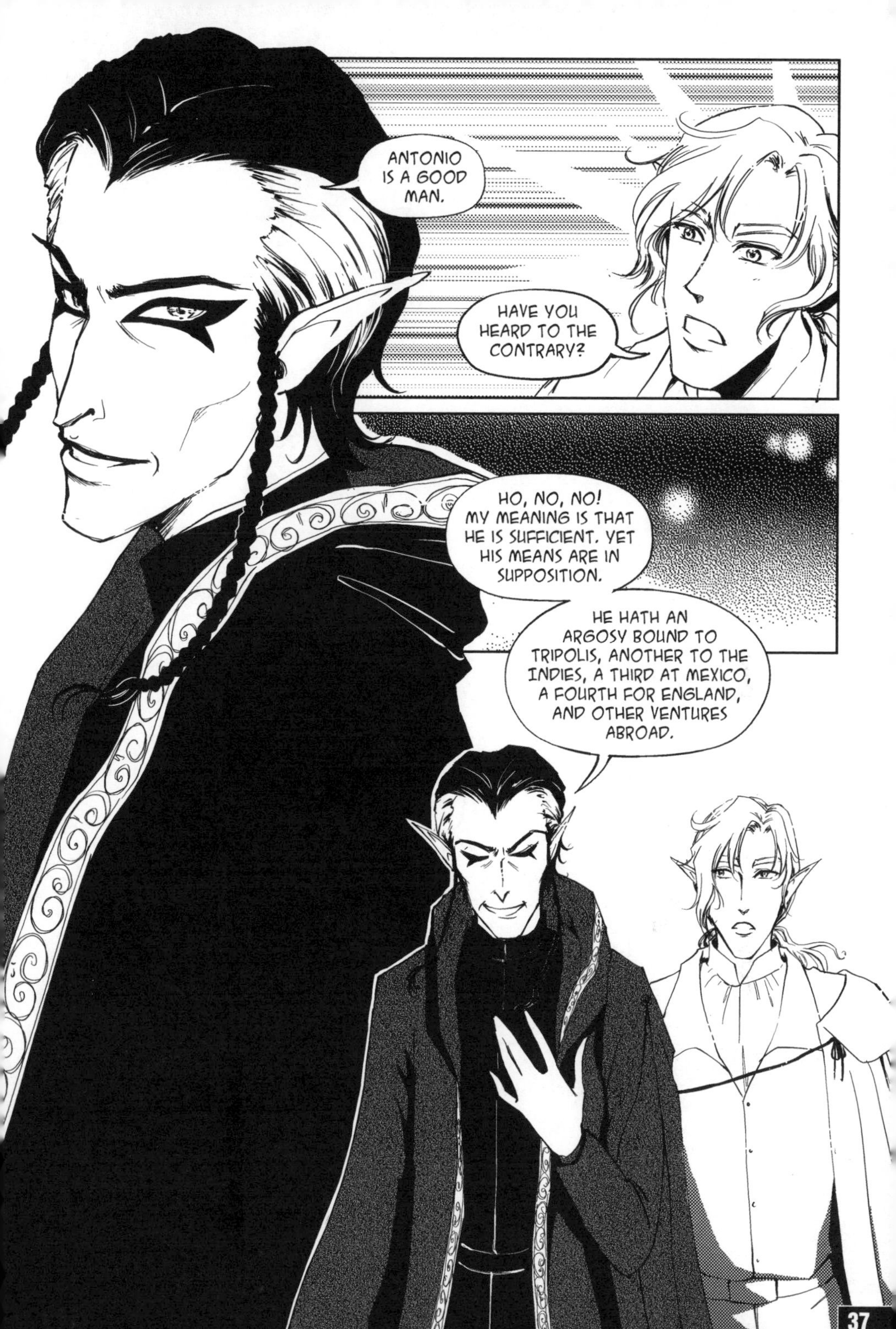

ANTONIO IS A GOOD MAN.
HAVE YOU HEARD TO THE CONTRARY?
HO, NO, NO! MY MEANING IS THAT HE IS SUFFICIENT. YET HIS MEANS ARE IN SUPPOSITION.
HE HATH AN ARGOSY BOUND TO TRIPOLIS, ANOTHER TO THE INDIES, A THIRD AT MEXICO, A FOURTH FOR ENGLAND, AND OTHER VENTURES ABROAD.

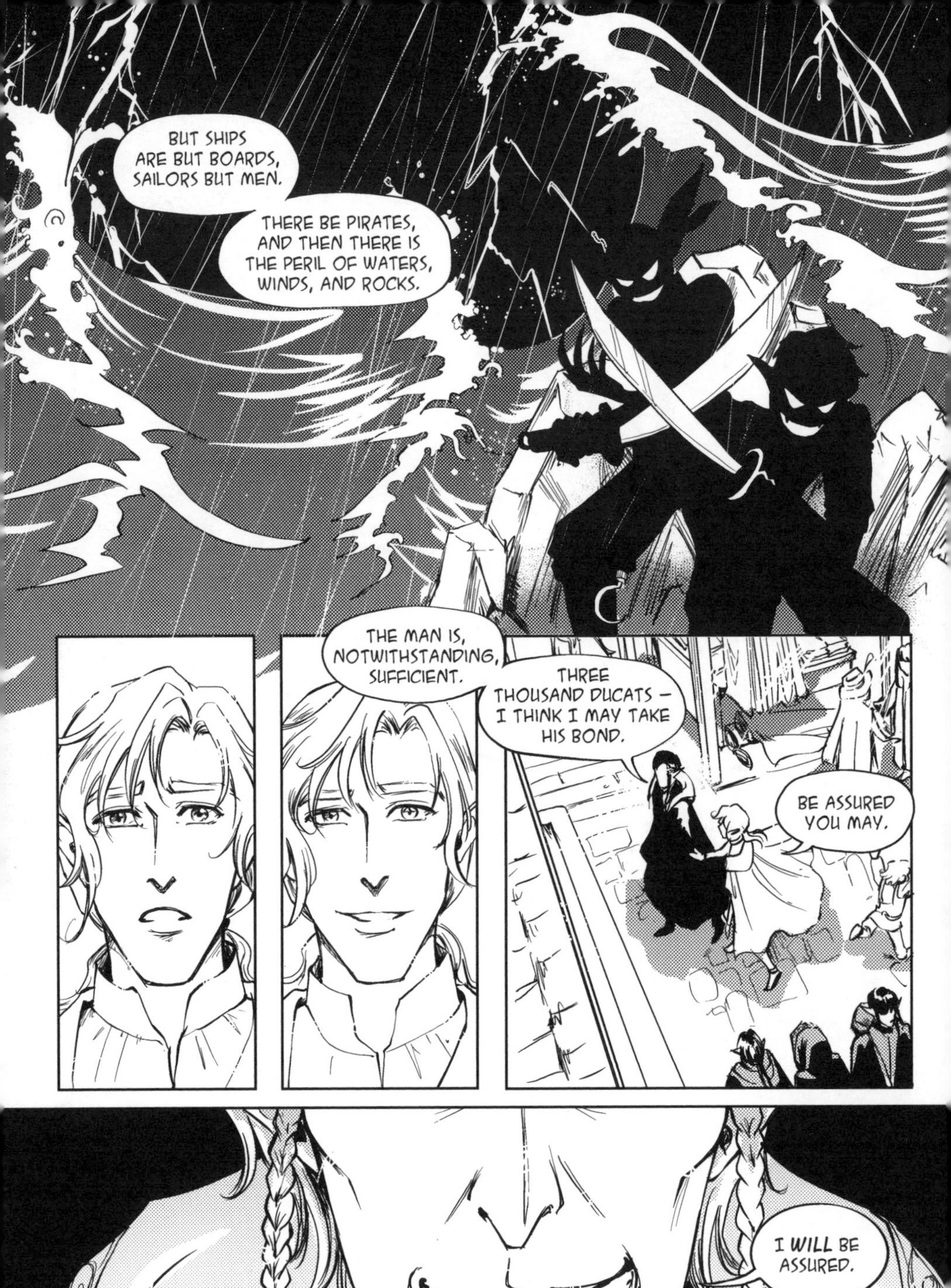
BUT SHIPS ARE BUT BOARDS, SAILORS BUT MEN.
THERE BE PIRATES, AND THEN THERE IS THE PERIL OF WATERS, WINDS, AND ROCKS.
THE MAN IS, NOTWITHSTANDING, SUFFICIENT.
THREE THOUSAND DUCATS — I THINK I MAY TAKE HIS BOND.
BE ASSURED YOU MAY.
I **WILL** BE ASSURED.

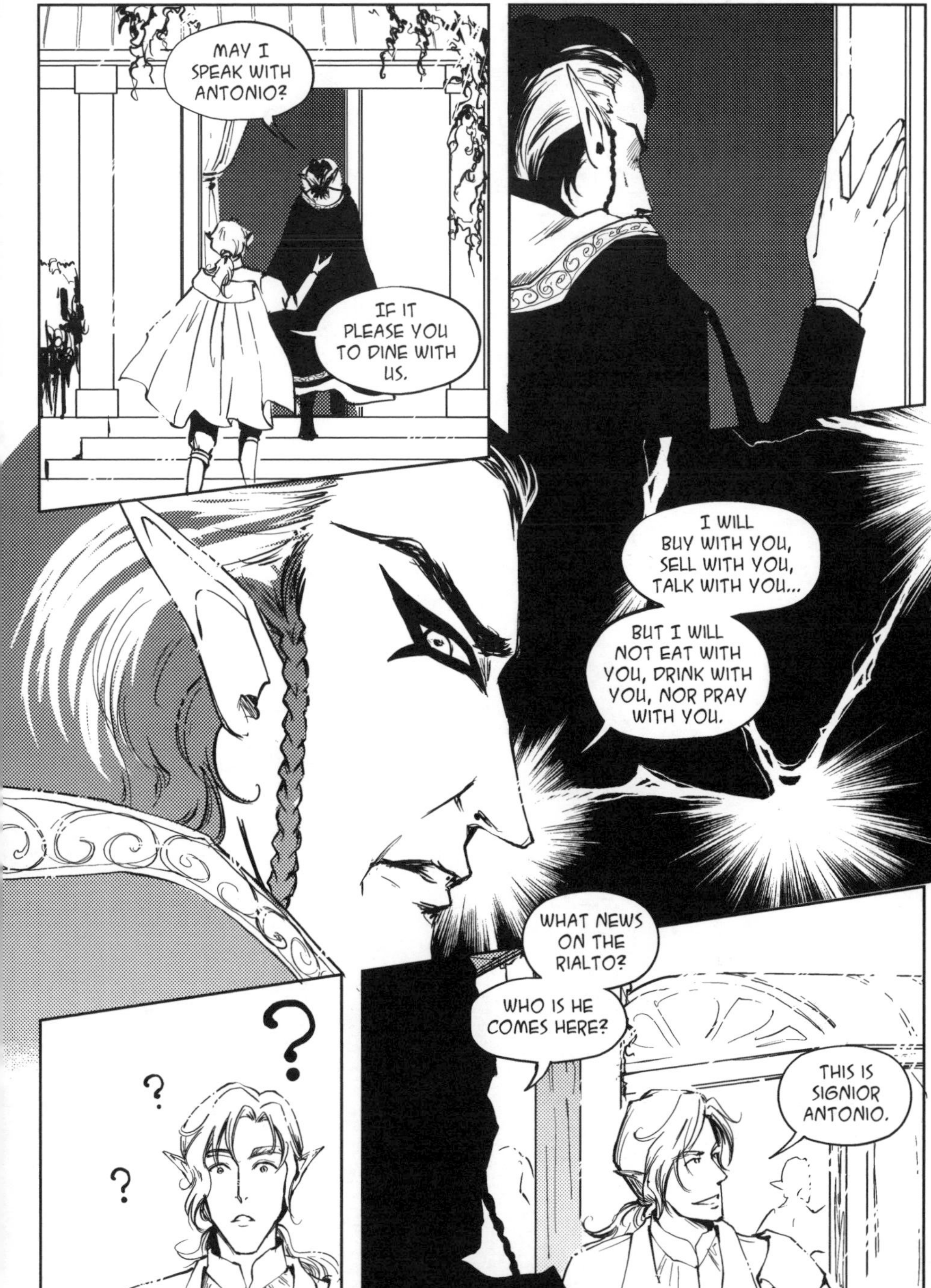
MAY I SPEAK WITH ANTONIO?
IF IT PLEASE YOU TO DINE WITH US.
I WILL BUY WITH YOU, SELL WITH YOU, TALK WITH YOU...
BUT I WILL NOT EAT WITH YOU, DRINK WITH YOU, NOR PRAY WITH YOU.
?
?
?
WHAT NEWS ON THE RIALTO?
WHO IS HE COMES HERE?
THIS IS SIGNIOR ANTONIO.

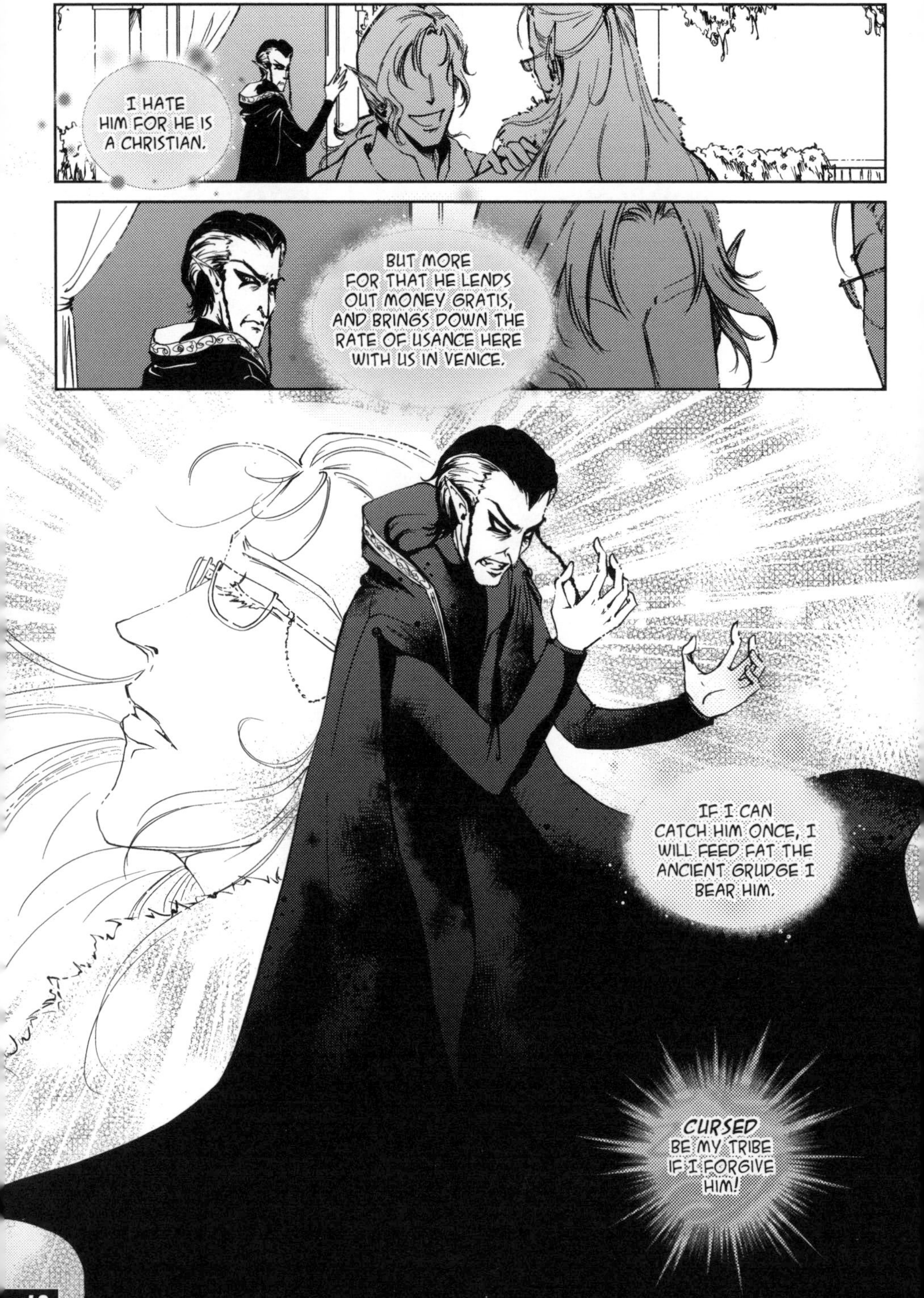
I HATE HIM FOR HE IS A CHRISTIAN.
BUT MORE FOR THAT HE LENDS OUT MONEY GRATIS, AND BRINGS DOWN THE RATE OF USANCE HERE WITH US IN VENICE.
IF I CAN CATCH HIM ONCE, I WILL FEED FAT THE ANCIENT GRUDGE I BEAR HIM.
CURSED BE MY TRIBE IF I FORGIVE HIM!

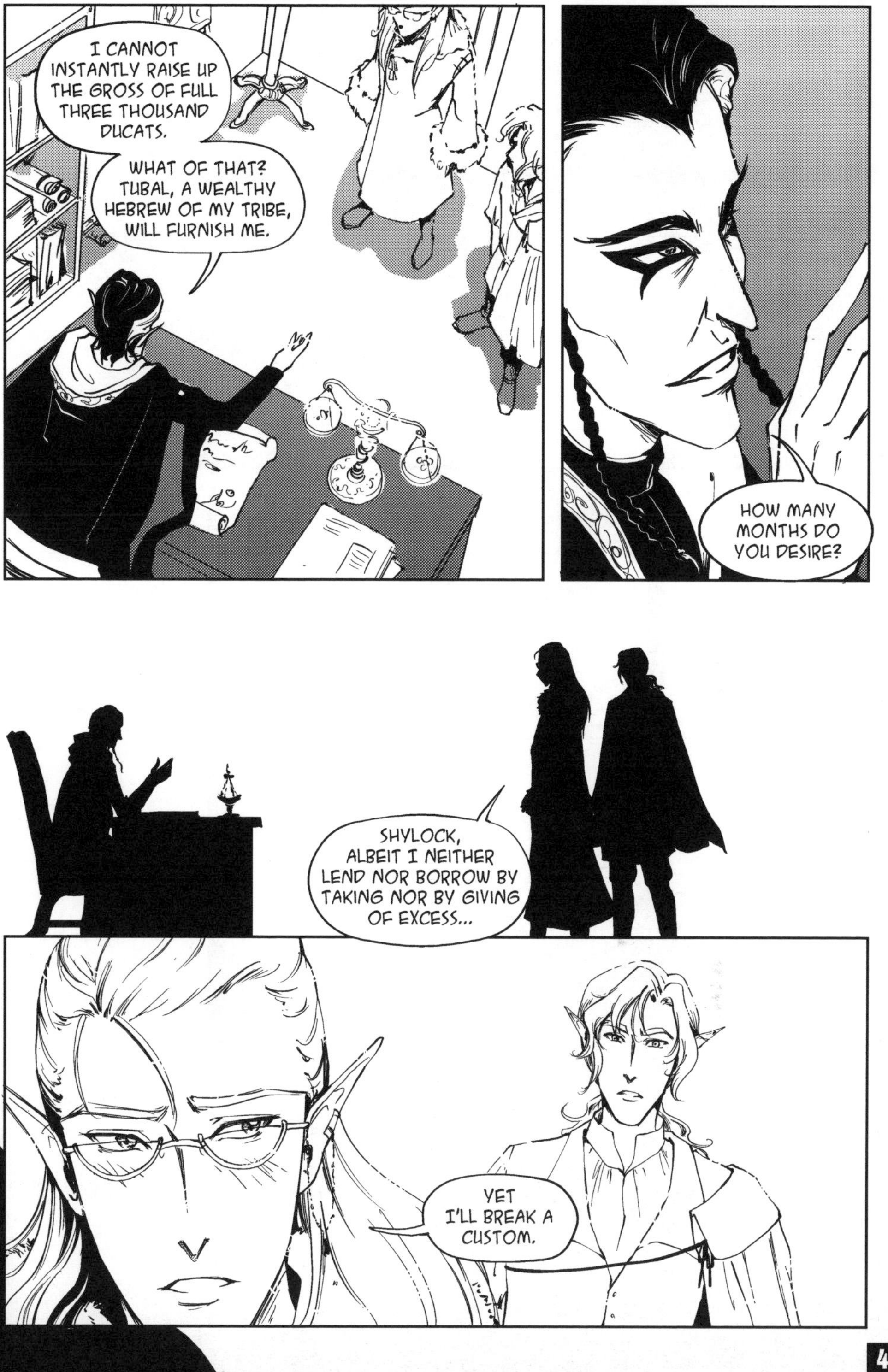
I CANNOT INSTANTLY RAISE UP THE GROSS OF FULL THREE THOUSAND DUCATS.
WHAT OF THAT? TUBAL, A WEALTHY HEBREW OF MY TRIBE, WILL FURNISH ME.
HOW MANY MONTHS DO YOU DESIRE?
SHYLOCK, ALBEIT I NEITHER LEND NOR BORROW BY TAKING NOR BY GIVING OF EXCESS...
YET I'LL BREAK A CUSTOM.

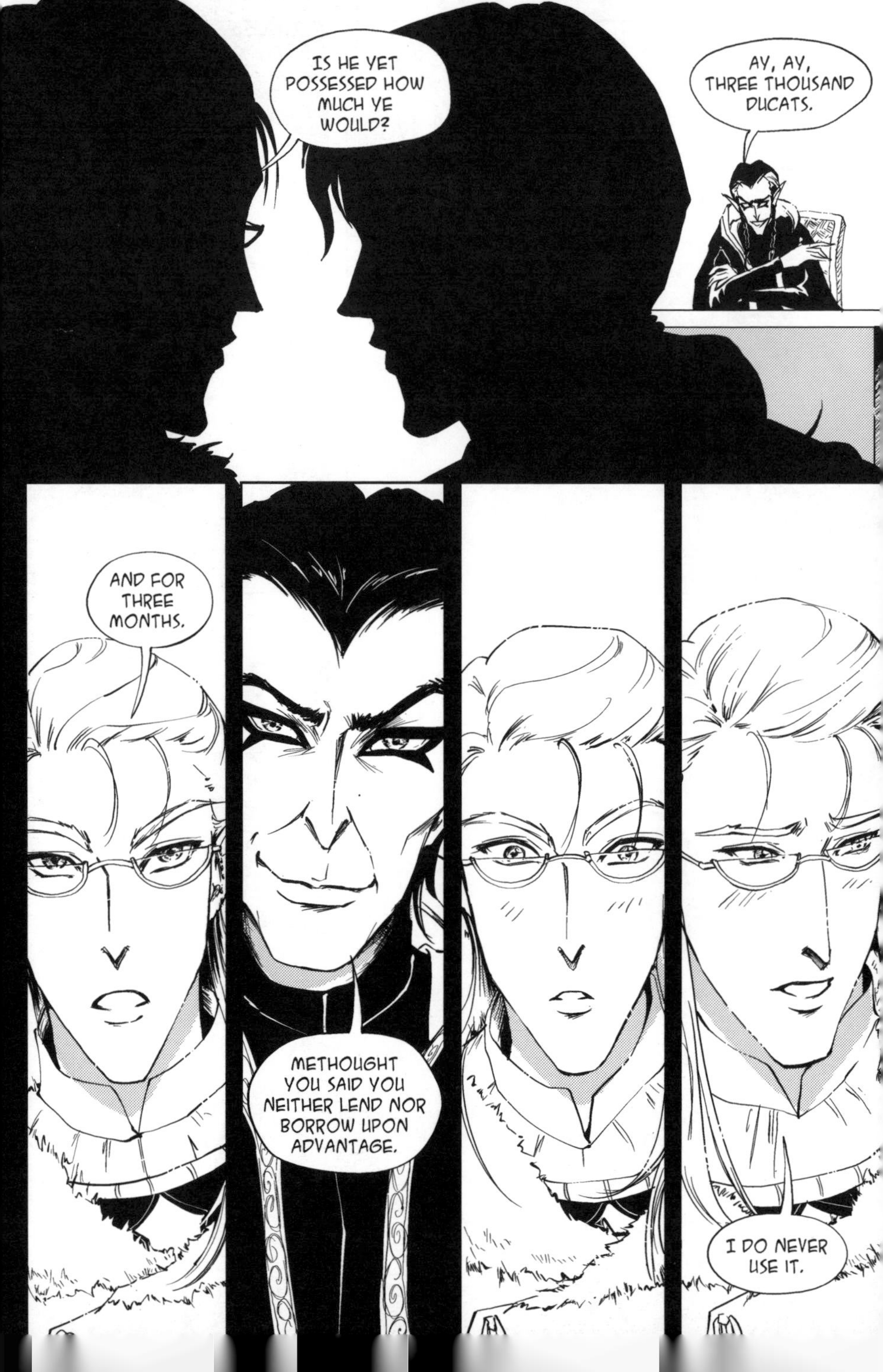
IS HE YET POSSESSED HOW MUCH YE WOULD?
AY, AY, THREE THOUSAND DUCATS.
AND FOR THREE MONTHS.
METHOUGHT YOU SAID YOU NEITHER LEND NOR BORROW UPON ADVANTAGE.
I DO NEVER USE IT.

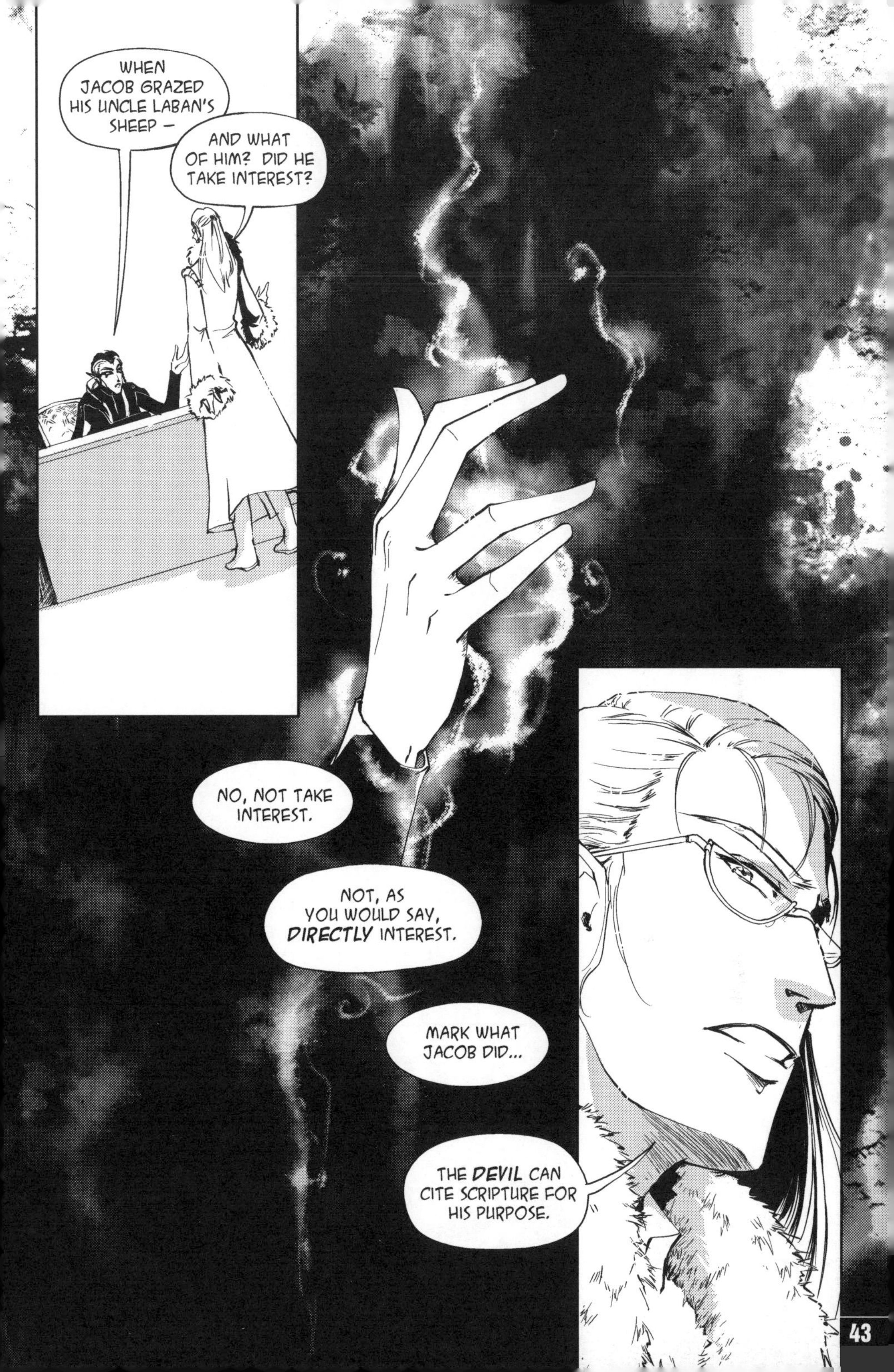
WHEN JACOB GRAZED HIS UNCLE LABAN'S SHEEP —
AND WHAT OF HIM? DID HE TAKE INTEREST?
NO, NOT TAKE INTEREST.
NOT, AS YOU WOULD SAY, **DIRECTLY** INTEREST.
MARK WHAT JACOB DID...
THE **DEVIL** CAN CITE SCRIPTURE FOR HIS PURPOSE.

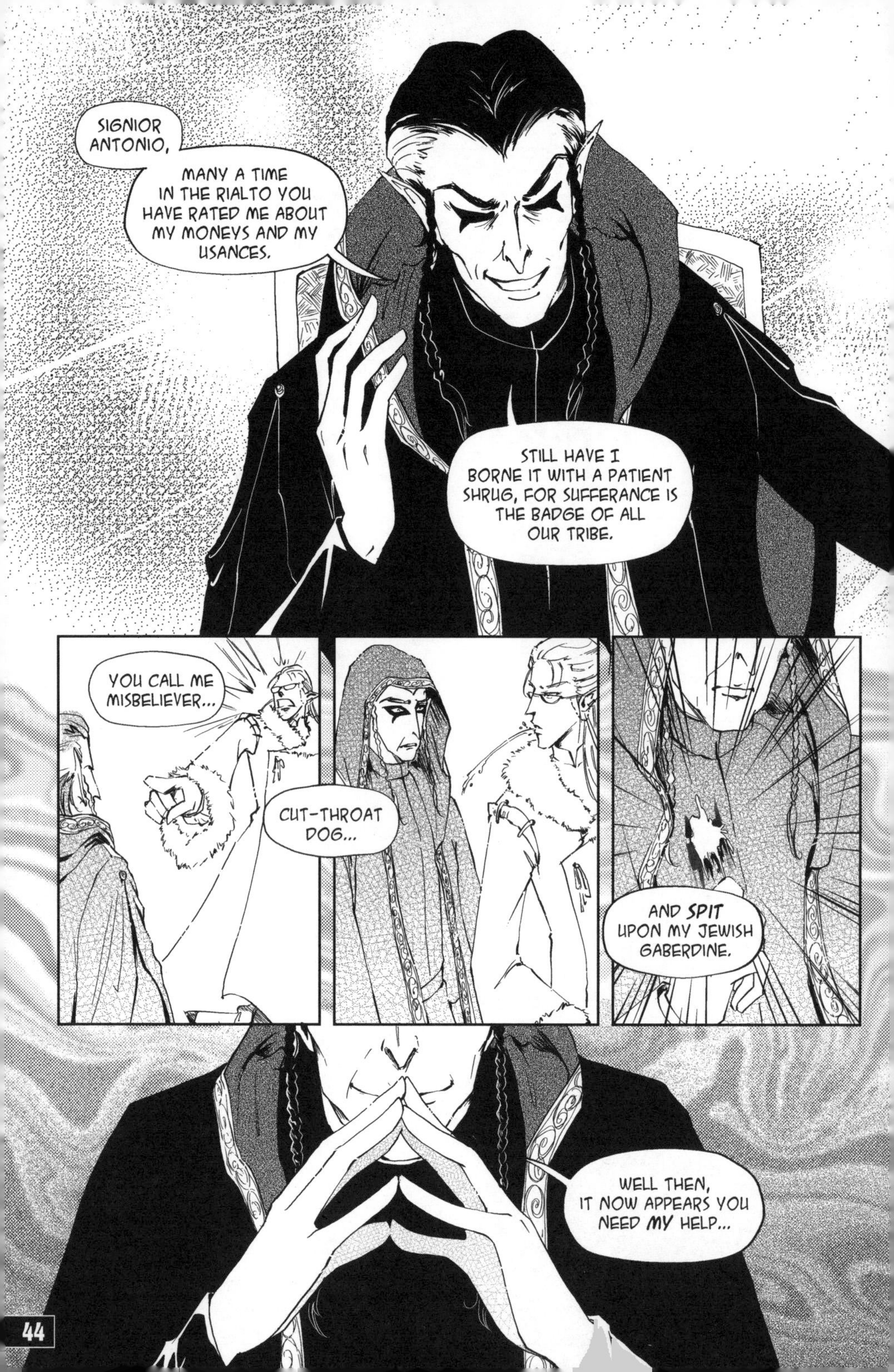
SIGNIOR ANTONIO,
MANY A TIME IN THE RIALTO YOU HAVE RATED ME ABOUT MY MONEYS AND MY USANCES.
STILL HAVE I BORNE IT WITH A PATIENT SHRUG, FOR SUFFERANCE IS THE BADGE OF ALL OUR TRIBE.
YOU CALL ME MISBELIEVER...
CUT-THROAT DOG...
AND SPIT UPON MY JEWISH GABERDINE.
WELL THEN, IT NOW APPEARS YOU NEED MY HELP...

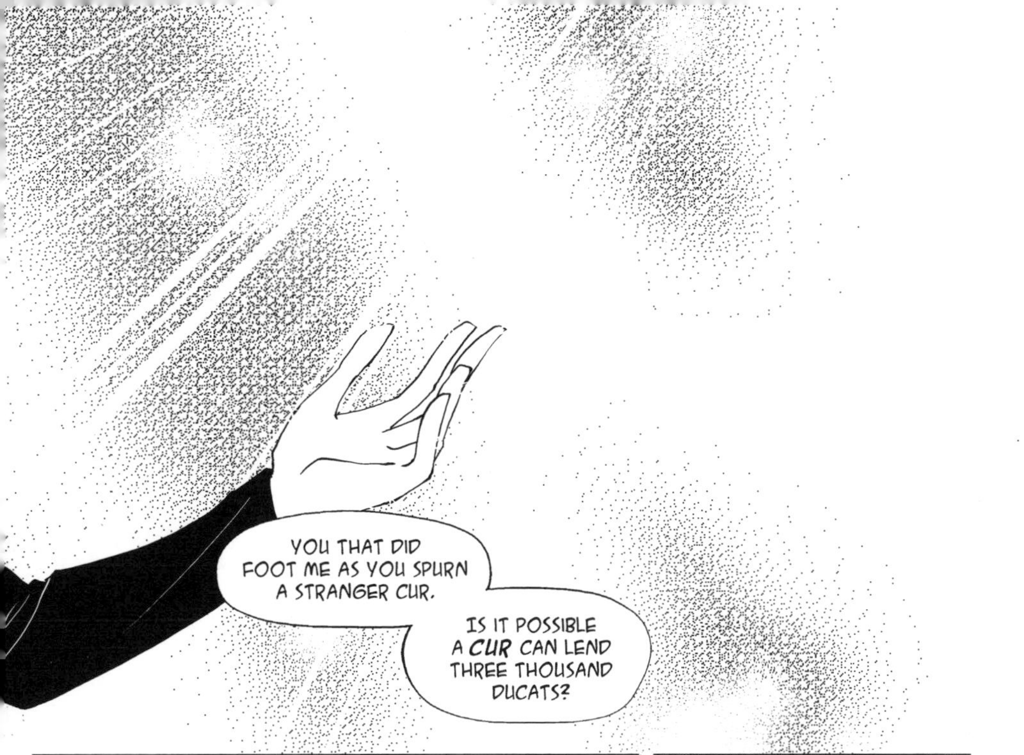
YOU THAT DID FOOT ME AS YOU SPURN A STRANGER CUR.
IS IT POSSIBLE A CUR CAN LEND THREE THOUSAND DUCATS?

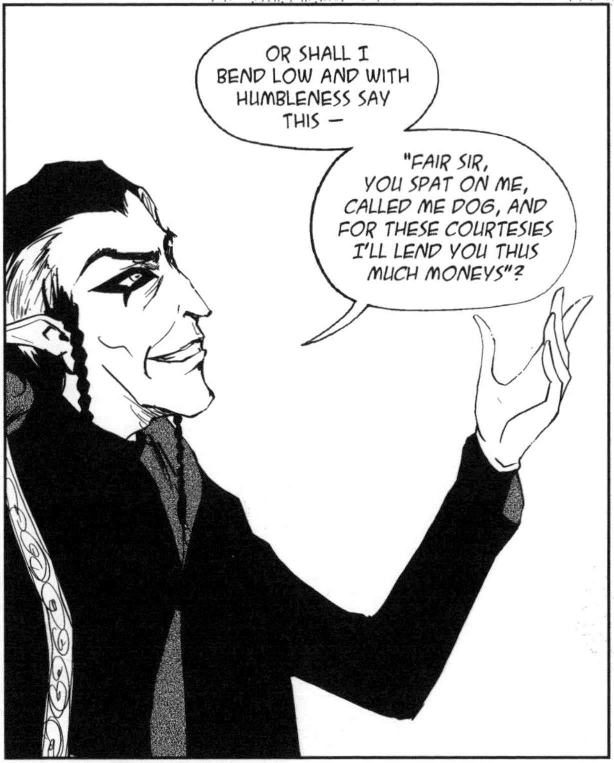
OR SHALL I BEND LOW AND WITH HUMBLENESS SAY THIS —
"FAIR SIR, YOU SPAT ON ME, CALLED ME DOG, AND FOR THESE COURTESIES I'LL LEND YOU THUS MUCH MONEYS"?

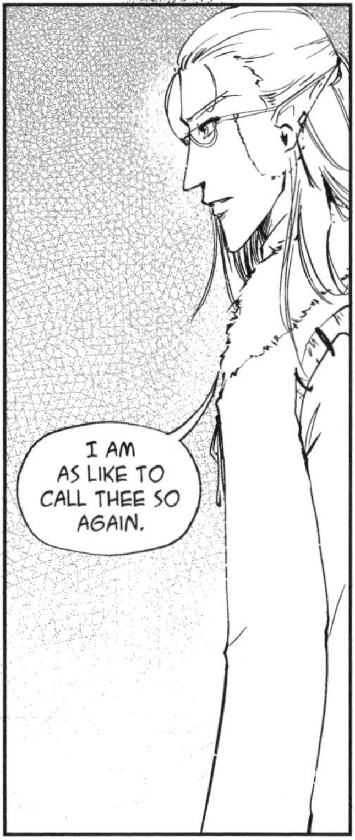
I AM AS LIKE TO CALL THEE SO AGAIN.

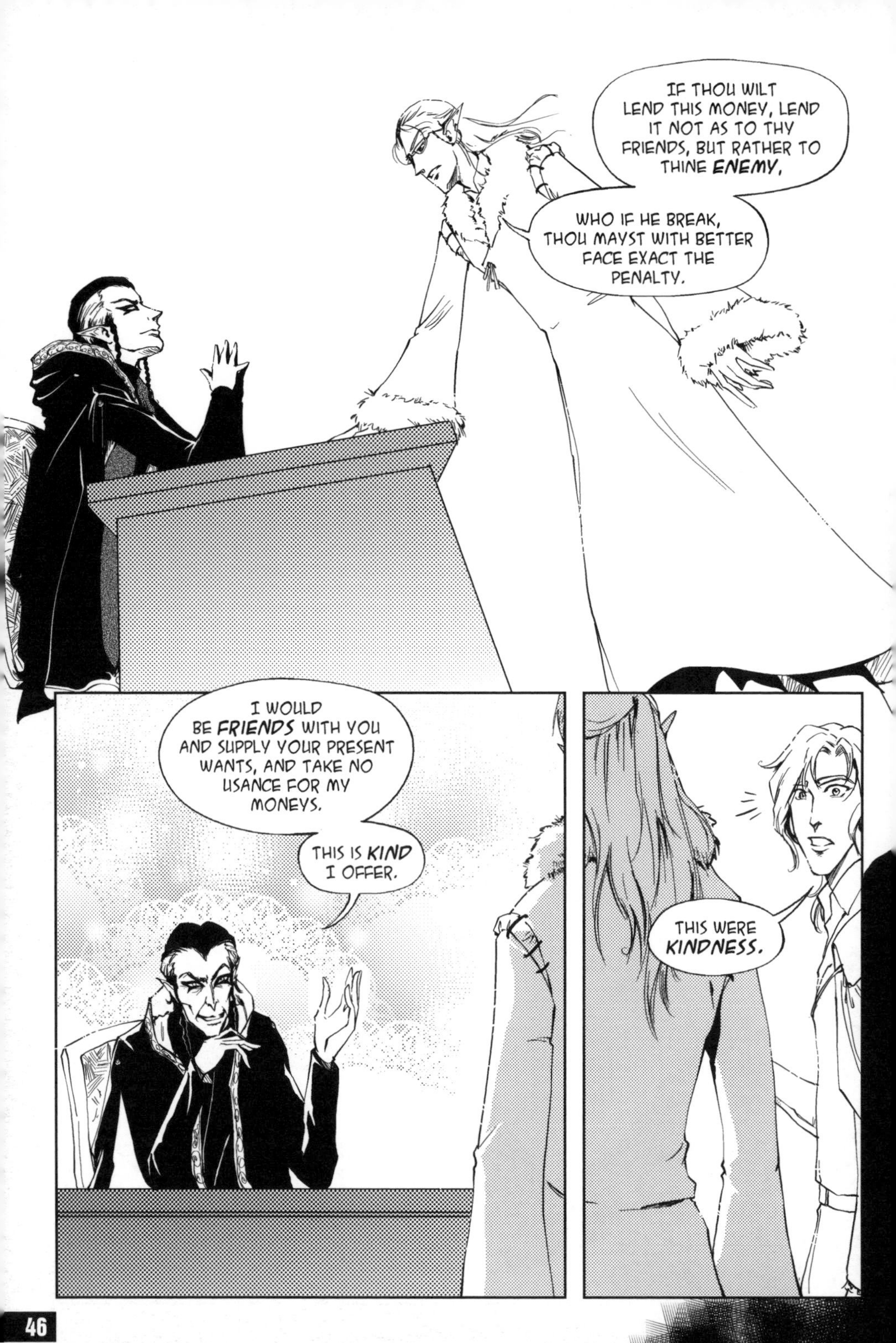
IF THOU WILT LEND THIS MONEY, LEND IT NOT AS TO THY FRIENDS, BUT RATHER TO THINE ENEMY,
WHO IF HE BREAK, THOU MAYST WITH BETTER FACE EXACT THE PENALTY.
I WOULD BE FRIENDS WITH YOU AND SUPPLY YOUR PRESENT WANTS, AND TAKE NO USANCE FOR MY MONEYS.
THIS IS KIND I OFFER.
THIS WERE KINDNESS.

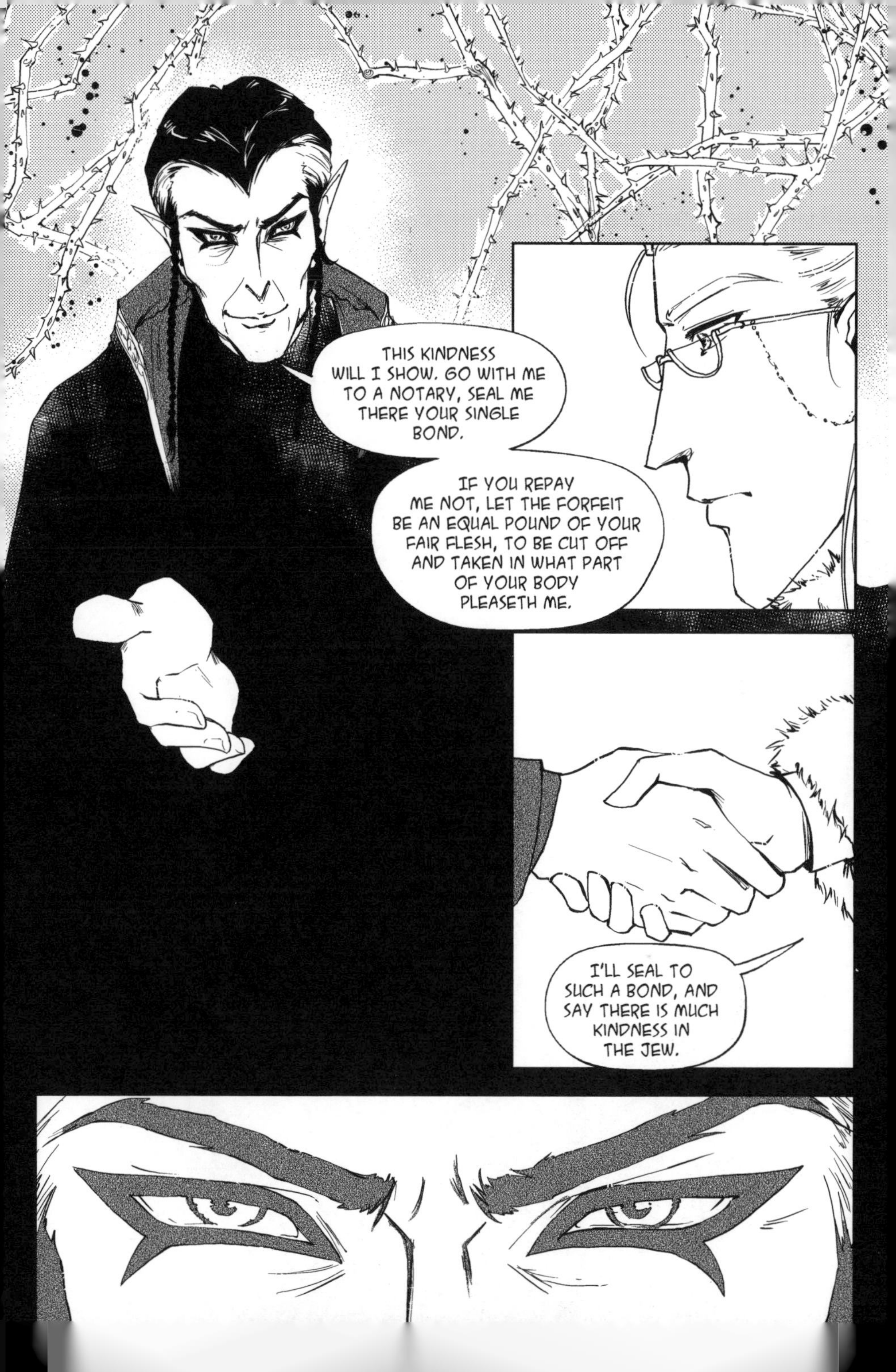
THIS KINDNESS WILL I SHOW. GO WITH ME TO A NOTARY, SEAL ME THERE YOUR SINGLE BOND.
IF YOU REPAY ME NOT, LET THE FORFEIT BE AN EQUAL POUND OF YOUR FAIR FLESH, TO BE CUT OFF AND TAKEN IN WHAT PART OF YOUR BODY PLEASETH ME.
I'LL SEAL TO SUCH A BOND, AND SAY THERE IS MUCH KINDNESS IN THE JEW.

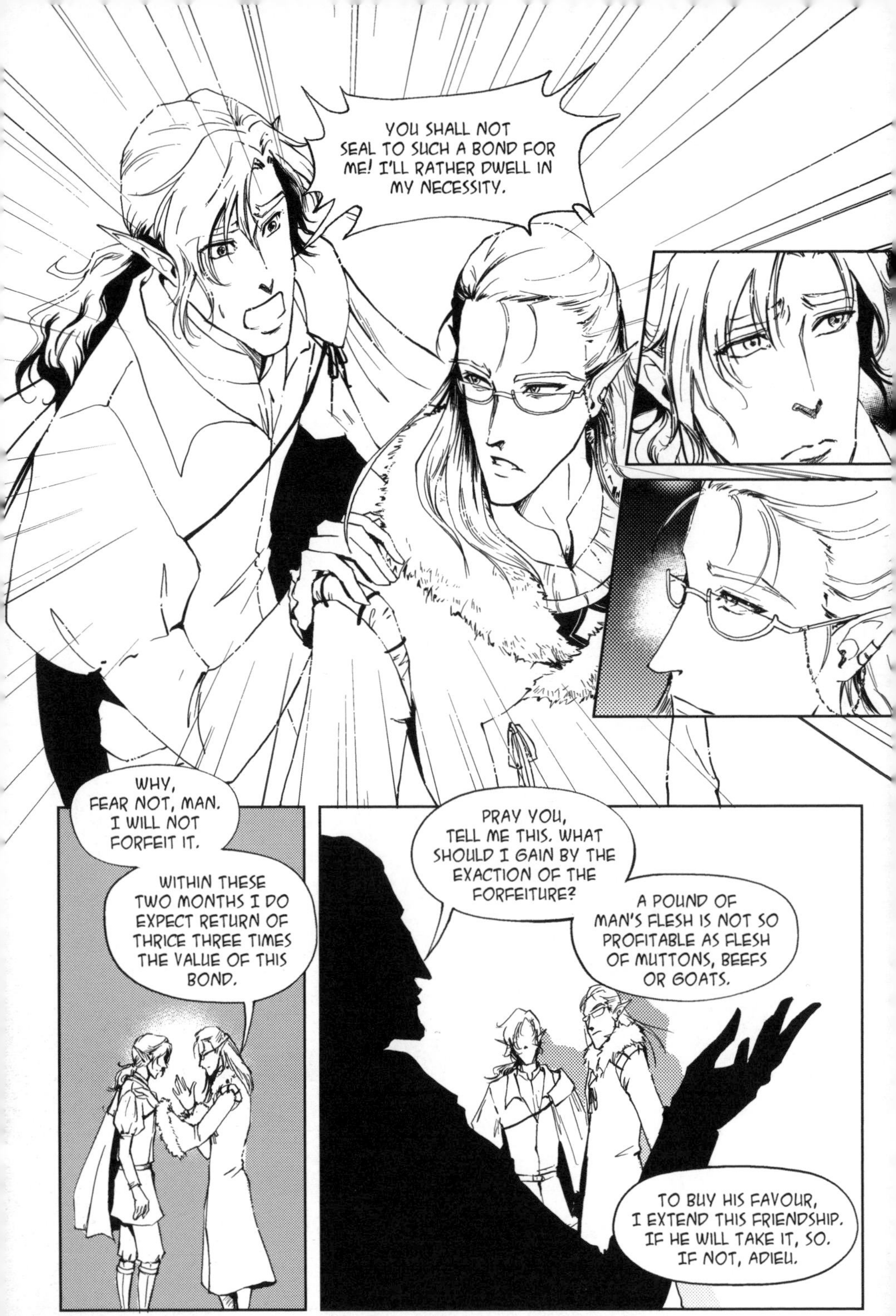
YOU SHALL NOT SEAL TO SUCH A BOND FOR ME! I'LL RATHER DWELL IN MY NECESSITY.
WHY, FEAR NOT, MAN. I WILL NOT FORFEIT IT.
WITHIN THESE TWO MONTHS I DO EXPECT RETURN OF THRICE THREE TIMES THE VALUE OF THIS BOND.
PRAY YOU, TELL ME THIS. WHAT SHOULD I GAIN BY THE EXACTION OF THE FORFEITURE?
A POUND OF MAN'S FLESH IS NOT SO PROFITABLE AS FLESH OF MUTTONS, BEEFS OR GOATS.
TO BUY HIS FAVOUR, I EXTEND THIS FRIENDSHIP. IF HE WILL TAKE IT, SO. IF NOT, ADIEU.

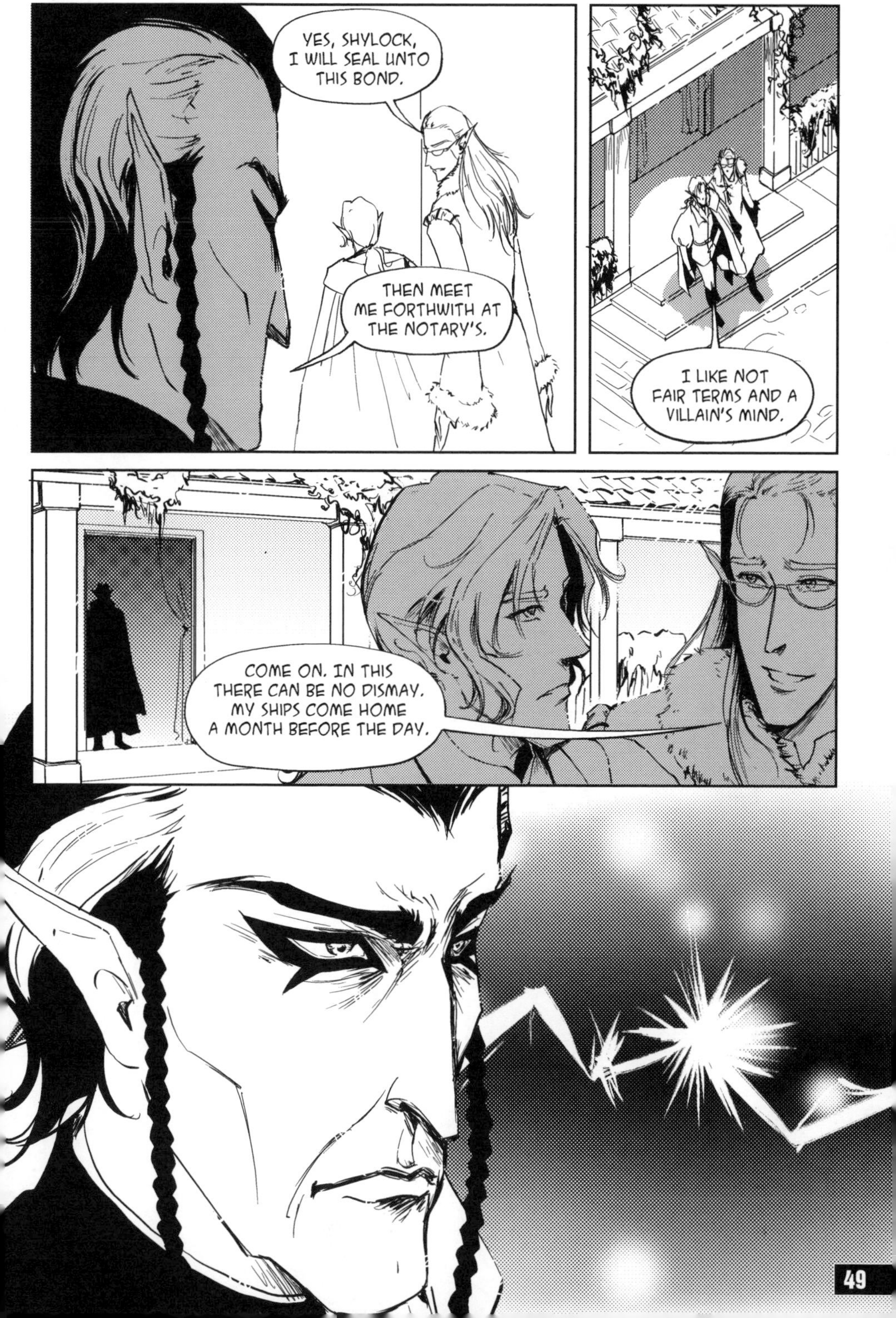
YES, SHYLOCK, I WILL SEAL UNTO THIS BOND.
THEN MEET ME FORTHWITH AT THE NOTARY'S.
I LIKE NOT FAIR TERMS AND A VILLAIN'S MIND.
COME ON. IN THIS THERE CAN BE NO DISMAY. MY SHIPS COME HOME A MONTH BEFORE THE DAY.

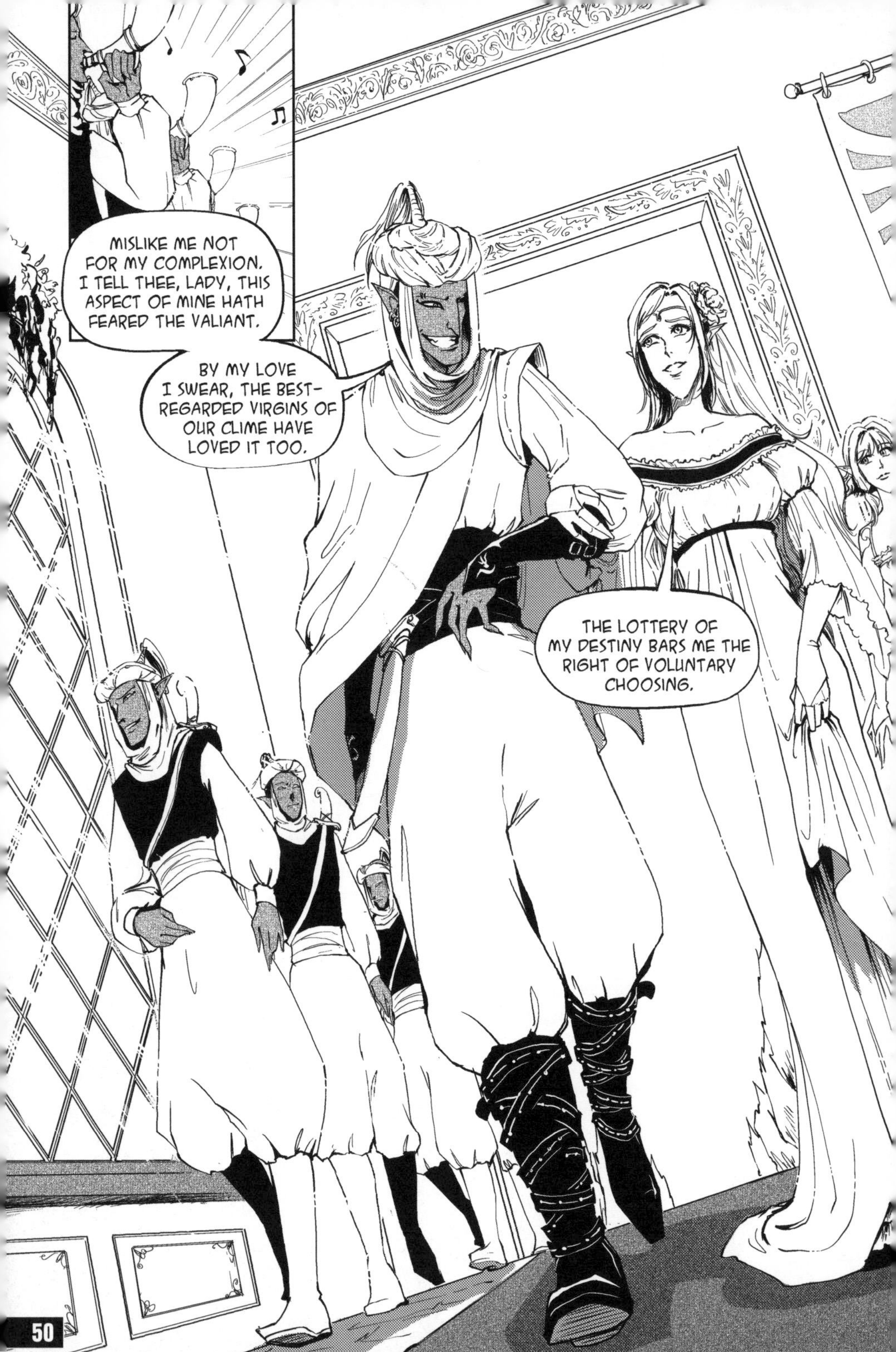
MISLIKE ME NOT FOR MY COMPLEXION. I TELL THEE, LADY, THIS ASPECT OF MINE HATH FEARED THE VALIANT.
BY MY LOVE I SWEAR, THE BEST-REGARDED VIRGINS OF OUR CLIME HAVE LOVED IT TOO.
THE LOTTERY OF MY DESTINY BARS ME THE RIGHT OF VOLUNTARY CHOOSING.

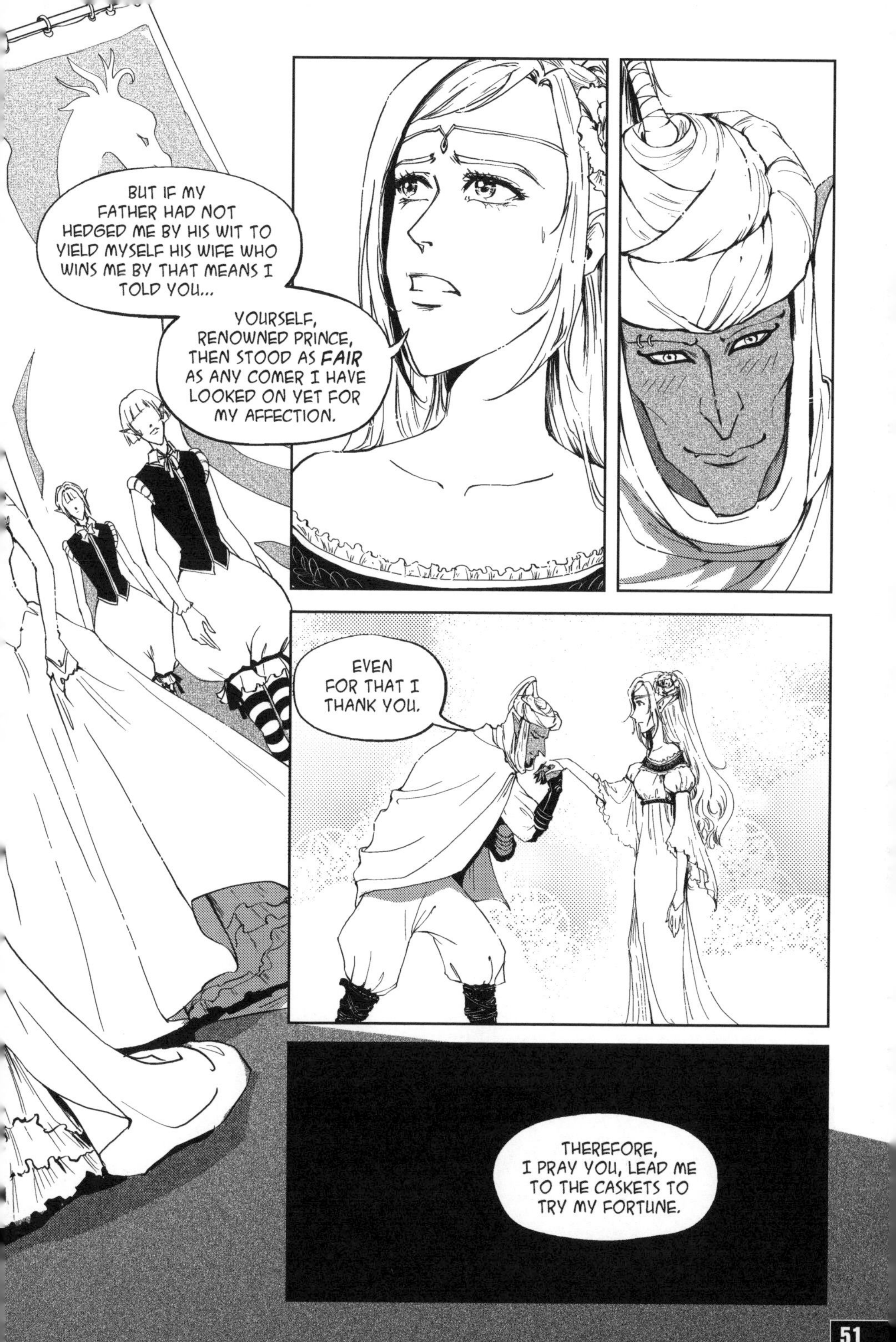
BUT IF MY FATHER HAD NOT HEDGED ME BY HIS WIT TO YIELD MYSELF HIS WIFE WHO WINS ME BY THAT MEANS I TOLD YOU...
YOURSELF, RENOWNED PRINCE, THEN STOOD AS **FAIR** AS ANY COMER I HAVE LOOKED ON YET FOR MY AFFECTION.
EVEN FOR THAT I THANK YOU.
THEREFORE, I PRAY YOU, LEAD ME TO THE CASKETS TO TRY MY FORTUNE.

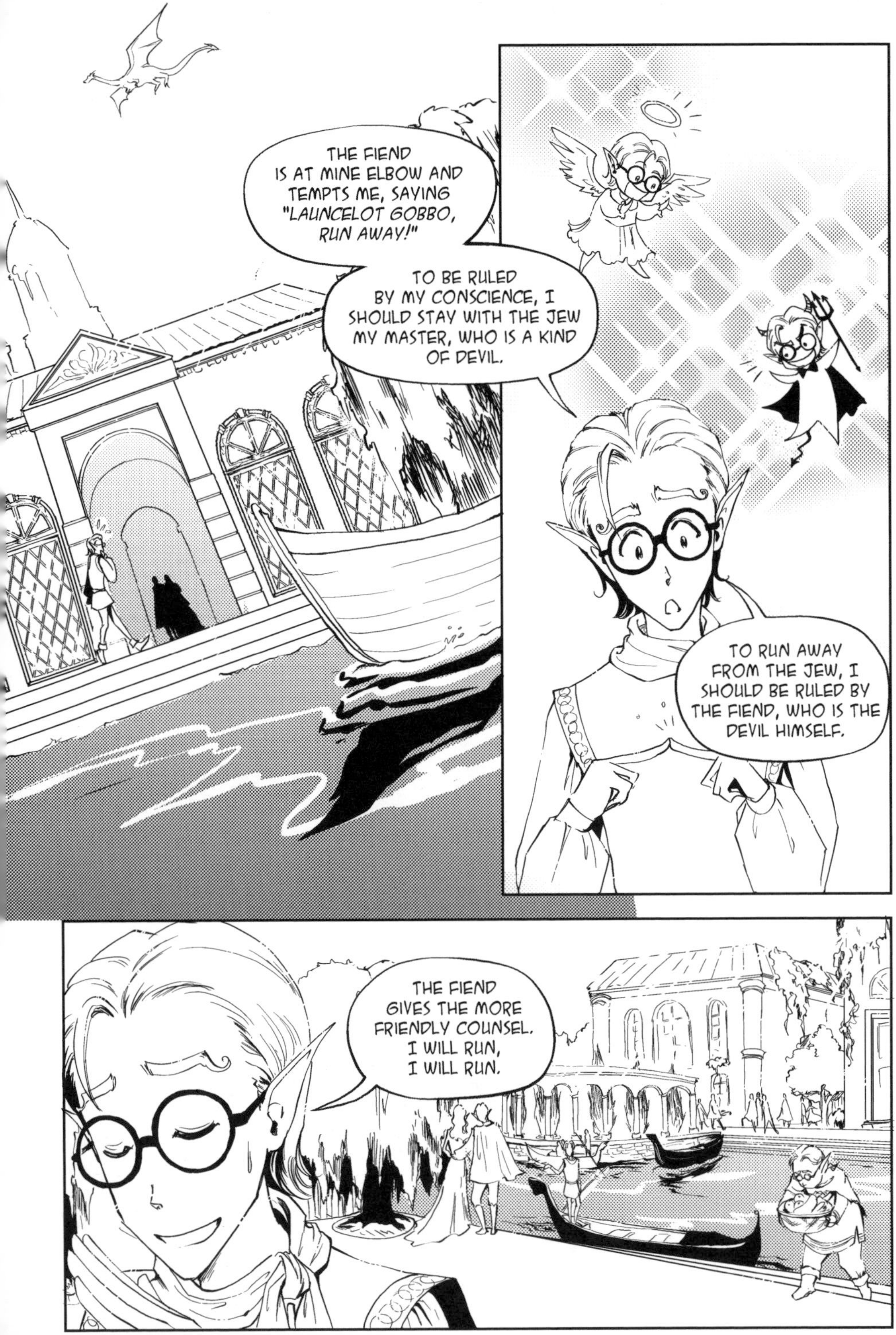
THE FIEND IS AT MINE ELBOW AND TEMPTS ME, SAYING "LAUNCELOT GOBBO, RUN AWAY!"
TO BE RULED BY MY CONSCIENCE, I SHOULD STAY WITH THE JEW MY MASTER, WHO IS A KIND OF DEVIL.
TO RUN AWAY FROM THE JEW, I SHOULD BE RULED BY THE FIEND, WHO IS THE DEVIL HIMSELF.
THE FIEND GIVES THE MORE FRIENDLY COUNSEL. I WILL RUN, I WILL RUN.

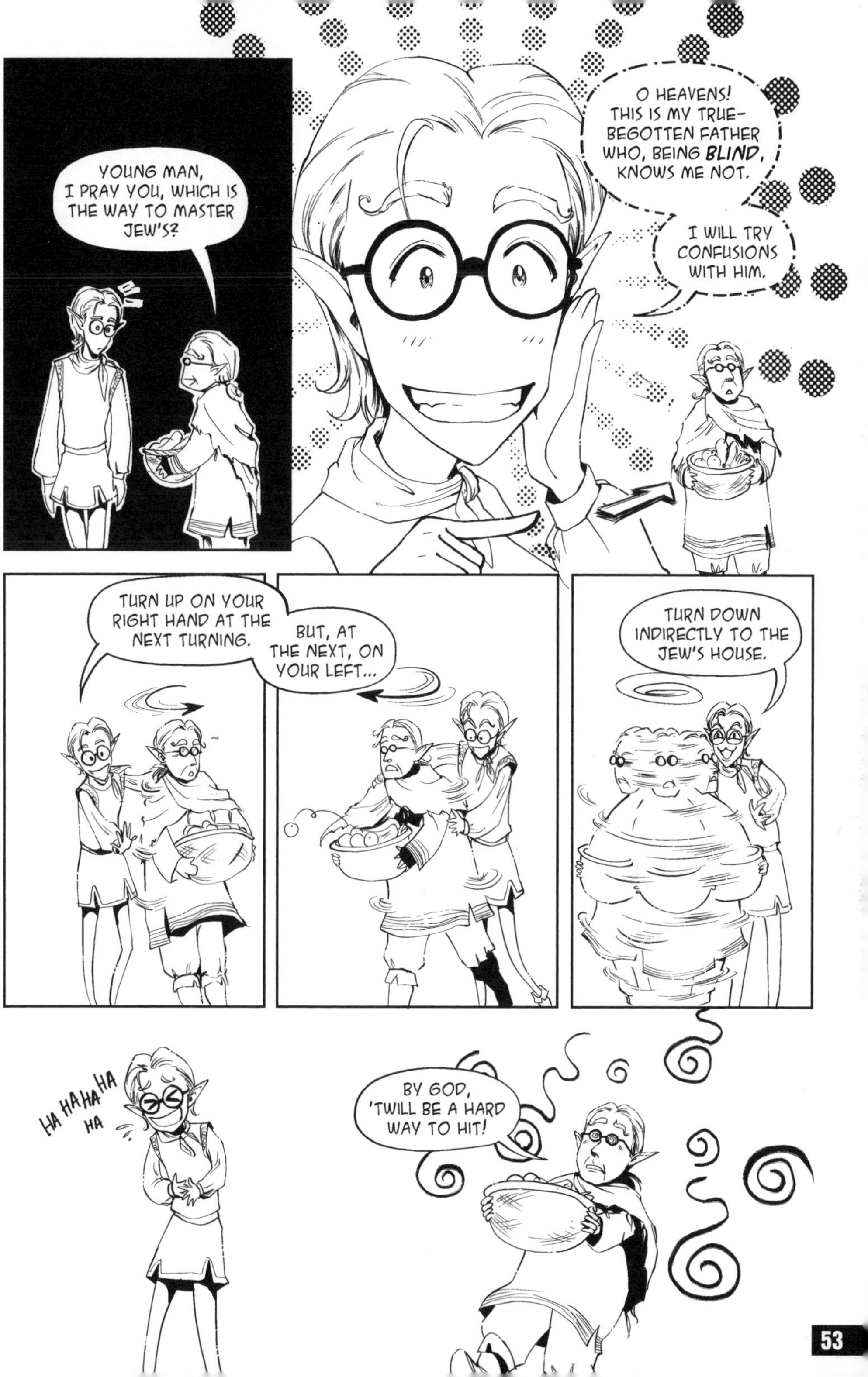
YOUNG MAN, I PRAY YOU, WHICH IS THE WAY TO MASTER JEW'S?
O HEAVENS! THIS IS MY TRUE-BEGOTTEN FATHER WHO, BEING *BLIND*, KNOWS ME NOT.
I WILL TRY CONFUSIONS WITH HIM.
TURN UP ON YOUR RIGHT HAND AT THE NEXT TURNING.
BUT, AT THE NEXT, ON YOUR LEFT...
TURN DOWN INDIRECTLY TO THE JEW'S HOUSE.
HA HAHAHA HA HA
BY GOD, 'TWILL BE A HARD WAY TO HIT!

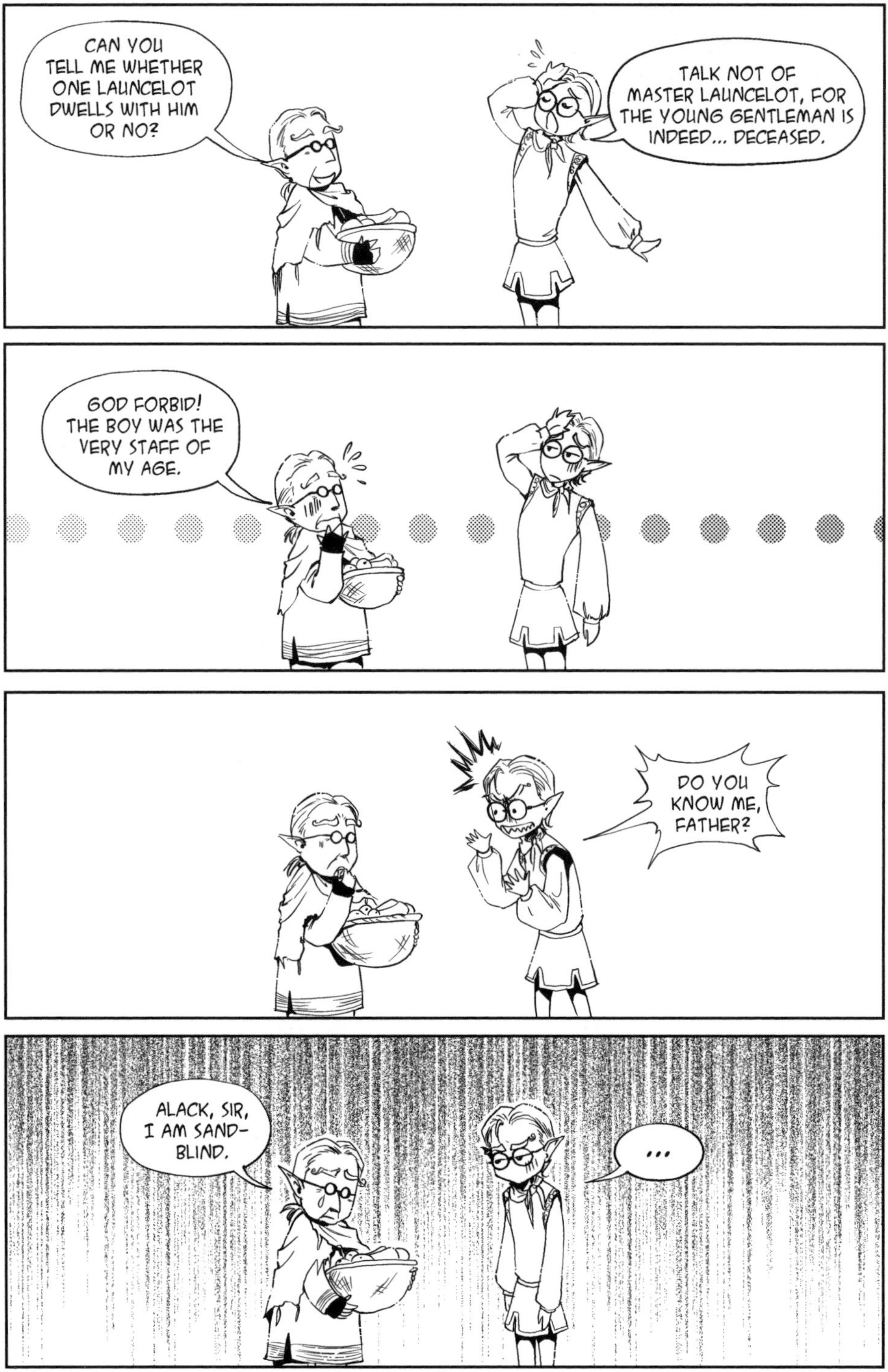
CAN YOU TELL ME WHETHER ONE LAUNCELOT DWELLS WITH HIM OR NO?
TALK NOT OF MASTER LAUNCELOT, FOR THE YOUNG GENTLEMAN IS INDEED... DECEASED.
GOD FORBID! THE BOY WAS THE VERY STAFF OF MY AGE.
DO YOU KNOW ME, FATHER?
ALACK, SIR, I AM SAND-BLIND.
...

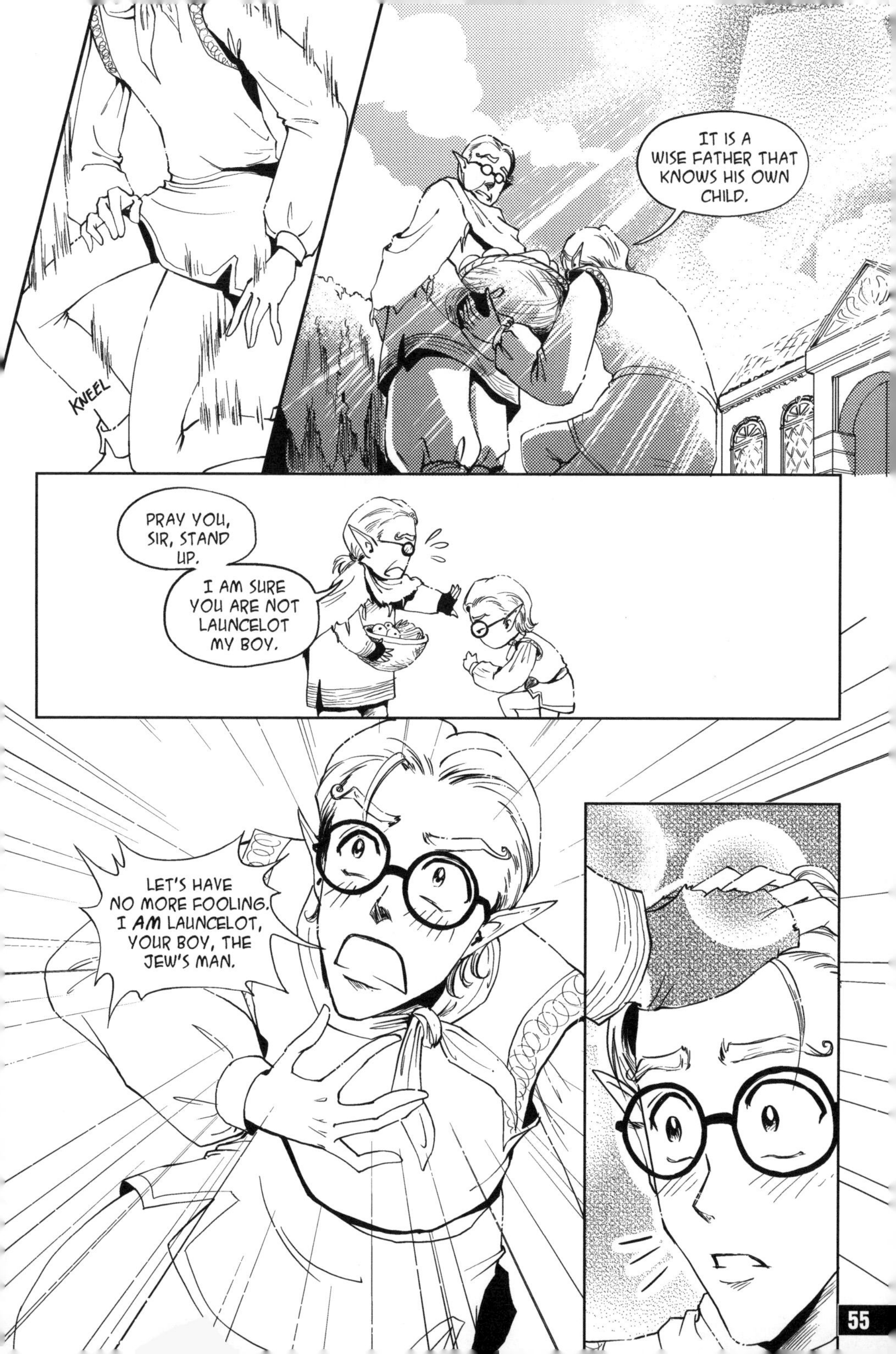
KNEEL
IT IS A WISE FATHER THAT KNOWS HIS OWN CHILD.
PRAY YOU, SIR, STAND UP.
I AM SURE YOU ARE NOT LAUNCELOT MY BOY.
LET'S HAVE NO MORE FOOLING. I *AM* LAUNCELOT, YOUR BOY, THE JEW'S MAN.

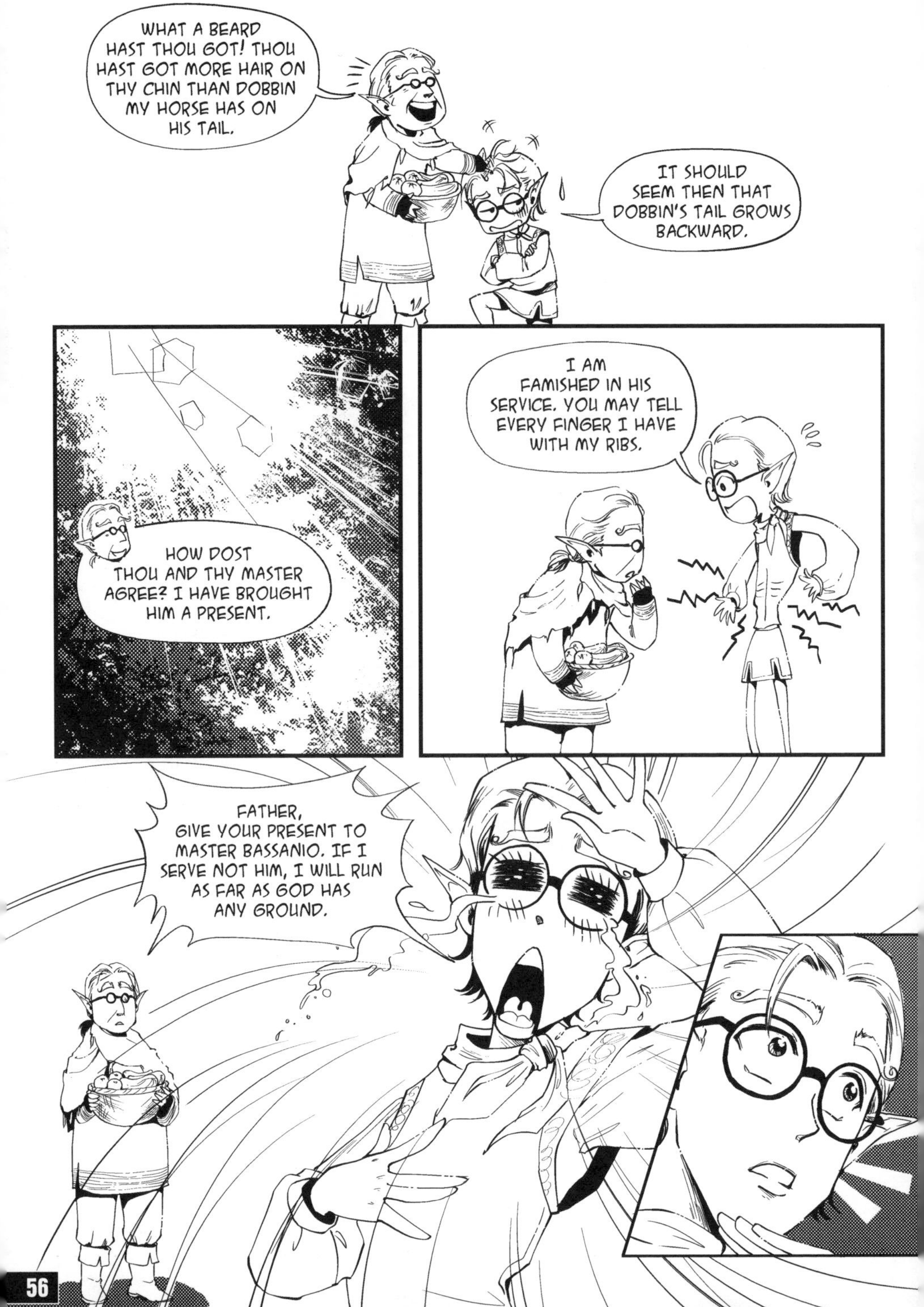
WHAT A BEARD HAST THOU GOT! THOU HAST GOT MORE HAIR ON THY CHIN THAN DOBBIN MY HORSE HAS ON HIS TAIL.
IT SHOULD SEEM THEN THAT DOBBIN'S TAIL GROWS BACKWARD.
HOW DOST THOU AND THY MASTER AGREE? I HAVE BROUGHT HIM A PRESENT.
I AM FAMISHED IN HIS SERVICE. YOU MAY TELL EVERY FINGER I HAVE WITH MY RIBS.
FATHER, GIVE YOUR PRESENT TO MASTER BASSANIO. IF I SERVE NOT HIM, I WILL RUN AS FAR AS GOD HAS ANY GROUND.

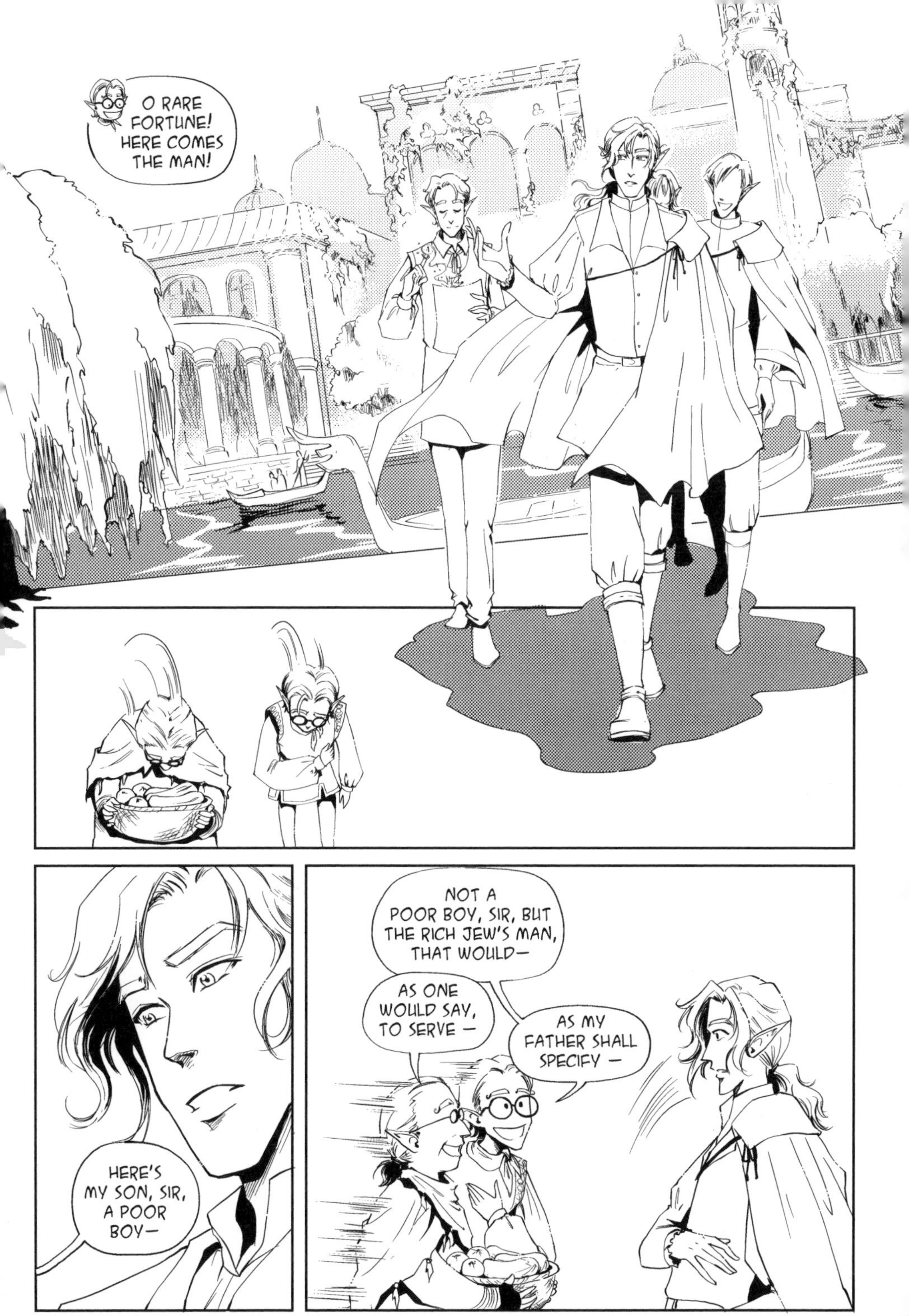
O RARE FORTUNE! HERE COMES THE MAN!
HERE'S MY SON, SIR, A POOR BOY—
NOT A POOR BOY, SIR, BUT THE RICH JEW'S MAN, THAT WOULD—
AS ONE WOULD SAY, TO SERVE —
AS MY FATHER SHALL SPECIFY —

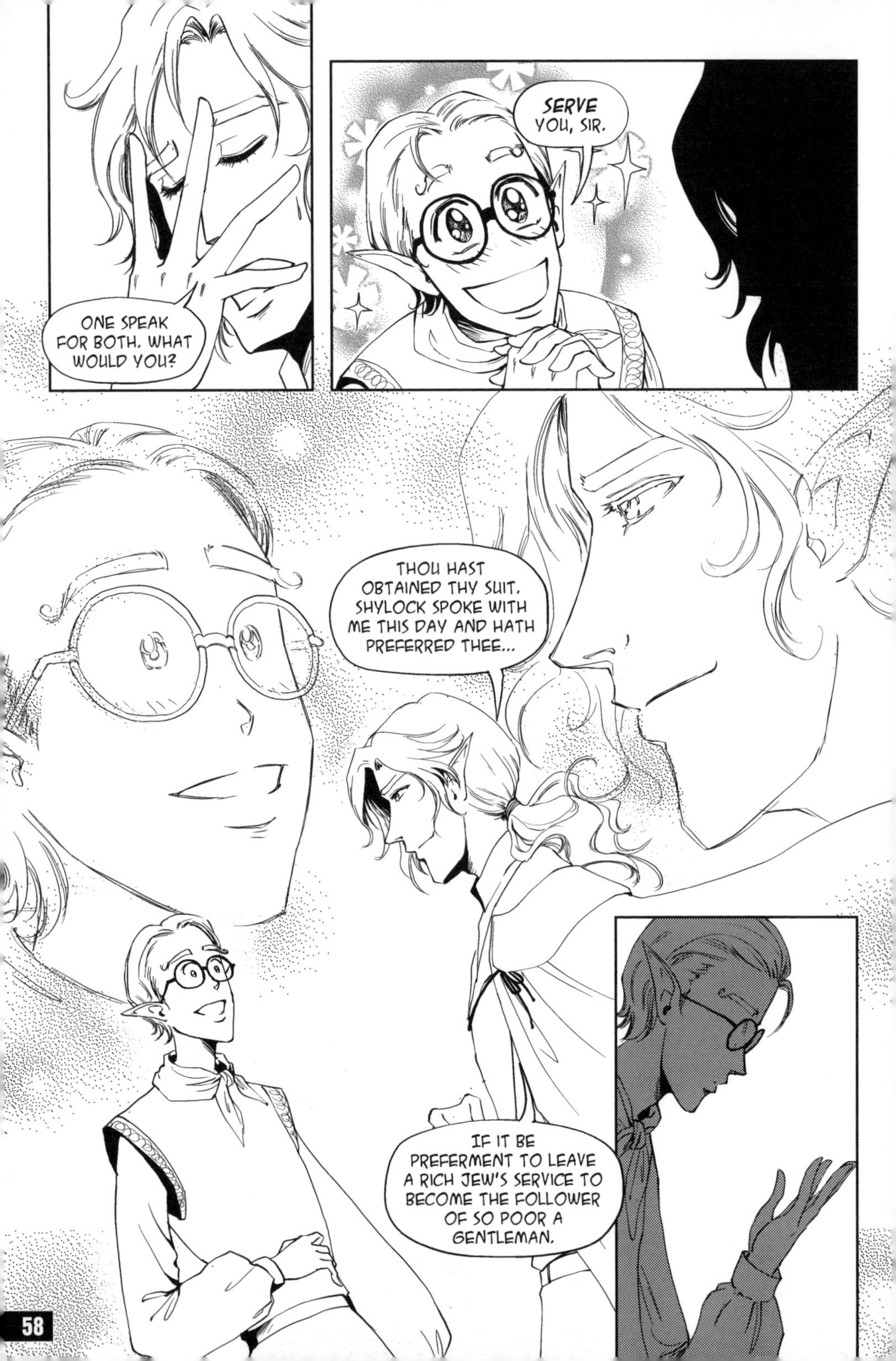
ONE SPEAK FOR BOTH. WHAT WOULD YOU?
SERVE YOU, SIR.
THOU HAST OBTAINED THY SUIT. SHYLOCK SPOKE WITH ME THIS DAY AND HATH PREFERRED THEE...
IF IT BE PREFERMENT TO LEAVE A RICH JEW'S SERVICE TO BECOME THE FOLLOWER OF SO POOR A GENTLEMAN.

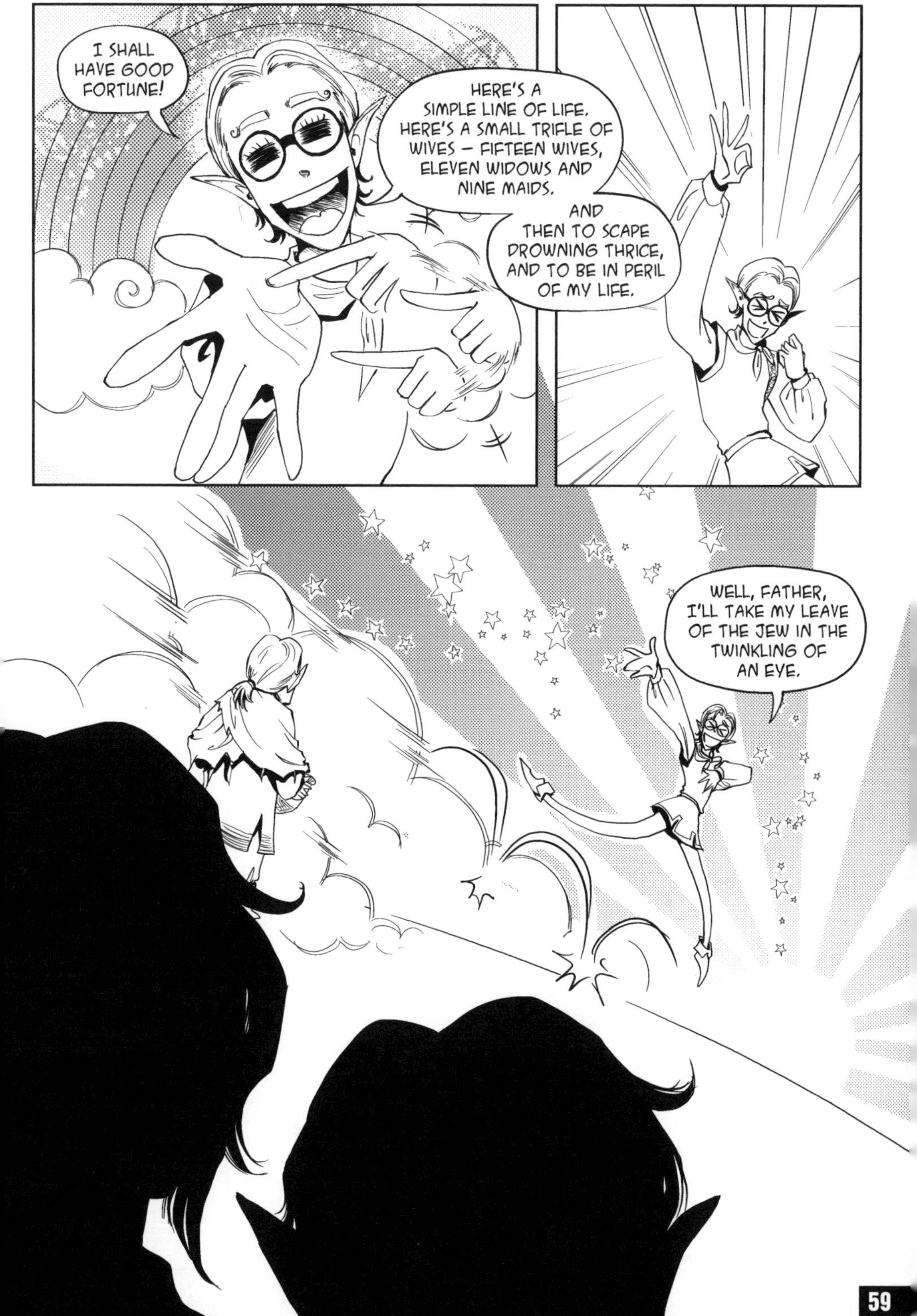
I SHALL HAVE GOOD FORTUNE!
HERE'S A SIMPLE LINE OF LIFE. HERE'S A SMALL TRIFLE OF WIVES – FIFTEEN WIVES, ELEVEN WIDOWS AND NINE MAIDS.
AND THEN TO SCAPE DROWNING THRICE, AND TO BE IN PERIL OF MY LIFE.
WELL, FATHER, I'LL TAKE MY LEAVE OF THE JEW IN THE TWINKLING OF AN EYE.

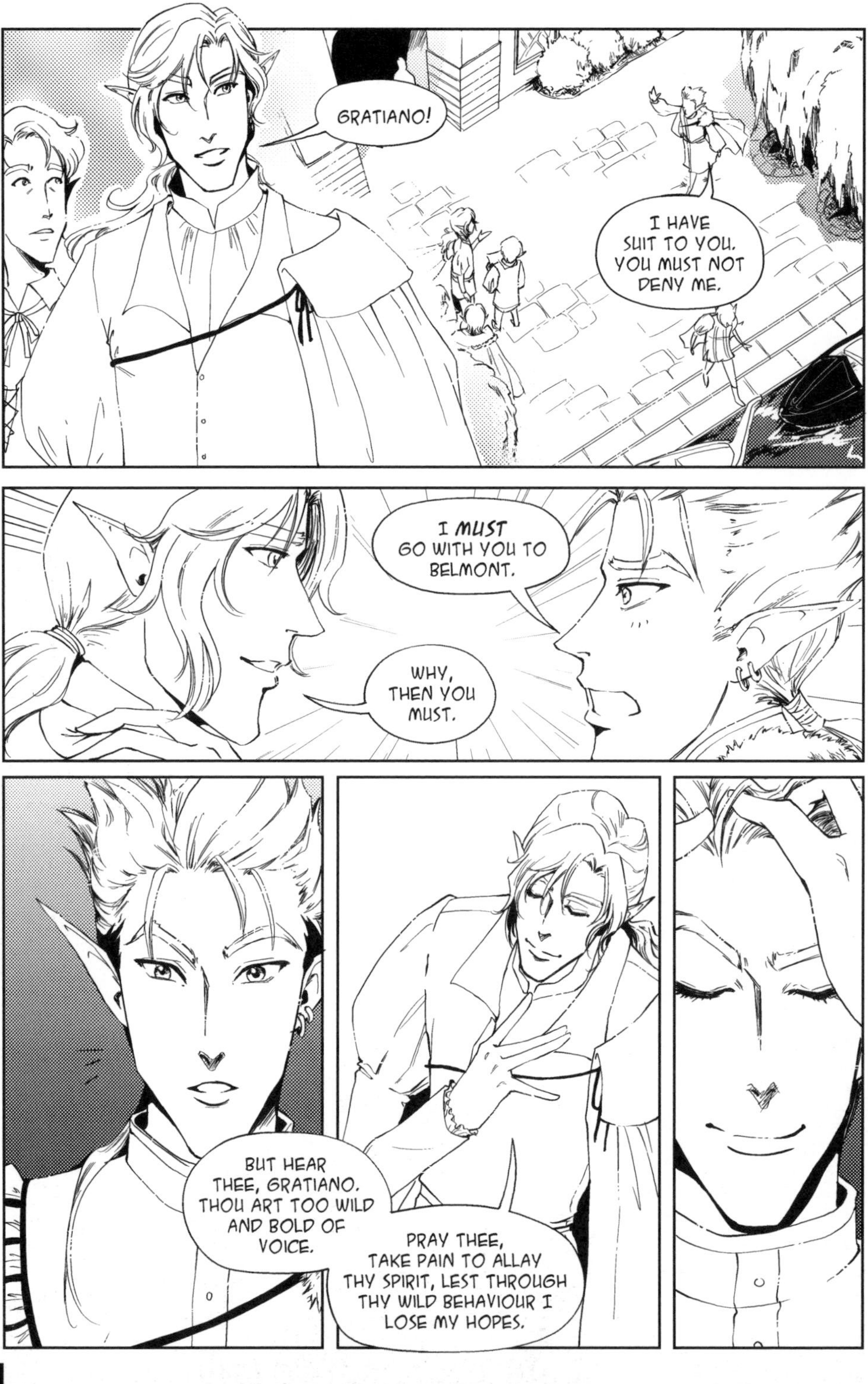
GRATIANO!
I HAVE SUIT TO YOU. YOU MUST NOT DENY ME.
I *MUST* GO WITH YOU TO BELMONT.
WHY, THEN YOU MUST.
BUT HEAR THEE, GRATIANO. THOU ART TOO WILD AND BOLD OF VOICE.
PRAY THEE, TAKE PAIN TO ALLAY THY SPIRIT, LEST THROUGH THY WILD BEHAVIOUR I LOSE MY HOPES.

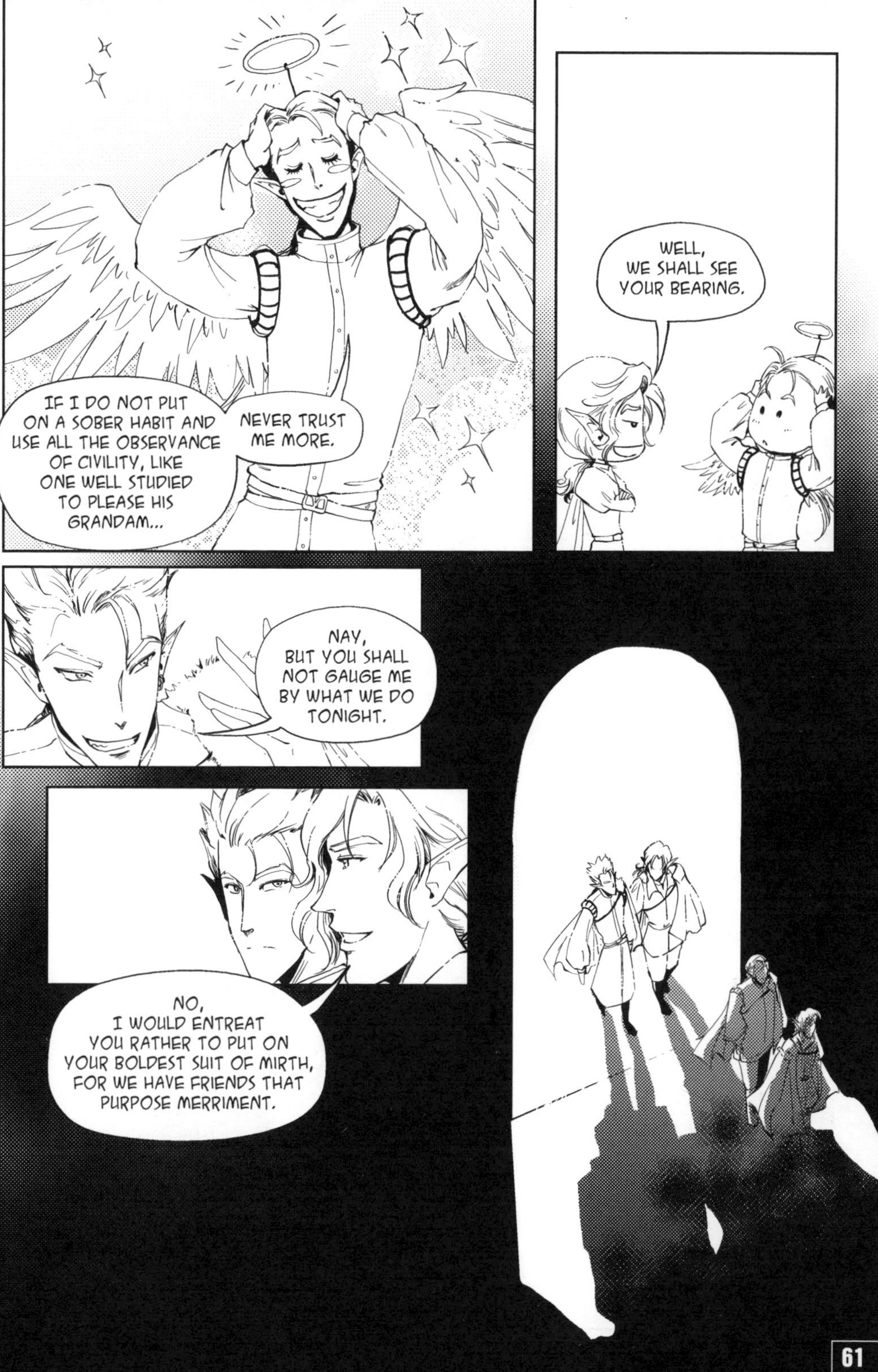
IF I DO NOT PUT ON A SOBER HABIT AND USE ALL THE OBSERVANCE OF CIVILITY, LIKE ONE WELL STUDIED TO PLEASE HIS GRANDAM...
NEVER TRUST ME MORE.
WELL, WE SHALL SEE YOUR BEARING.
NAY, BUT YOU SHALL NOT GAUGE ME BY WHAT WE DO TONIGHT.
NO, I WOULD ENTREAT YOU RATHER TO PUT ON YOUR BOLDEST SUIT OF MIRTH, FOR WE HAVE FRIENDS THAT PURPOSE MERRIMENT.

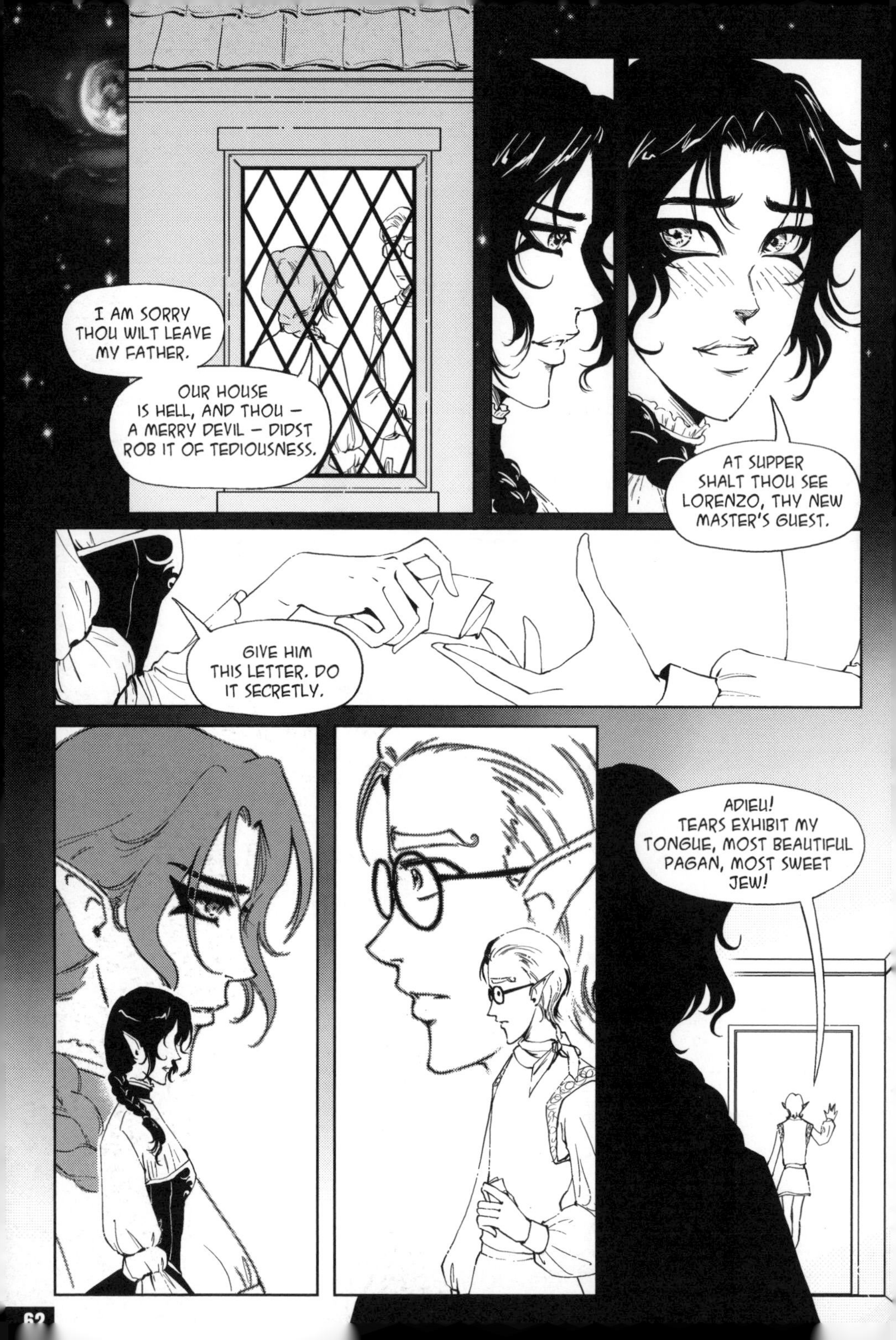
I AM SORRY THOU WILT LEAVE MY FATHER.
OUR HOUSE IS HELL, AND THOU — A MERRY DEVIL — DIDST ROB IT OF TEDIOUSNESS.
AT SUPPER SHALT THOU SEE LORENZO, THY NEW MASTER'S GUEST.
GIVE HIM THIS LETTER. DO IT SECRETLY.
ADIEU! TEARS EXHIBIT MY TONGUE, MOST BEAUTIFUL PAGAN, MOST SWEET JEW!

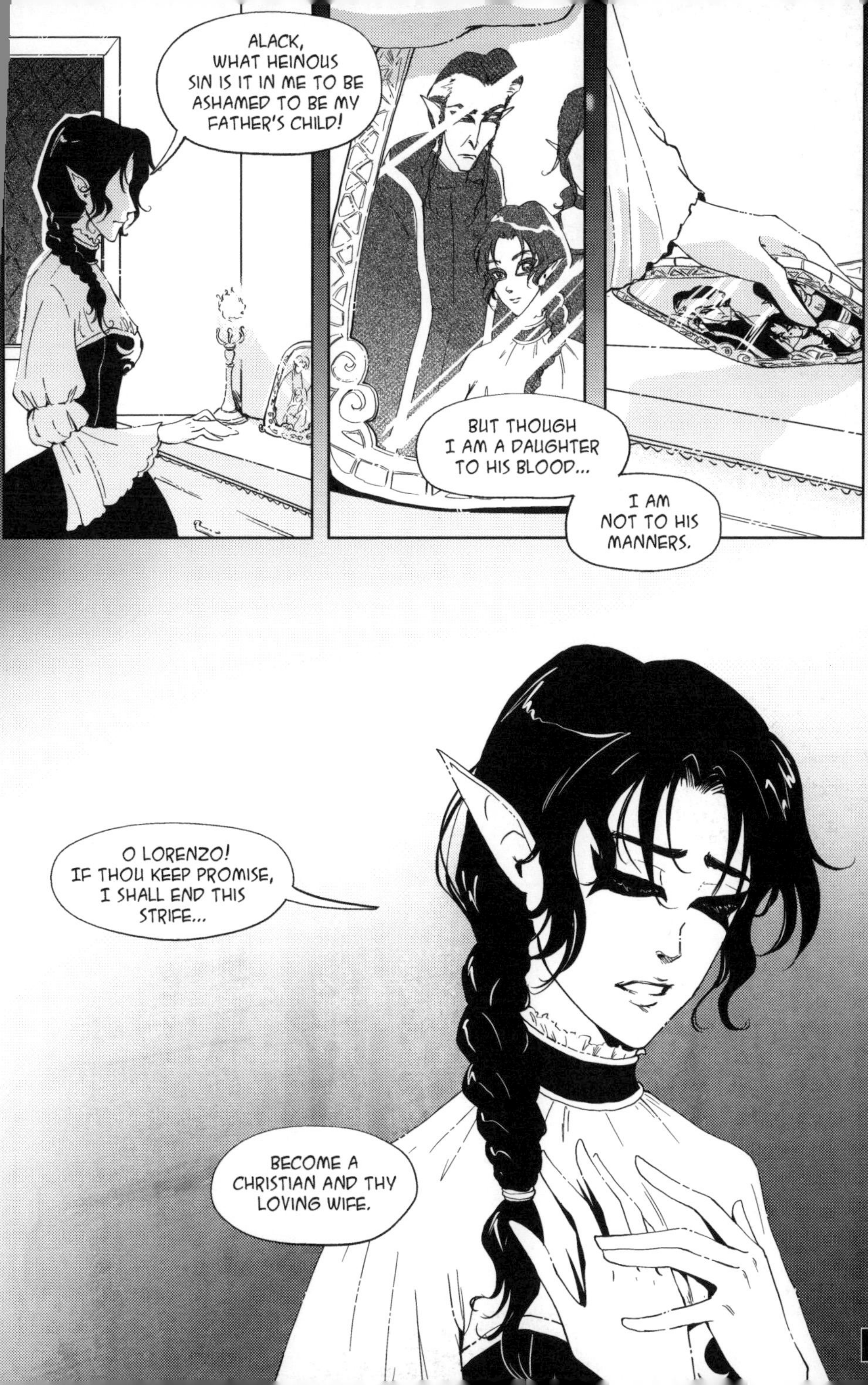
ALACK, WHAT HEINOUS SIN IS IT IN ME TO BE ASHAMED TO BE MY FATHER'S CHILD!
BUT THOUGH I AM A DAUGHTER TO HIS BLOOD...
I AM NOT TO HIS MANNERS.
O LORENZO! IF THOU KEEP PROMISE, I SHALL END THIS STRIFE...
BECOME A CHRISTIAN AND THY LOVING WIFE.

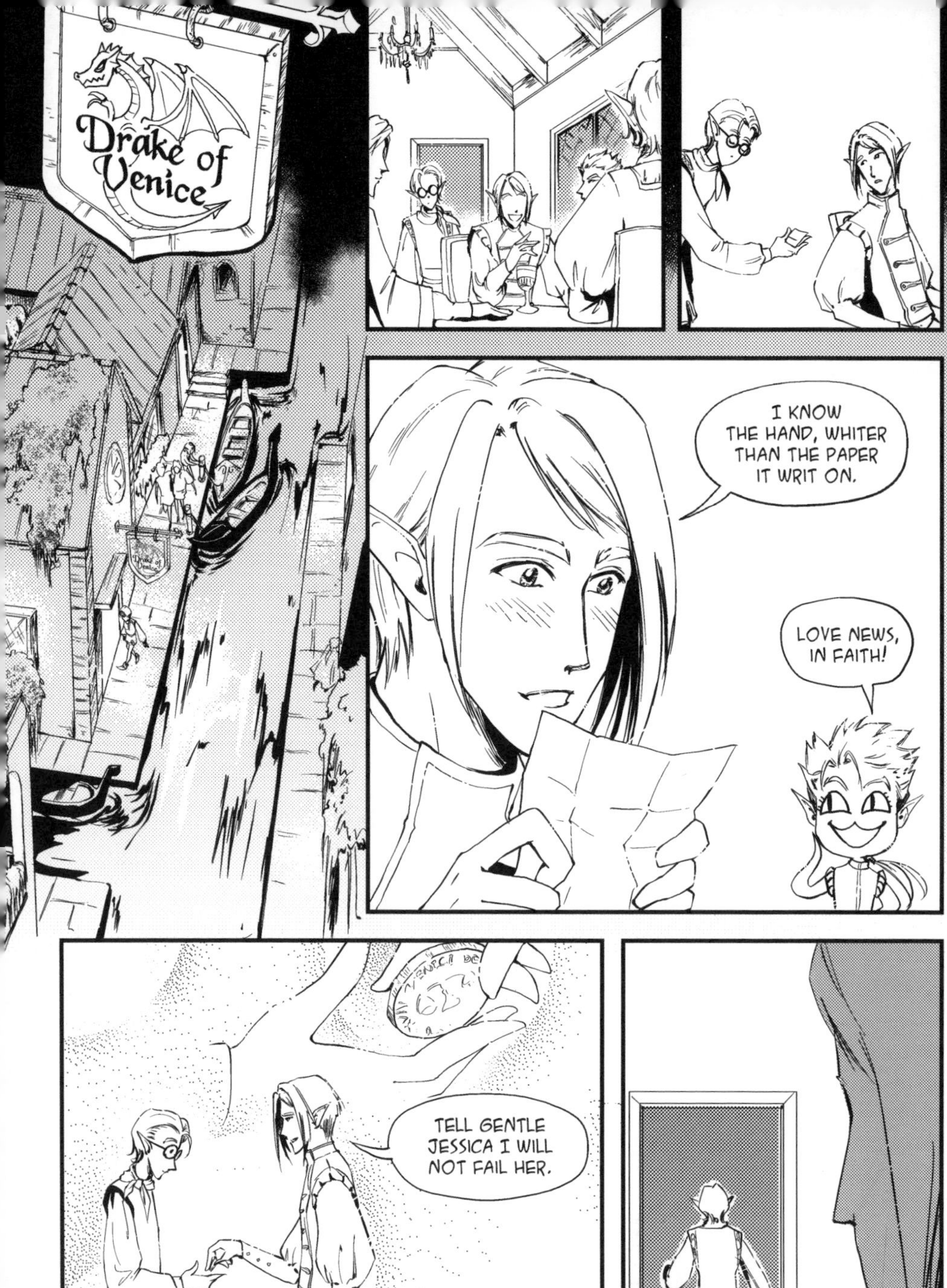
Drake of Venice
Drake of Venice
I KNOW THE HAND, WHITER THAN THE PAPER IT WRIT ON.
LOVE NEWS, IN FAITH!
TELL GENTLE JESSICA I WILL NOT FAIL HER.

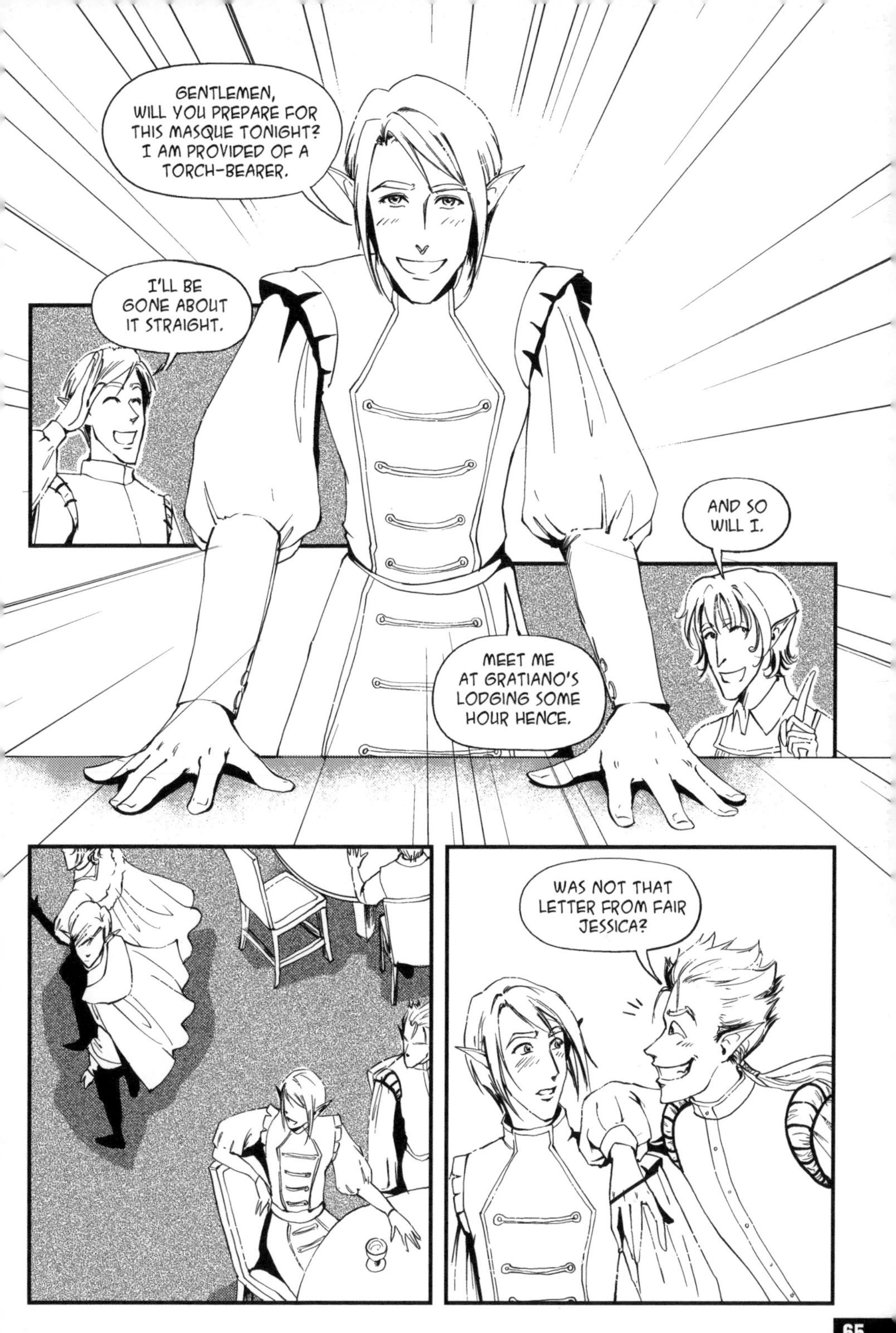
GENTLEMEN, WILL YOU PREPARE FOR THIS MASQUE TONIGHT? I AM PROVIDED OF A TORCH-BEARER.
I'LL BE GONE ABOUT IT STRAIGHT.
AND SO WILL I.
MEET ME AT GRATIANO'S LODGING SOME HOUR HENCE.
WAS NOT THAT LETTER FROM FAIR JESSICA?

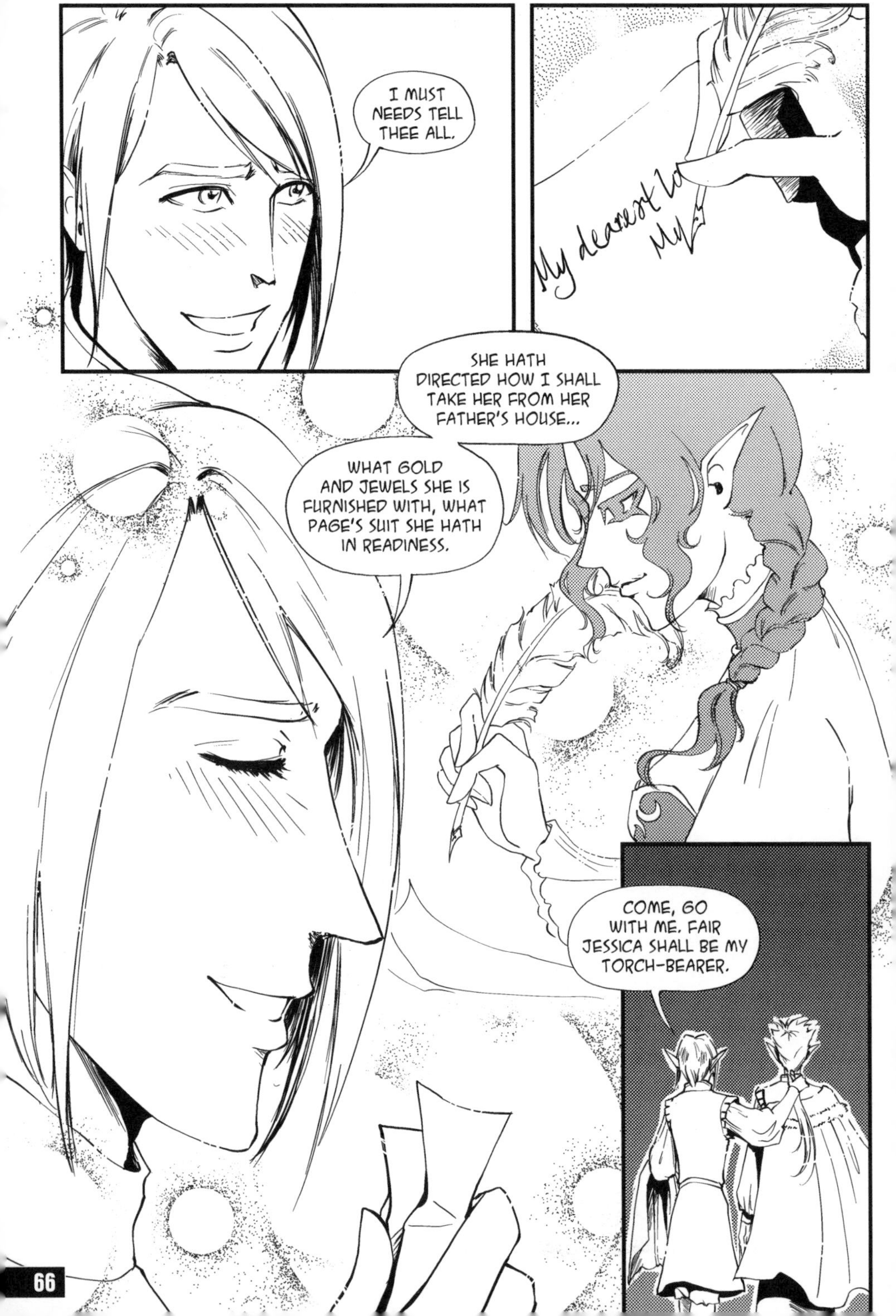
I MUST NEEDS TELL THEE ALL.
My dearest lo
My
SHE HATH DIRECTED HOW I SHALL TAKE HER FROM HER FATHER'S HOUSE...
WHAT GOLD AND JEWELS SHE IS FURNISHED WITH, WHAT PAGE'S SUIT SHE HATH IN READINESS.
COME, GO WITH ME. FAIR JESSICA SHALL BE MY TORCH-BEARER.

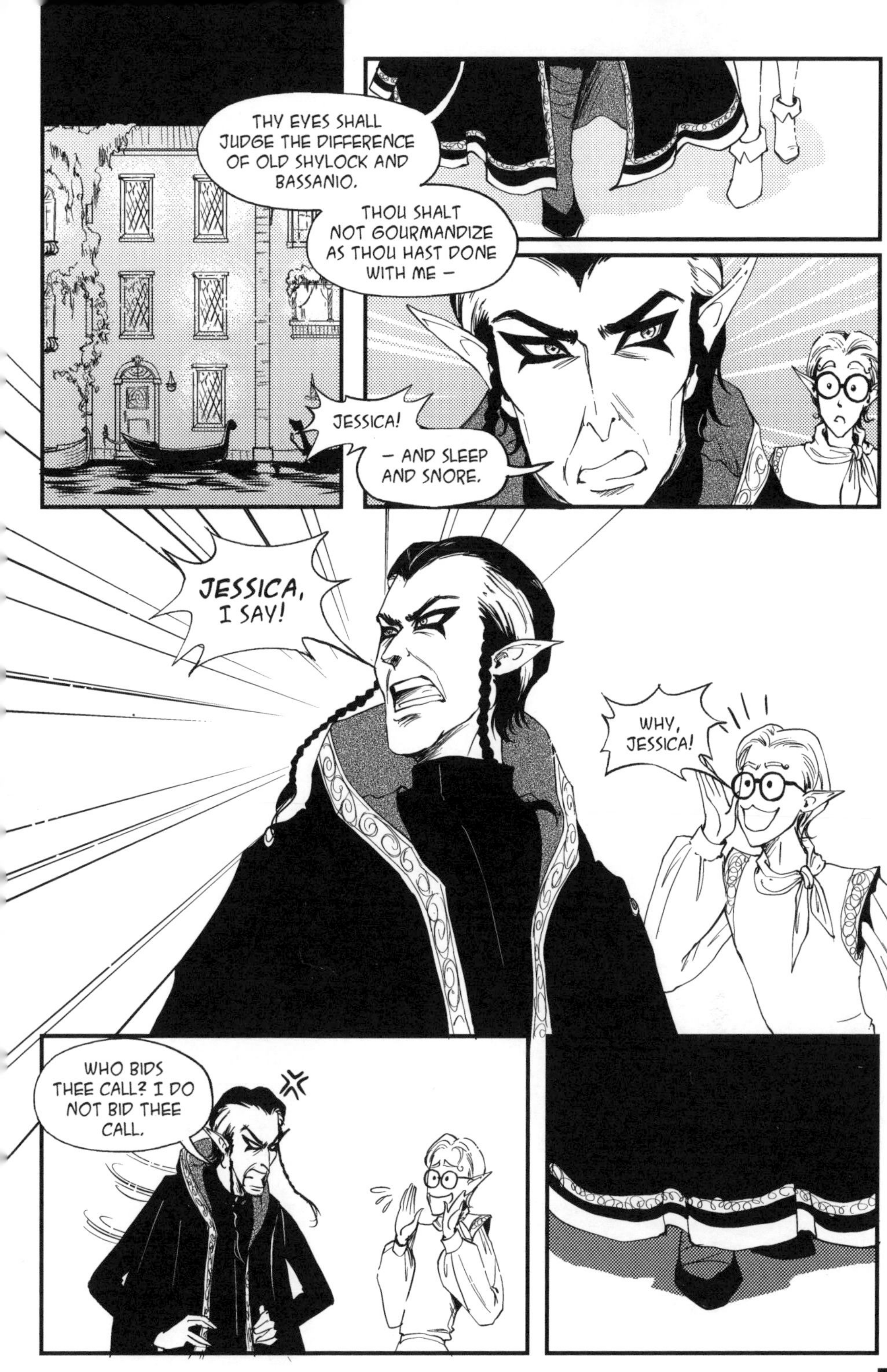
THY EYES SHALL JUDGE THE DIFFERENCE OF OLD SHYLOCK AND BASSANIO.
THOU SHALT NOT GOURMANDIZE AS THOU HAST DONE WITH ME –
JESSICA!
– AND SLEEP AND SNORE.
JESSICA, I SAY!
WHY, JESSICA!
WHO BIDS THEE CALL? I DO NOT BID THEE CALL.

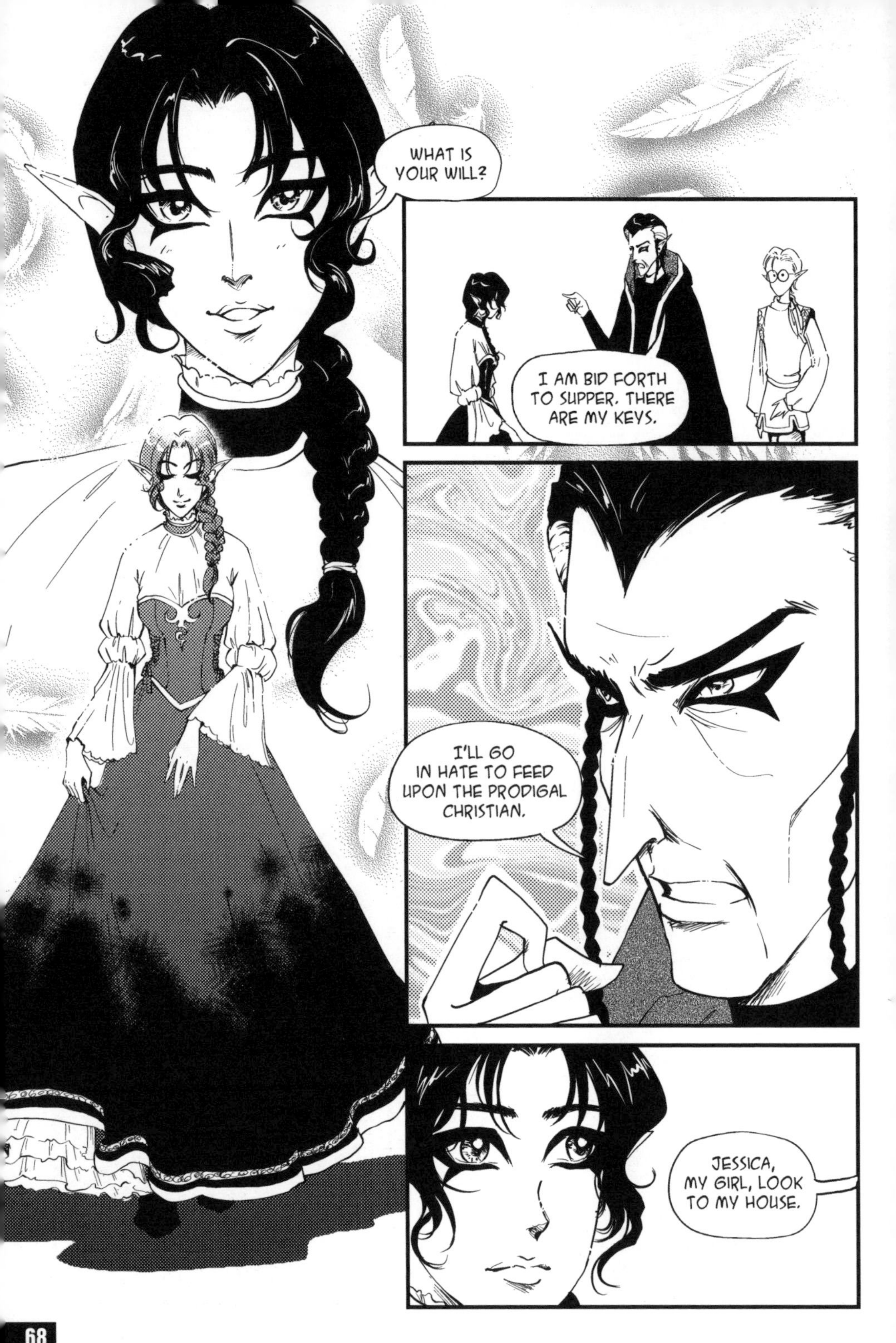
WHAT IS YOUR WILL?
I AM BID FORTH TO SUPPER. THERE ARE MY KEYS.
I'LL GO IN HATE TO FEED UPON THE PRODIGAL CHRISTIAN.
JESSICA, MY GIRL, LOOK TO MY HOUSE.

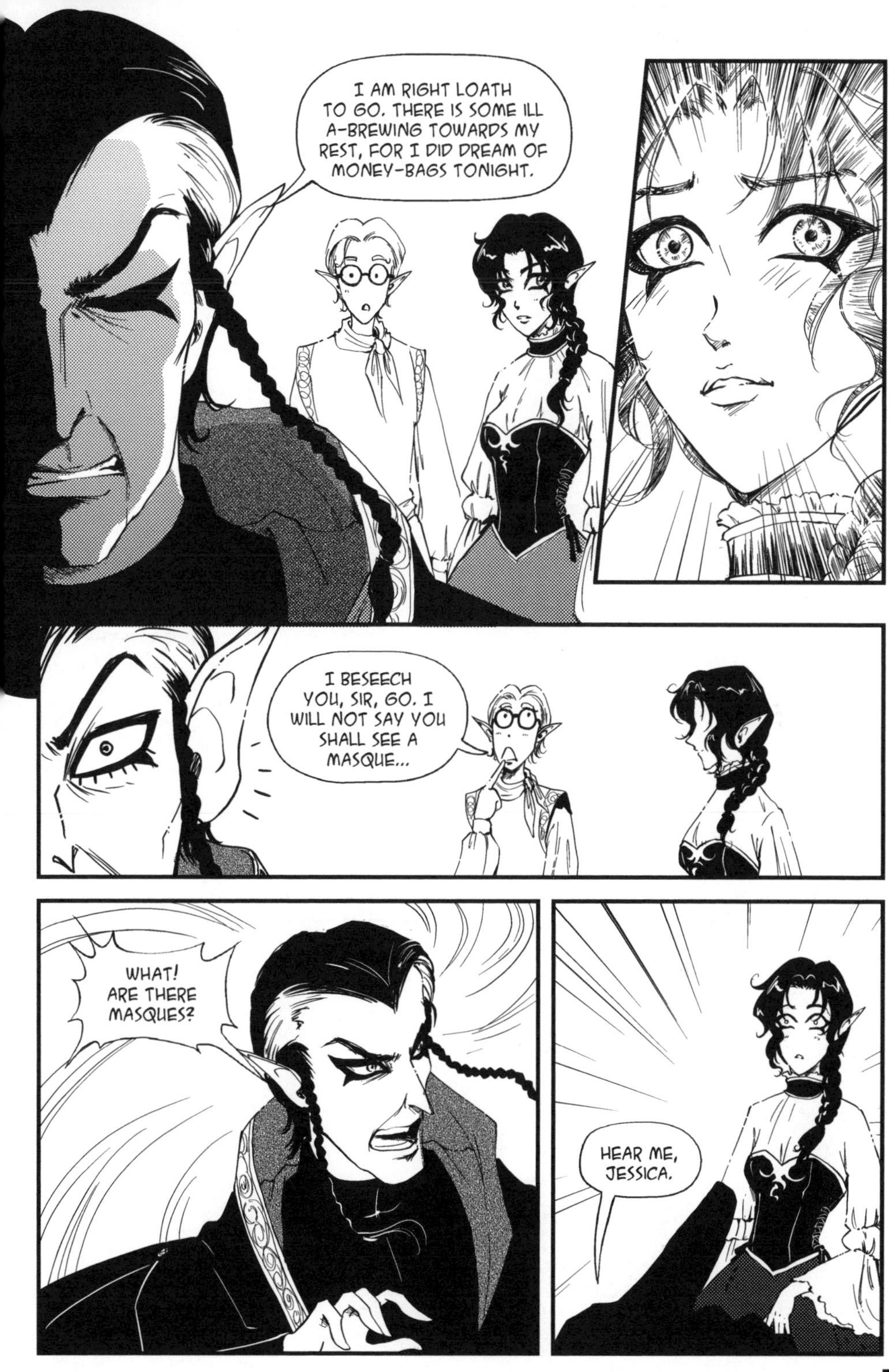
I AM RIGHT LOATH TO GO. THERE IS SOME ILL A-BREWING TOWARDS MY REST, FOR I DID DREAM OF MONEY-BAGS TONIGHT.
I BESEECH YOU, SIR, GO. I WILL NOT SAY YOU SHALL SEE A MASQUE...
WHAT! ARE THERE MASQUES?
HEAR ME, JESSICA.

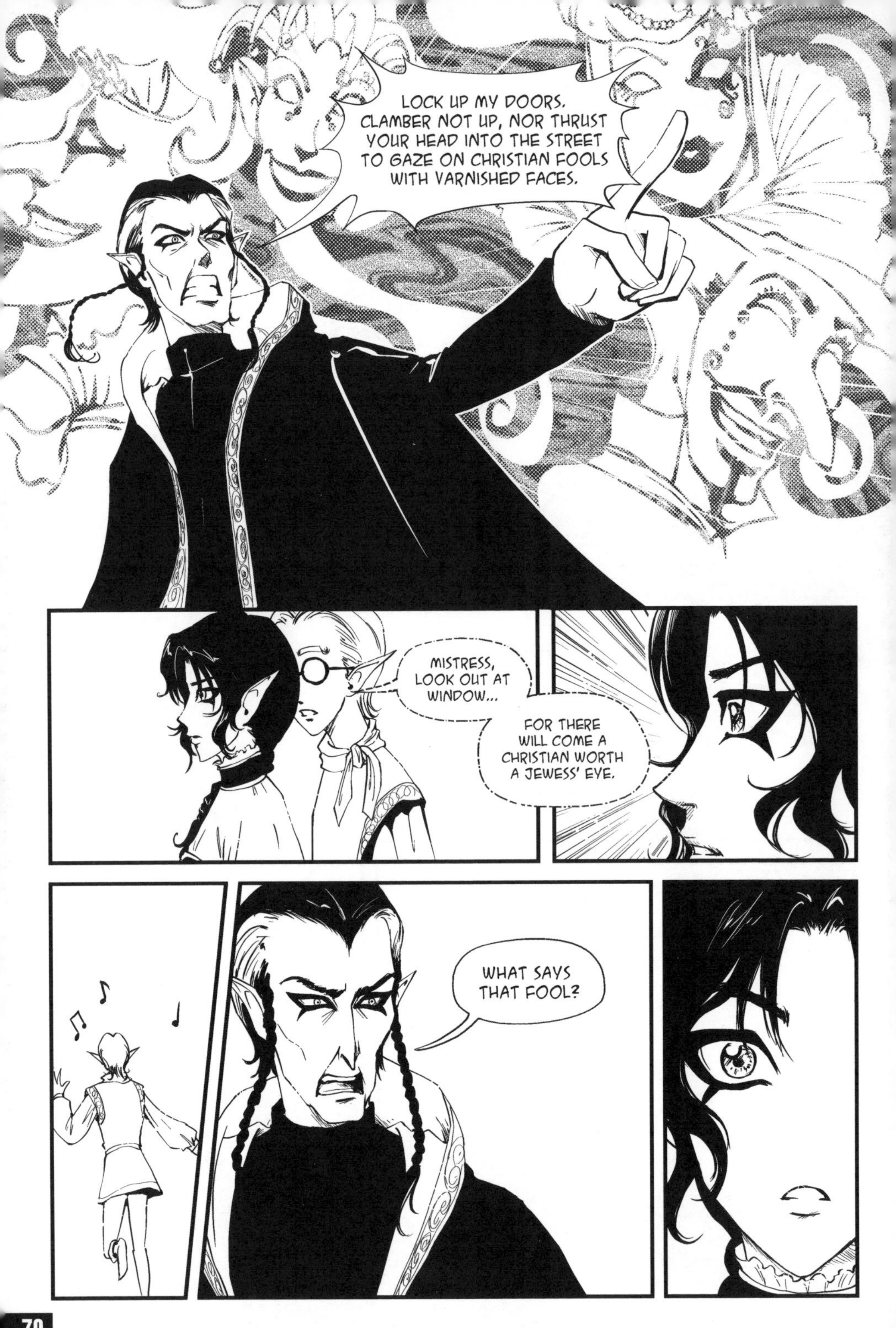
LOCK UP MY DOORS. CLAMBER NOT UP, NOR THRUST YOUR HEAD INTO THE STREET TO GAZE ON CHRISTIAN FOOLS WITH VARNISHED FACES.
MISTRESS, LOOK OUT AT WINDOW...
FOR THERE WILL COME A CHRISTIAN WORTH A JEWESS' EYE.
WHAT SAYS THAT FOOL?

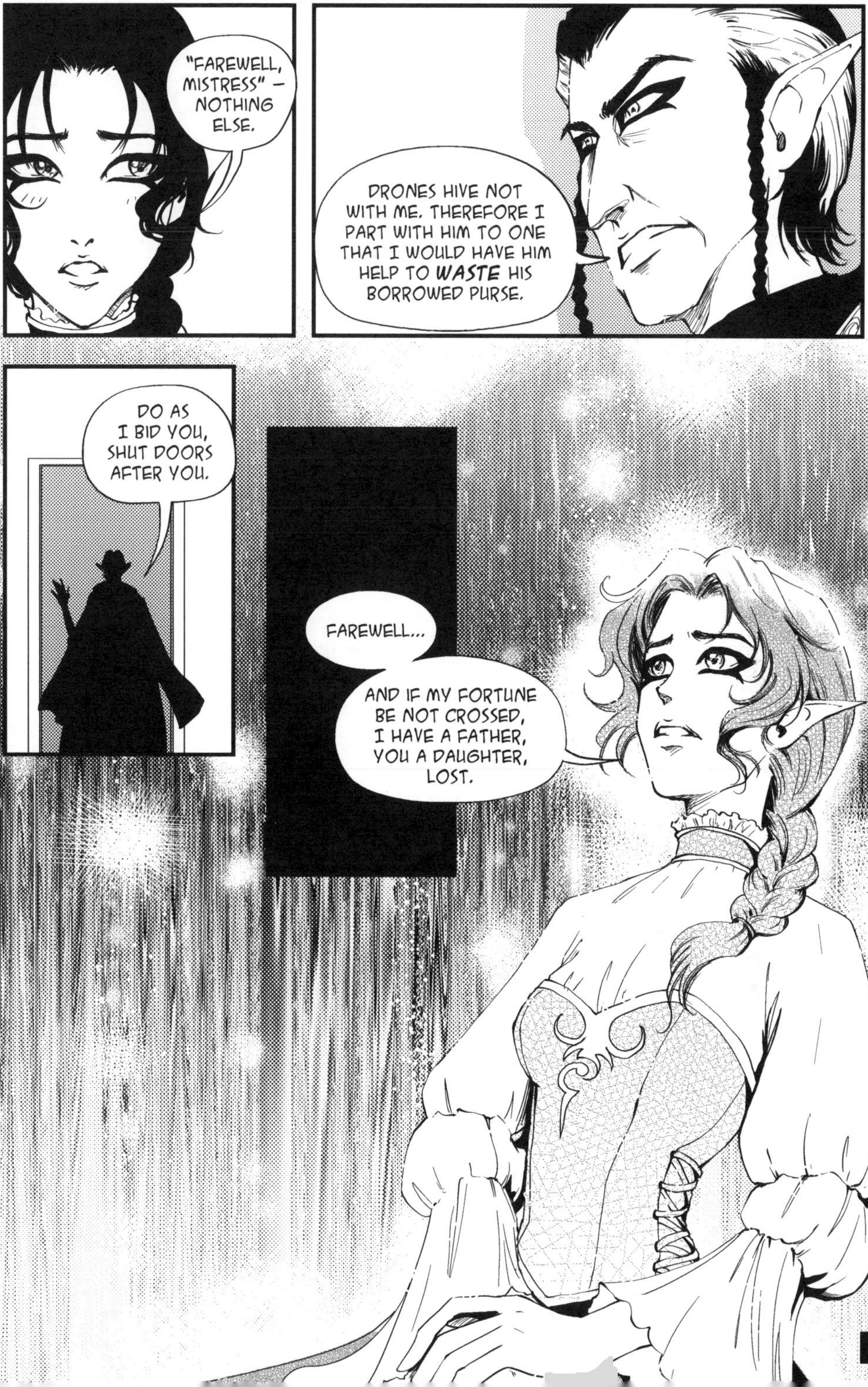
"FAREWELL, MISTRESS" — NOTHING ELSE.
DRONES HIVE NOT WITH ME. THEREFORE I PART WITH HIM TO ONE THAT I WOULD HAVE HIM HELP TO WASTE HIS BORROWED PURSE.
DO AS I BID YOU, SHUT DOORS AFTER YOU.
FAREWELL...
AND IF MY FORTUNE BE NOT CROSSED, I HAVE A FATHER, YOU A DAUGHTER, LOST.

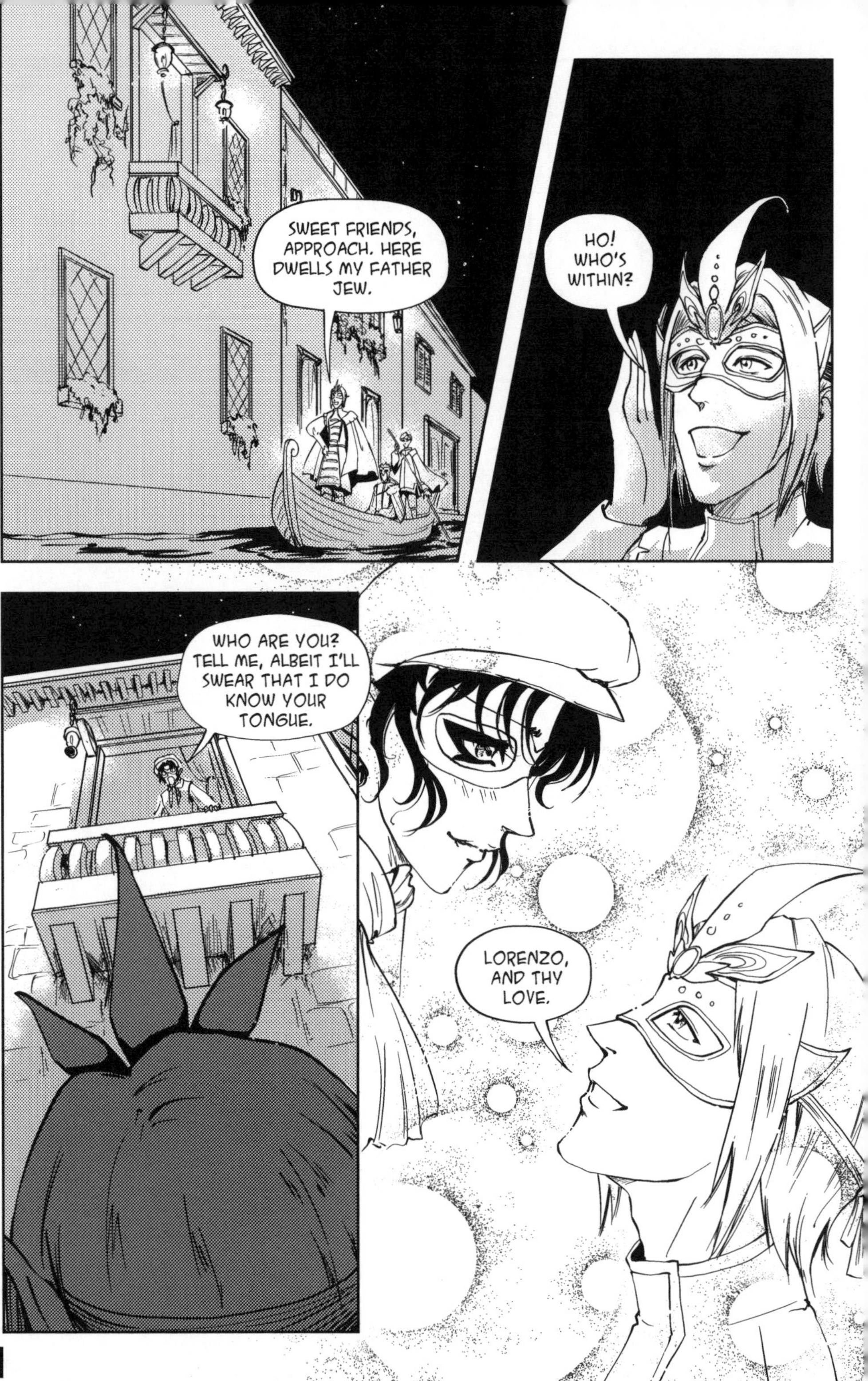
SWEET FRIENDS, APPROACH. HERE DWELLS MY FATHER JEW.
HO! WHO'S WITHIN?
WHO ARE YOU? TELL ME, ALBEIT I'LL SWEAR THAT I DO KNOW YOUR TONGUE.
LORENZO, AND THY LOVE.

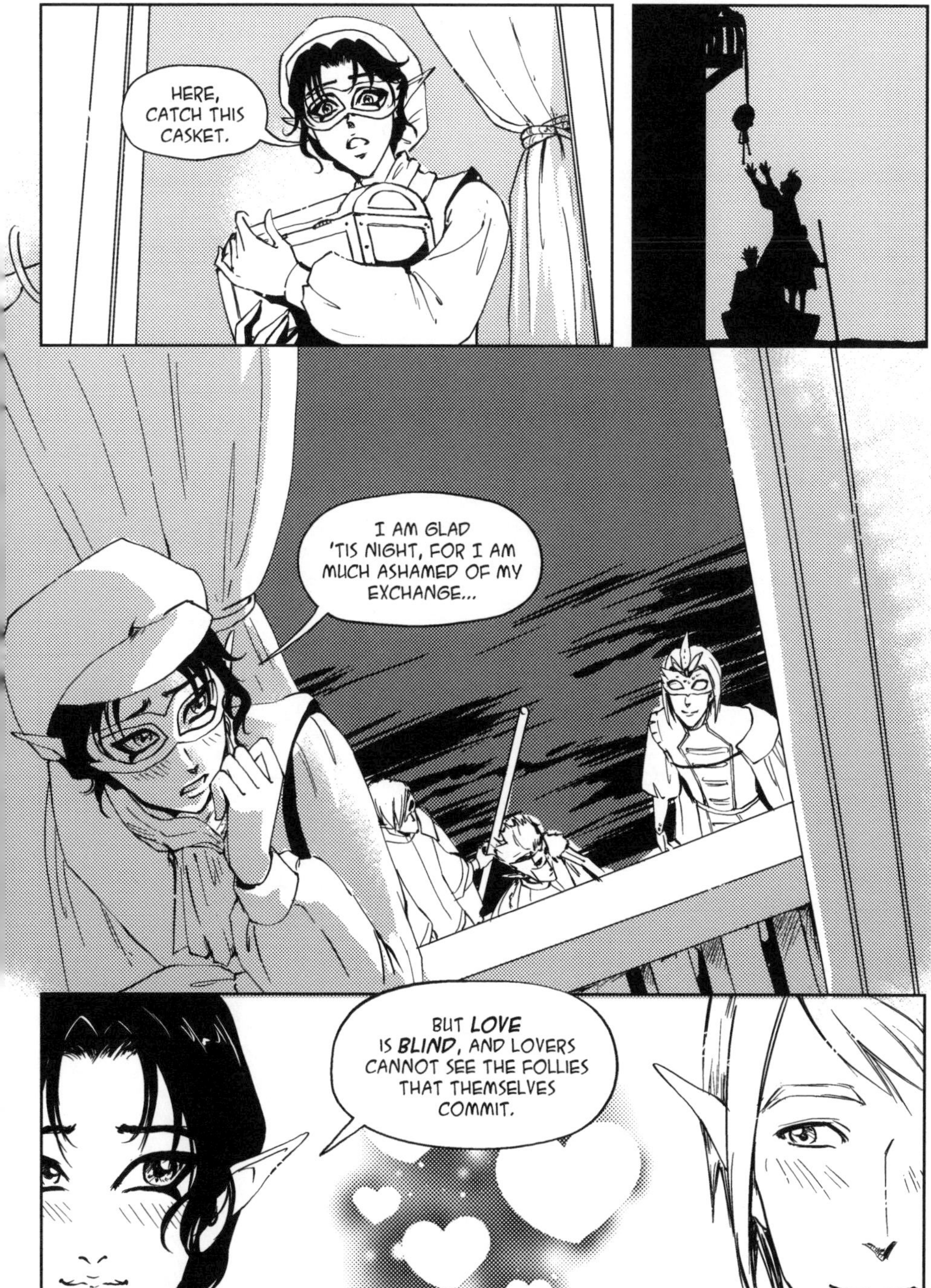
HERE, CATCH THIS CASKET.
I AM GLAD 'TIS NIGHT, FOR I AM MUCH ASHAMED OF MY EXCHANGE...
BUT **LOVE** IS **BLIND**, AND LOVERS CANNOT SEE THE FOLLIES THAT THEMSELVES COMMIT.

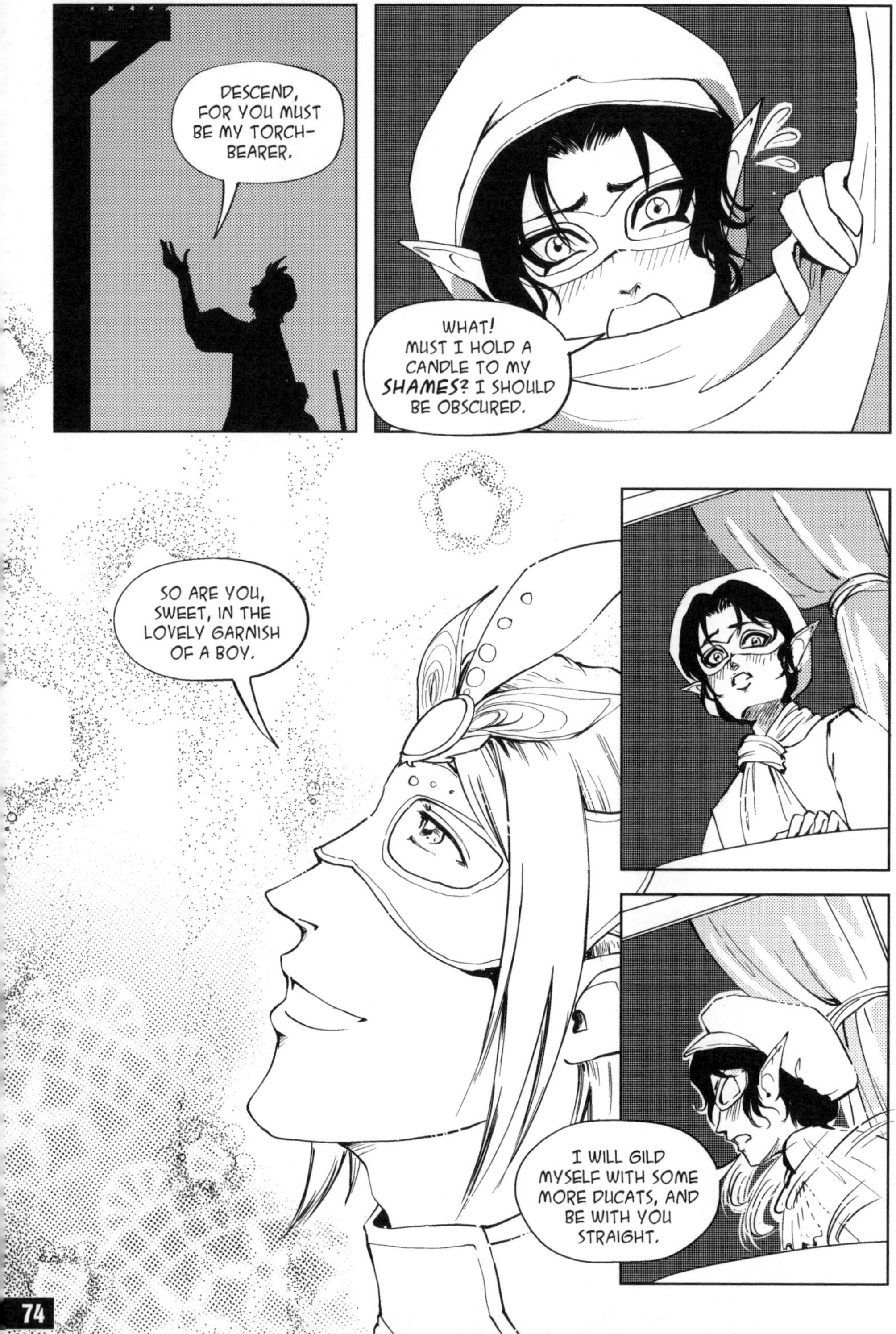
DESCEND, FOR YOU MUST BE MY TORCH-BEARER.
WHAT! MUST I HOLD A CANDLE TO MY SHAMES? I SHOULD BE OBSCURED.
SO ARE YOU, SWEET, IN THE LOVELY GARNISH OF A BOY.
I WILL GILD MYSELF WITH SOME MORE DUCATS, AND BE WITH YOU STRAIGHT.

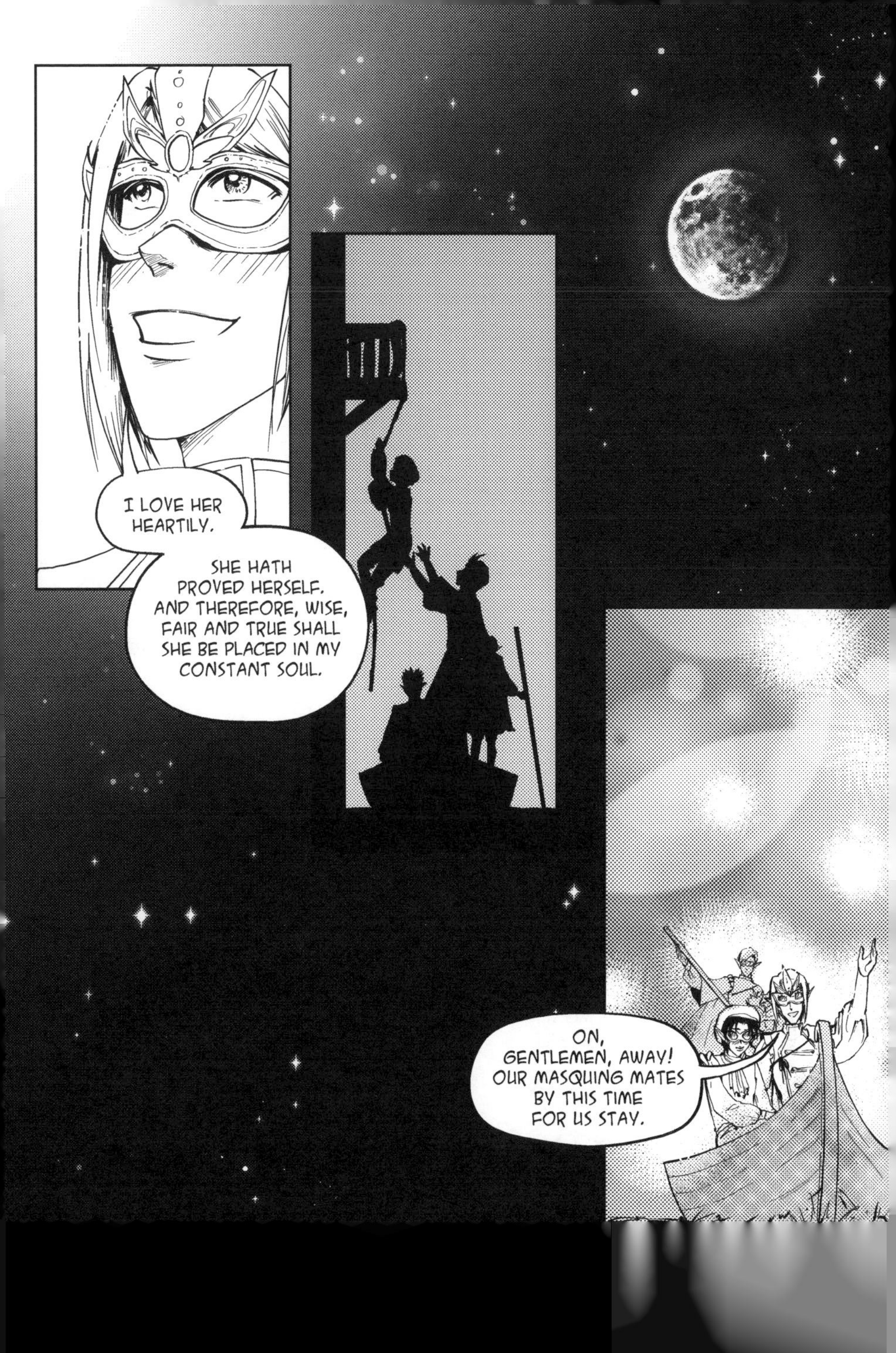
I LOVE HER HEARTILY.
SHE HATH PROVED HERSELF. AND THEREFORE, WISE, FAIR AND TRUE SHALL SHE BE PLACED IN MY CONSTANT SOUL.
ON, GENTLEMEN, AWAY! OUR MASQUING MATES BY THIS TIME FOR US STAY.

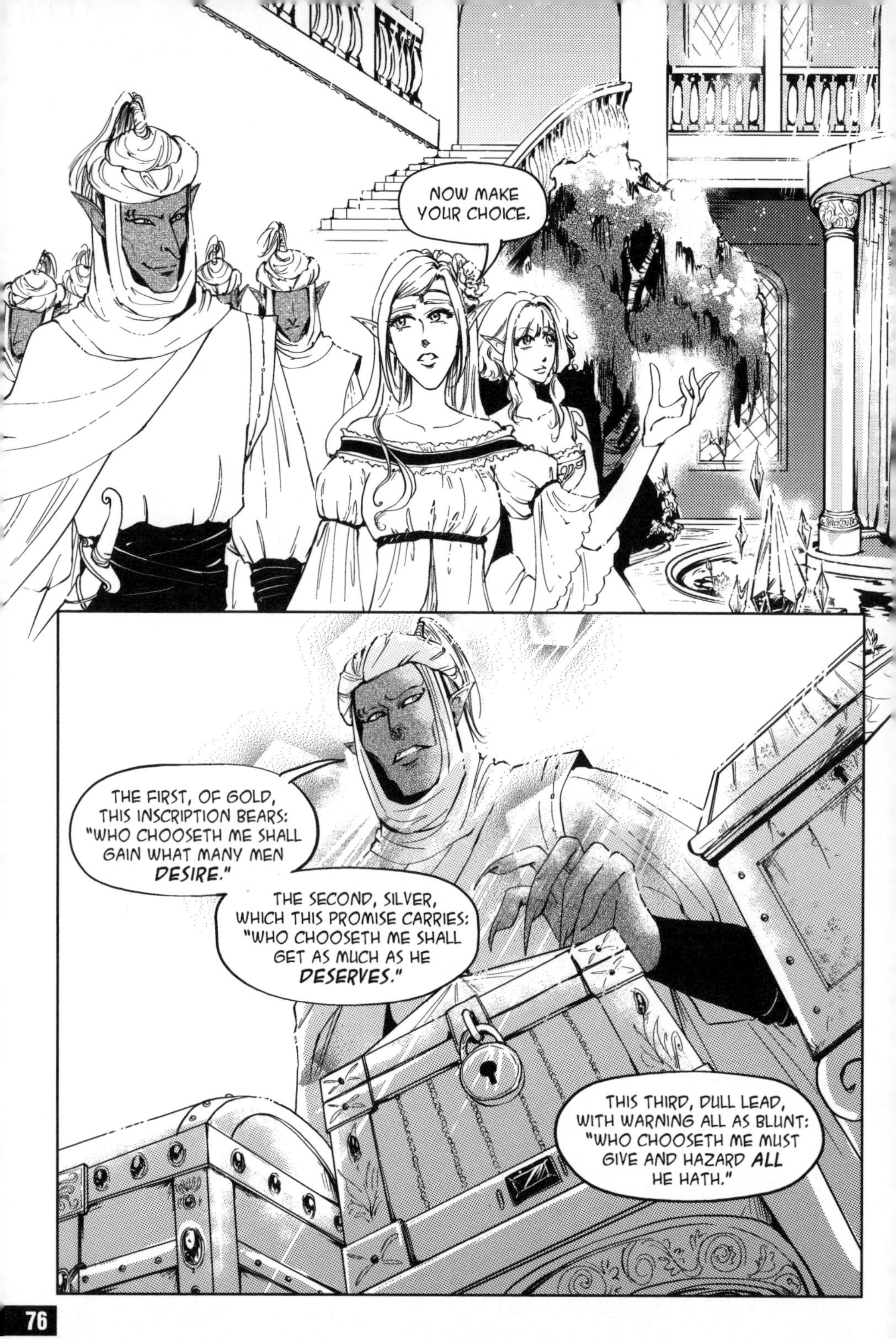
NOW MAKE YOUR CHOICE.
THE FIRST, OF GOLD, THIS INSCRIPTION BEARS: "WHO CHOOSETH ME SHALL GAIN WHAT MANY MEN DESIRE."
THE SECOND, SILVER, WHICH THIS PROMISE CARRIES: "WHO CHOOSETH ME SHALL GET AS MUCH AS HE DESERVES."
THIS THIRD, DULL LEAD, WITH WARNING ALL AS BLUNT: "WHO CHOOSETH ME MUST GIVE AND HAZARD ALL HE HATH."

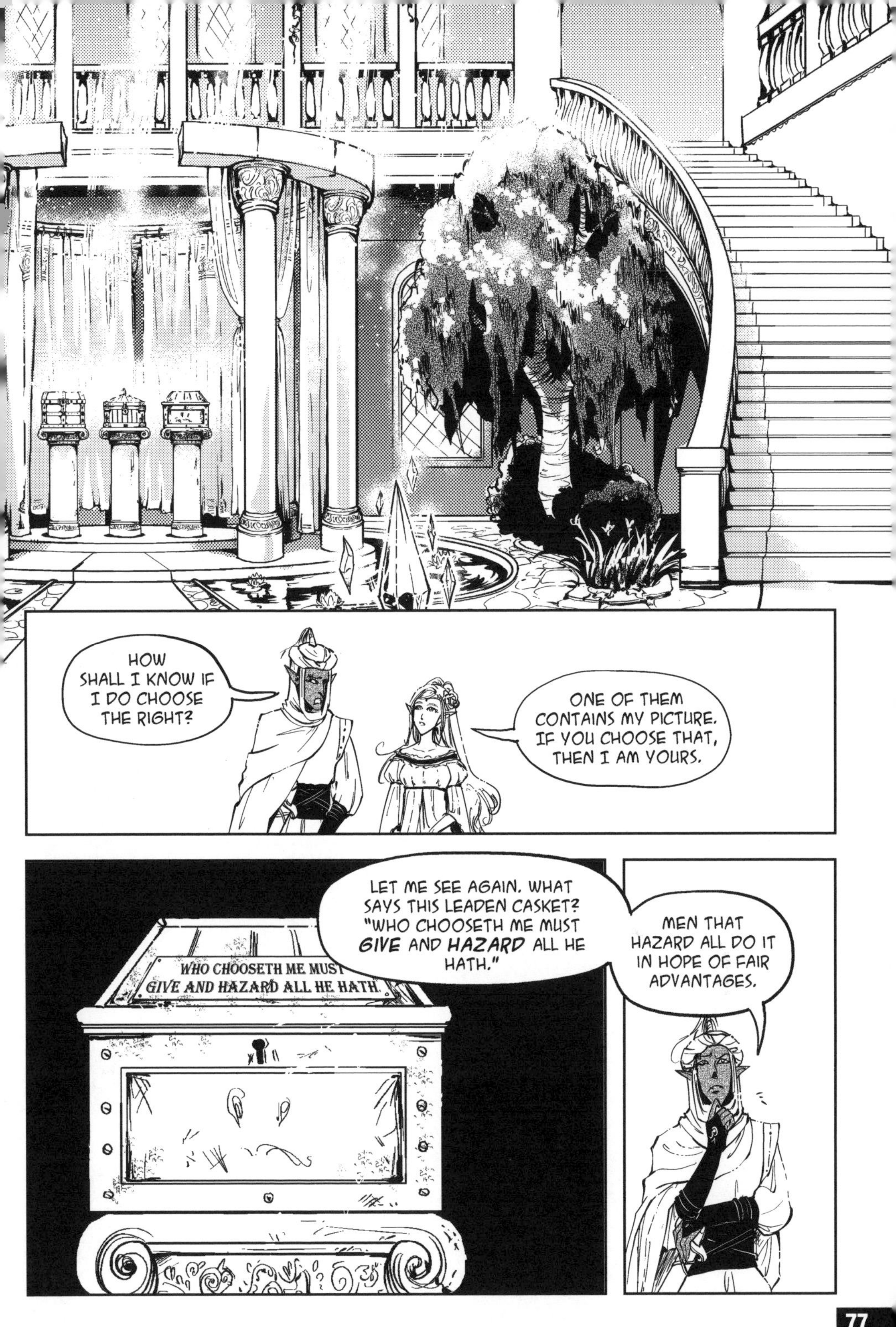
HOW SHALL I KNOW IF I DO CHOOSE THE RIGHT?
ONE OF THEM CONTAINS MY PICTURE. IF YOU CHOOSE THAT, THEN I AM YOURS.
WHO CHOOSETH ME MUST GIVE AND HAZARD ALL HE HATH.
LET ME SEE AGAIN. WHAT SAYS THIS LEADEN CASKET? "WHO CHOOSETH ME MUST **GIVE** AND **HAZARD** ALL HE HATH."
MEN THAT HAZARD ALL DO IT IN HOPE OF FAIR ADVANTAGES.

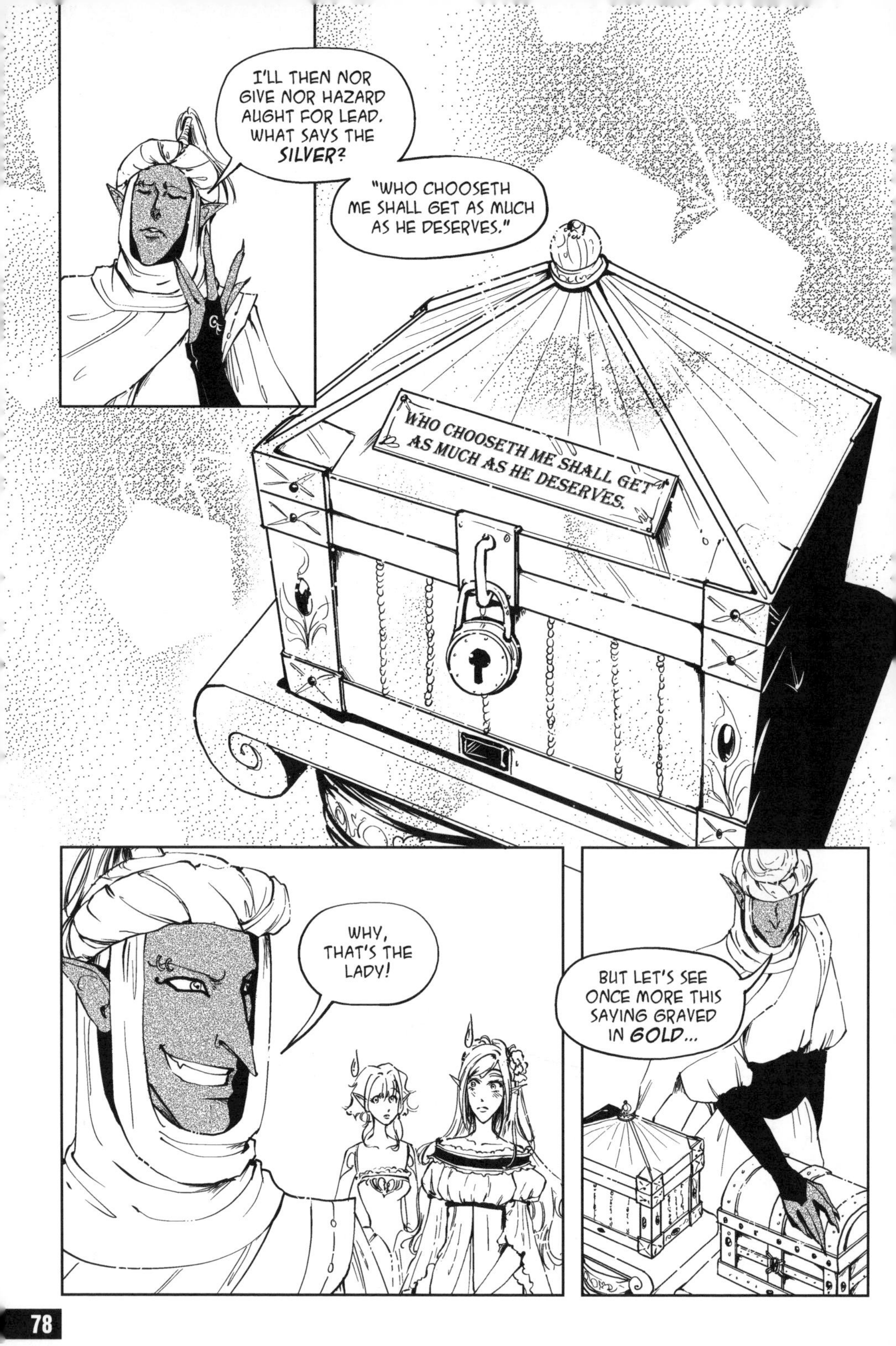
I'LL THEN NOR GIVE NOR HAZARD AUGHT FOR LEAD. WHAT SAYS THE SILVER?
"WHO CHOOSETH ME SHALL GET AS MUCH AS HE DESERVES."
WHO CHOOSETH ME SHALL GET AS MUCH AS HE DESERVES.
WHY, THAT'S THE LADY!
BUT LET'S SEE ONCE MORE THIS SAYING GRAVED IN GOLD...

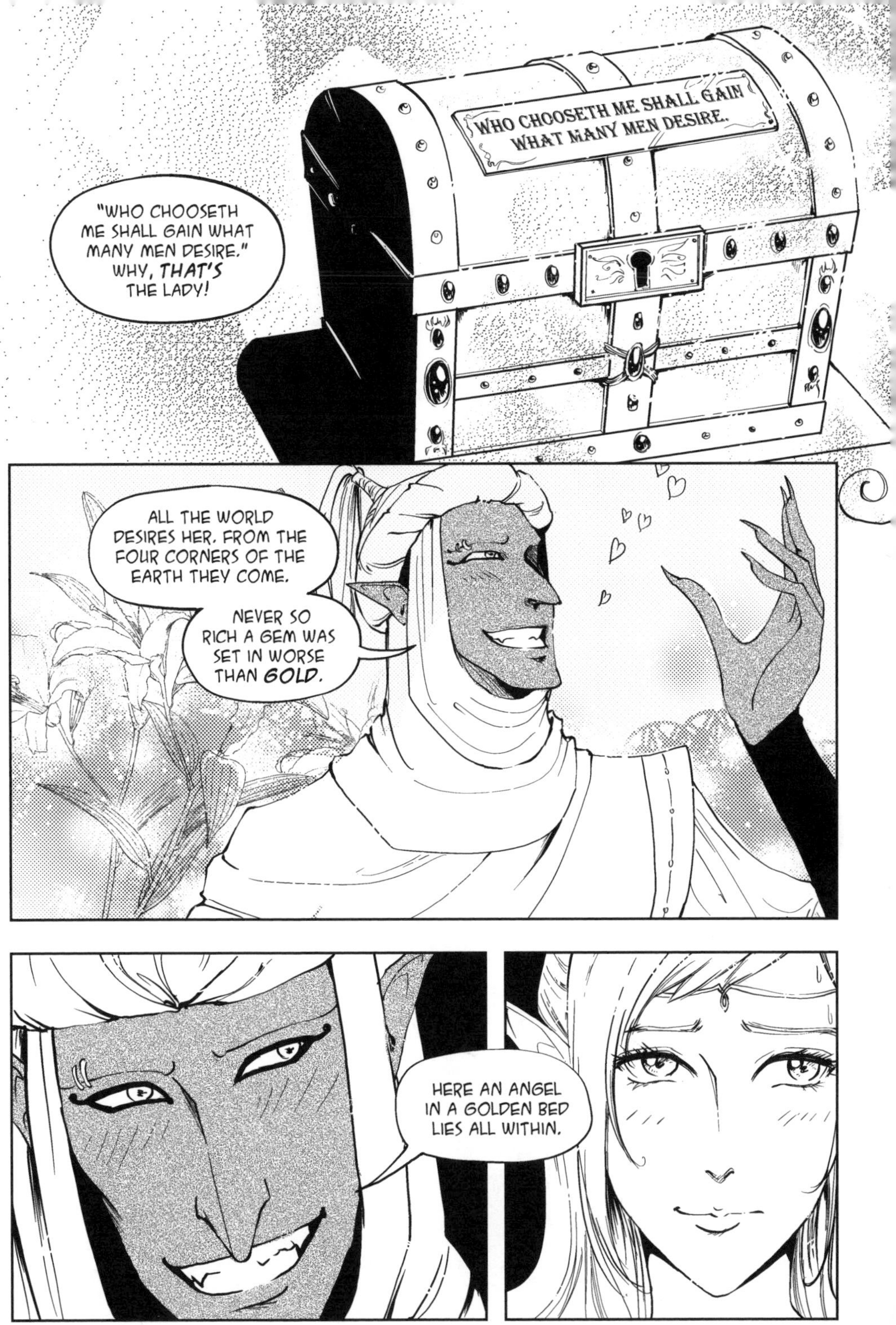
WHO CHOOSETH ME SHALL GAIN WHAT MANY MEN DESIRE.
"WHO CHOOSETH ME SHALL GAIN WHAT MANY MEN DESIRE." WHY, THAT'S THE LADY!
ALL THE WORLD DESIRES HER. FROM THE FOUR CORNERS OF THE EARTH THEY COME.
NEVER SO RICH A GEM WAS SET IN WORSE THAN GOLD.
HERE AN ANGEL IN A GOLDEN BED LIES ALL WITHIN.

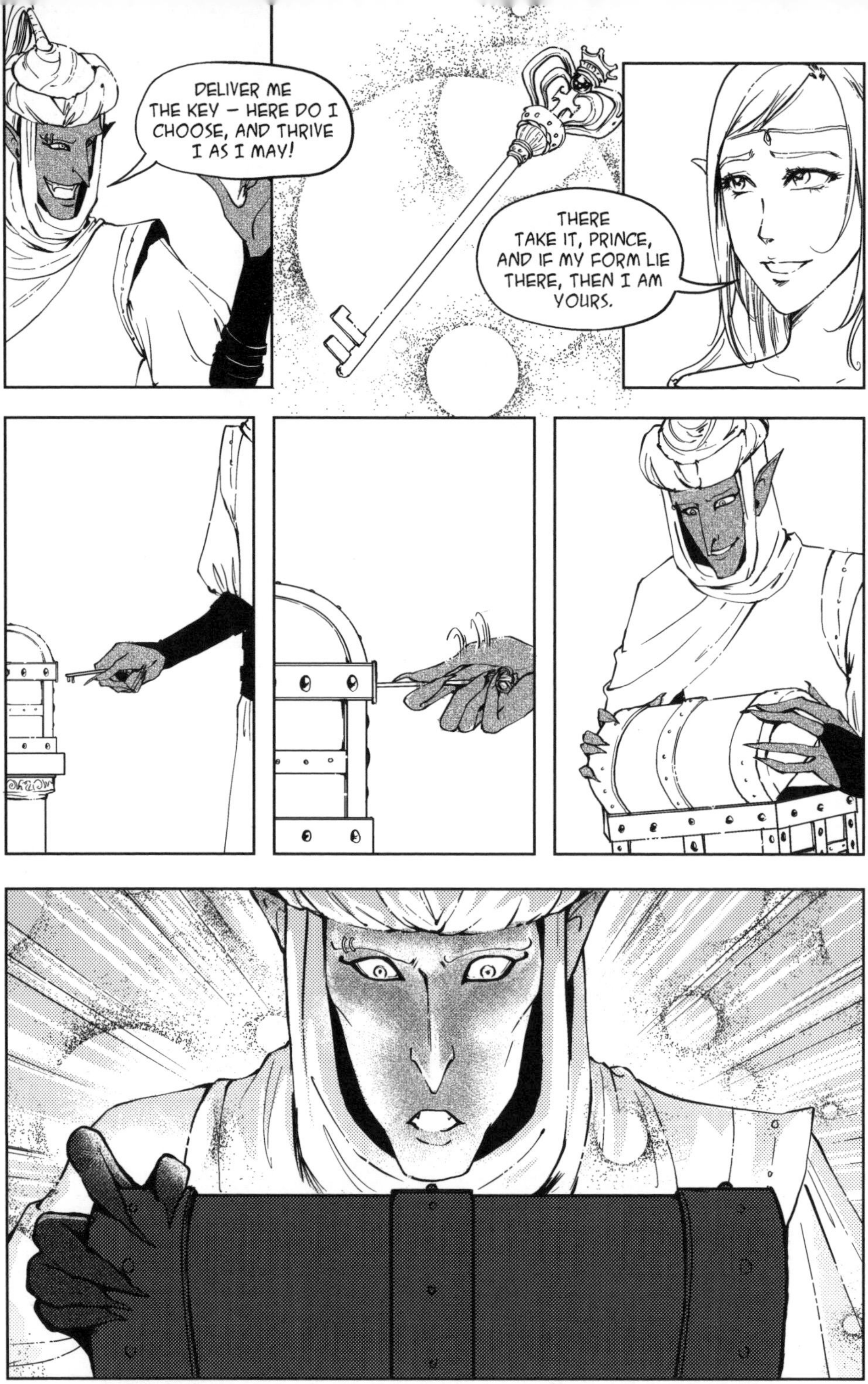
DELIVER ME THE KEY — HERE DO I CHOOSE, AND THRIVE I AS I MAY!
THERE TAKE IT, PRINCE, AND IF MY FORM LIE THERE, THEN I AM YOURS.

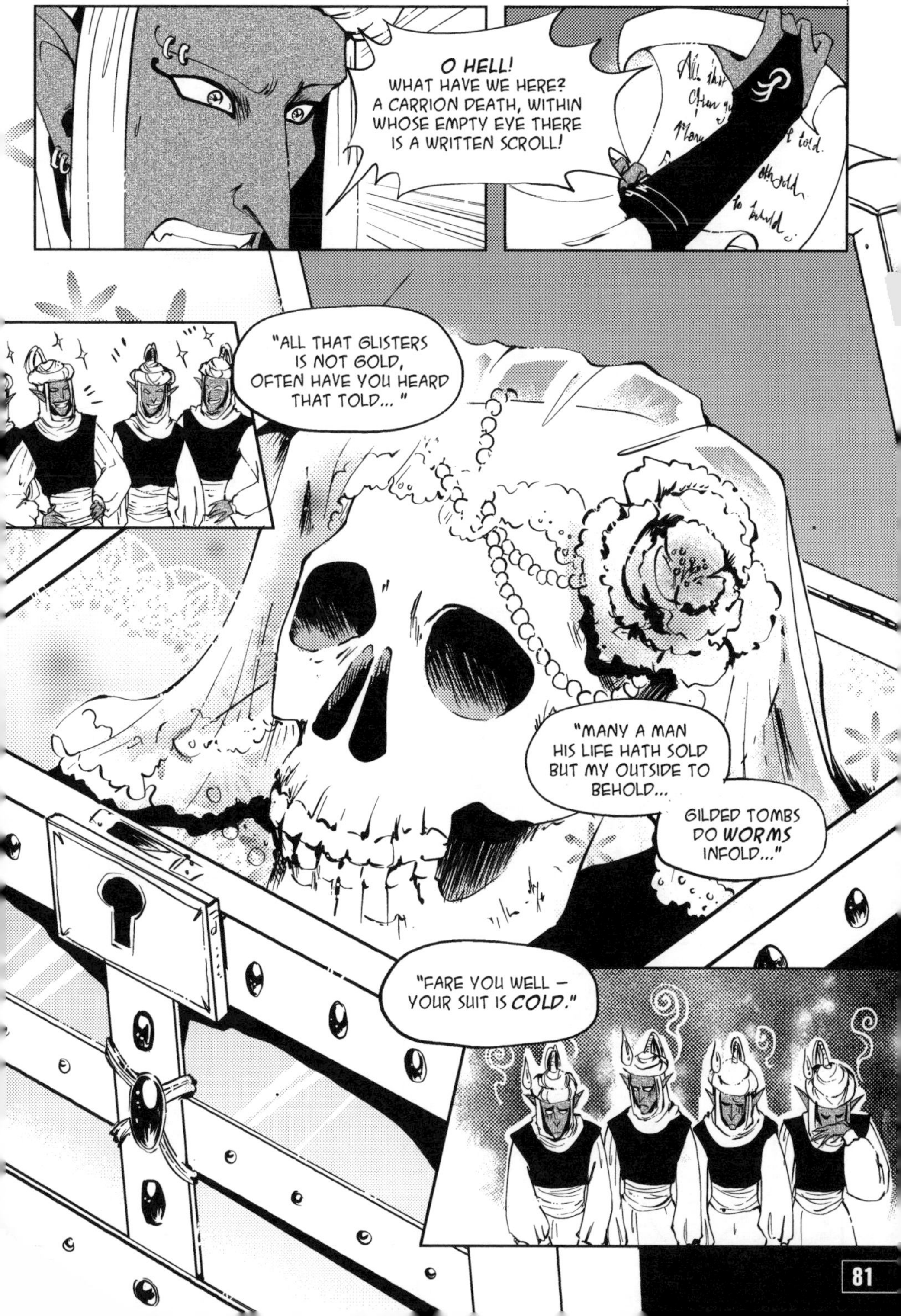
O **HELL!** WHAT HAVE WE HERE? A CARRION DEATH, WITHIN WHOSE EMPTY EYE THERE IS A WRITTEN SCROLL!
"ALL THAT GLISTERS IS NOT GOLD, OFTEN HAVE YOU HEARD THAT TOLD..."
"MANY A MAN HIS LIFE HATH SOLD BUT MY OUTSIDE TO BEHOLD...
GILDED TOMBS DO **WORMS** INFOLD..."
"FARE YOU WELL — YOUR SUIT IS **COLD.**"

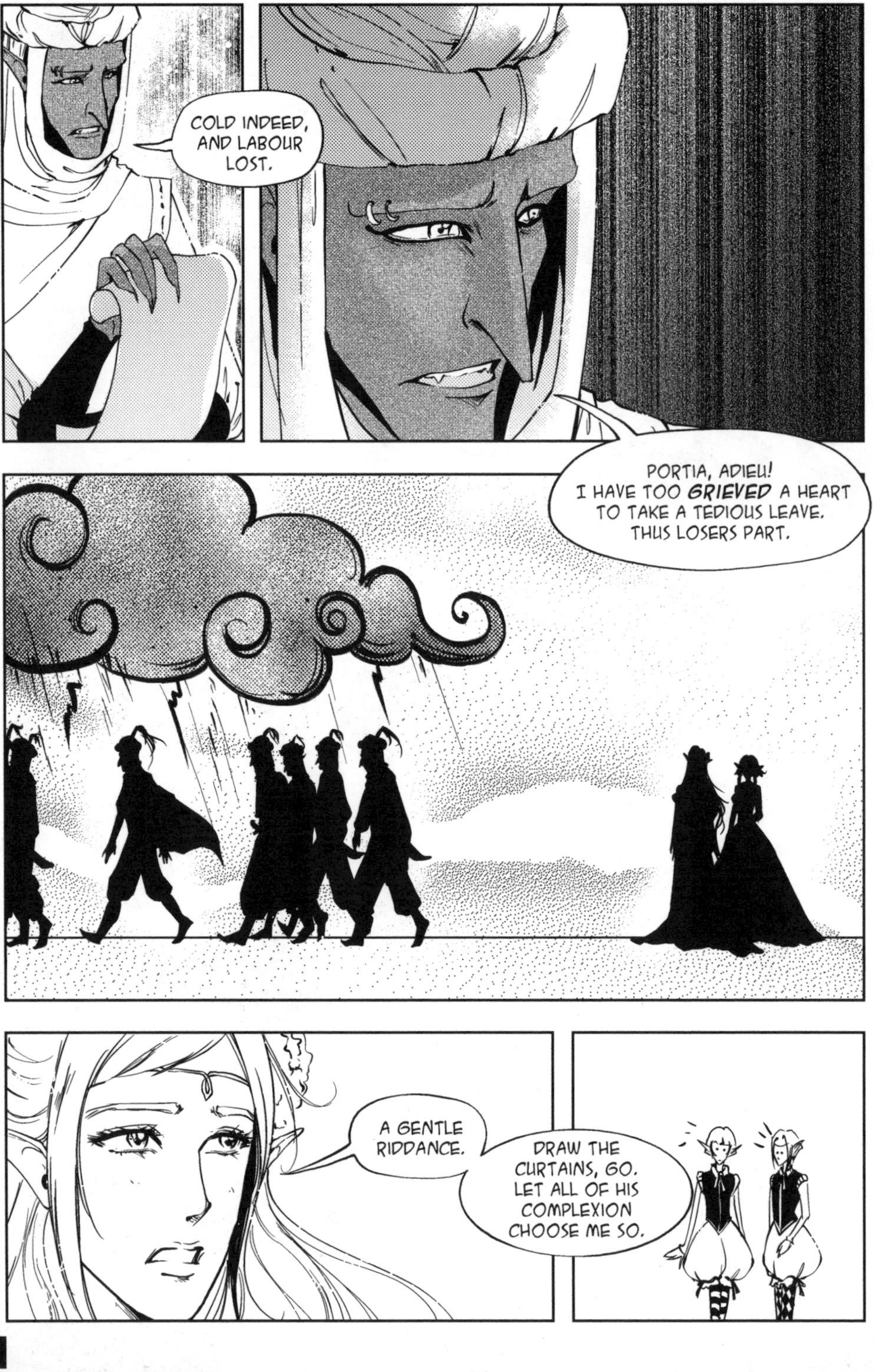
COLD INDEED, AND LABOUR LOST.
PORTIA, ADIEU! I HAVE TOO GRIEVED A HEART TO TAKE A TEDIOUS LEAVE. THUS LOSERS PART.
A GENTLE RIDDANCE.
DRAW THE CURTAINS, GO. LET ALL OF HIS COMPLEXION CHOOSE ME SO.

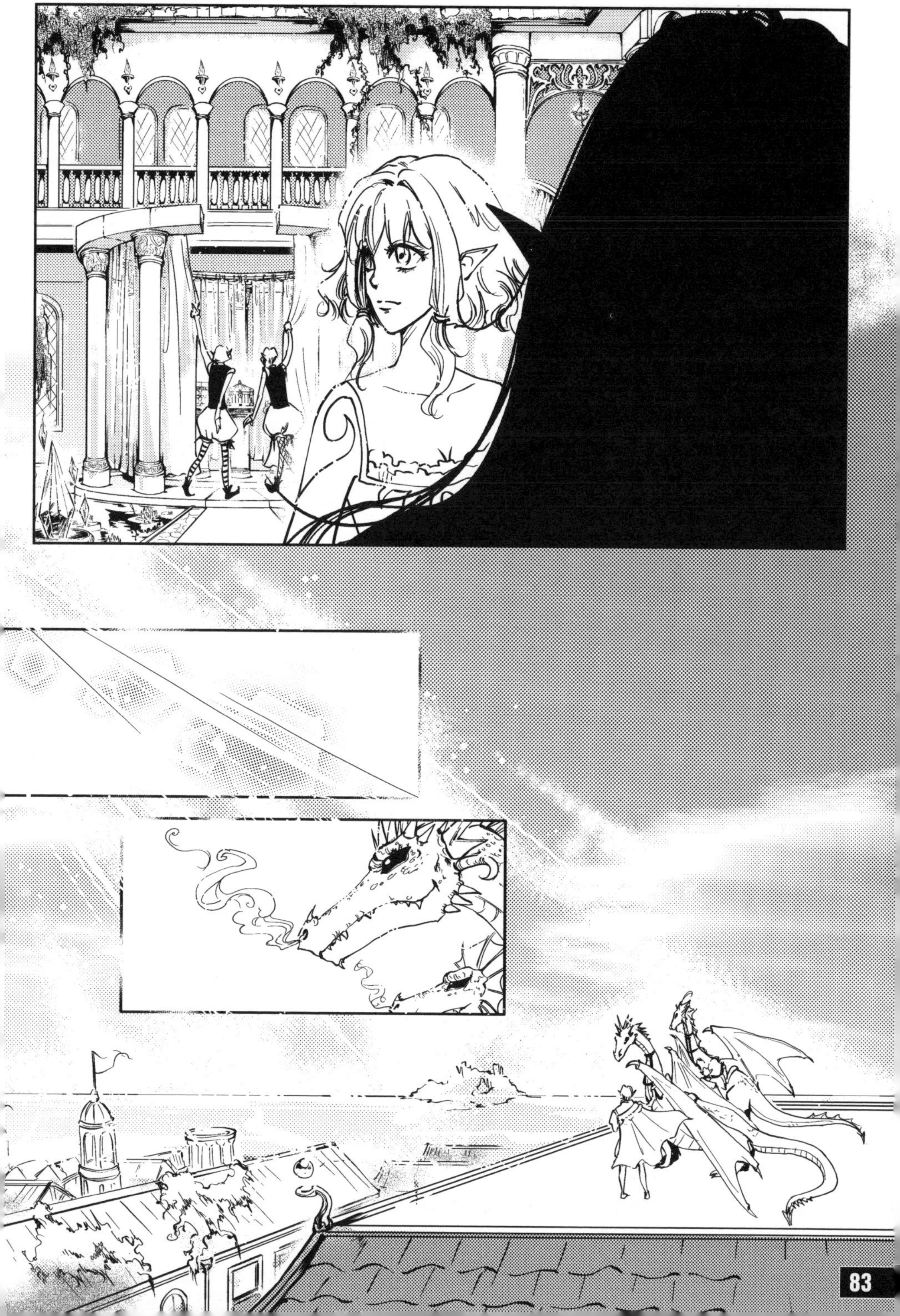

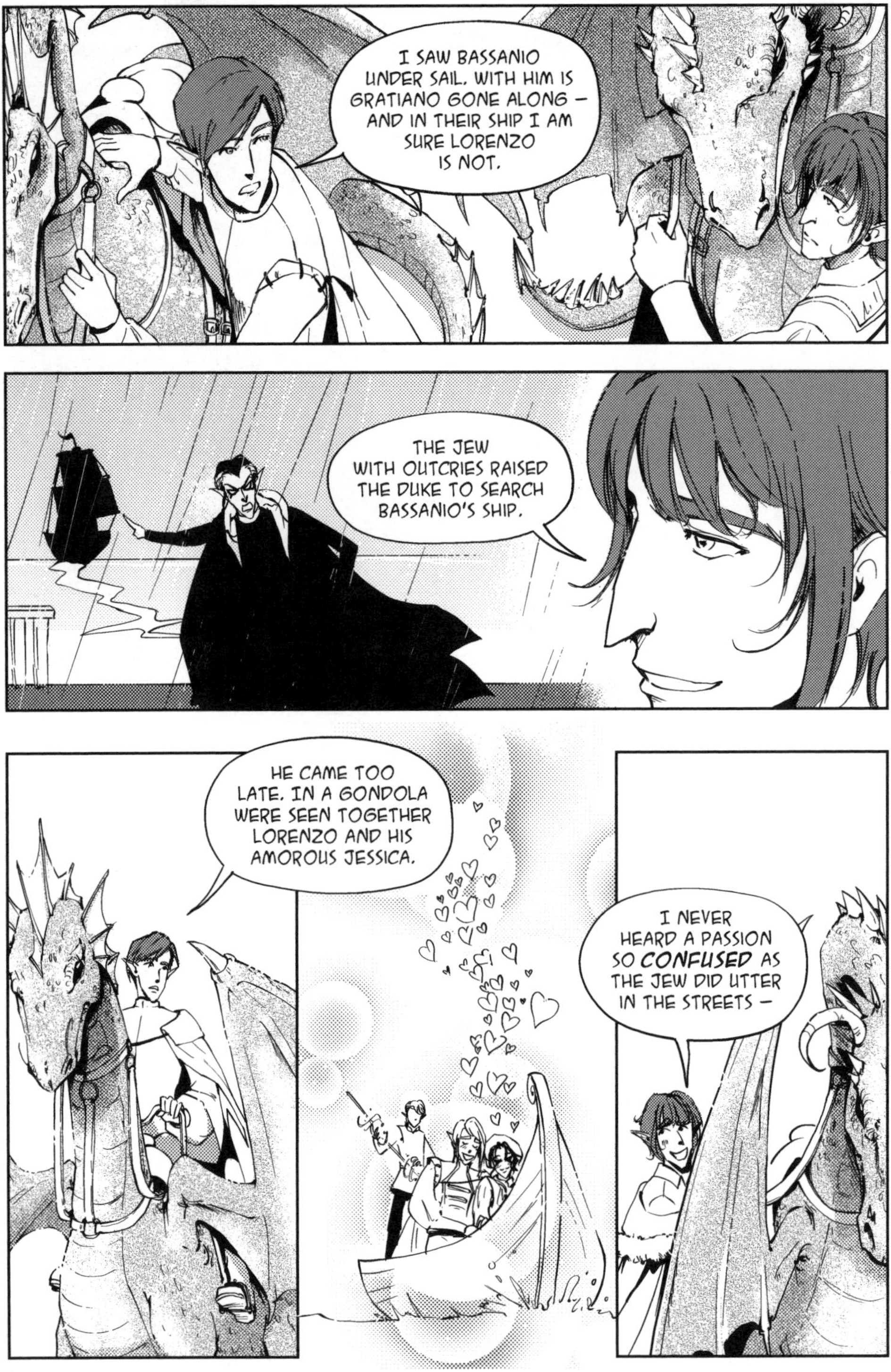
I SAW BASSANIO UNDER SAIL. WITH HIM IS GRATIANO GONE ALONG — AND IN THEIR SHIP I AM SURE LORENZO IS NOT.
THE JEW WITH OUTCRIES RAISED THE DUKE TO SEARCH BASSANIO'S SHIP.
HE CAME TOO LATE. IN A GONDOLA WERE SEEN TOGETHER LORENZO AND HIS AMOROUS JESSICA.
I NEVER HEARD A PASSION SO **CONFUSED** AS THE JEW DID UTTER IN THE STREETS —

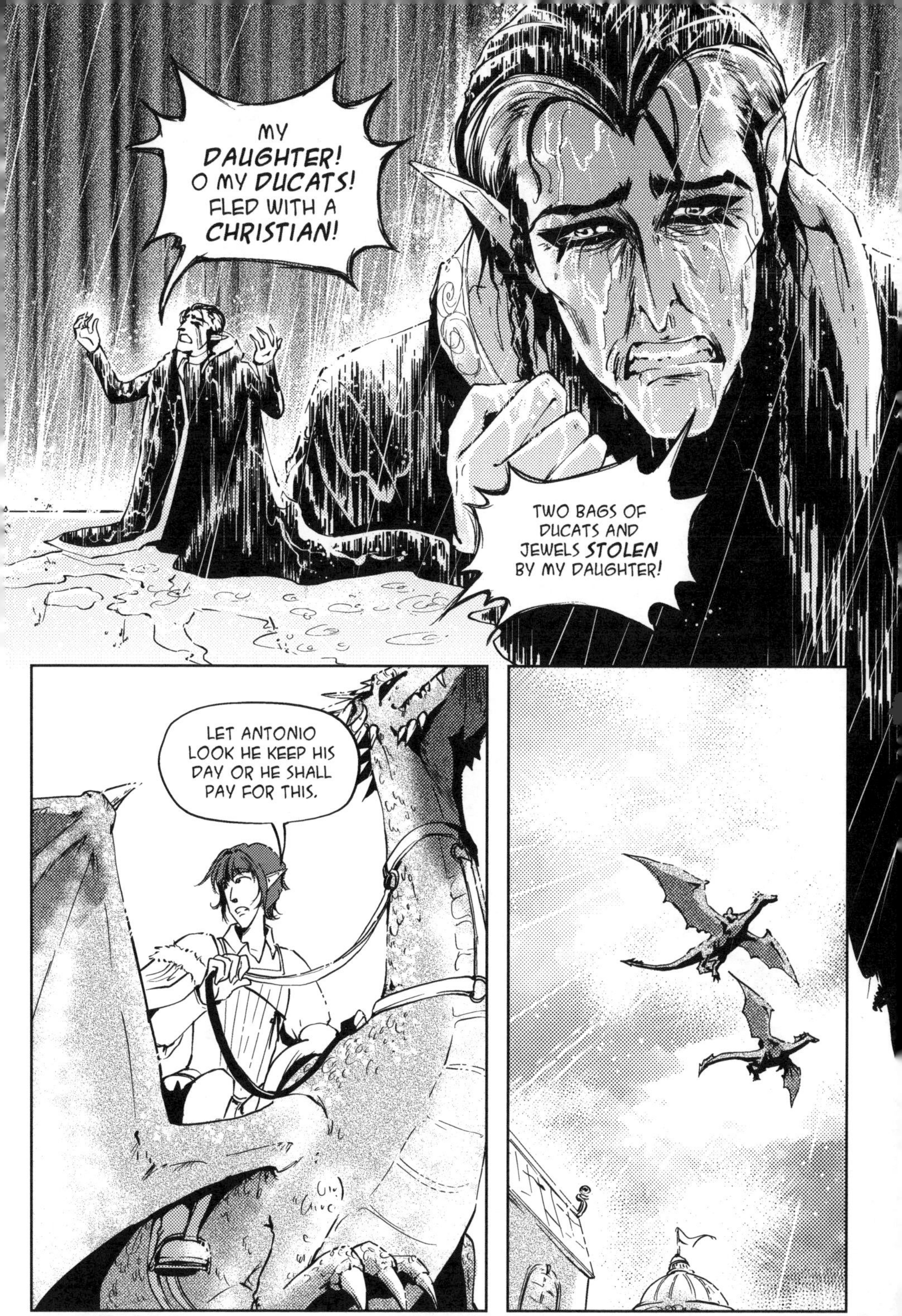
MY DAUGHTER! O MY DUCATS! FLED WITH A CHRISTIAN!
TWO BAGS OF DUCATS AND JEWELS STOLEN BY MY DAUGHTER!
LET ANTONIO LOOK HE KEEP HIS DAY OR HE SHALL PAY FOR THIS.

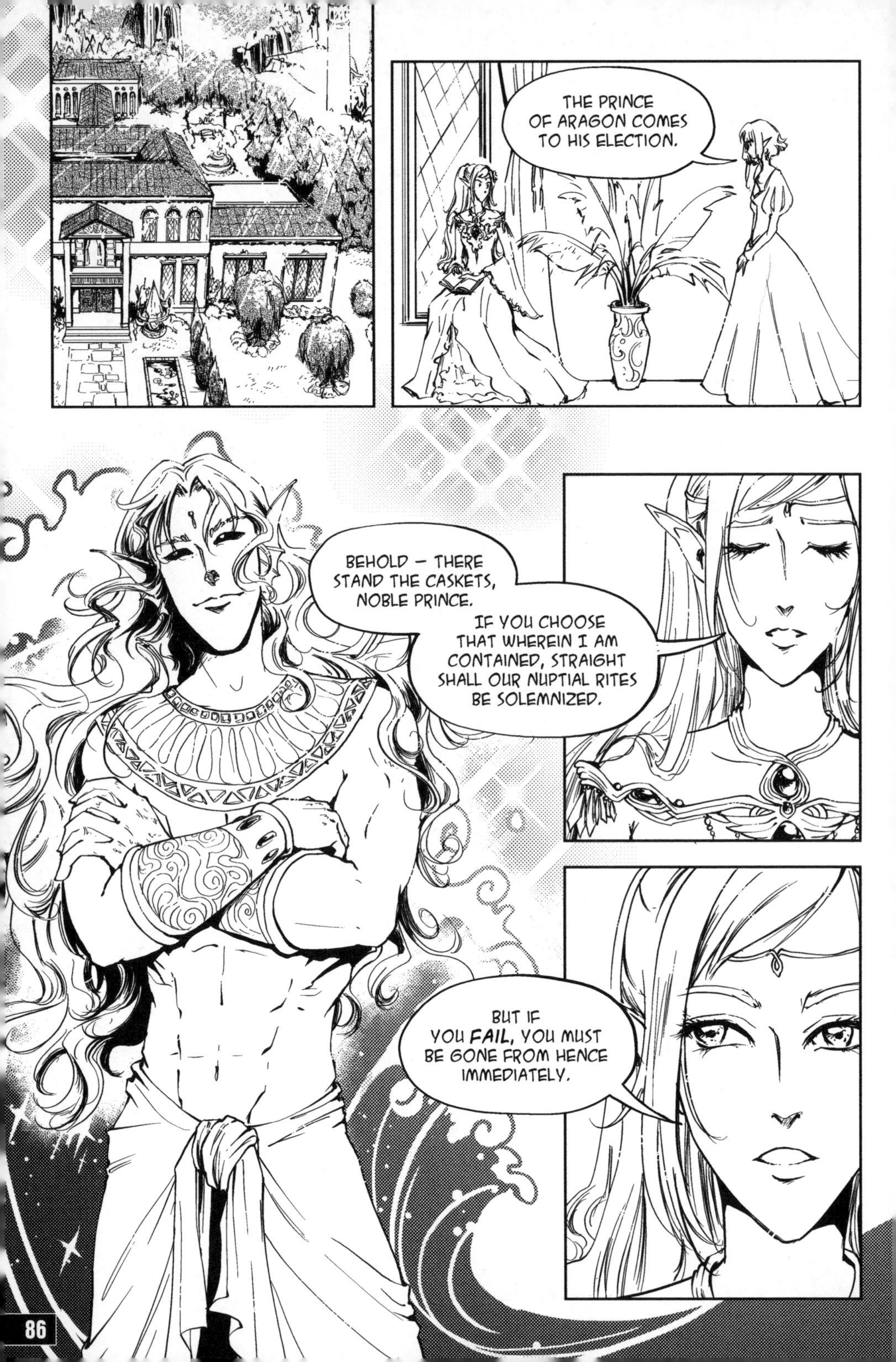
THE PRINCE OF ARAGON COMES TO HIS ELECTION.
BEHOLD – THERE STAND THE CASKETS, NOBLE PRINCE.
IF YOU CHOOSE THAT WHEREIN I AM CONTAINED, STRAIGHT SHALL OUR NUPTIAL RITES BE SOLEMNIZED.
BUT IF YOU **FAIL**, YOU MUST BE GONE FROM HENCE IMMEDIATELY.

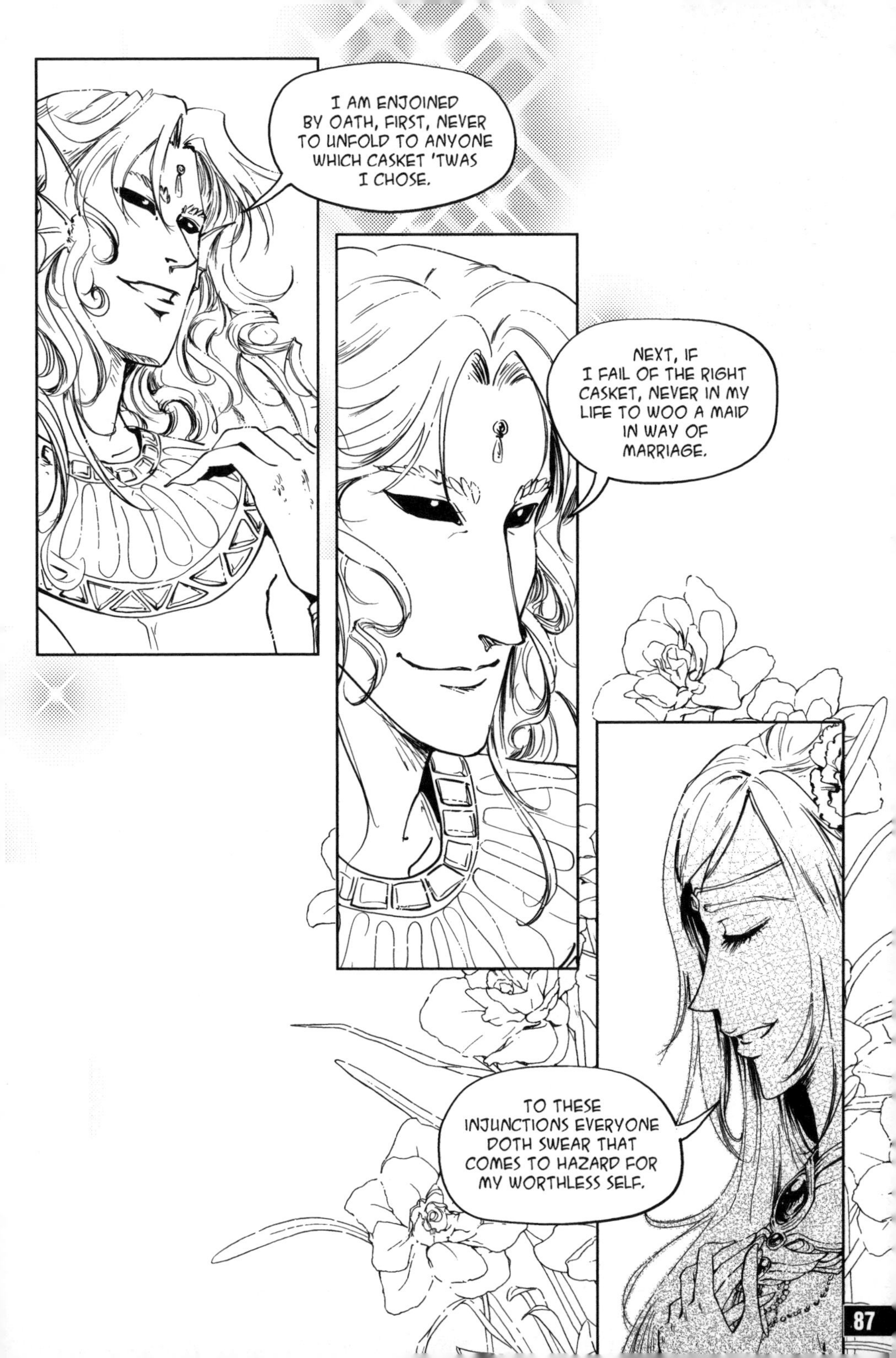
I AM ENJOINED BY OATH, FIRST, NEVER TO UNFOLD TO ANYONE WHICH CASKET 'TWAS I CHOSE.
NEXT, IF I FAIL OF THE RIGHT CASKET, NEVER IN MY LIFE TO WOO A MAID IN WAY OF MARRIAGE.
TO THESE INJUNCTIONS EVERYONE DOTH SWEAR THAT COMES TO HAZARD FOR MY WORTHLESS SELF.

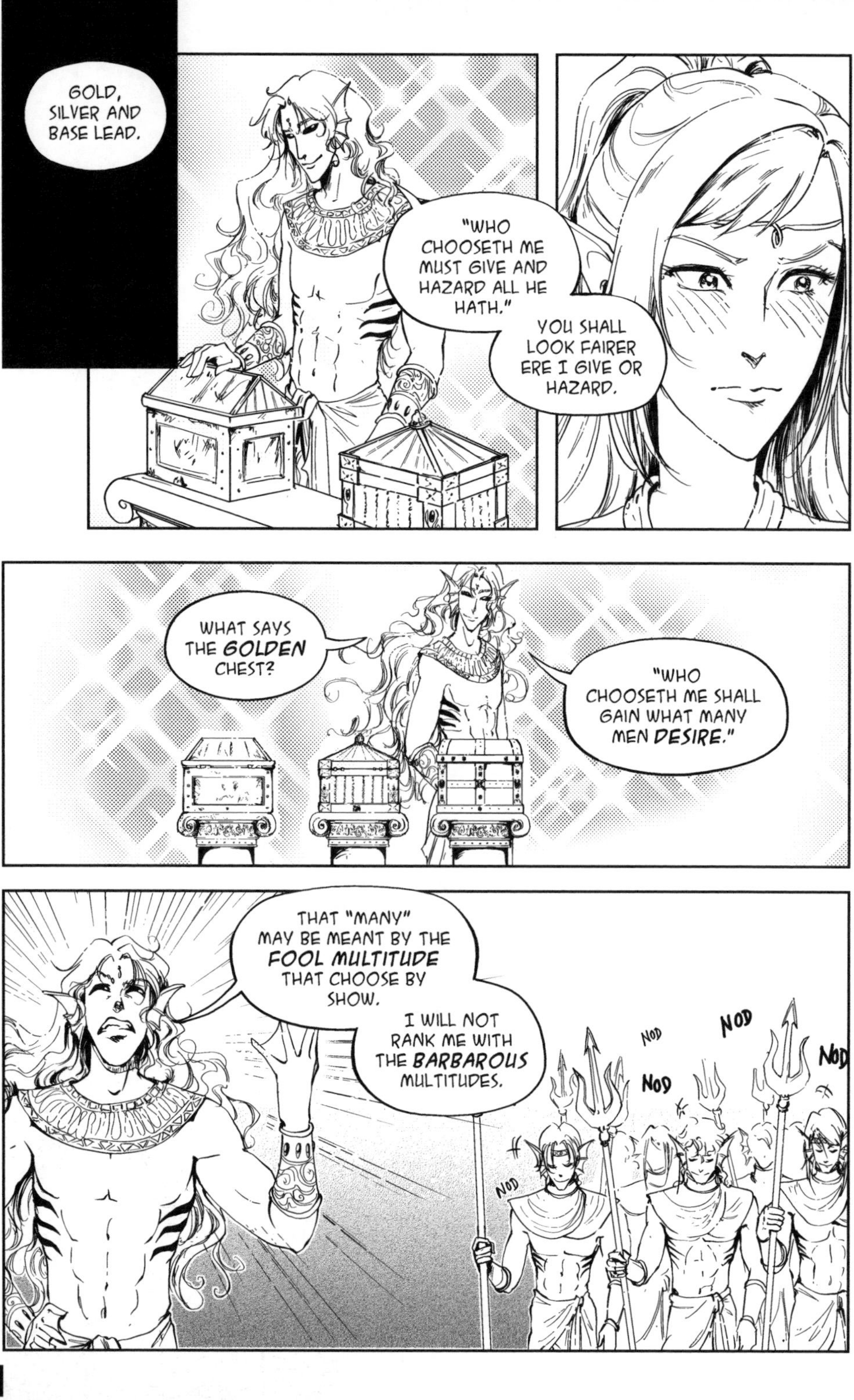
GOLD, SILVER AND BASE LEAD.
"WHO CHOOSETH ME MUST GIVE AND HAZARD ALL HE HATH."
YOU SHALL LOOK FAIRER ERE I GIVE OR HAZARD.
WHAT SAYS THE GOLDEN CHEST?
"WHO CHOOSETH ME SHALL GAIN WHAT MANY MEN DESIRE."
THAT "MANY" MAY BE MEANT BY THE FOOL MULTITUDE THAT CHOOSE BY SHOW.
I WILL NOT RANK ME WITH THE BARBAROUS MULTITUDES.
NOD
NOD
NOD
NOD
NOD

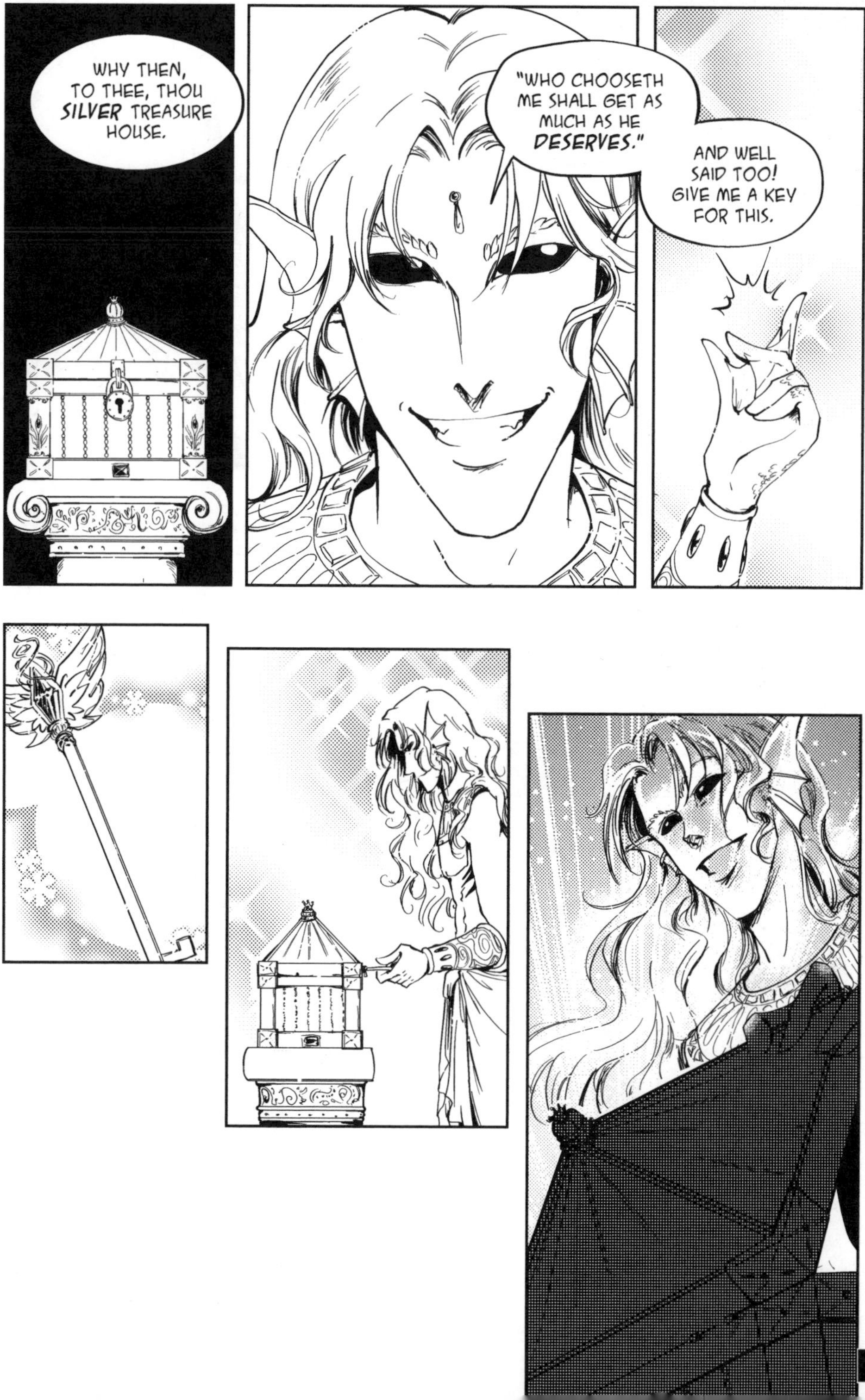
WHY THEN, TO THEE, THOU **SILVER** TREASURE HOUSE.
"WHO CHOOSETH ME SHALL GET AS MUCH AS HE **DESERVES.**"
AND WELL SAID TOO! GIVE ME A KEY FOR THIS.

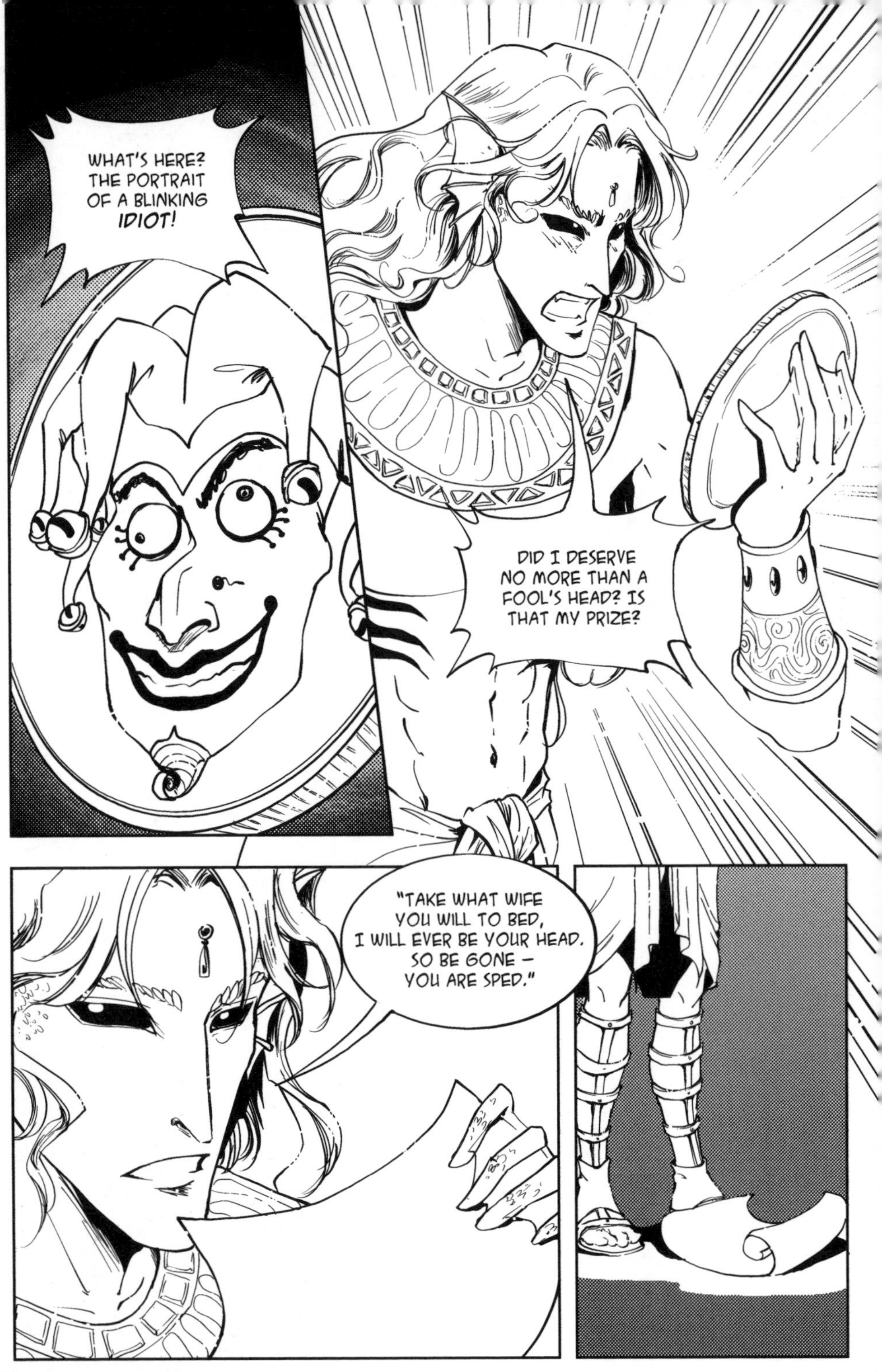
WHAT'S HERE? THE PORTRAIT OF A BLINKING IDIOT!
DID I DESERVE NO MORE THAN A FOOL'S HEAD? IS THAT MY PRIZE?
"TAKE WHAT WIFE YOU WILL TO BED, I WILL EVER BE YOUR HEAD. SO BE GONE – YOU ARE SPED."

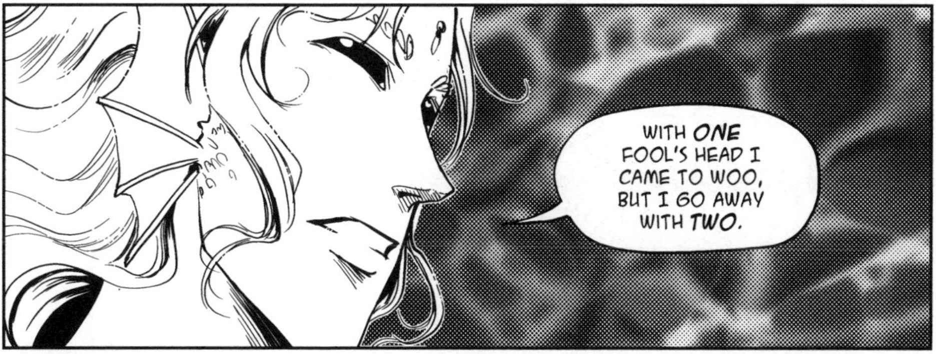
WITH ONE FOOL'S HEAD I CAME TO WOO, BUT I GO AWAY WITH TWO.

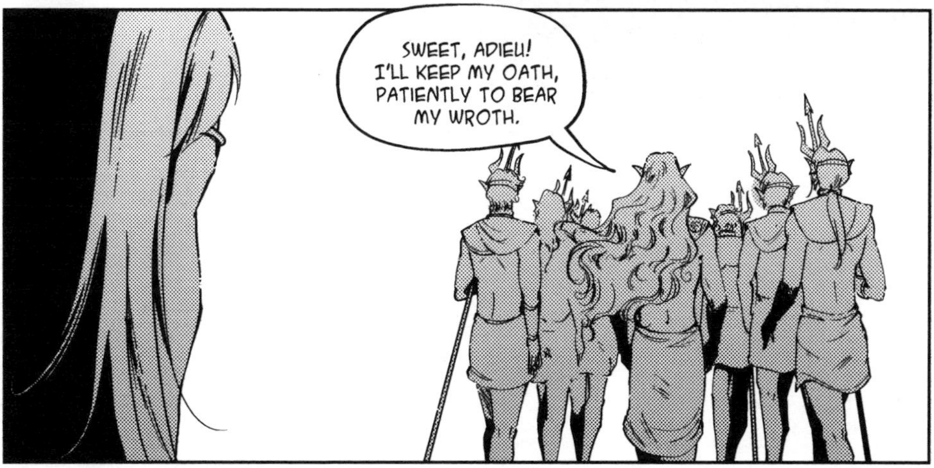
SWEET, ADIEU! I'LL KEEP MY OATH, PATIENTLY TO BEAR MY WROTH.

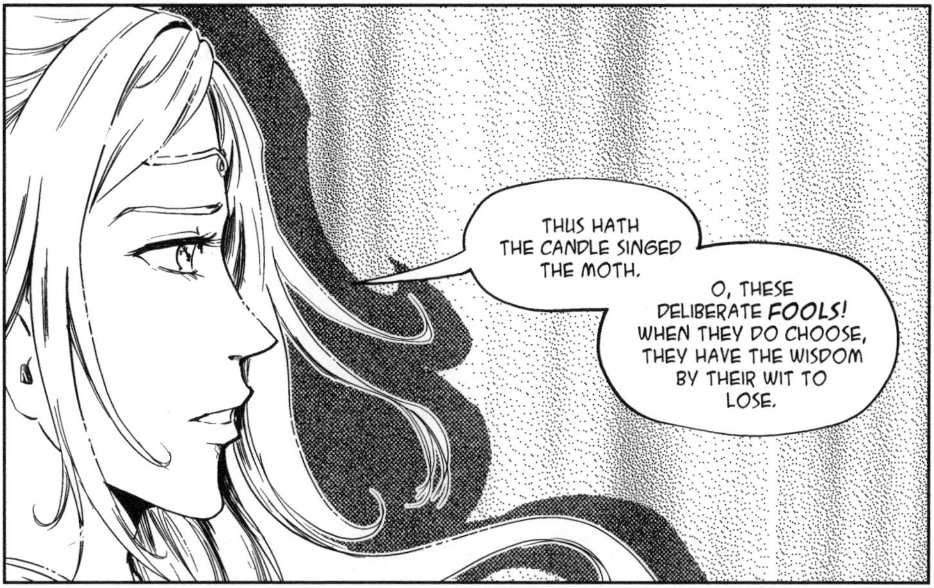
THUS HATH THE CANDLE SINGED THE MOTH.
O, THESE DELIBERATE FOOLS! WHEN THEY DO CHOOSE, THEY HAVE THE WISDOM BY THEIR WIT TO LOSE.

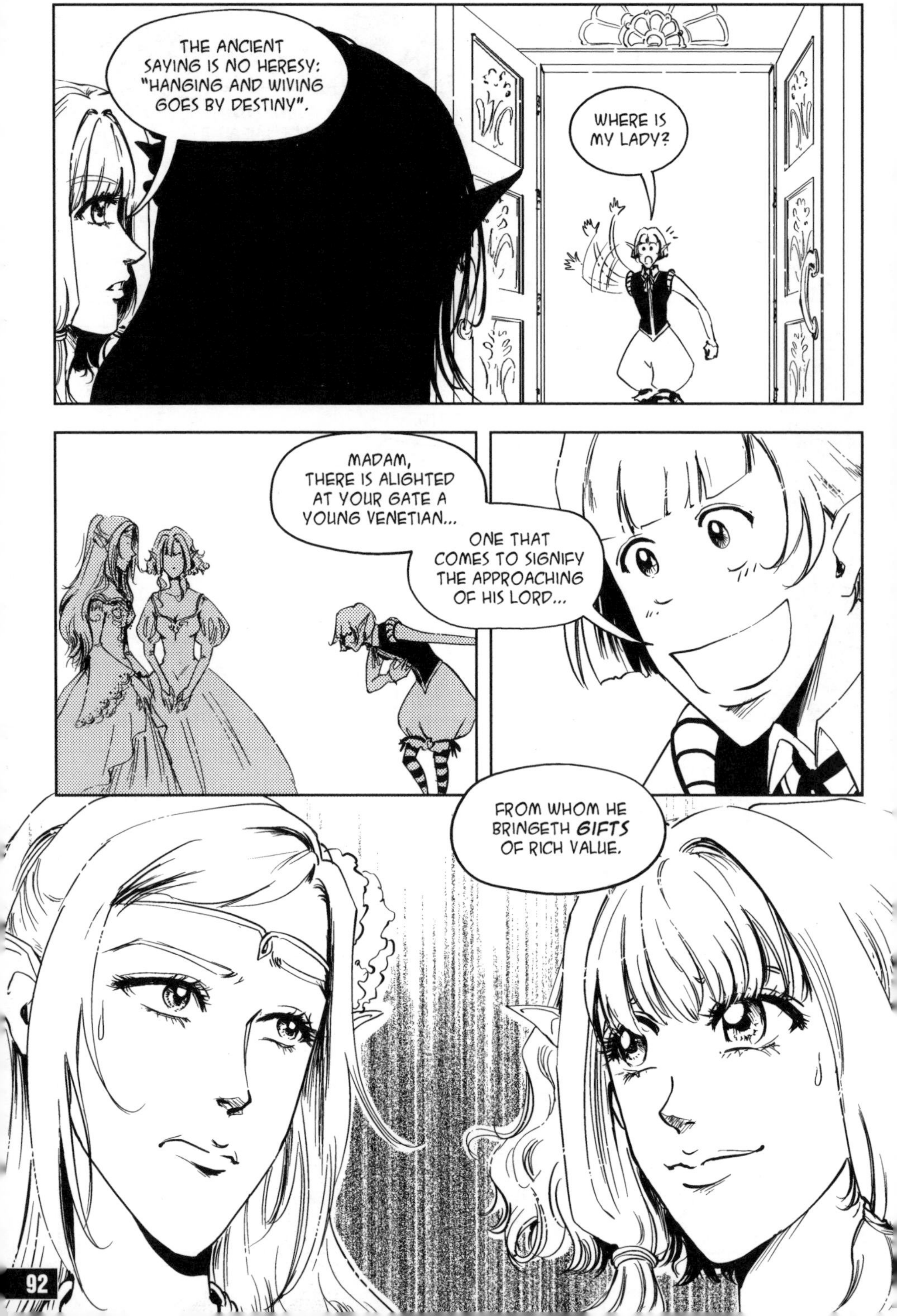

THE ANCIENT SAYING IS NO HERESY: "HANGING AND WIVING GOES BY DESTINY".
WHERE IS MY LADY?
MADAM, THERE IS ALIGHTED AT YOUR GATE A YOUNG VENETIAN...
ONE THAT COMES TO SIGNIFY THE APPROACHING OF HIS LORD...
FROM WHOM HE BRINGETH GIFTS OF RICH VALUE.

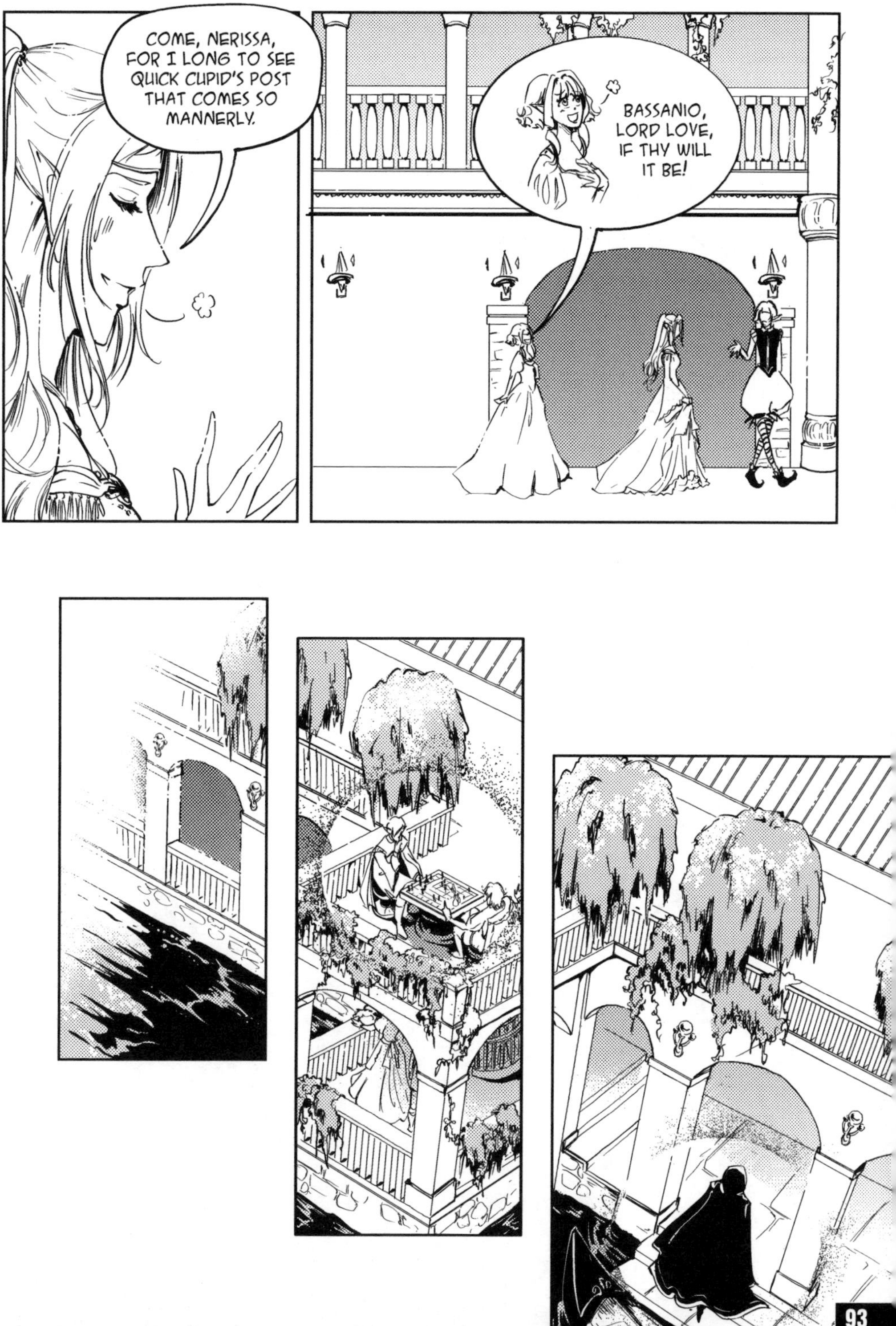
COME, NERISSA, FOR I LONG TO SEE QUICK CUPID'S POST THAT COMES SO MANNERLY.
BASSANIO, LORD LOVE, IF THY WILL IT BE!

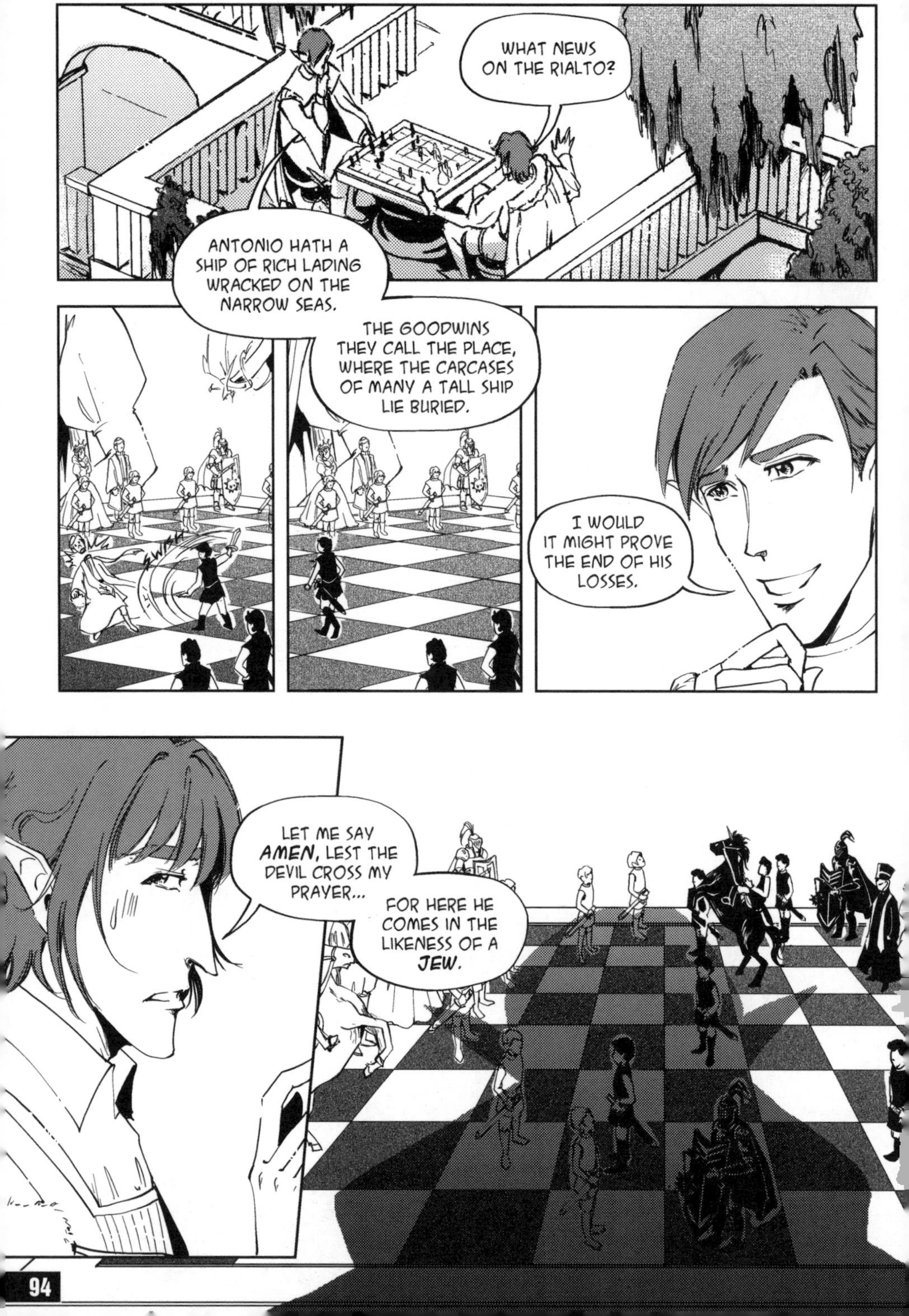
WHAT NEWS ON THE RIALTO?
ANTONIO HATH A SHIP OF RICH LADING WRACKED ON THE NARROW SEAS.
SWISH
THE GOODWINS THEY CALL THE PLACE, WHERE THE CARCASES OF MANY A TALL SHIP LIE BURIED.
I WOULD IT MIGHT PROVE THE END OF HIS LOSSES.
LET ME SAY **AMEN**, LEST THE DEVIL CROSS MY PRAYER...
FOR HERE HE COMES IN THE LIKENESS OF A **JEW**.

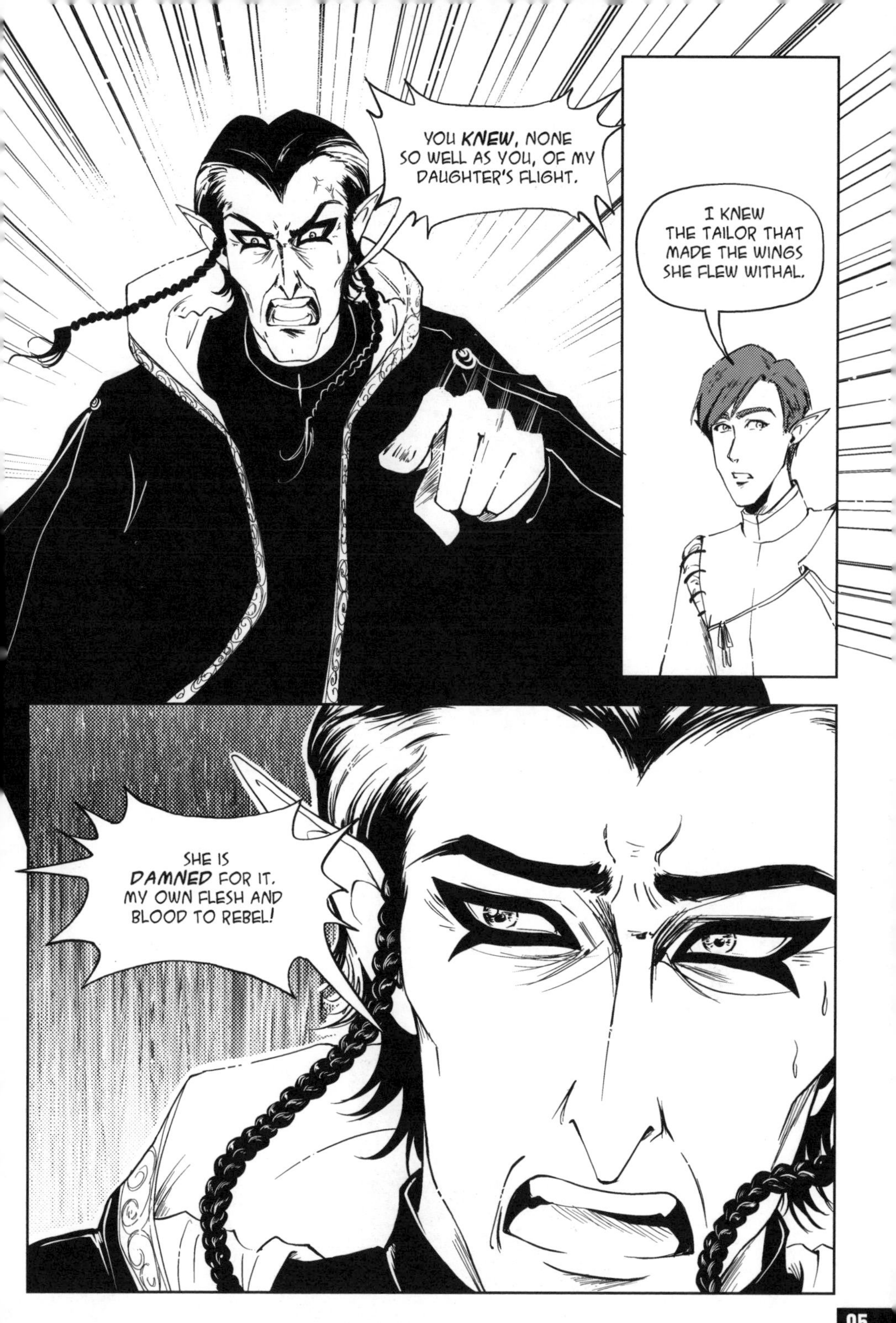
YOU **KNEW**, NONE SO WELL AS YOU, OF MY DAUGHTER'S FLIGHT.
I KNEW THE TAILOR THAT MADE THE WINGS SHE FLEW WITHAL.
SHE IS **DAMNED** FOR IT. MY OWN FLESH AND BLOOD TO REBEL!

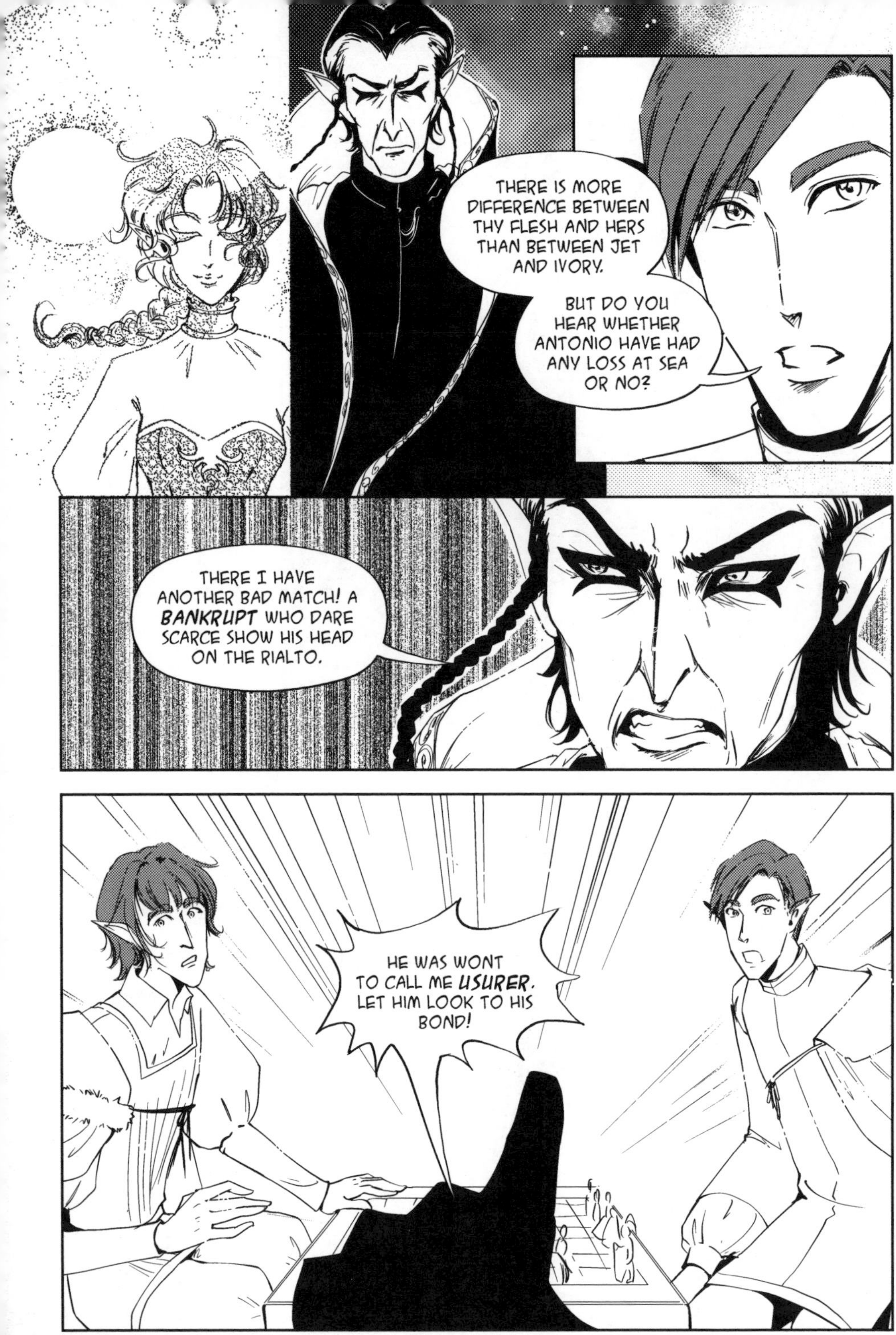
THERE IS MORE DIFFERENCE BETWEEN THY FLESH AND HERS THAN BETWEEN JET AND IVORY.
BUT DO YOU HEAR WHETHER ANTONIO HAVE HAD ANY LOSS AT SEA OR NO?
THERE I HAVE ANOTHER BAD MATCH! A BANKRUPT WHO DARE SCARCE SHOW HIS HEAD ON THE RIALTO.
HE WAS WONT TO CALL ME USURER. LET HIM LOOK TO HIS BOND!

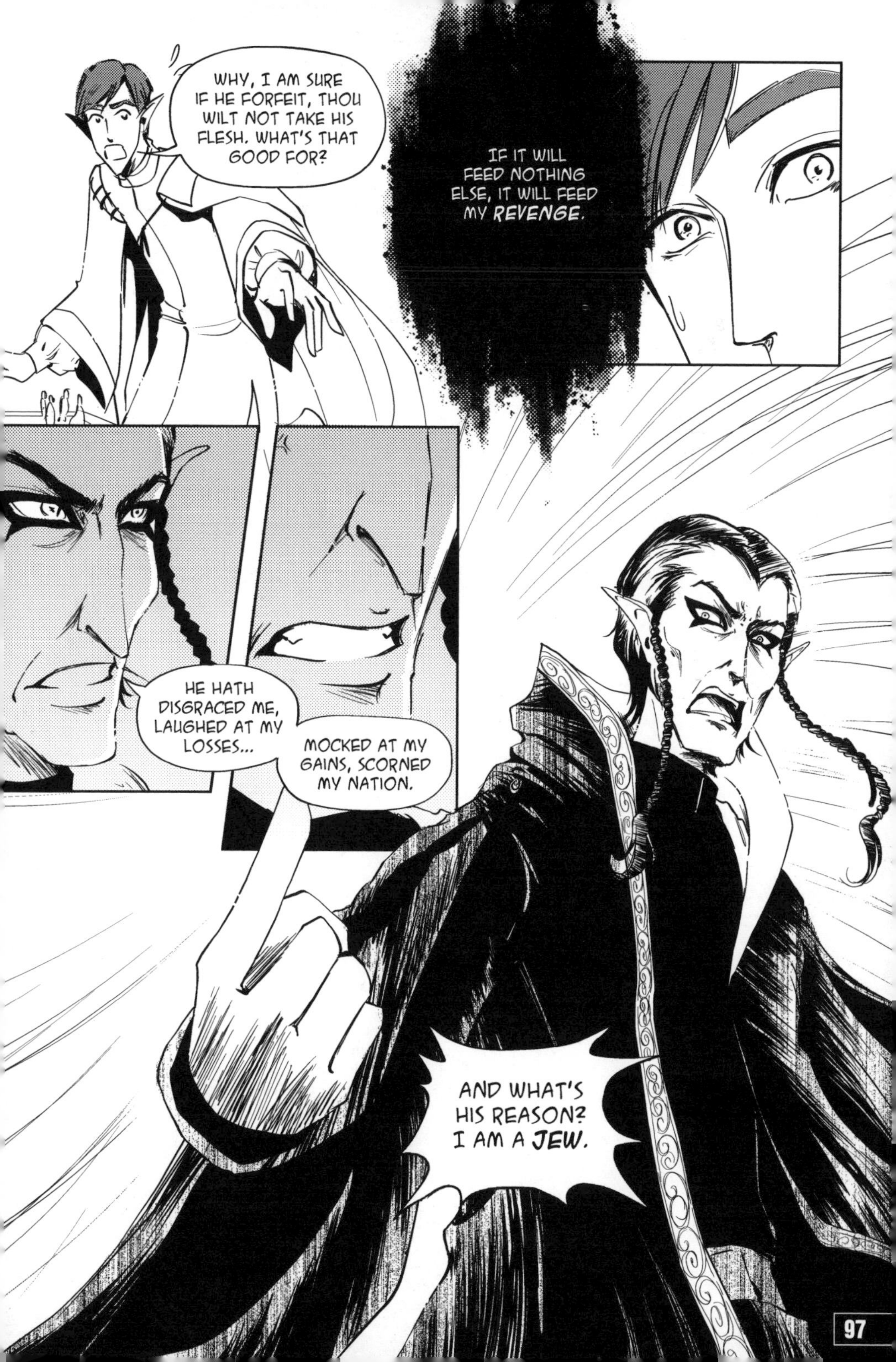
WHY, I AM SURE IF HE FORFEIT, THOU WILT NOT TAKE HIS FLESH. WHAT'S THAT GOOD FOR?
IF IT WILL FEED NOTHING ELSE, IT WILL FEED MY REVENGE.
HE HATH DISGRACED ME, LAUGHED AT MY LOSSES...
MOCKED AT MY GAINS, SCORNED MY NATION.
AND WHAT'S HIS REASON? I AM A JEW.

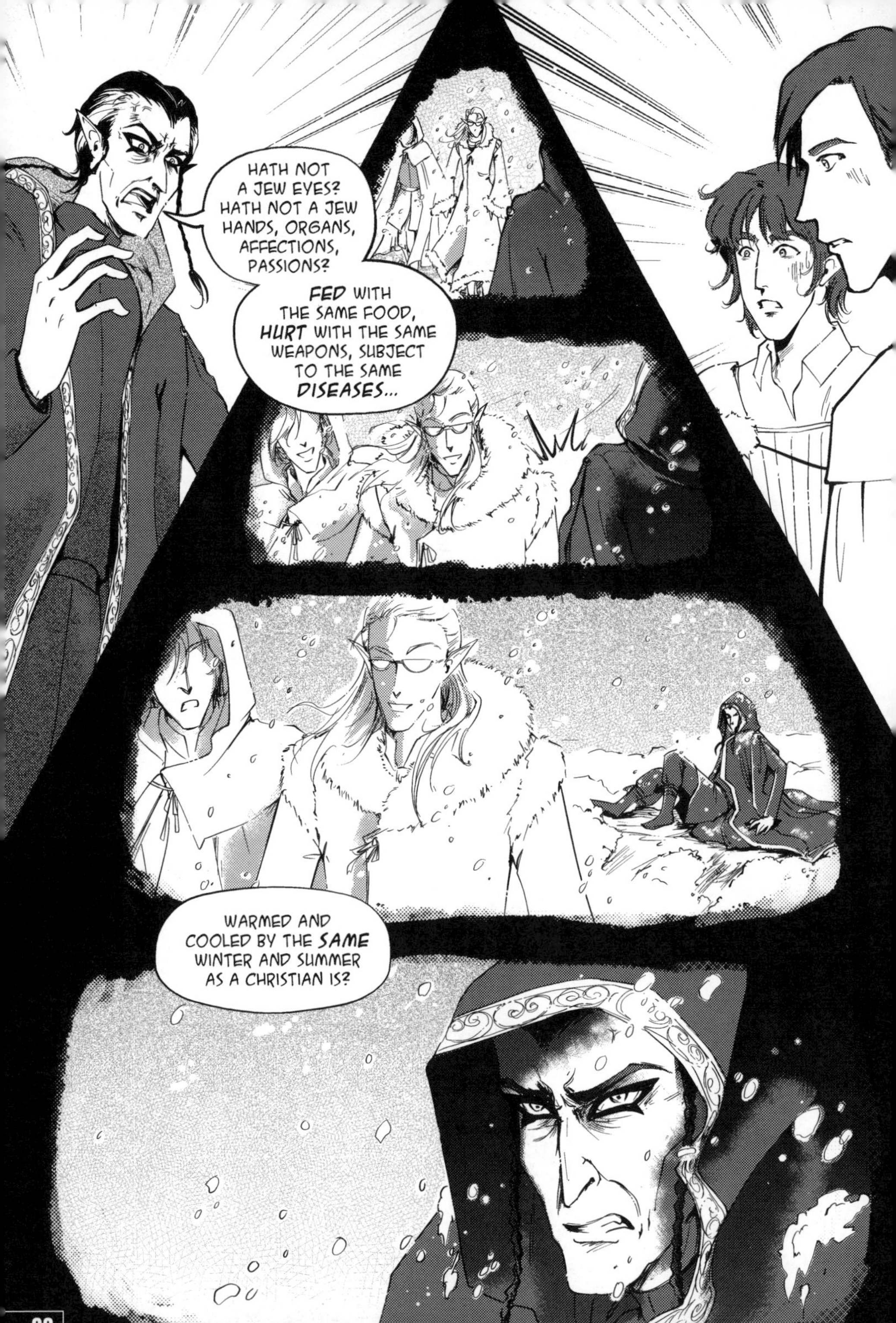
HATH NOT A JEW EYES? HATH NOT A JEW HANDS, ORGANS, AFFECTIONS, PASSIONS?
FED WITH THE SAME FOOD, **HURT** WITH THE SAME WEAPONS, SUBJECT TO THE SAME **DISEASES**...
WARMED AND COOLED BY THE **SAME** WINTER AND SUMMER AS A CHRISTIAN IS?

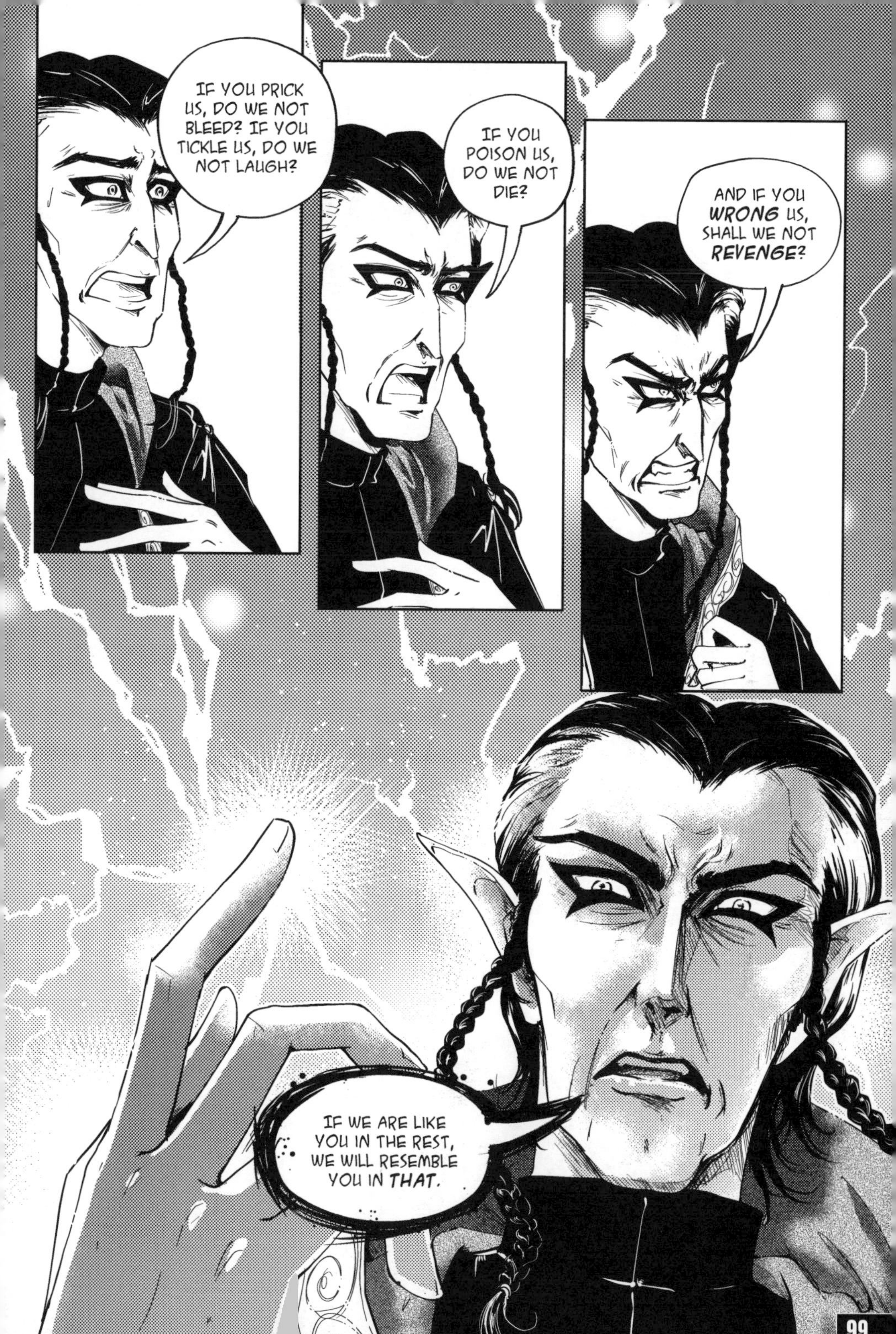
IF YOU PRICK US, DO WE NOT BLEED? IF YOU TICKLE US, DO WE NOT LAUGH?
IF YOU POISON US, DO WE NOT DIE?
AND IF YOU WRONG US, SHALL WE NOT REVENGE?
IF WE ARE LIKE YOU IN THE REST, WE WILL RESEMBLE YOU IN THAT.

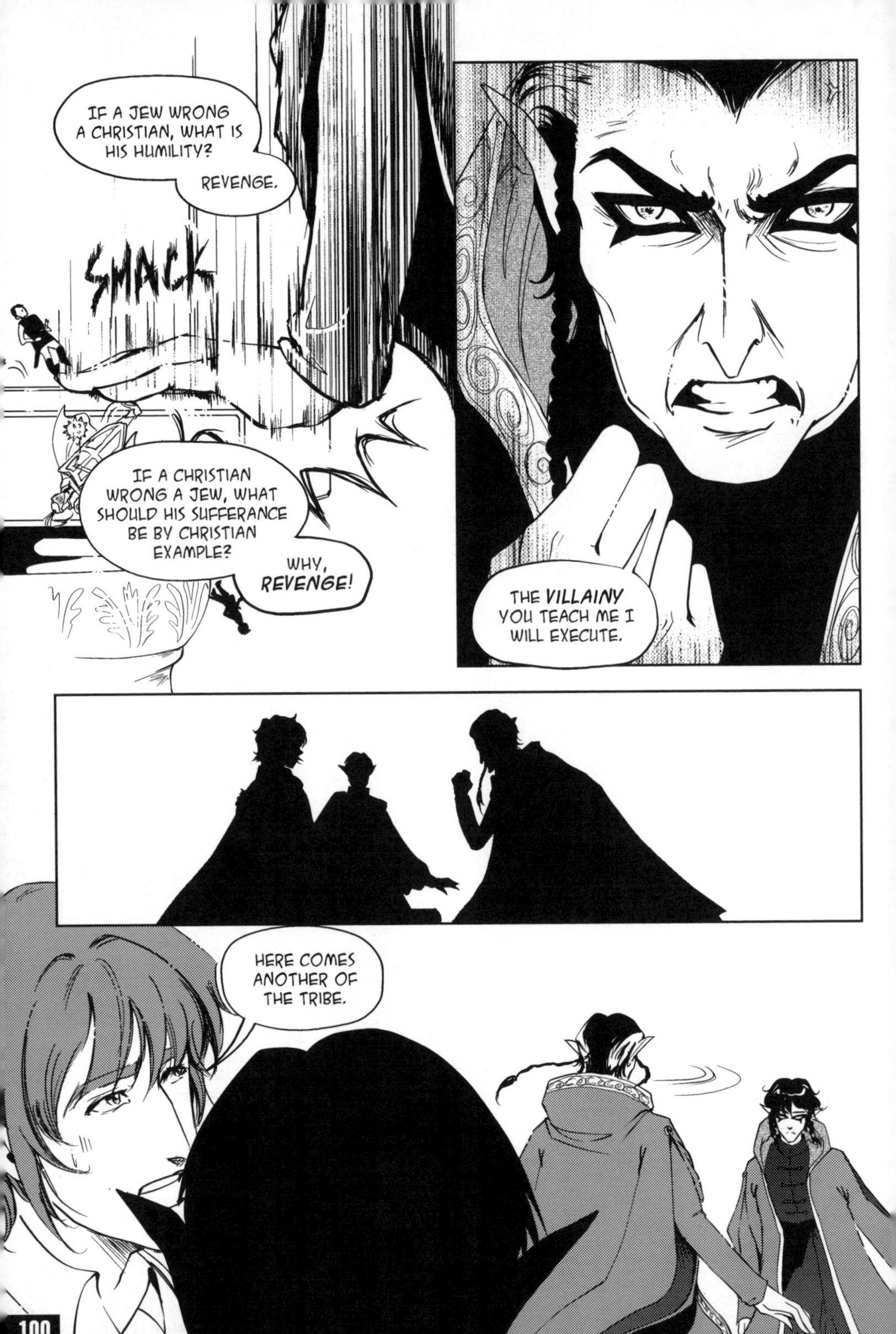
IF A JEW WRONG A CHRISTIAN, WHAT IS HIS HUMILITY?
REVENGE.
SMACK
IF A CHRISTIAN WRONG A JEW, WHAT SHOULD HIS SUFFERANCE BE BY CHRISTIAN EXAMPLE?
WHY, *REVENGE!*
THE *VILLAINY* YOU TEACH ME I WILL EXECUTE.
HERE COMES ANOTHER OF THE TRIBE.

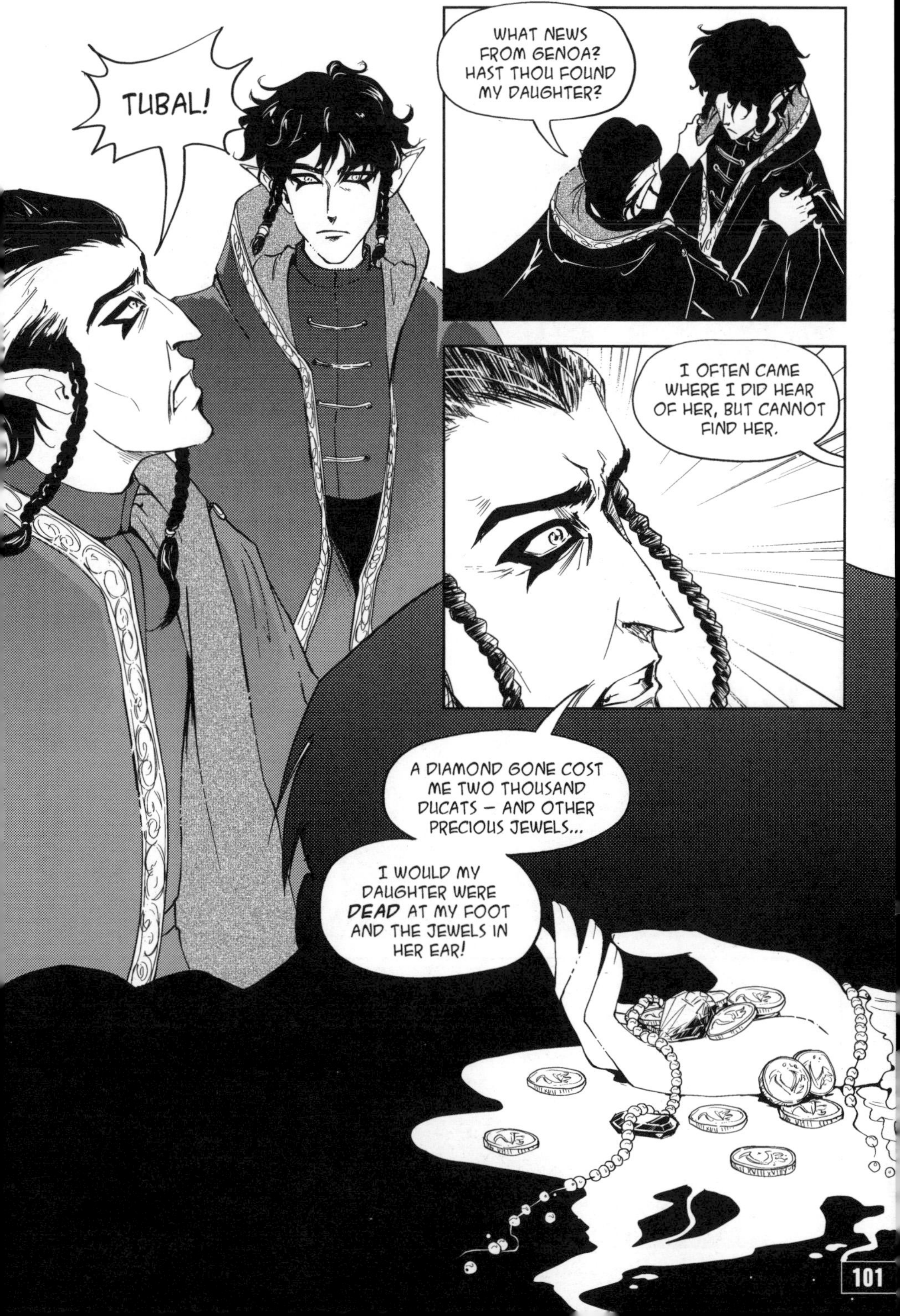
TUBAL!
WHAT NEWS FROM GENOA? HAST THOU FOUND MY DAUGHTER?
I OFTEN CAME WHERE I DID HEAR OF HER, BUT CANNOT FIND HER.
A DIAMOND GONE COST ME TWO THOUSAND DUCATS – AND OTHER PRECIOUS JEWELS...
I WOULD MY DAUGHTER WERE **DEAD** AT MY FOOT AND THE JEWELS IN HER EAR!

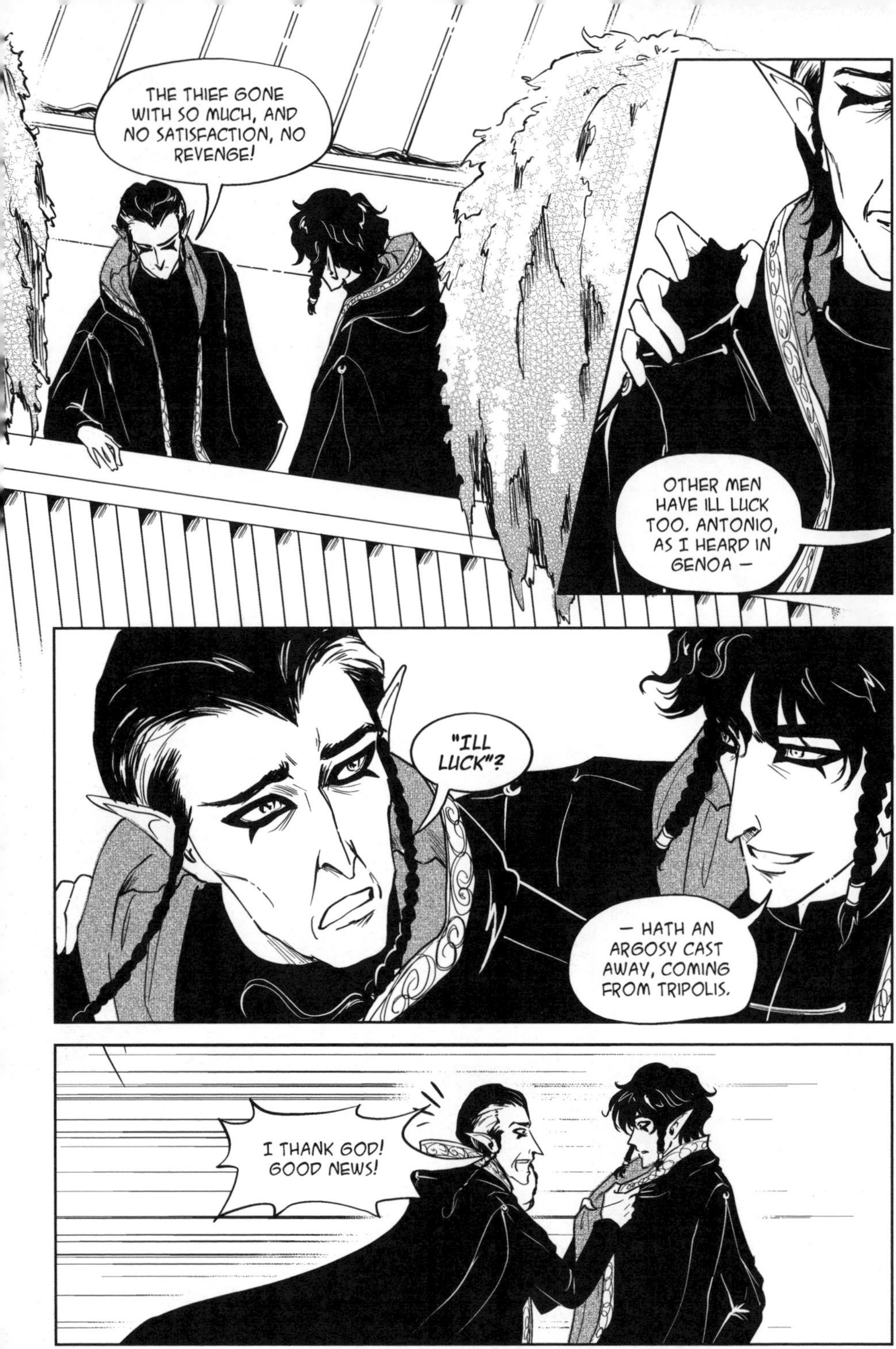
THE THIEF GONE WITH SO MUCH, AND NO SATISFACTION, NO REVENGE!
OTHER MEN HAVE ILL LUCK TOO. ANTONIO, AS I HEARD IN GENOA —
"ILL LUCK"?
— HATH AN ARGOSY CAST AWAY, COMING FROM TRIPOLIS.
I THANK GOD! GOOD NEWS!

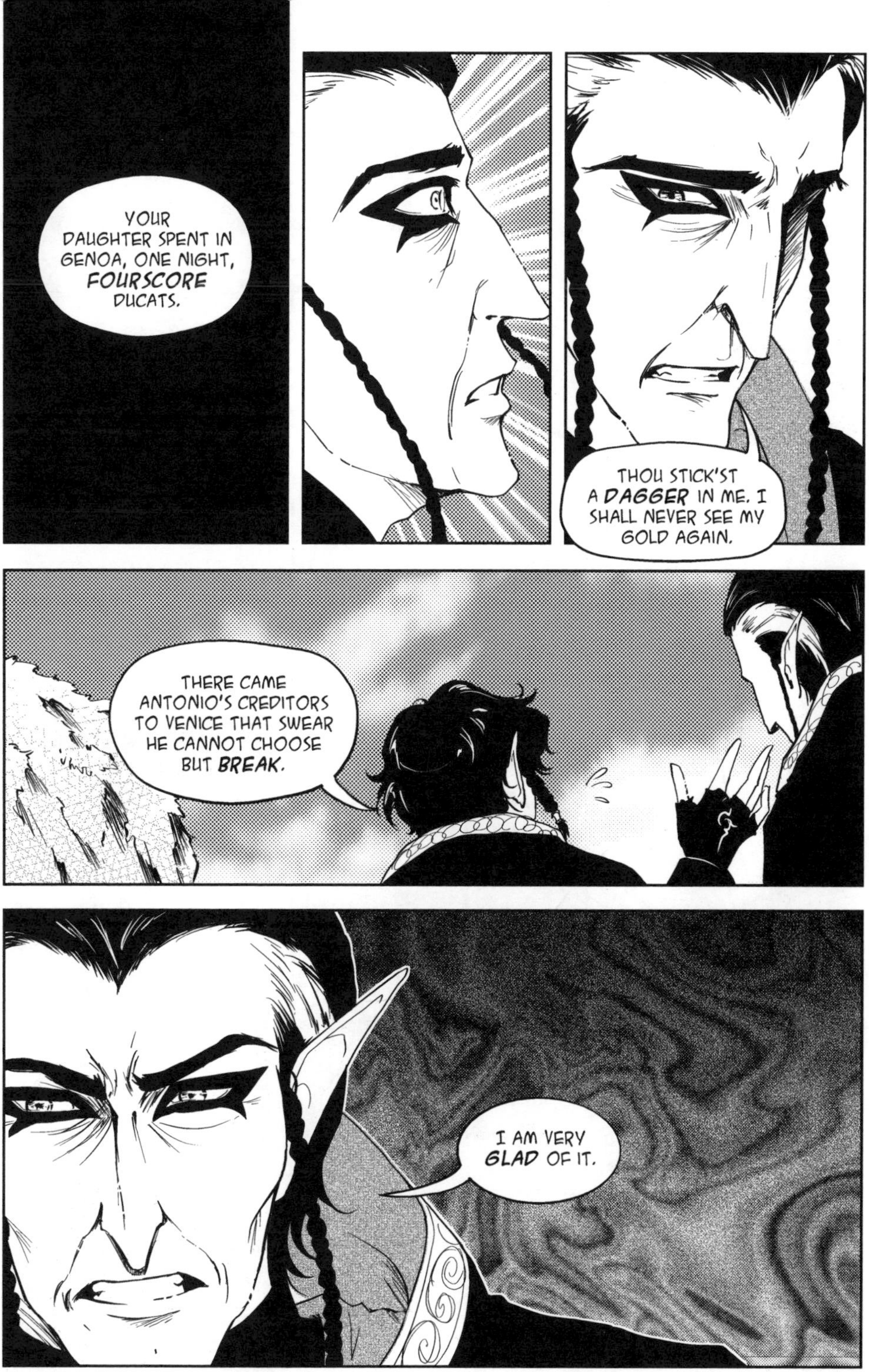
YOUR DAUGHTER SPENT IN GENOA, ONE NIGHT, FOURSCORE DUCATS.
THOU STICK'ST A DAGGER IN ME. I SHALL NEVER SEE MY GOLD AGAIN.
THERE CAME ANTONIO'S CREDITORS TO VENICE THAT SWEAR HE CANNOT CHOOSE BUT BREAK.
I AM VERY GLAD OF IT.

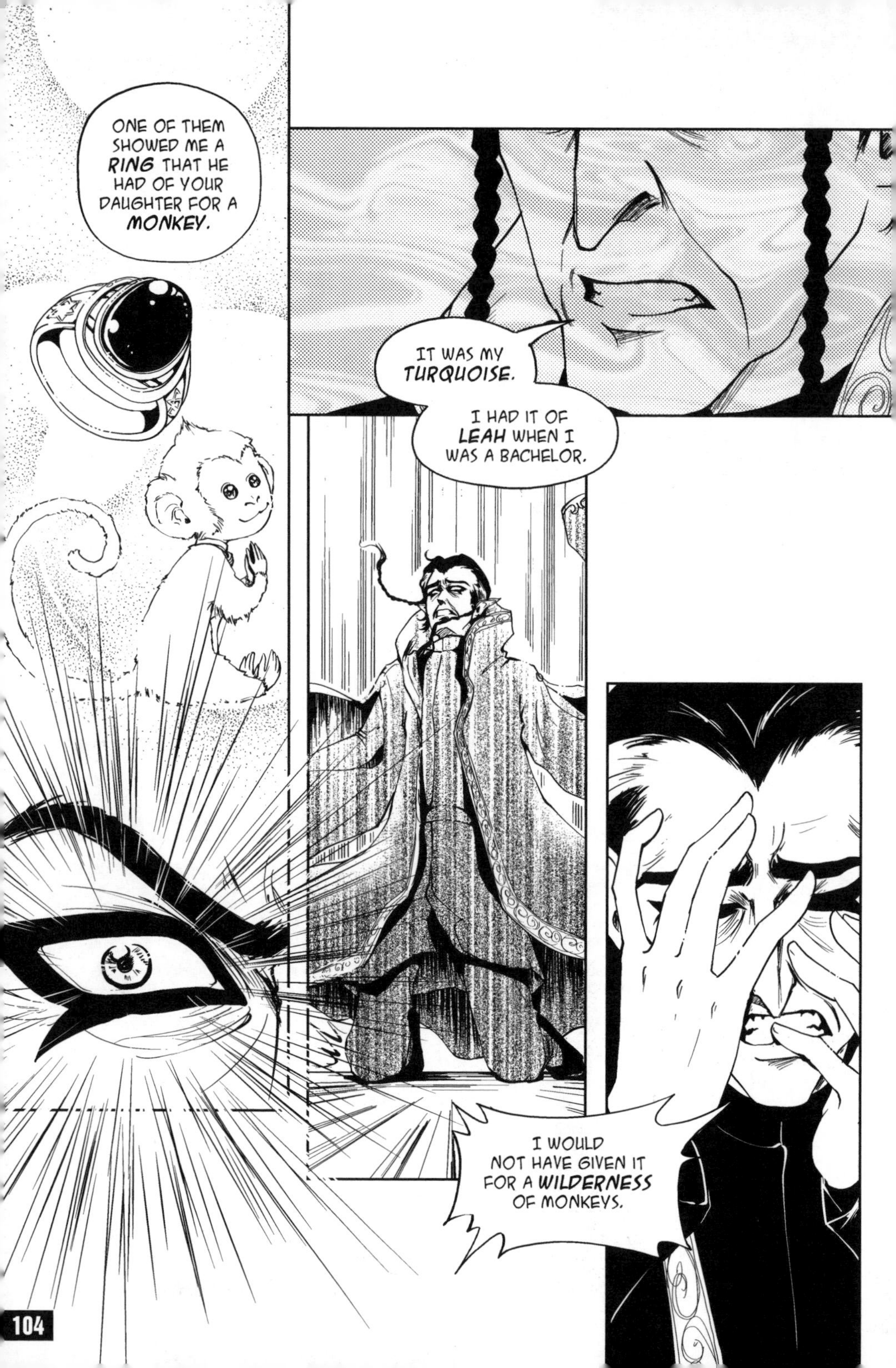
ONE OF THEM SHOWED ME A RING THAT HE HAD OF YOUR DAUGHTER FOR A MONKEY.
IT WAS MY TURQUOISE.
I HAD IT OF LEAH WHEN I WAS A BACHELOR.
I WOULD NOT HAVE GIVEN IT FOR A WILDERNESS OF MONKEYS.

BUT ANTONIO IS CERTAINLY *UNDONE.*

THAT'S VERY TRUE.

GO, TUBAL, FEE ME AN OFFICER. I WILL HAVE THE *HEART* OF HIM IF HE FORFEIT.

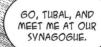

GO, TUBAL, AND MEET ME AT OUR SYNAGOGUE.

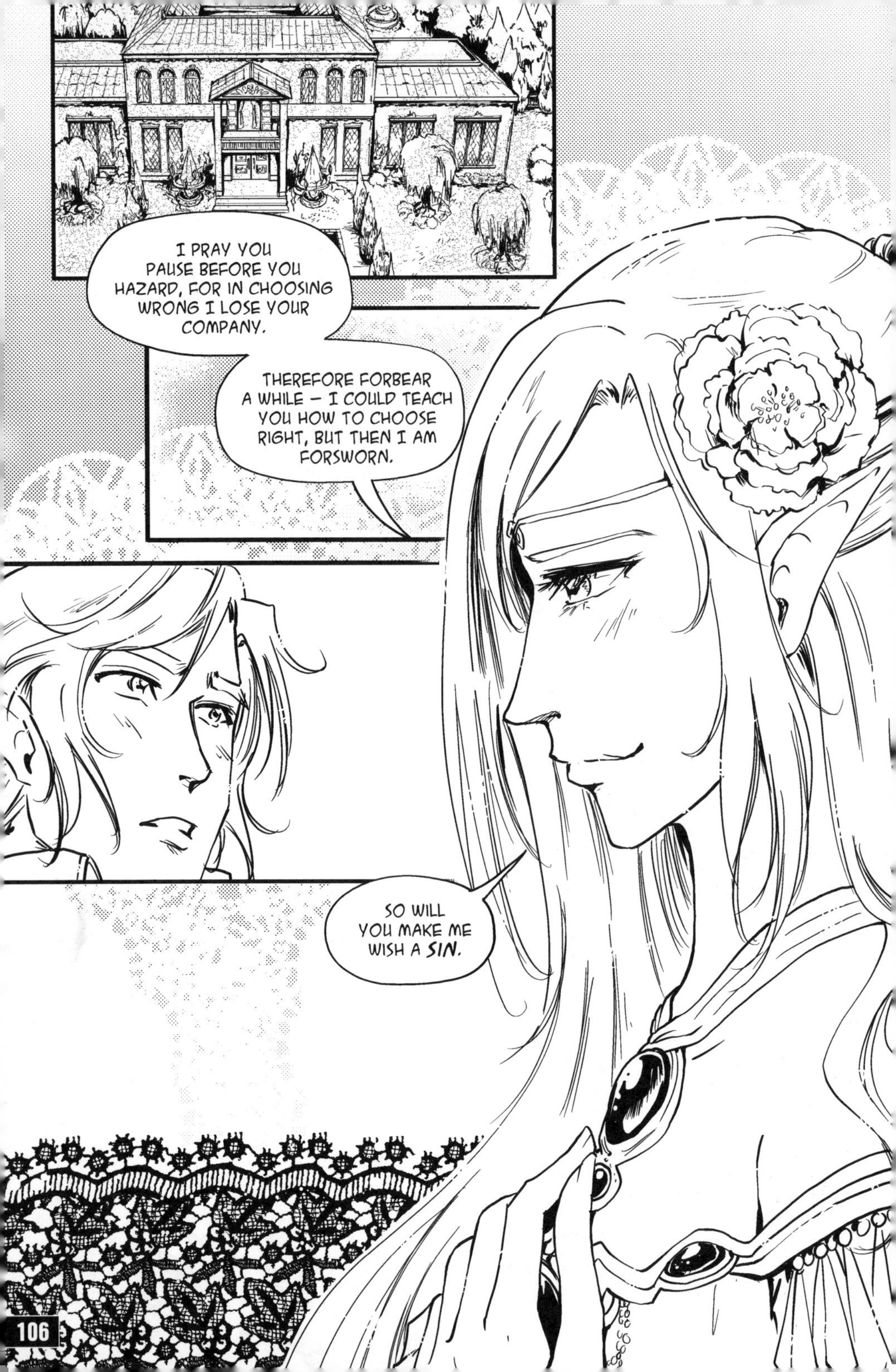
I PRAY YOU PAUSE BEFORE YOU HAZARD, FOR IN CHOOSING WRONG I LOSE YOUR COMPANY.
THEREFORE FORBEAR A WHILE – I COULD TEACH YOU HOW TO CHOOSE RIGHT, BUT THEN I AM FORSWORN.
SO WILL YOU MAKE ME WISH A SIN.

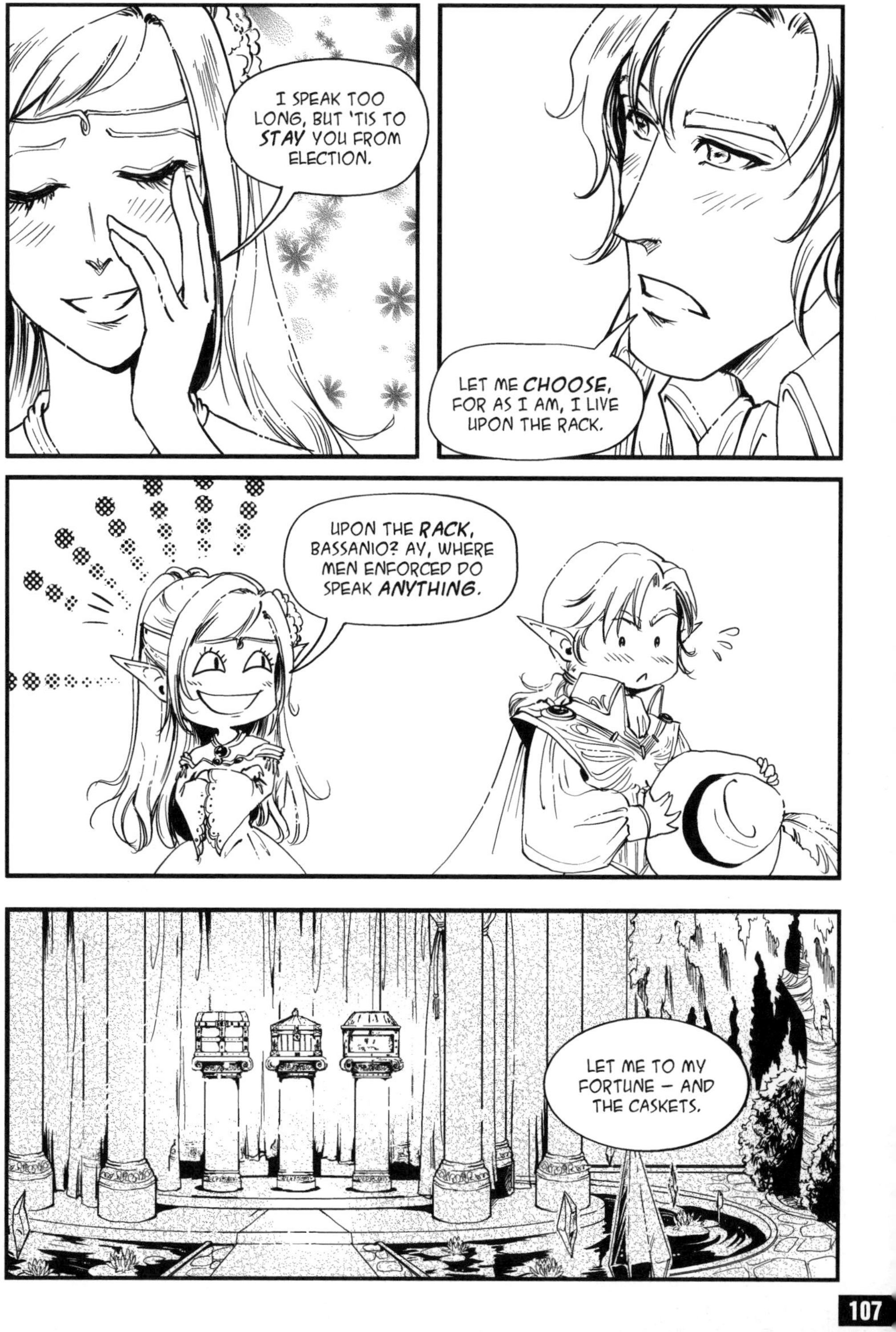
I SPEAK TOO LONG, BUT 'TIS TO STAY YOU FROM ELECTION.
LET ME CHOOSE, FOR AS I AM, I LIVE UPON THE RACK.
UPON THE RACK, BASSANIO? AY, WHERE MEN ENFORCED DO SPEAK ANYTHING.
LET ME TO MY FORTUNE – AND THE CASKETS.

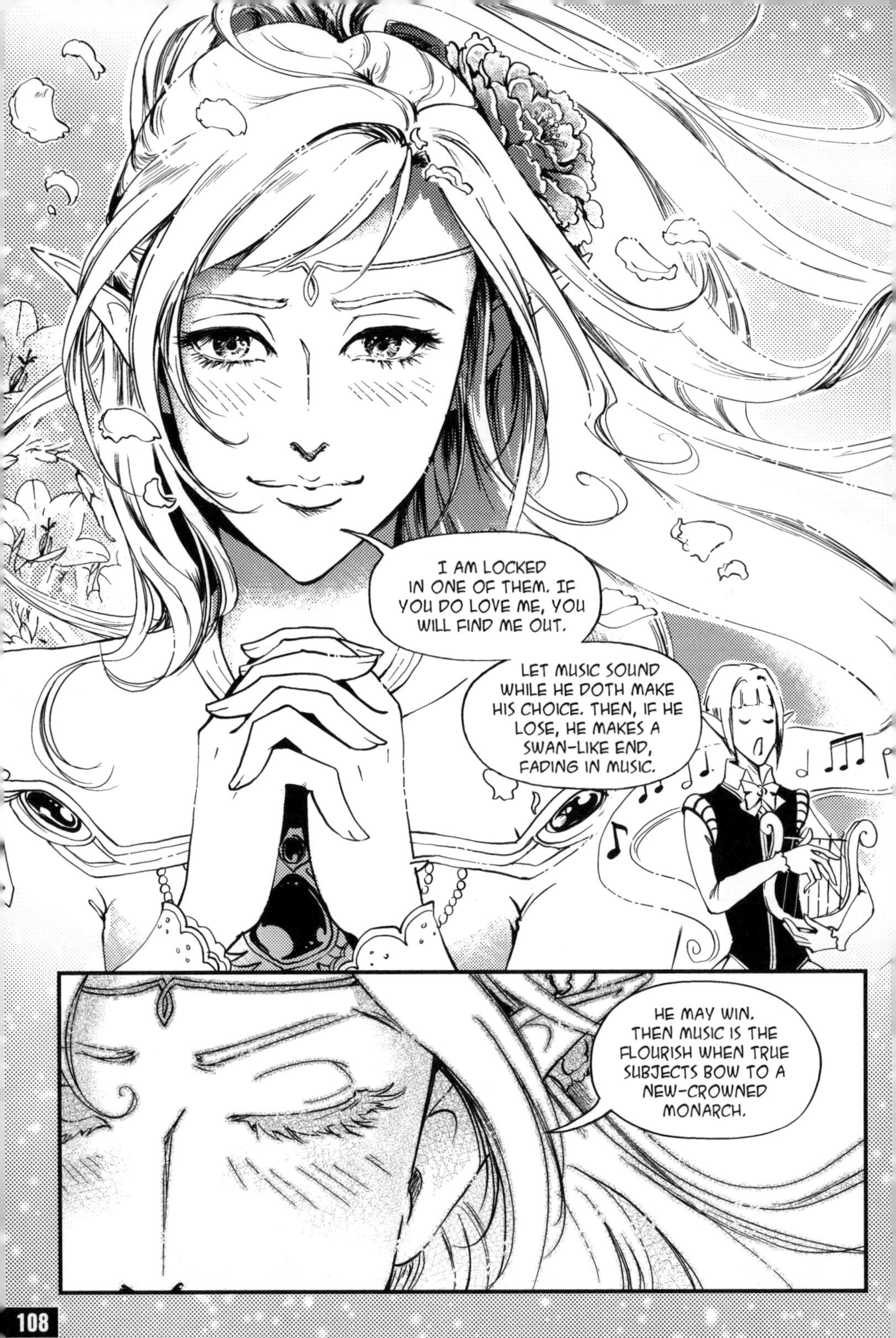
I AM LOCKED IN ONE OF THEM. IF YOU DO LOVE ME, YOU WILL FIND ME OUT.
LET MUSIC SOUND WHILE HE DOTH MAKE HIS CHOICE. THEN, IF HE LOSE, HE MAKES A SWAN-LIKE END, FADING IN MUSIC.
HE MAY WIN. THEN MUSIC IS THE FLOURISH WHEN TRUE SUBJECTS BOW TO A NEW-CROWNED MONARCH.

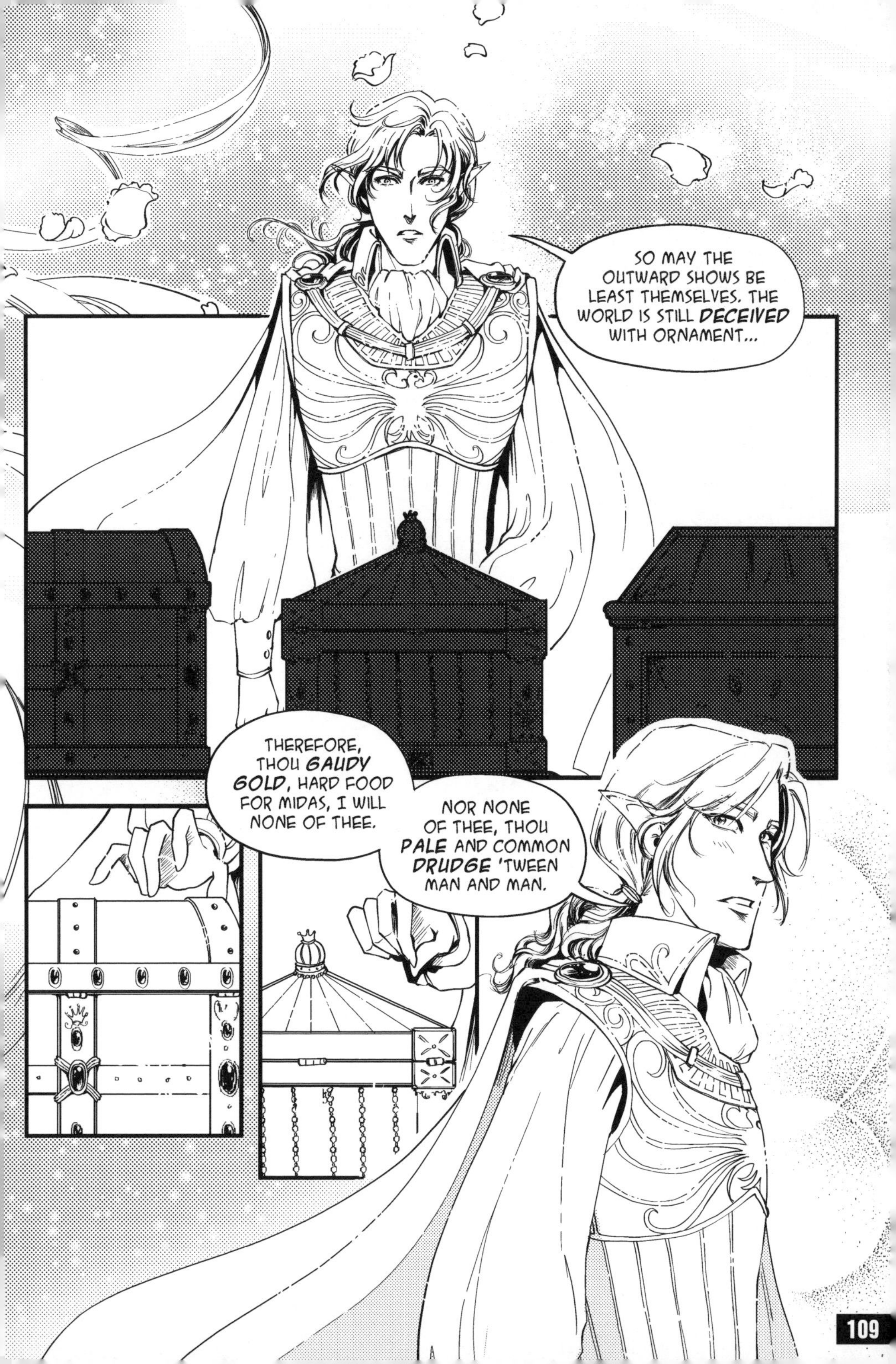
SO MAY THE OUTWARD SHOWS BE LEAST THEMSELVES. THE WORLD IS STILL DECEIVED WITH ORNAMENT...
THEREFORE, THOU GAUDY GOLD, HARD FOOD FOR MIDAS, I WILL NONE OF THEE.
NOR NONE OF THEE, THOU PALE AND COMMON DRUDGE 'TWEEN MAN AND MAN.

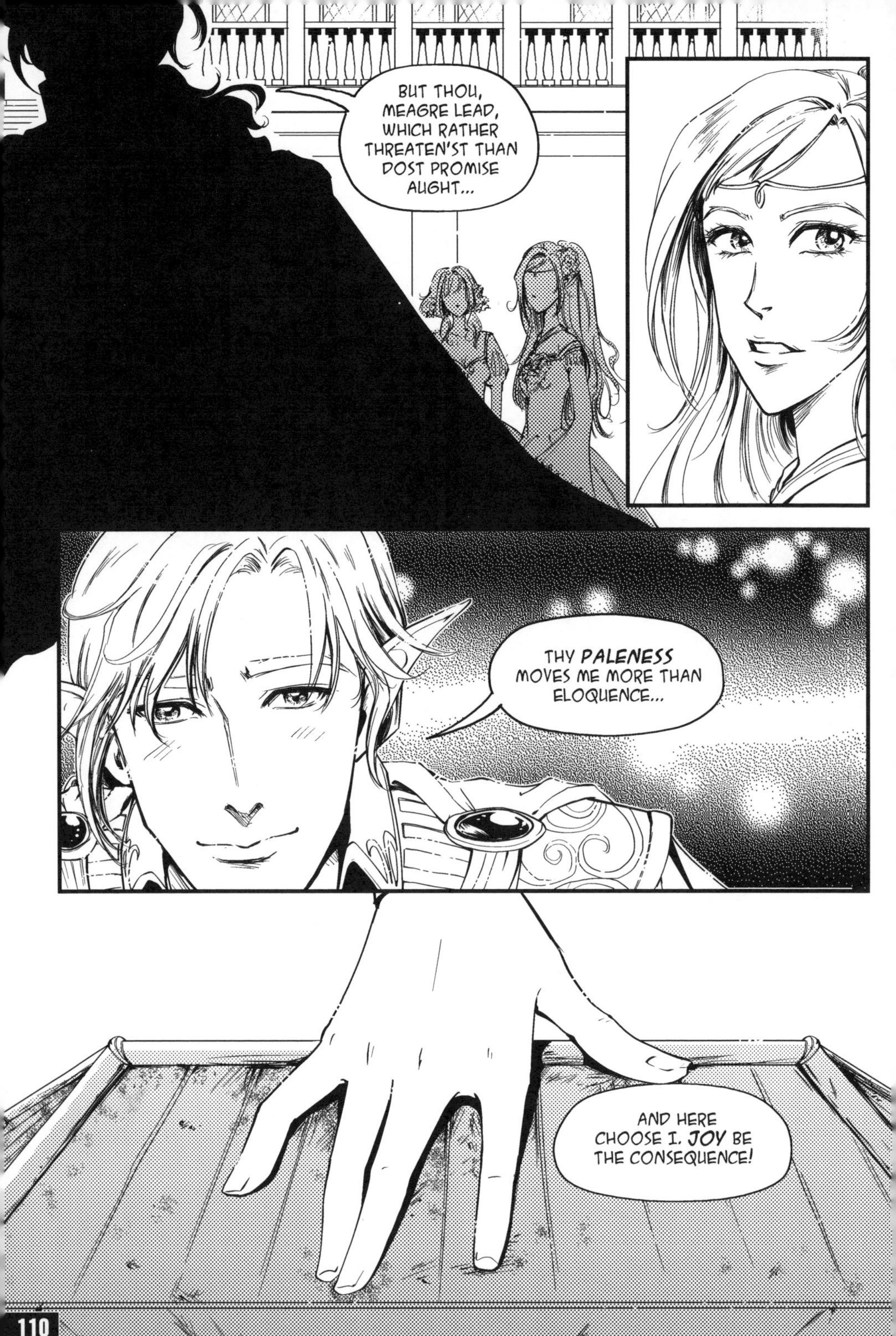
BUT THOU, MEAGRE LEAD, WHICH RATHER THREATEN'ST THAN DOST PROMISE AUGHT...
THY **PALENESS** MOVES ME MORE THAN ELOQUENCE...
AND HERE CHOOSE I. **JOY** BE THE CONSEQUENCE!

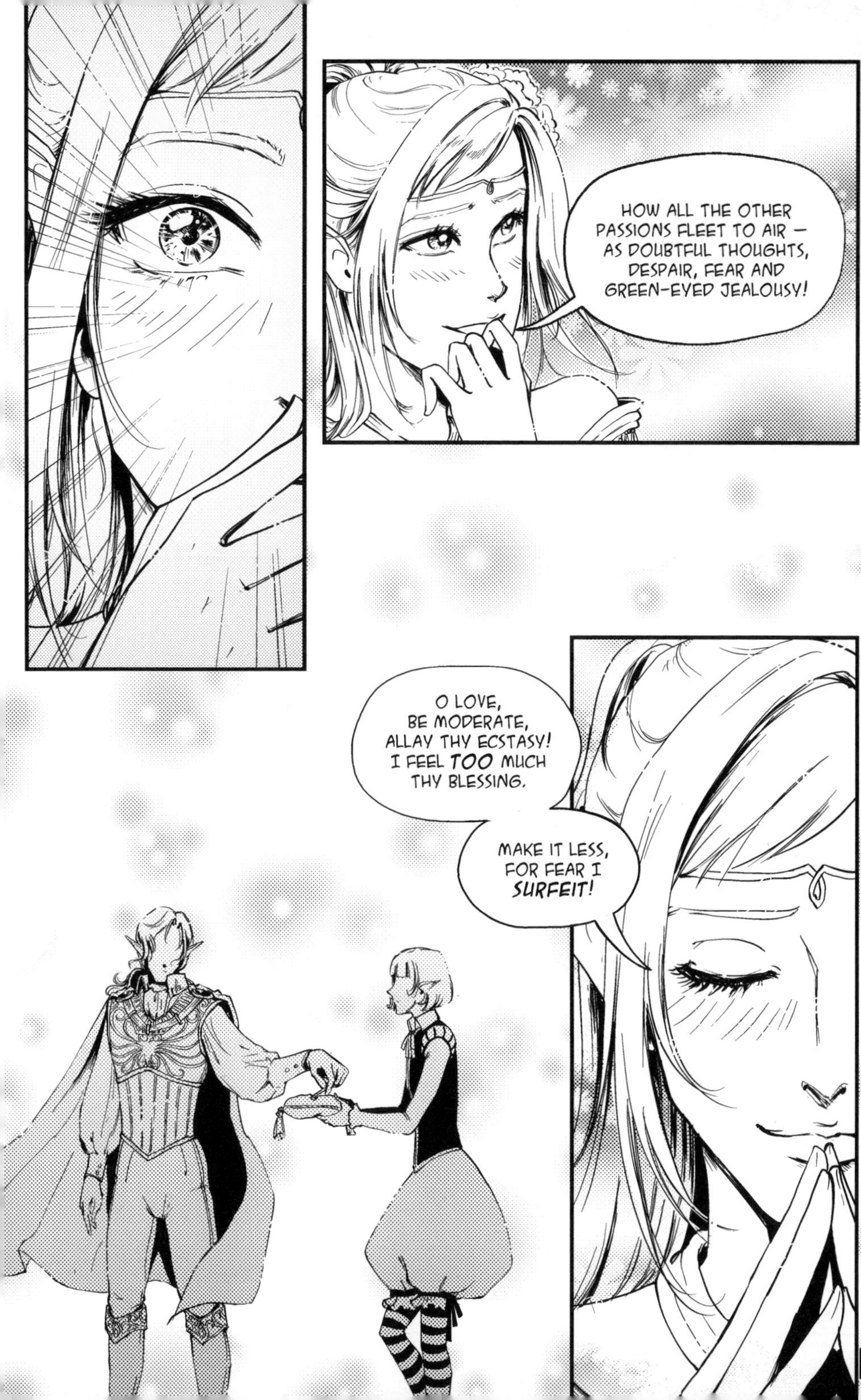
HOW ALL THE OTHER PASSIONS FLEET TO AIR — AS DOUBTFUL THOUGHTS, DESPAIR, FEAR AND GREEN-EYED JEALOUSY!
O LOVE, BE MODERATE, ALLAY THY ECSTASY! I FEEL *TOO* MUCH THY BLESSING.
MAKE IT LESS, FOR FEAR I ***SURFEIT***!

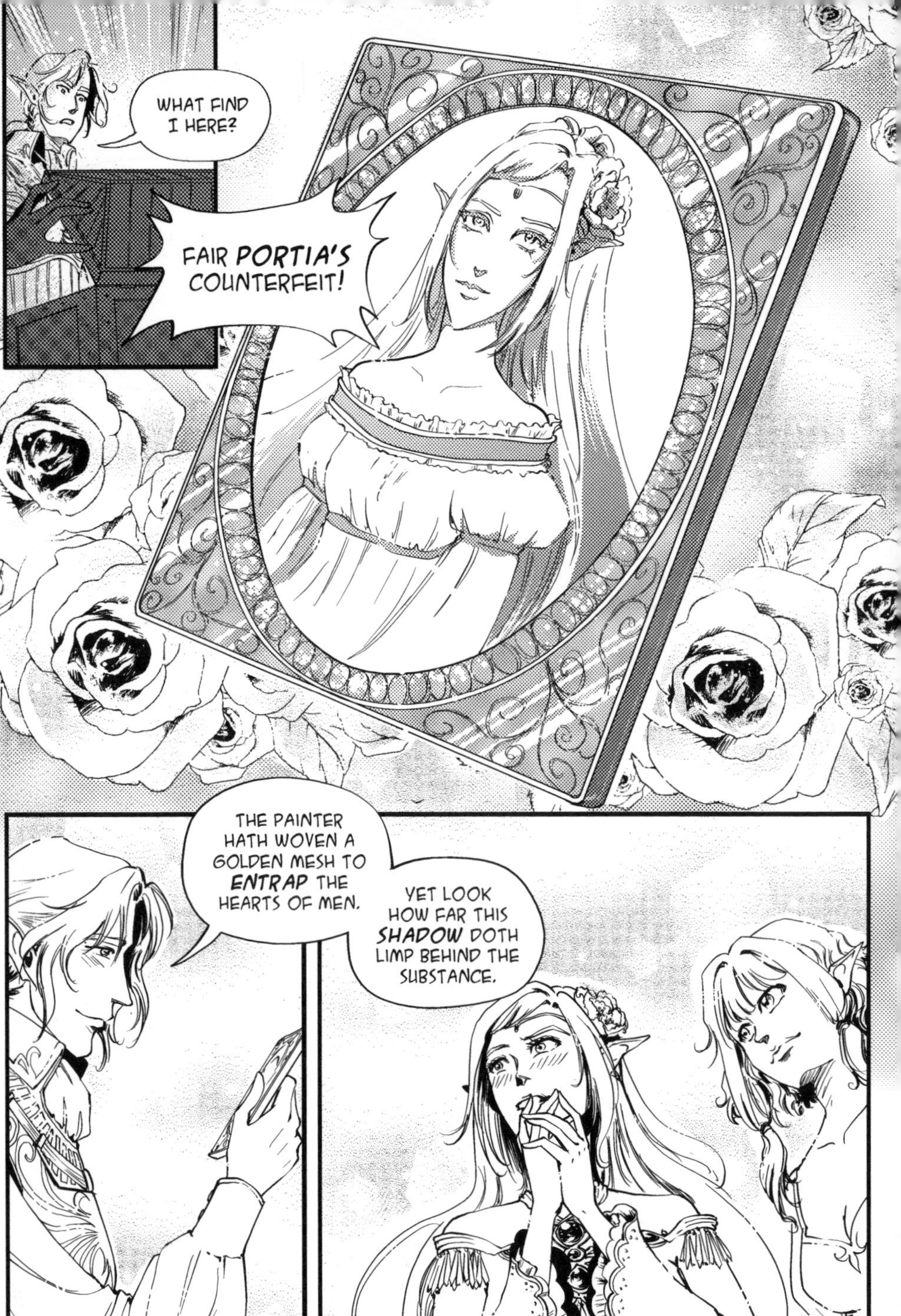
WHAT FIND I HERE?
FAIR PORTIA'S COUNTERFEIT!
THE PAINTER HATH WOVEN A GOLDEN MESH TO ENTRAP THE HEARTS OF MEN.
YET LOOK HOW FAR THIS SHADOW DOTH LIMP BEHIND THE SUBSTANCE.

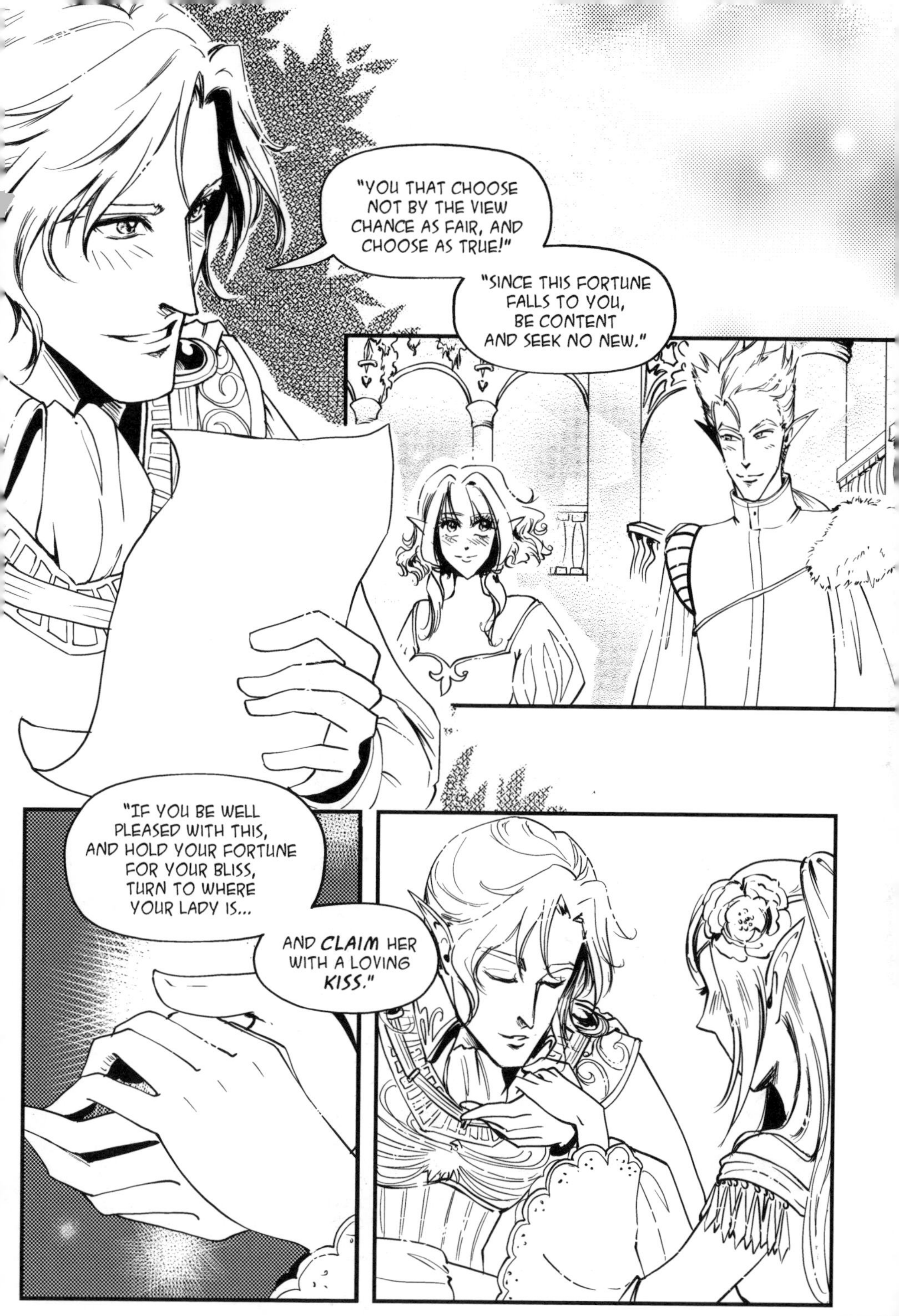
"YOU THAT CHOOSE NOT BY THE VIEW CHANCE AS FAIR, AND CHOOSE AS TRUE!"
"SINCE THIS FORTUNE FALLS TO YOU, BE CONTENT AND SEEK NO NEW."
"IF YOU BE WELL PLEASED WITH THIS, AND HOLD YOUR FORTUNE FOR YOUR BLISS, TURN TO WHERE YOUR LADY IS...
AND CLAIM HER WITH A LOVING KISS."

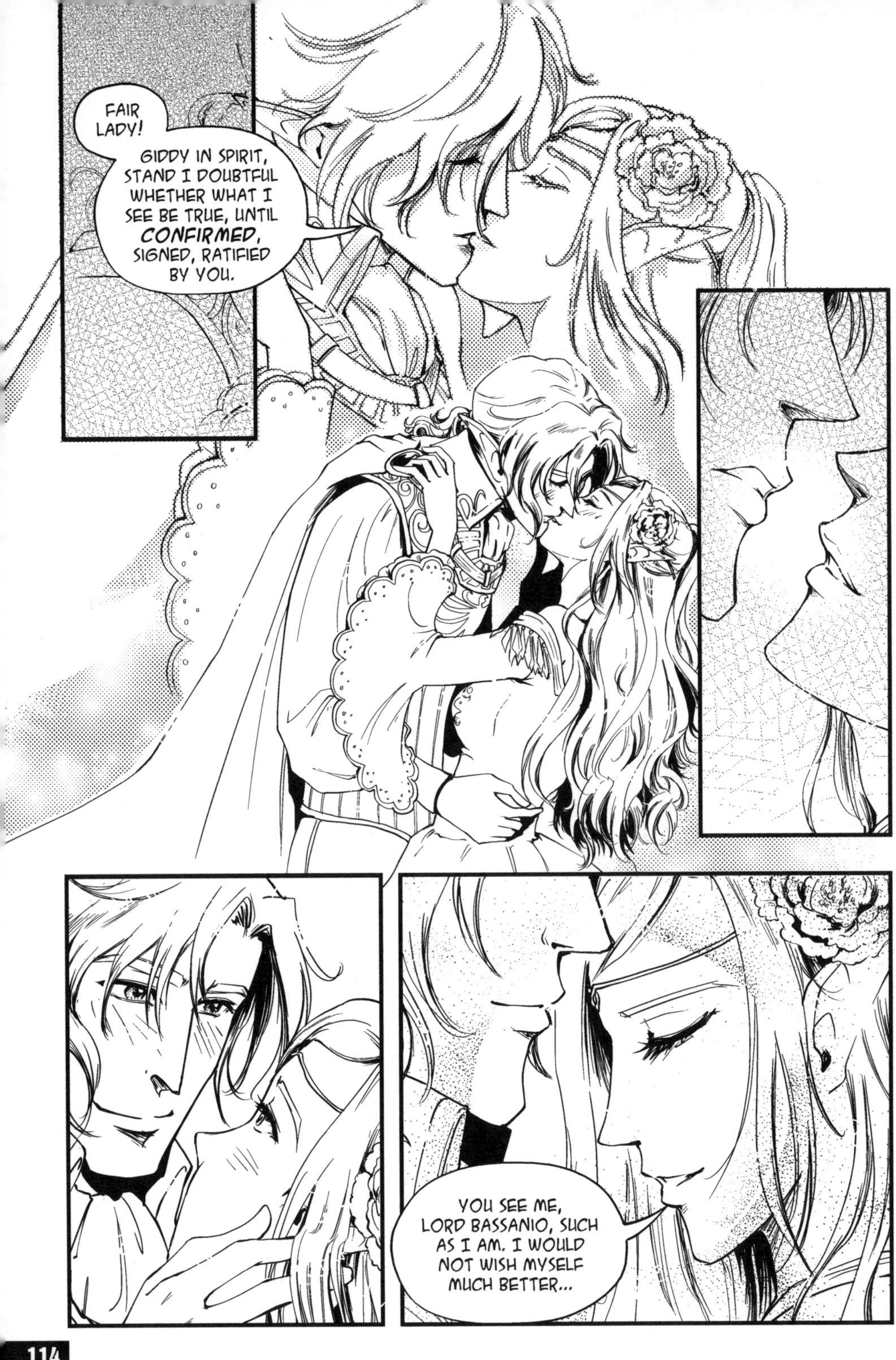
FAIR LADY!
GIDDY IN SPIRIT, STAND I DOUBTFUL WHETHER WHAT I SEE BE TRUE, UNTIL ***CONFIRMED***, SIGNED, RATIFIED BY YOU.
YOU SEE ME, LORD BASSANIO, SUCH AS I AM. I WOULD NOT WISH MYSELF MUCH BETTER...

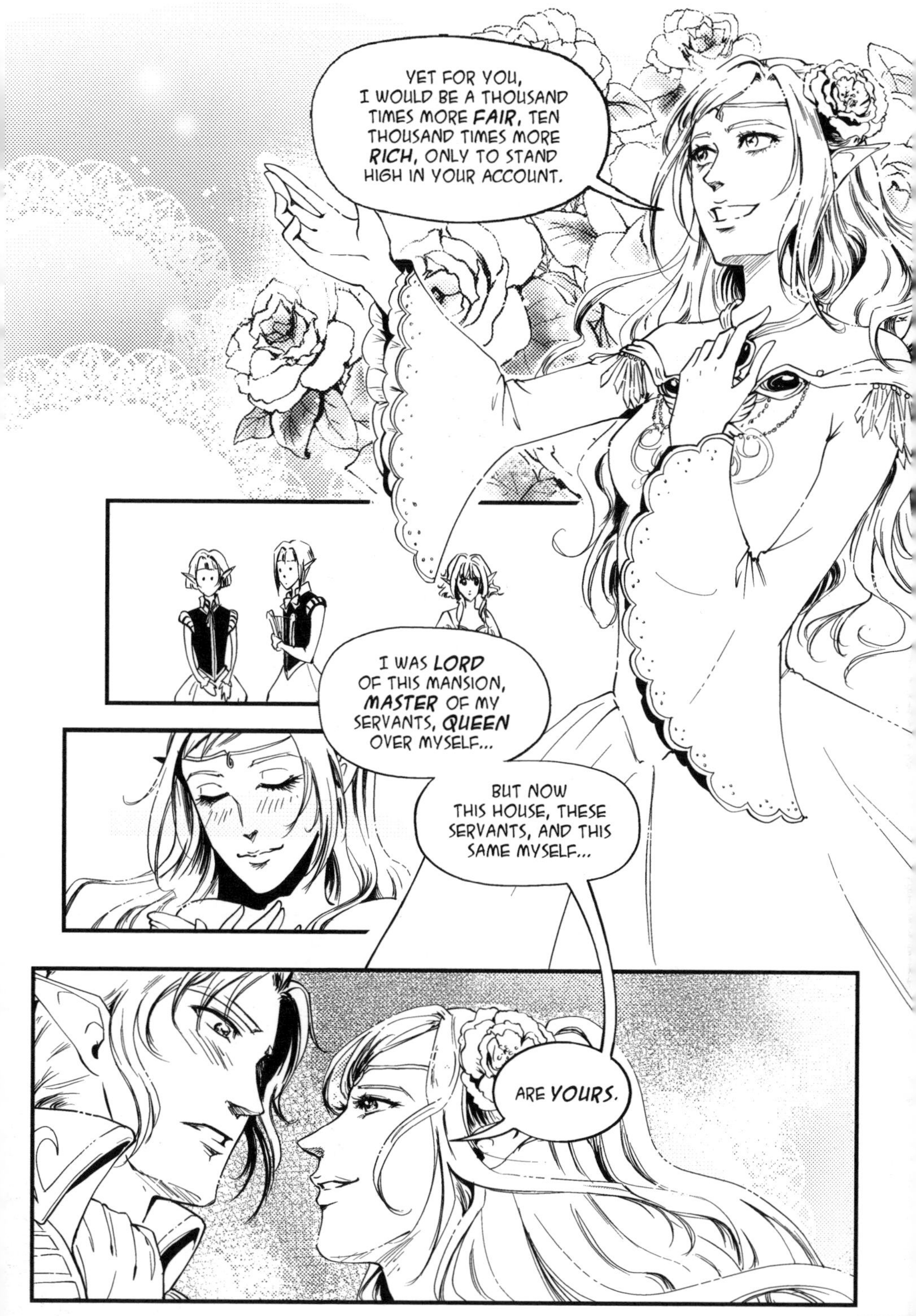
YET FOR YOU, I WOULD BE A THOUSAND TIMES MORE FAIR, TEN THOUSAND TIMES MORE RICH, ONLY TO STAND HIGH IN YOUR ACCOUNT.
I WAS LORD OF THIS MANSION, MASTER OF MY SERVANTS, QUEEN OVER MYSELF...
BUT NOW THIS HOUSE, THESE SERVANTS, AND THIS SAME MYSELF...
ARE YOURS.

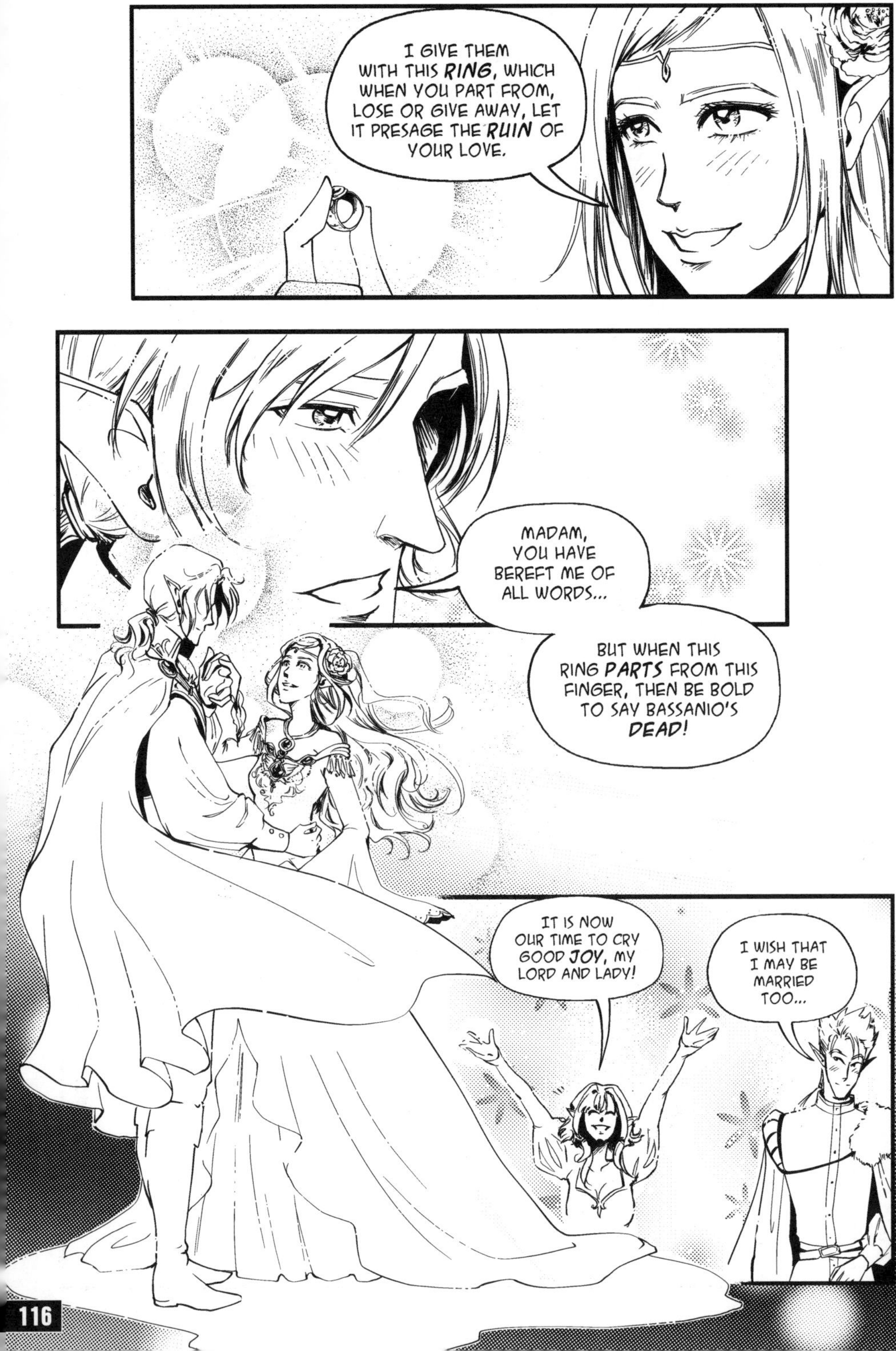
I GIVE THEM WITH THIS RING, WHICH WHEN YOU PART FROM, LOSE OR GIVE AWAY, LET IT PRESAGE THE RUIN OF YOUR LOVE.
MADAM, YOU HAVE BEREFT ME OF ALL WORDS...
BUT WHEN THIS RING PARTS FROM THIS FINGER, THEN BE BOLD TO SAY BASSANIO'S DEAD!
IT IS NOW OUR TIME TO CRY GOOD JOY, MY LORD AND LADY!
I WISH THAT I MAY BE MARRIED TOO...

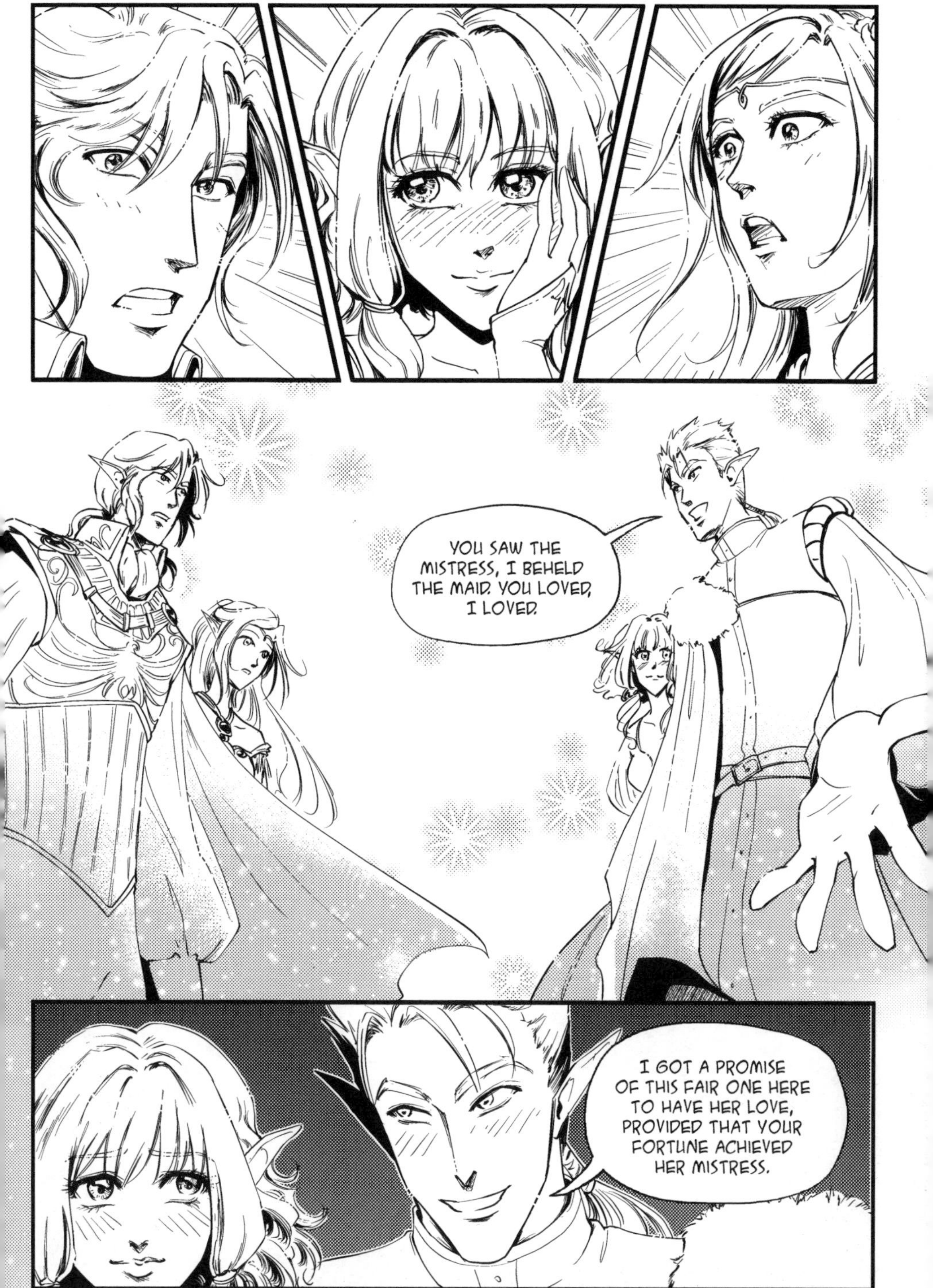
YOU SAW THE MISTRESS, I BEHELD THE MAID. YOU LOVED, I LOVED.
I GOT A PROMISE OF THIS FAIR ONE HERE TO HAVE HER LOVE, PROVIDED THAT YOUR FORTUNE ACHIEVED HER MISTRESS.

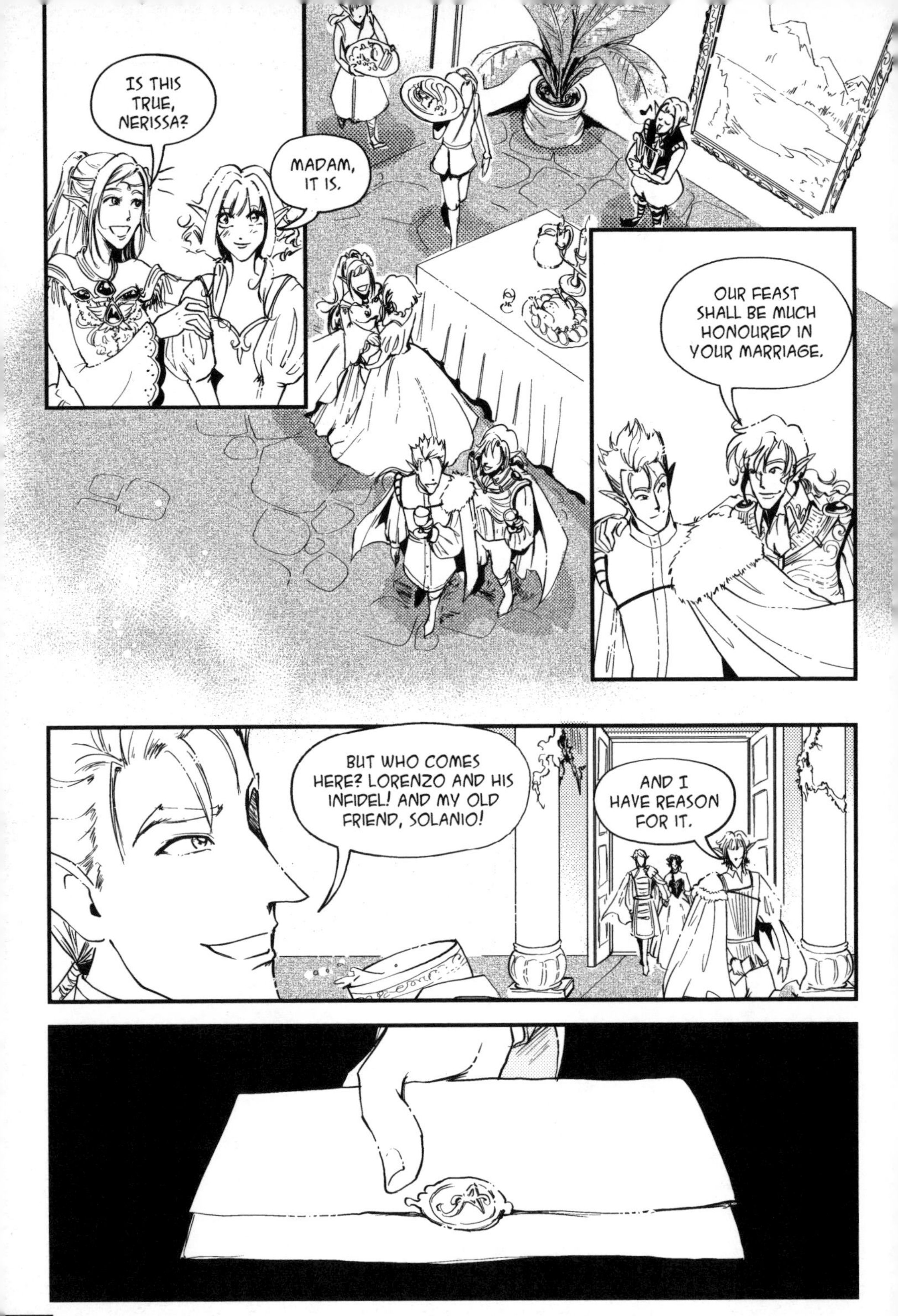
IS THIS TRUE, NERISSA?
MADAM, IT IS.
OUR FEAST SHALL BE MUCH HONOURED IN YOUR MARRIAGE.
BUT WHO COMES HERE? LORENZO AND HIS INFIDEL! AND MY OLD FRIEND, SOLANIO!
AND I HAVE REASON FOR IT.

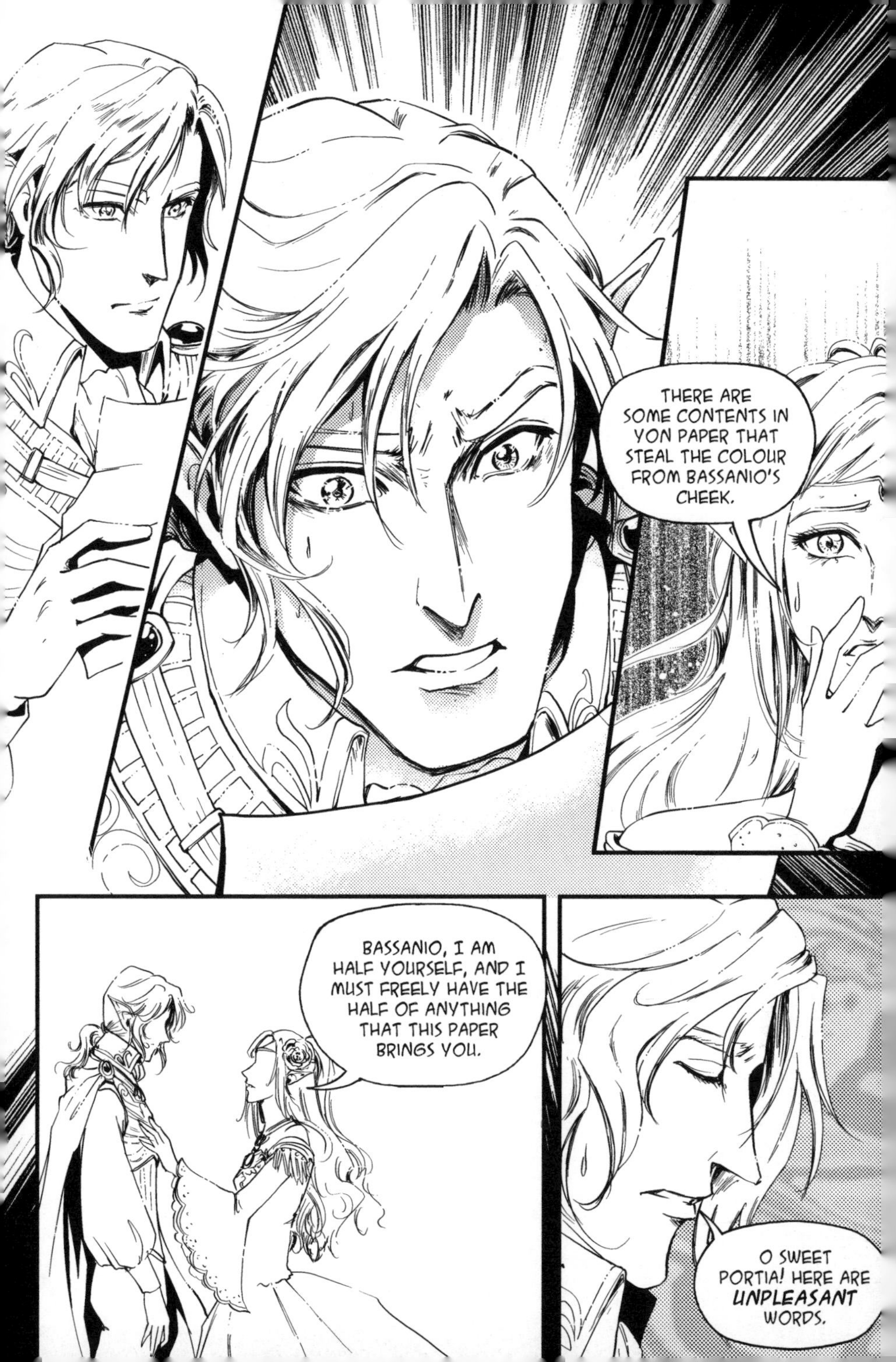
THERE ARE SOME CONTENTS IN YON PAPER THAT STEAL THE COLOUR FROM BASSANIO'S CHEEK.
BASSANIO, I AM HALF YOURSELF, AND I MUST FREELY HAVE THE HALF OF ANYTHING THAT THIS PAPER BRINGS YOU.
O SWEET PORTIA! HERE ARE *UNPLEASANT* WORDS.

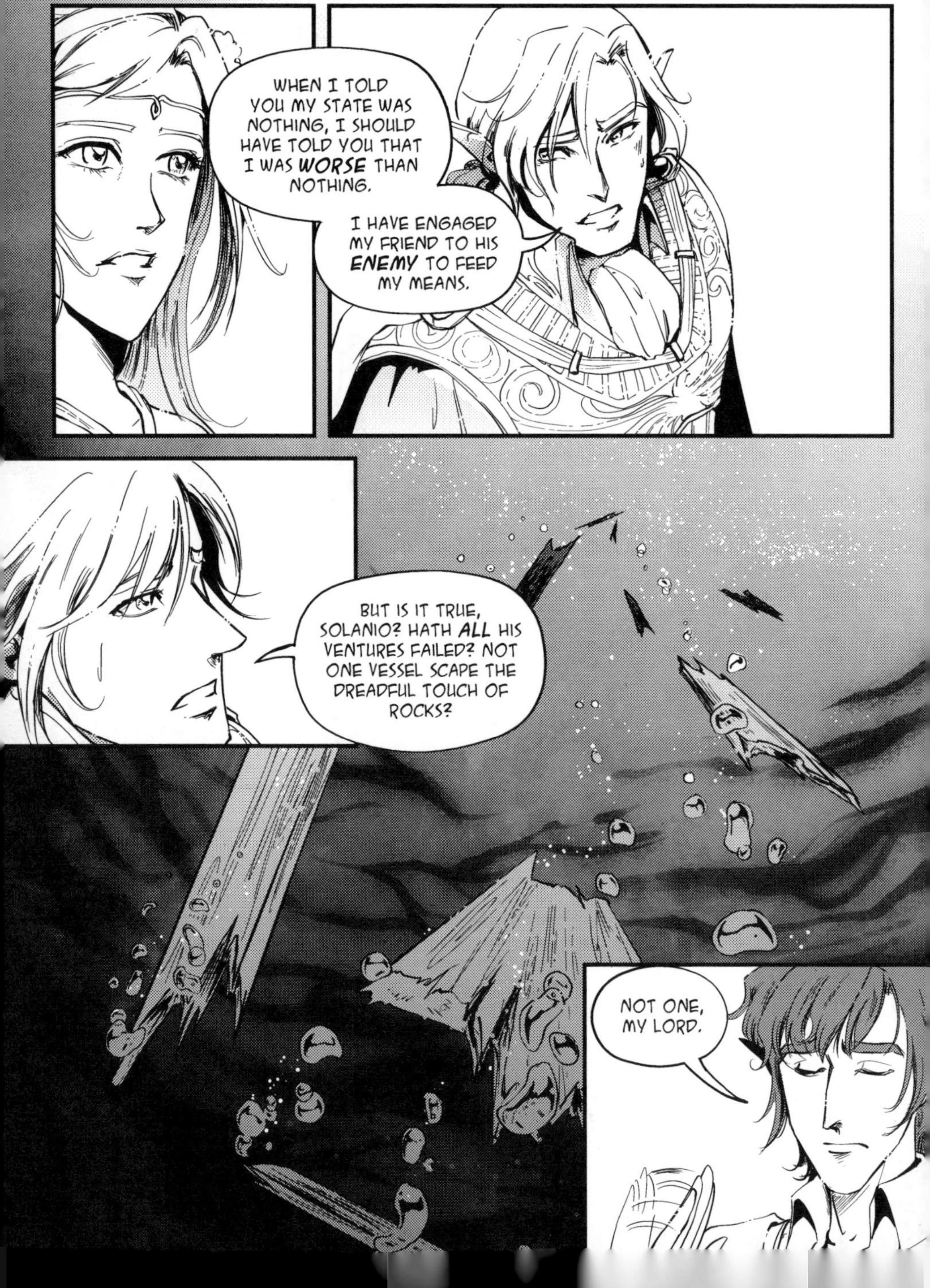
WHEN I TOLD YOU MY STATE WAS NOTHING, I SHOULD HAVE TOLD YOU THAT I WAS **WORSE** THAN NOTHING.
I HAVE ENGAGED MY FRIEND TO HIS **ENEMY** TO FEED MY MEANS.
BUT IS IT TRUE, SOLANIO? HATH **ALL** HIS VENTURES FAILED? NOT ONE VESSEL SCAPE THE DREADFUL TOUCH OF ROCKS?
NOT ONE, MY LORD.

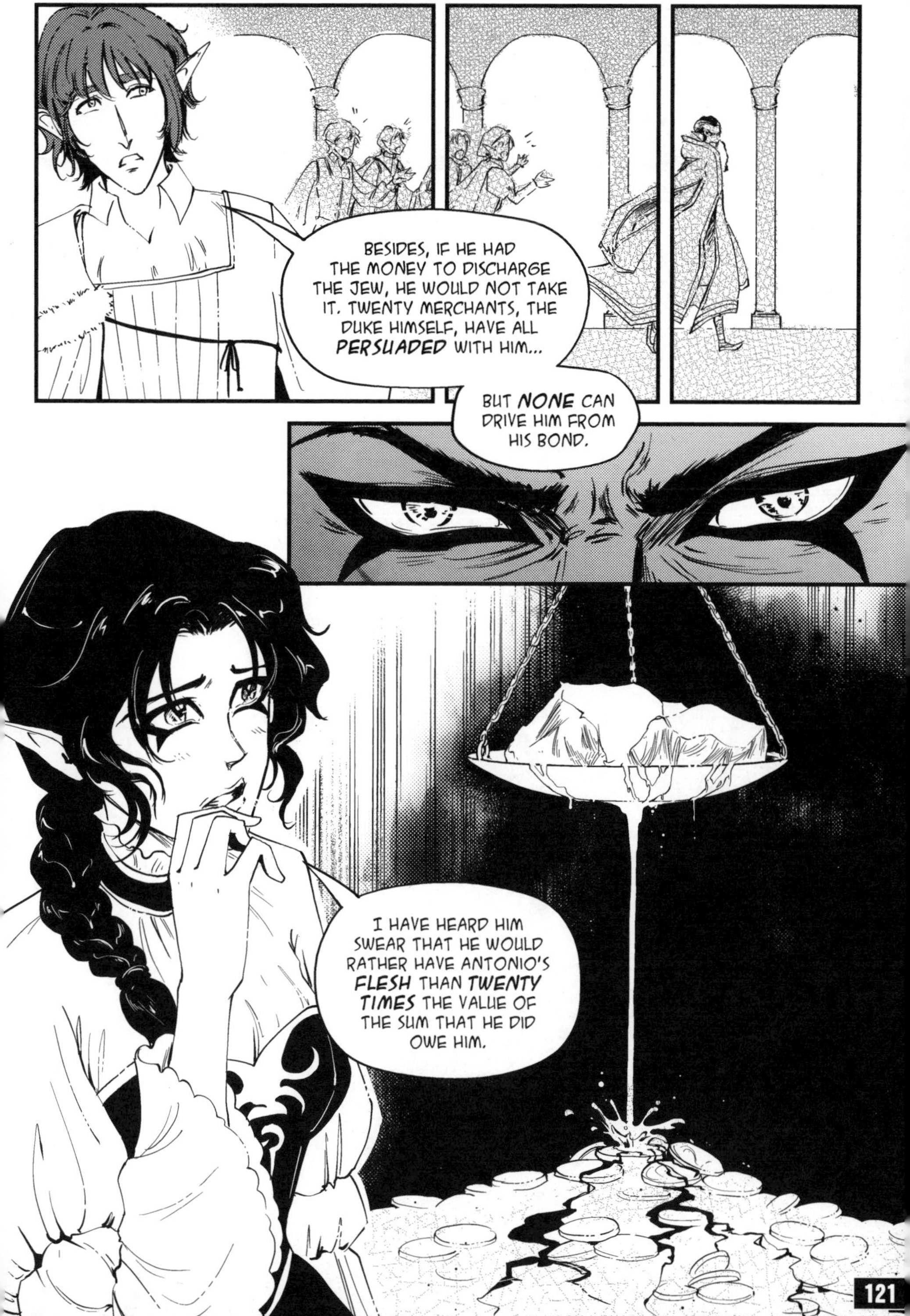
BESIDES, IF HE HAD THE MONEY TO DISCHARGE THE JEW, HE WOULD NOT TAKE IT. TWENTY MERCHANTS, THE DUKE HIMSELF, HAVE ALL **PERSUADED** WITH HIM...
BUT **NONE** CAN DRIVE HIM FROM HIS BOND.
I HAVE HEARD HIM SWEAR THAT HE WOULD RATHER HAVE ANTONIO'S **FLESH** THAN **TWENTY TIMES** THE VALUE OF THE SUM THAT HE DID OWE HIM.

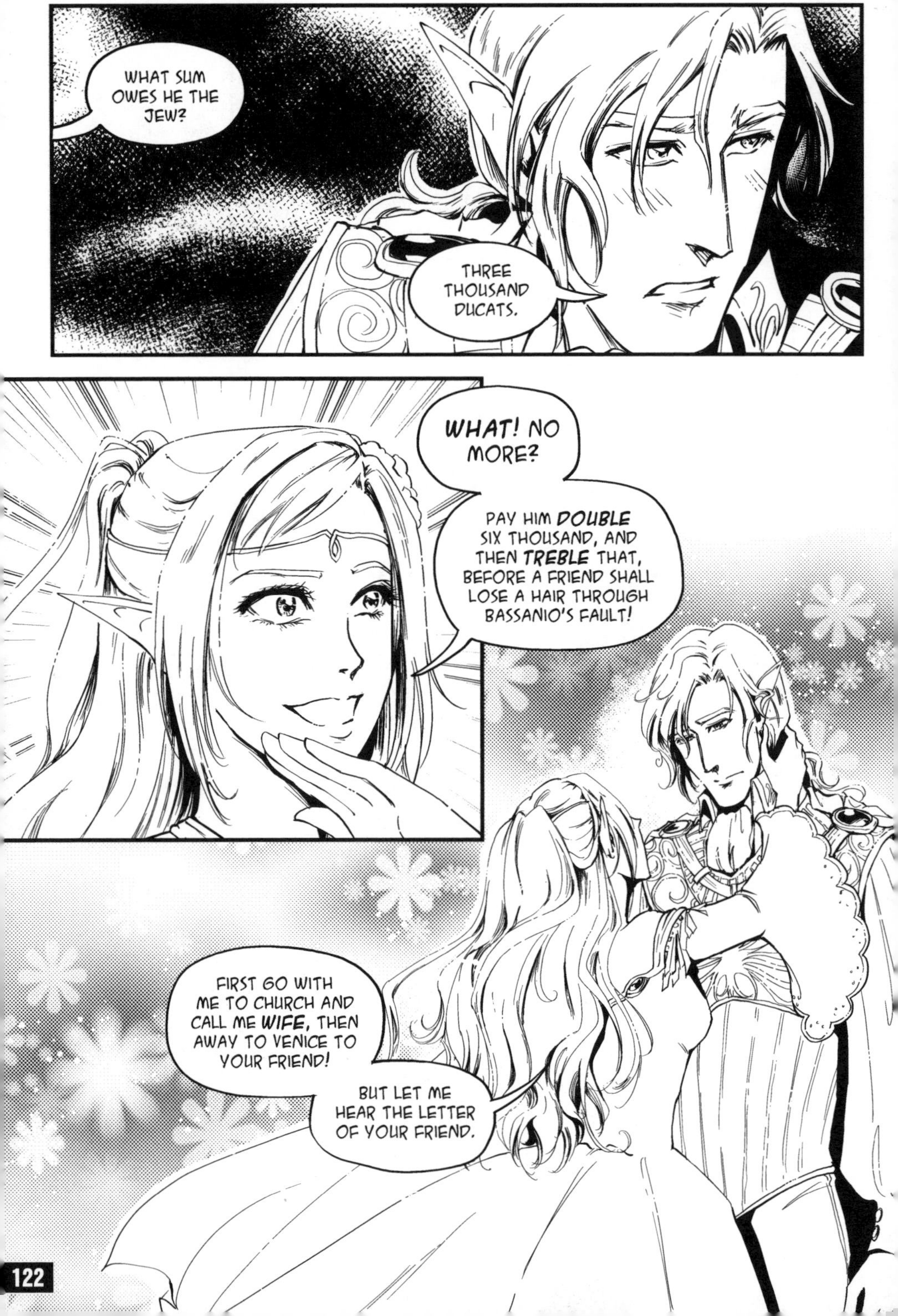
WHAT SUM OWES HE THE JEW?
THREE THOUSAND DUCATS.
WHAT! NO MORE?
PAY HIM DOUBLE SIX THOUSAND, AND THEN TREBLE THAT, BEFORE A FRIEND SHALL LOSE A HAIR THROUGH BASSANIO'S FAULT!
FIRST GO WITH ME TO CHURCH AND CALL ME WIFE, THEN AWAY TO VENICE TO YOUR FRIEND!
BUT LET ME HEAR THE LETTER OF YOUR FRIEND.

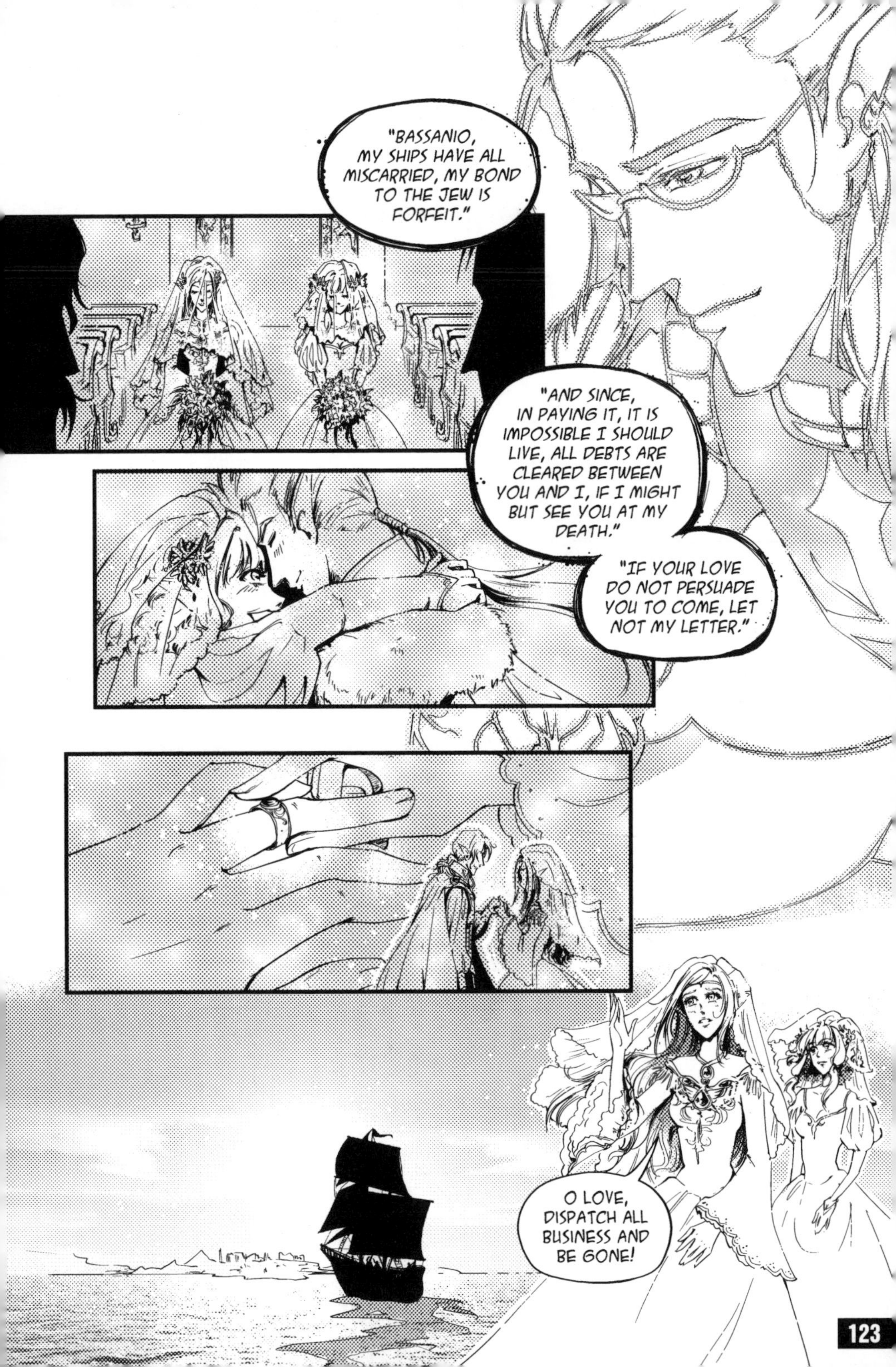
"BASSANIO, MY SHIPS HAVE ALL MISCARRIED, MY BOND TO THE JEW IS FORFEIT."
"AND SINCE, IN PAYING IT, IT IS IMPOSSIBLE I SHOULD LIVE, ALL DEBTS ARE CLEARED BETWEEN YOU AND I, IF I MIGHT BUT SEE YOU AT MY DEATH."
"IF YOUR LOVE DO NOT PERSUADE YOU TO COME, LET NOT MY LETTER."
O LOVE, DISPATCH ALL BUSINESS AND BE GONE!

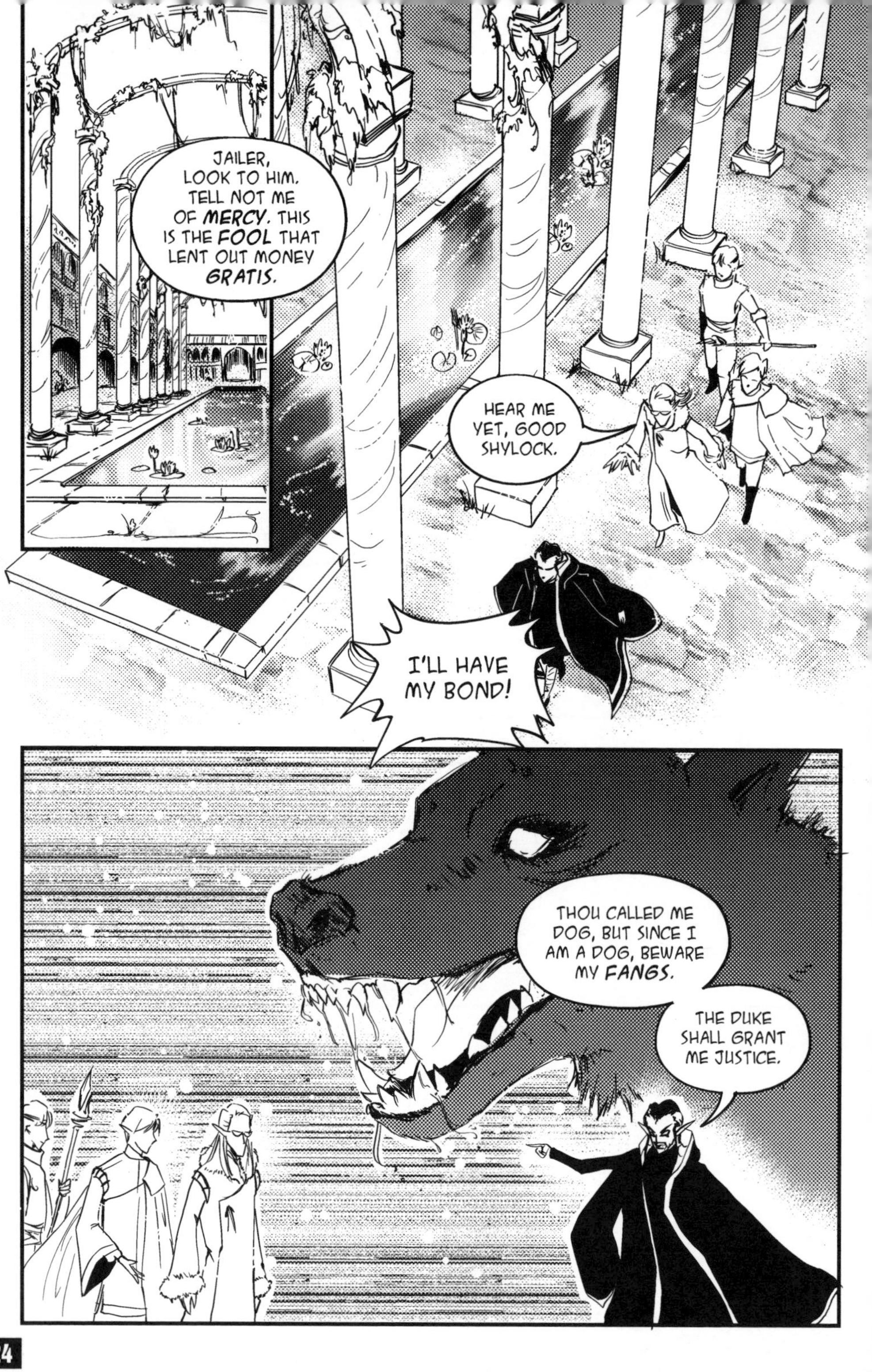

JAILER, LOOK TO HIM. TELL NOT ME OF MERCY. THIS IS THE FOOL THAT LENT OUT MONEY GRATIS.
HEAR ME YET, GOOD SHYLOCK.
I'LL HAVE MY BOND!
THOU CALLED ME DOG, BUT SINCE I AM A DOG, BEWARE MY FANGS.
THE DUKE SHALL GRANT ME JUSTICE.

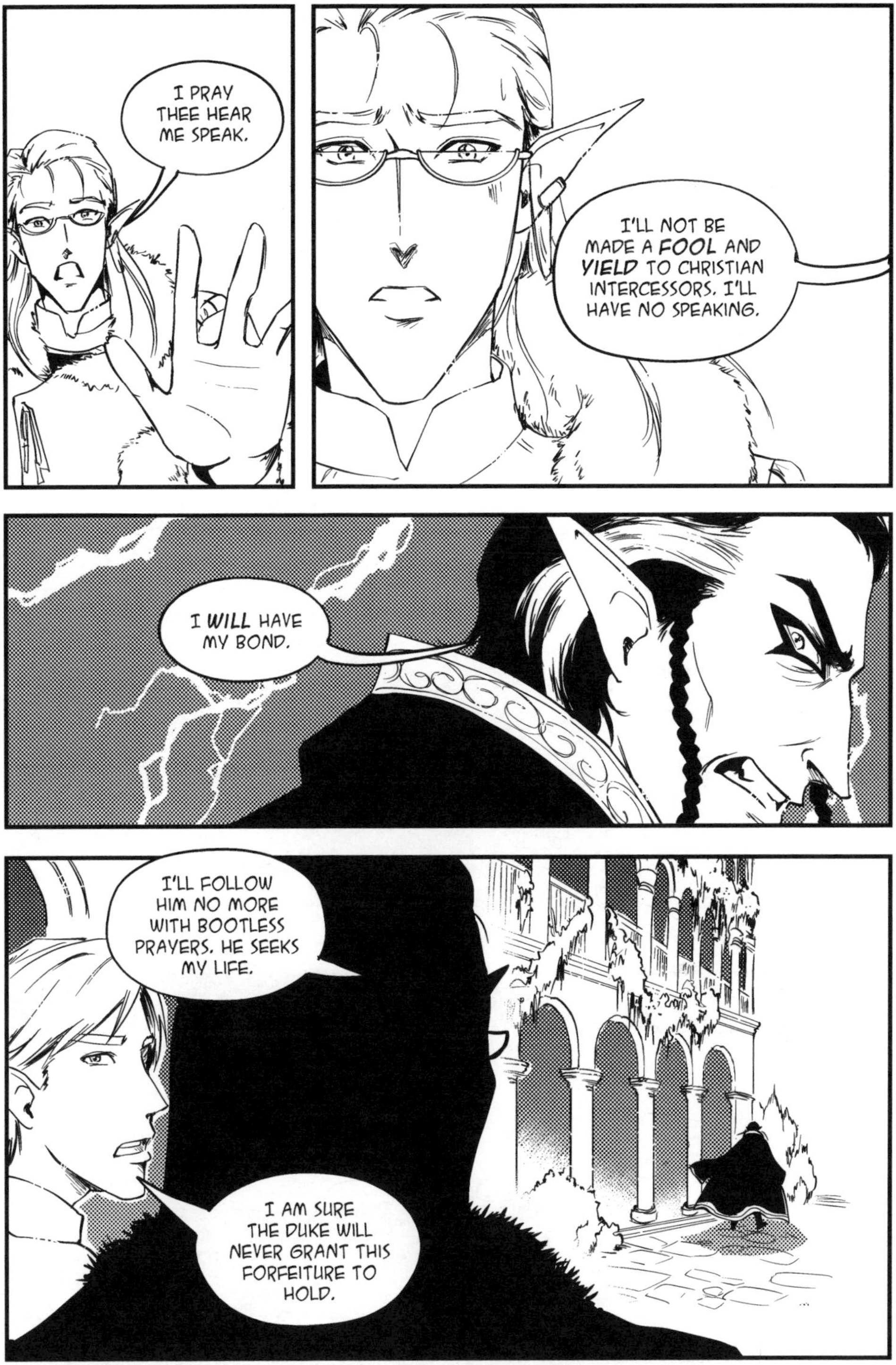
I PRAY THEE HEAR ME SPEAK.
I'LL NOT BE MADE A **FOOL** AND ***YIELD*** TO CHRISTIAN INTERCESSORS. I'LL HAVE NO SPEAKING.
I ***WILL*** HAVE MY BOND.
I'LL FOLLOW HIM NO MORE WITH BOOTLESS PRAYERS. HE SEEKS MY LIFE.
I AM SURE THE DUKE WILL NEVER GRANT THIS FORFEITURE TO HOLD.

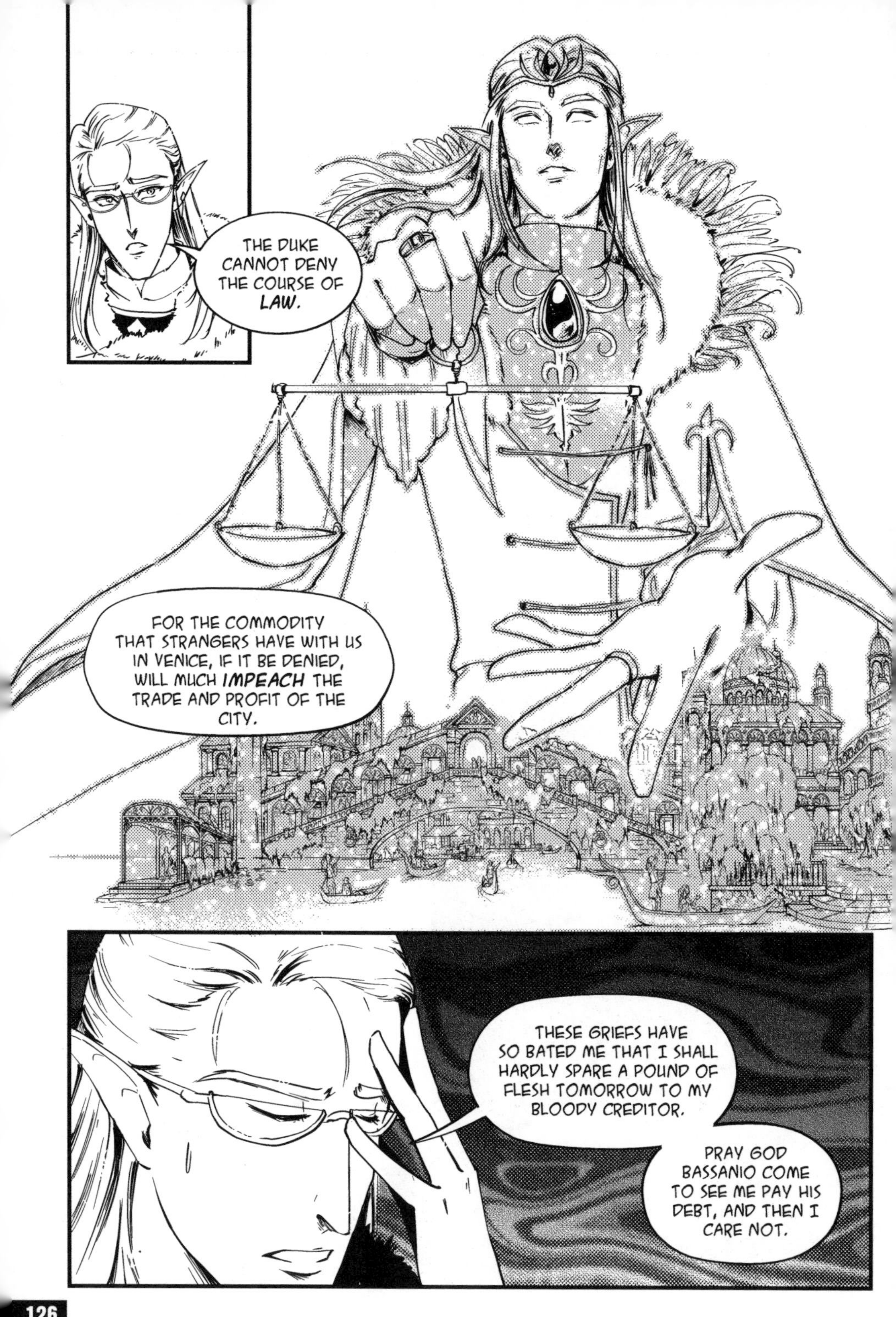
THE DUKE CANNOT DENY THE COURSE OF LAW.
FOR THE COMMODITY THAT STRANGERS HAVE WITH US IN VENICE, IF IT BE DENIED, WILL MUCH IMPEACH THE TRADE AND PROFIT OF THE CITY.
THESE GRIEFS HAVE SO BATED ME THAT I SHALL HARDLY SPARE A POUND OF FLESH TOMORROW TO MY BLOODY CREDITOR.
PRAY GOD BASSANIO COME TO SEE ME PAY HIS DEBT, AND THEN I CARE NOT.

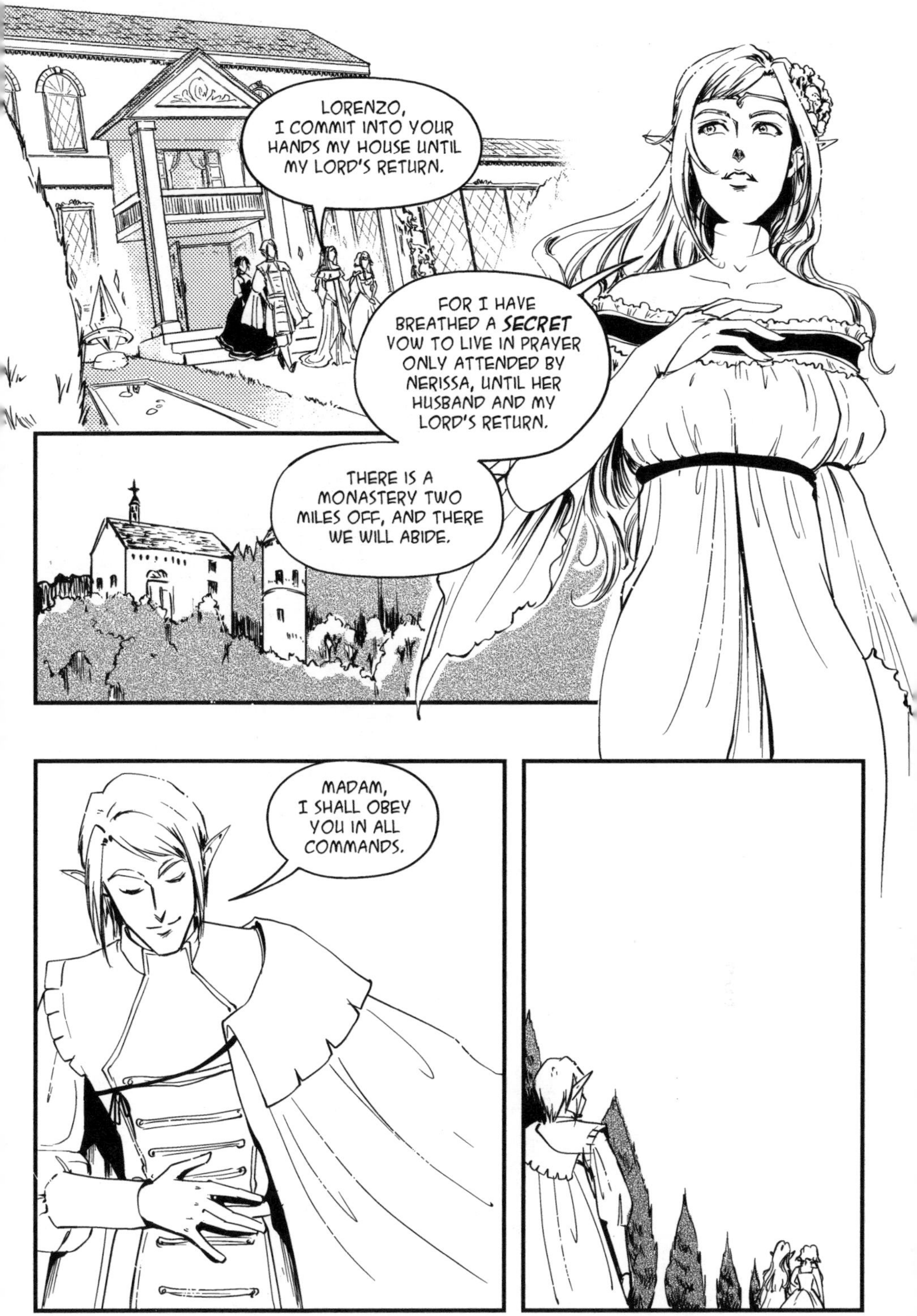
LORENZO, I COMMIT INTO YOUR HANDS MY HOUSE UNTIL MY LORD'S RETURN.
FOR I HAVE BREATHED A **SECRET** VOW TO LIVE IN PRAYER ONLY ATTENDED BY NERISSA, UNTIL HER HUSBAND AND MY LORD'S RETURN.
THERE IS A MONASTERY TWO MILES OFF, AND THERE WE WILL ABIDE.
MADAM, I SHALL OBEY YOU IN ALL COMMANDS.

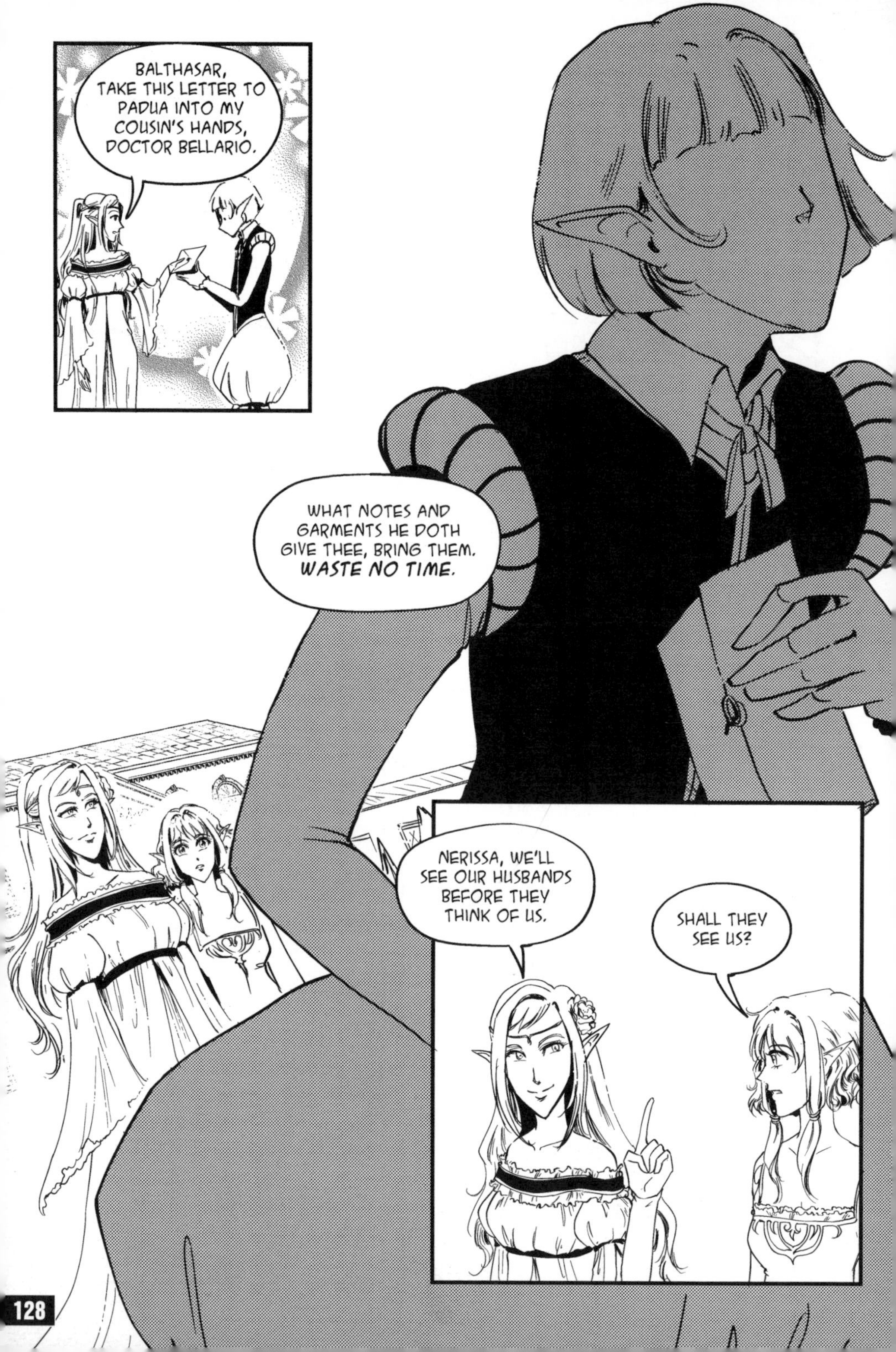
BALTHASAR, TAKE THIS LETTER TO PADUA INTO MY COUSIN'S HANDS, DOCTOR BELLARIO.
WHAT NOTES AND GARMENTS HE DOTH GIVE THEE, BRING THEM. *WASTE NO TIME.*
NERISSA, WE'LL SEE OUR HUSBANDS BEFORE THEY THINK OF US.
SHALL THEY SEE US?

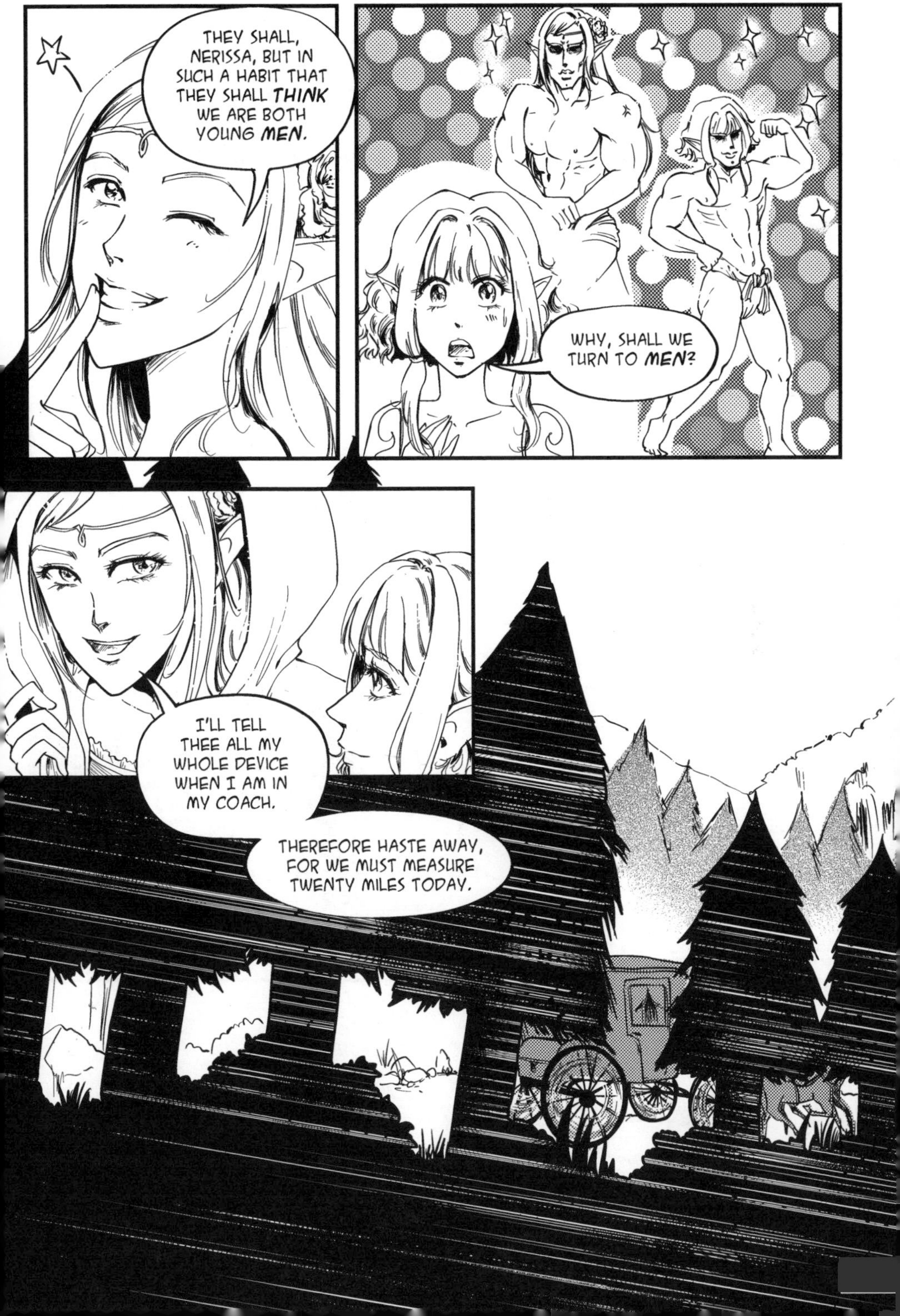
THEY SHALL, NERISSA, BUT IN SUCH A HABIT THAT THEY SHALL THINK WE ARE BOTH YOUNG MEN.
WHY, SHALL WE TURN TO MEN?
I'LL TELL THEE ALL MY WHOLE DEVICE WHEN I AM IN MY COACH.
THEREFORE HASTE AWAY, FOR WE MUST MEASURE TWENTY MILES TODAY.

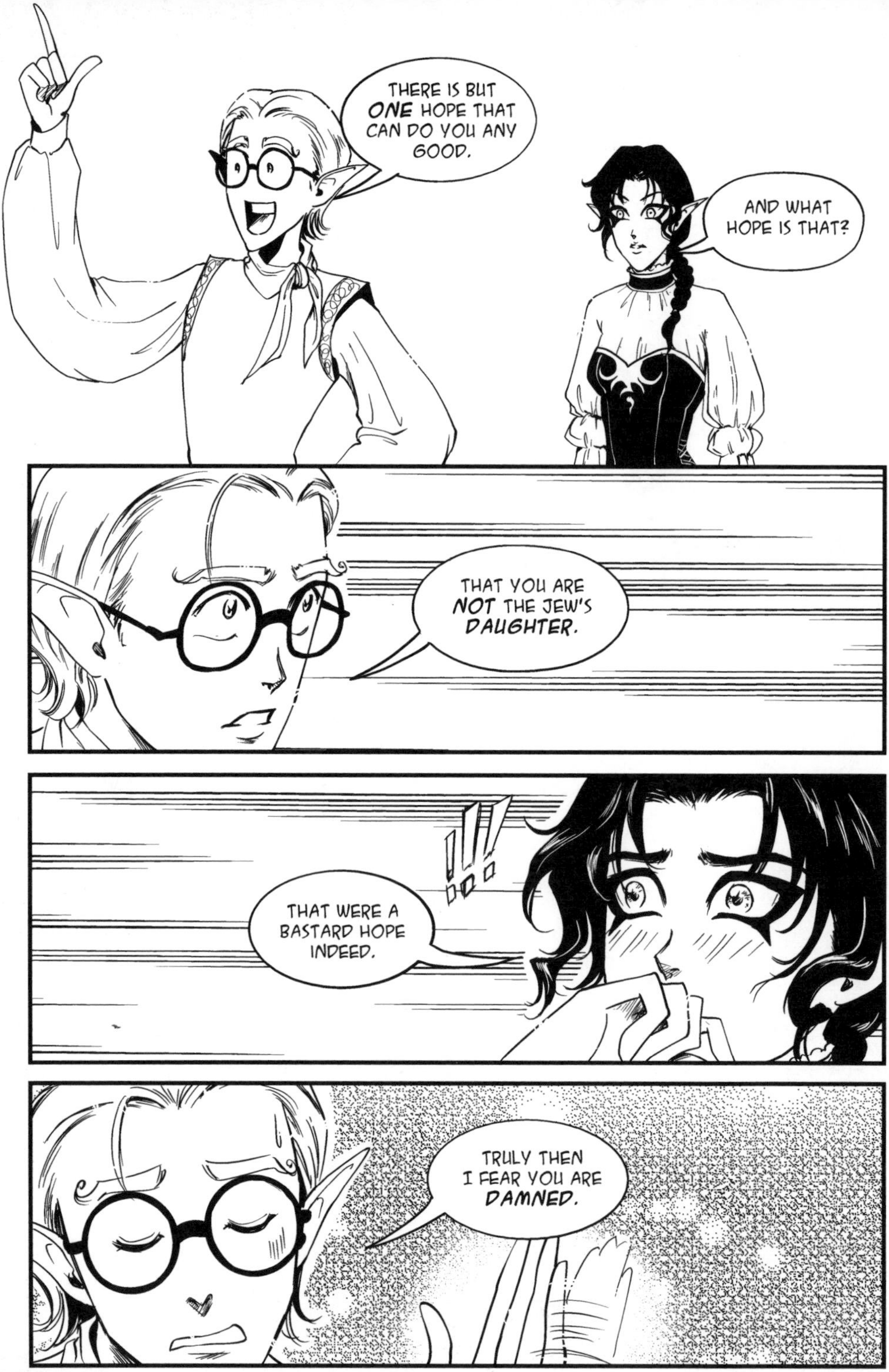
THERE IS BUT ONE HOPE THAT CAN DO YOU ANY GOOD.
AND WHAT HOPE IS THAT?
THAT YOU ARE NOT THE JEW'S DAUGHTER.
THAT WERE A BASTARD HOPE INDEED.
!!!
TRULY THEN I FEAR YOU ARE DAMNED.

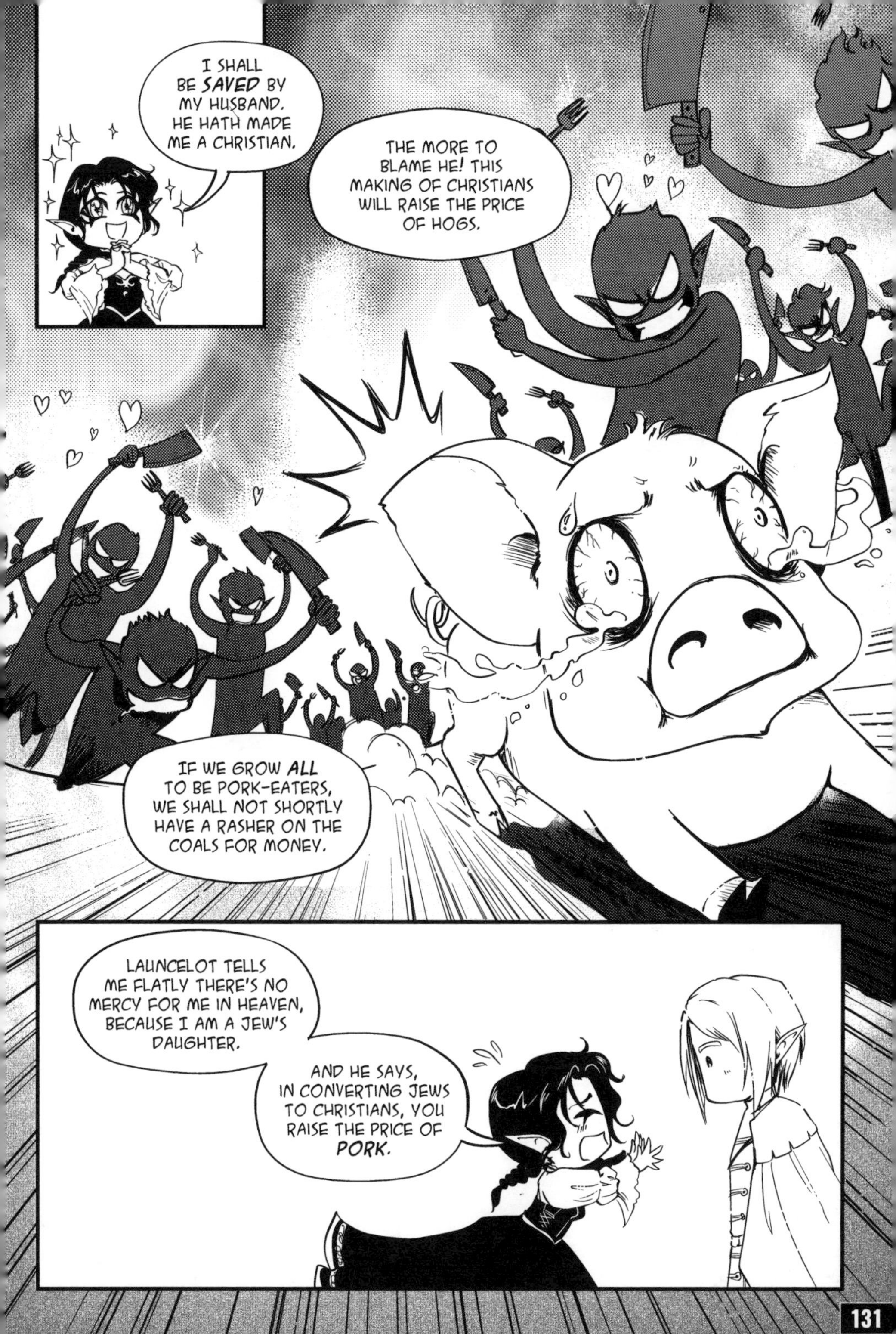
I SHALL BE *SAVED* BY MY HUSBAND. HE HATH MADE ME A CHRISTIAN.
THE MORE TO BLAME HE! THIS MAKING OF CHRISTIANS WILL RAISE THE PRICE OF HOGS.
IF WE GROW **ALL** TO BE PORK-EATERS, WE SHALL NOT SHORTLY HAVE A RASHER ON THE COALS FOR MONEY.
LAUNCELOT TELLS ME FLATLY THERE'S NO MERCY FOR ME IN HEAVEN, BECAUSE I AM A JEW'S DAUGHTER.
AND HE SAYS, IN CONVERTING JEWS TO CHRISTIANS, YOU RAISE THE PRICE OF **PORK**.

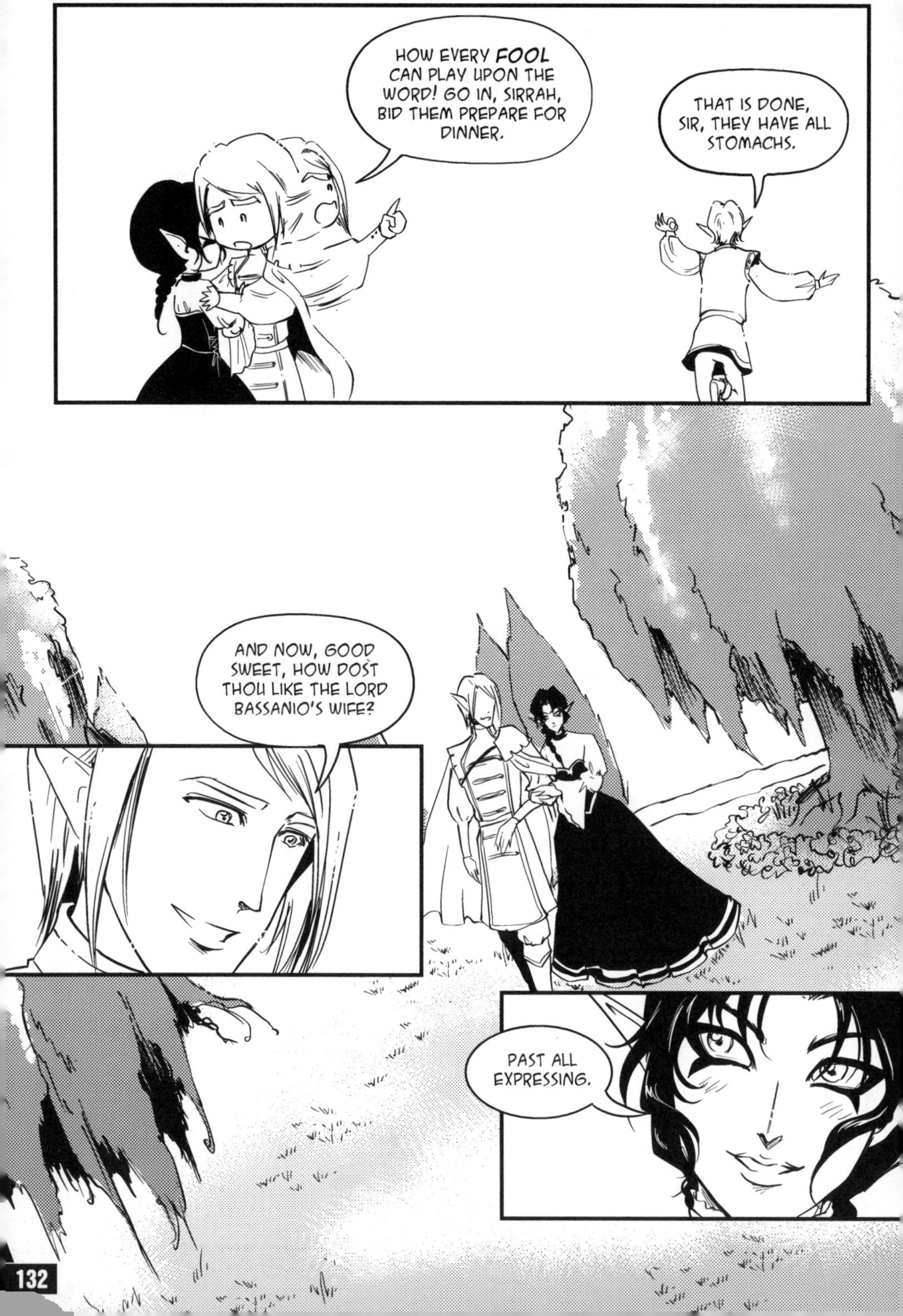
HOW EVERY **FOOL** CAN PLAY UPON THE WORD! GO IN, SIRRAH, BID THEM PREPARE FOR DINNER.
THAT IS DONE, SIR, THEY HAVE ALL STOMACHS.
AND NOW, GOOD SWEET, HOW DOST THOU LIKE THE LORD BASSANIO'S WIFE?
PAST ALL EXPRESSING.

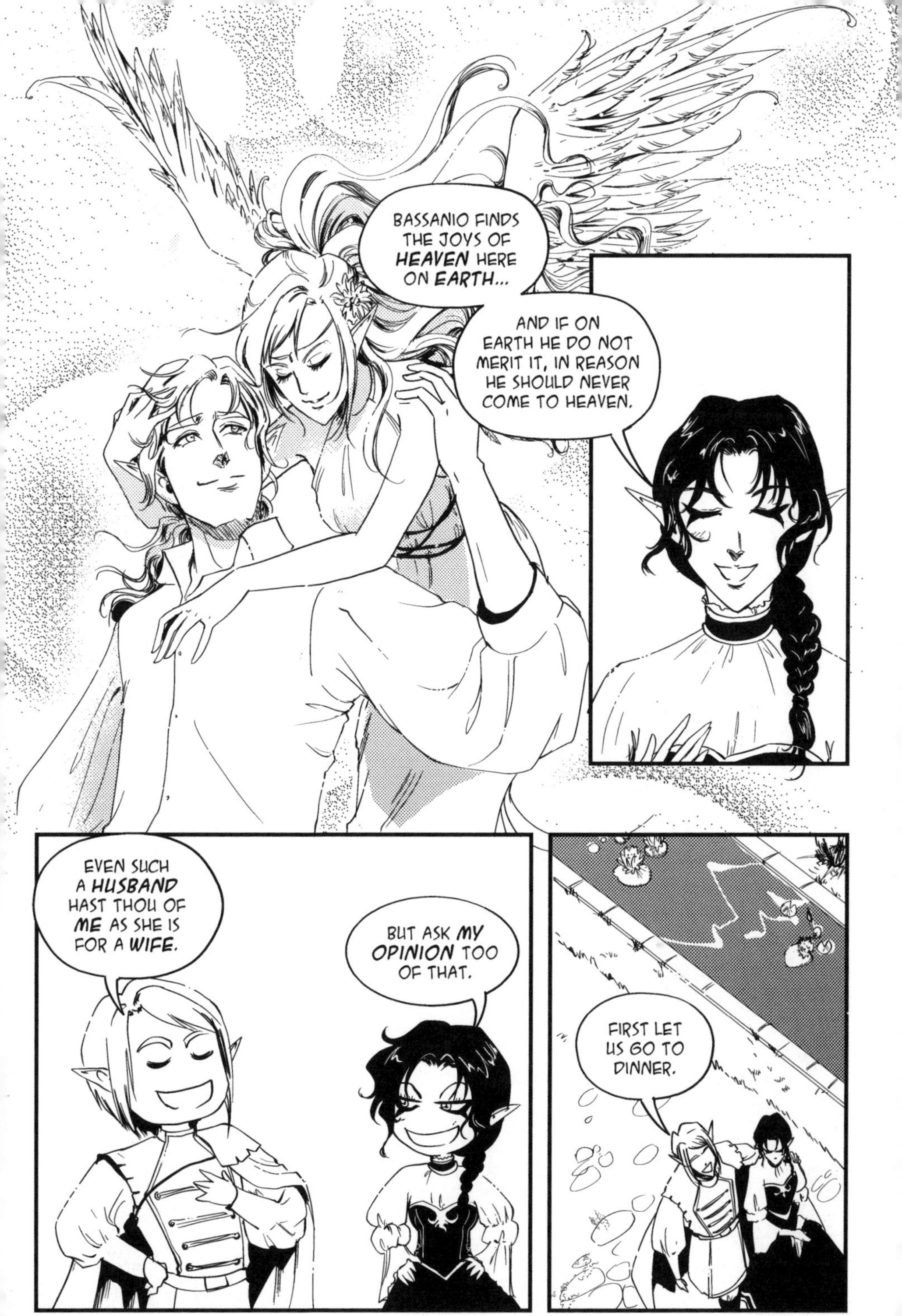
BASSANIO FINDS THE JOYS OF HEAVEN HERE ON EARTH...
AND IF ON EARTH HE DO NOT MERIT IT, IN REASON HE SHOULD NEVER COME TO HEAVEN.
EVEN SUCH A HUSBAND HAST THOU OF ME AS SHE IS FOR A WIFE.
BUT ASK MY OPINION TOO OF THAT.
FIRST LET US GO TO DINNER.

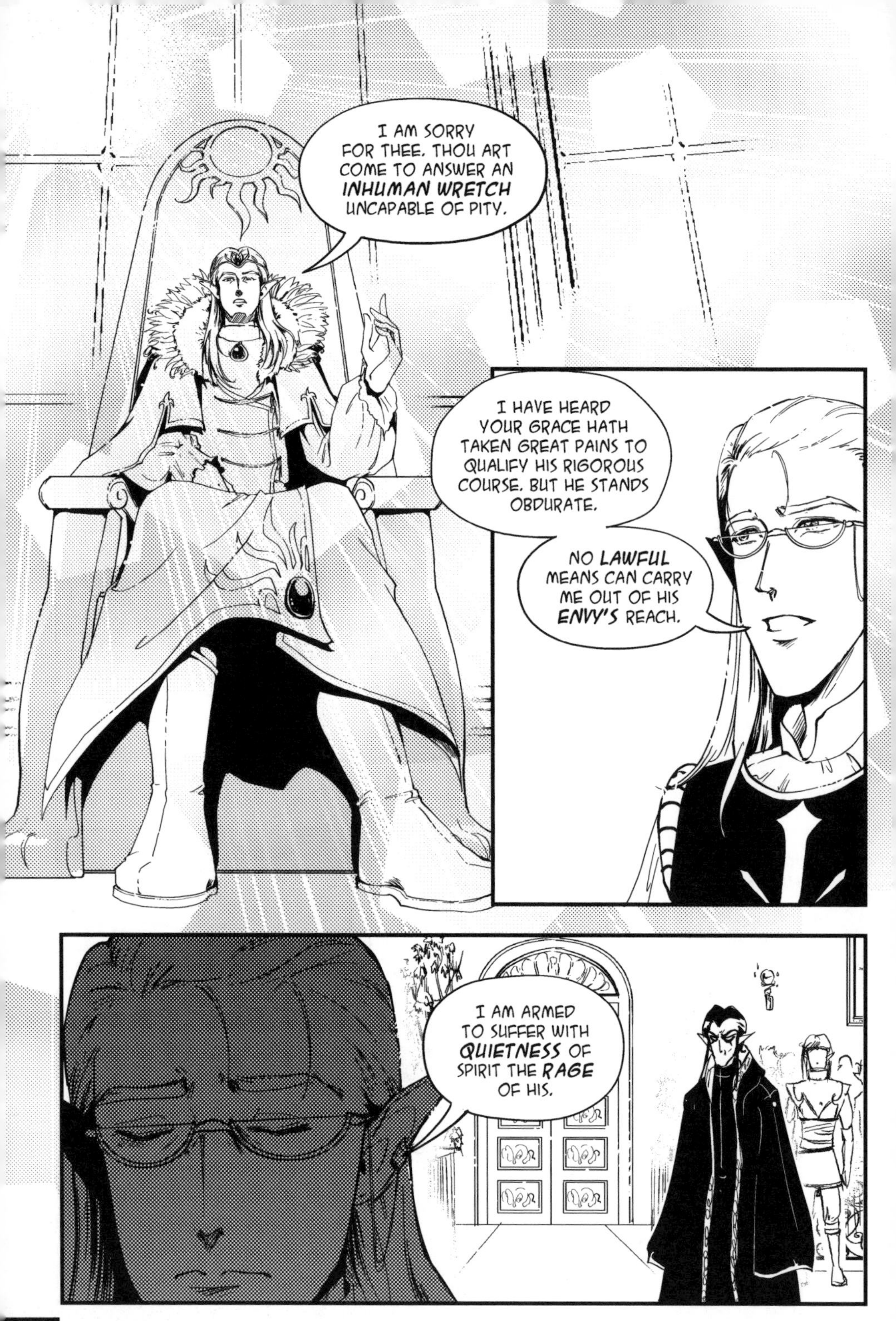
I AM SORRY FOR THEE. THOU ART COME TO ANSWER AN **INHUMAN WRETCH** UNCAPABLE OF PITY.
I HAVE HEARD YOUR GRACE HATH TAKEN GREAT PAINS TO QUALIFY HIS RIGOROUS COURSE. BUT HE STANDS OBDURATE.
NO **LAWFUL** MEANS CAN CARRY ME OUT OF HIS **ENVY'S** REACH.
I AM ARMED TO SUFFER WITH **QUIETNESS** OF SPIRIT THE **RAGE** OF HIS.

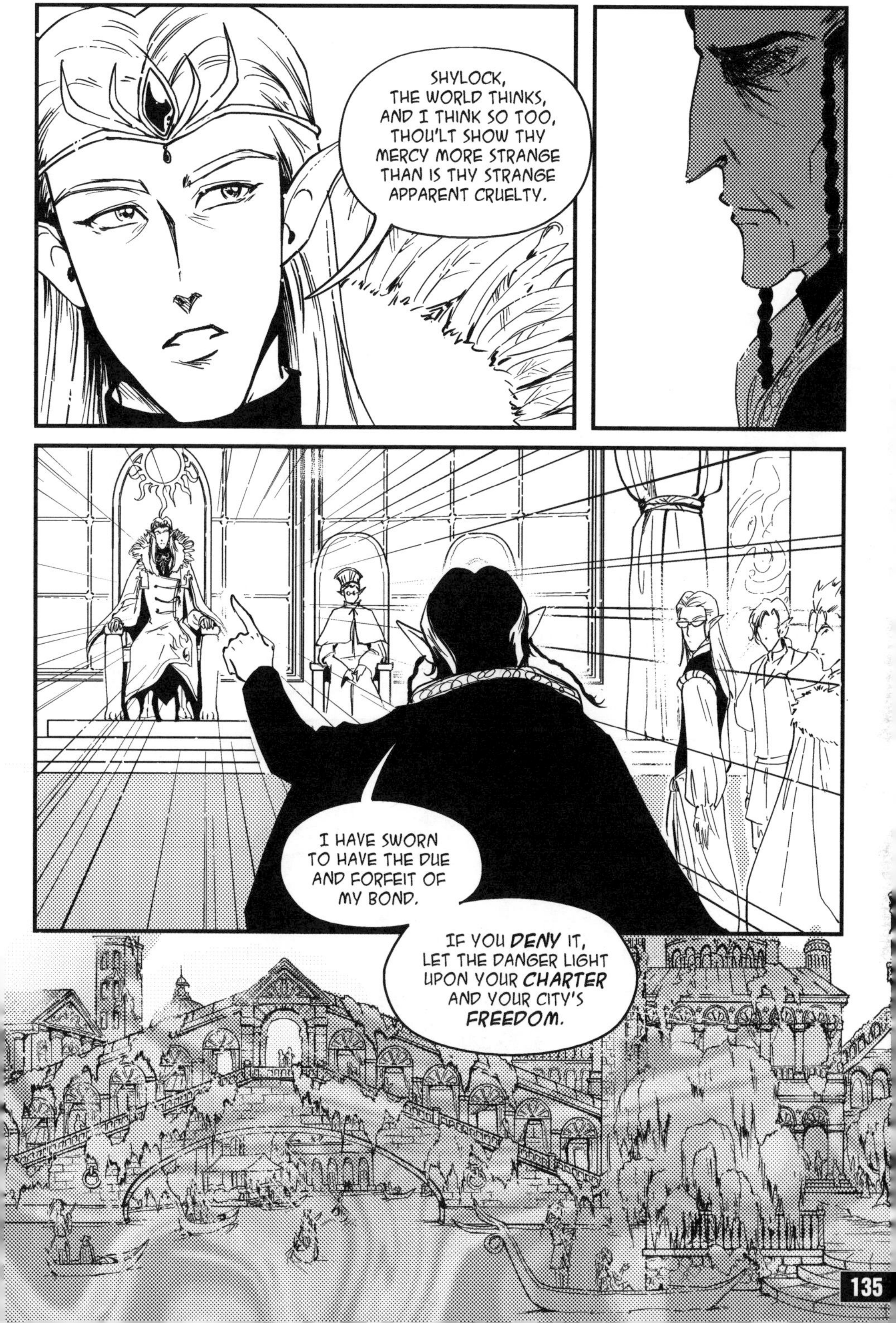
SHYLOCK, THE WORLD THINKS, AND I THINK SO TOO, THOU'LT SHOW THY MERCY MORE STRANGE THAN IS THY STRANGE APPARENT CRUELTY.
I HAVE SWORN TO HAVE THE DUE AND FORFEIT OF MY BOND.
IF YOU **DENY** IT, LET THE DANGER LIGHT UPON YOUR **CHARTER** AND YOUR CITY'S **FREEDOM.**

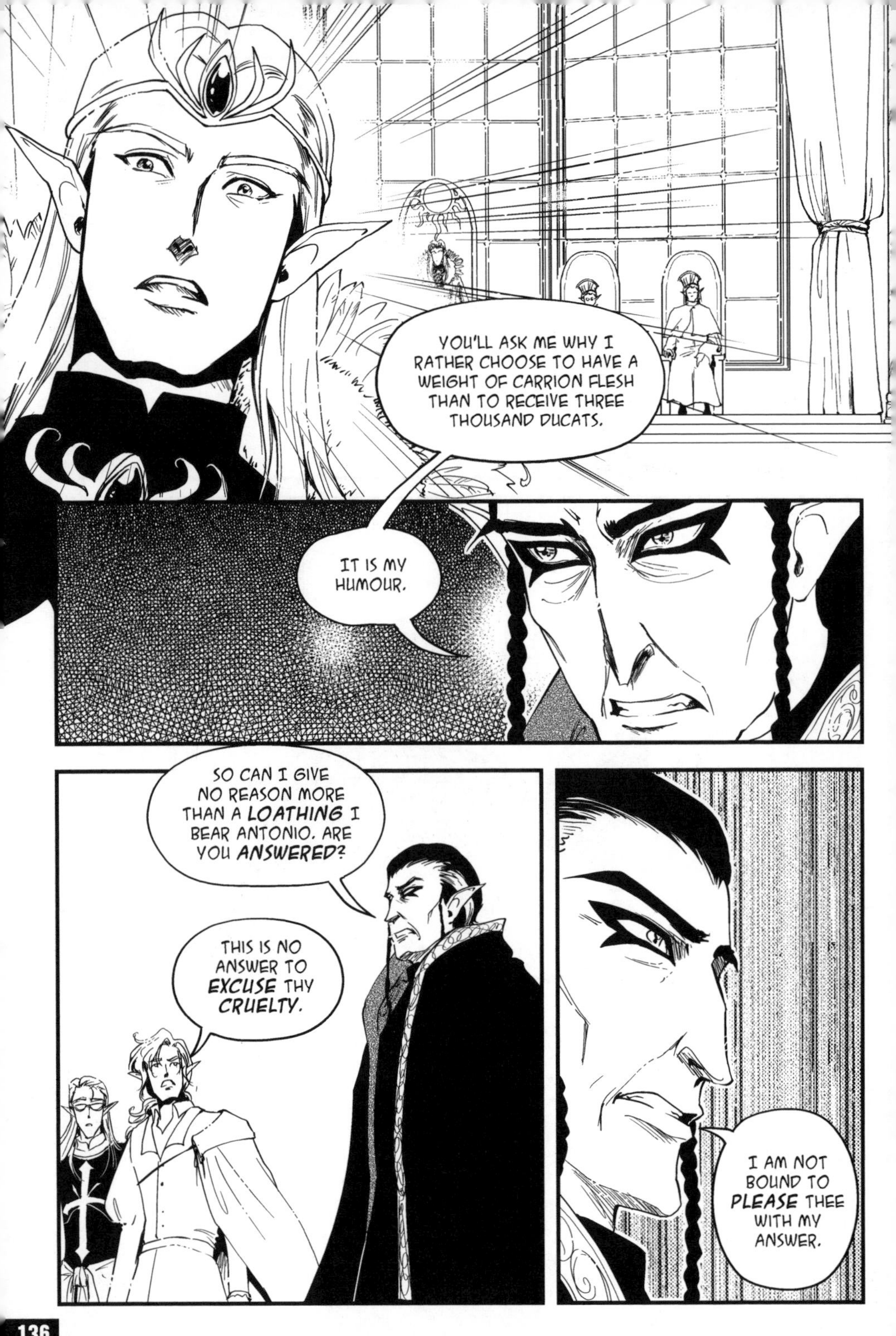
YOU'LL ASK ME WHY I RATHER CHOOSE TO HAVE A WEIGHT OF CARRION FLESH THAN TO RECEIVE THREE THOUSAND DUCATS.
IT IS MY HUMOUR.
SO CAN I GIVE NO REASON MORE THAN A LOATHING I BEAR ANTONIO. ARE YOU ANSWERED?
THIS IS NO ANSWER TO EXCUSE THY CRUELTY.
I AM NOT BOUND TO PLEASE THEE WITH MY ANSWER.

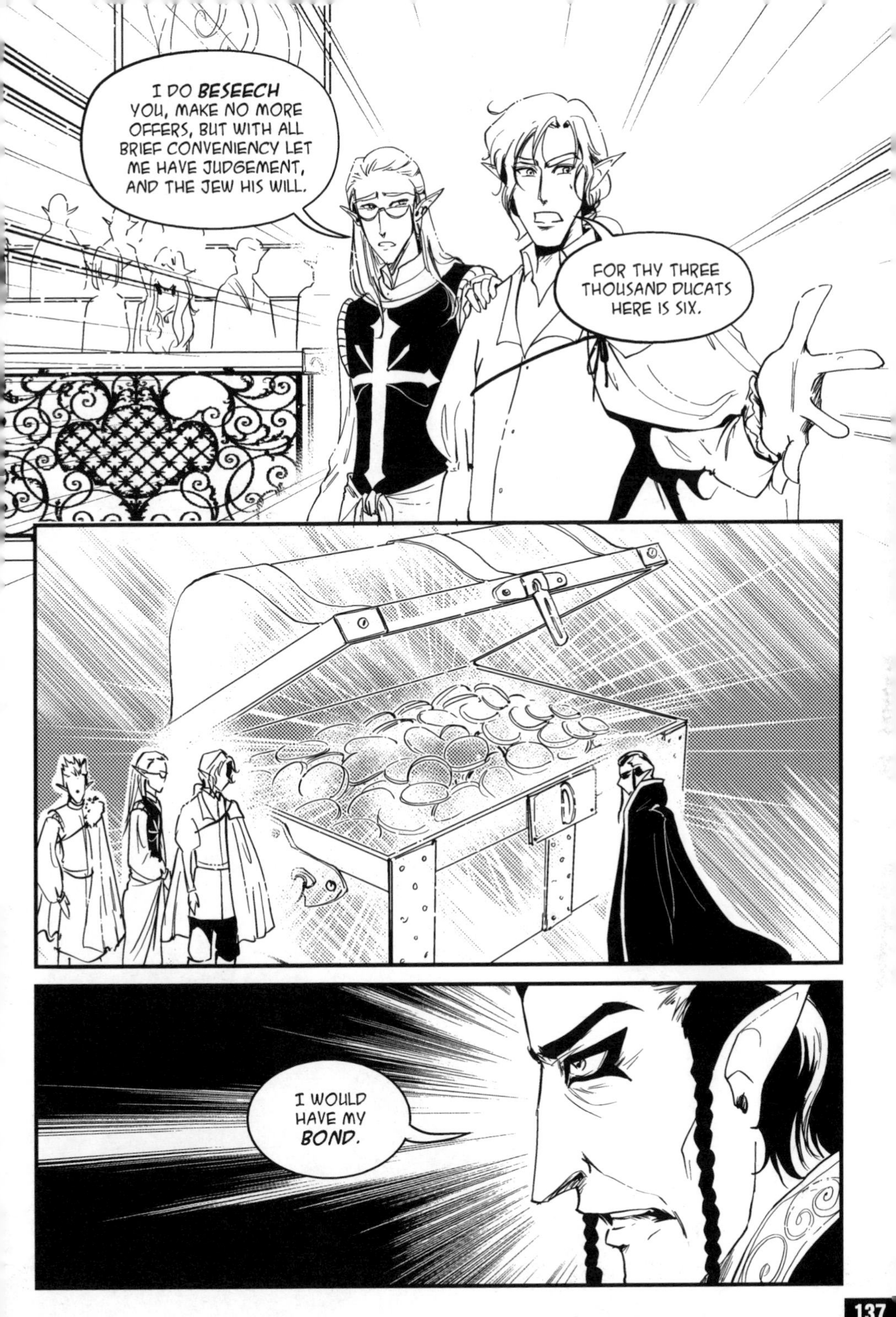

I DO BESEECH YOU, MAKE NO MORE OFFERS, BUT WITH ALL BRIEF CONVENIENCY LET ME HAVE JUDGEMENT, AND THE JEW HIS WILL.
FOR THY THREE THOUSAND DUCATS HERE IS SIX.
I WOULD HAVE MY BOND.

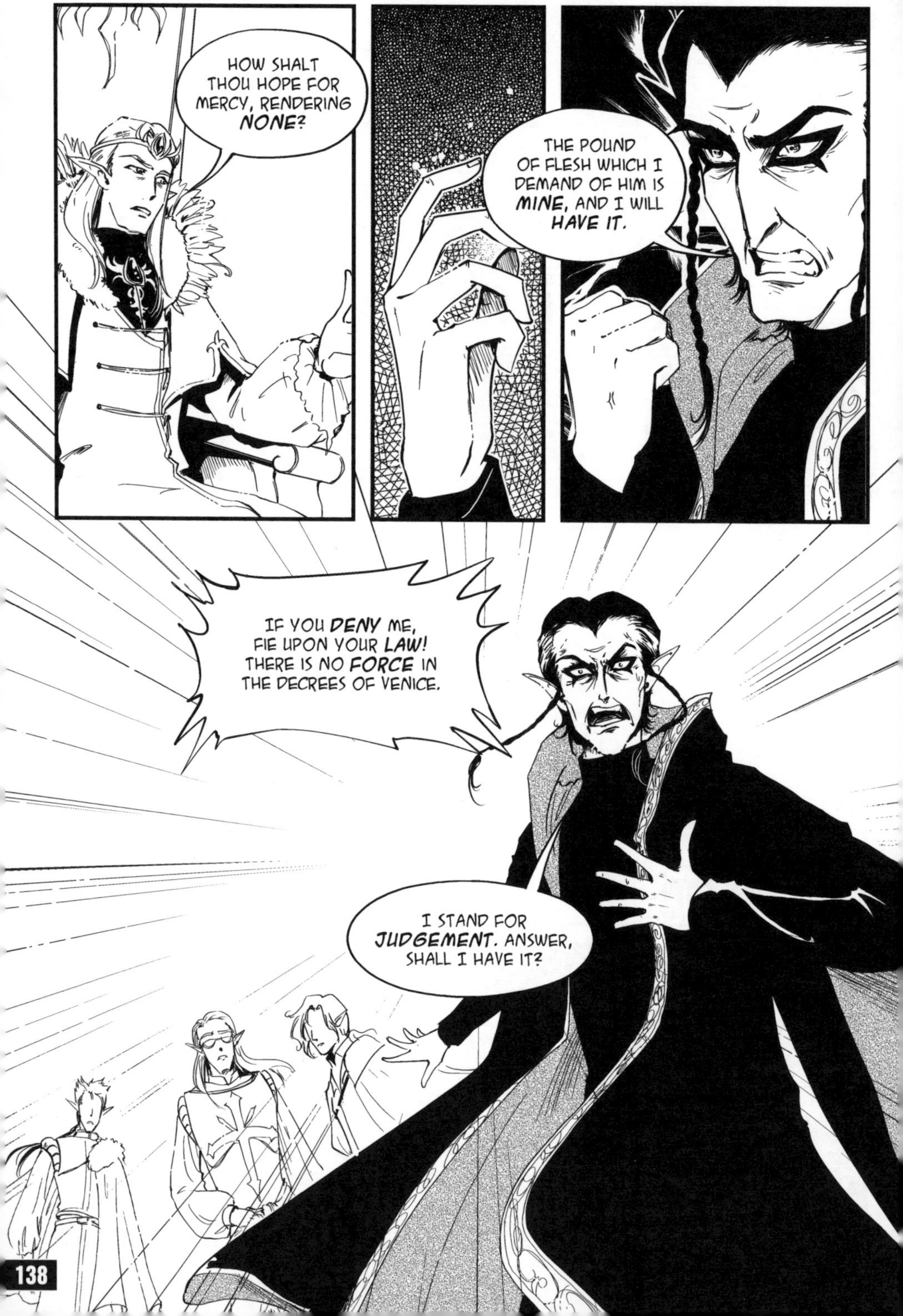
HOW SHALT THOU HOPE FOR MERCY, RENDERING NONE?
THE POUND OF FLESH WHICH I DEMAND OF HIM IS MINE, AND I WILL HAVE IT.
IF YOU DENY ME, FIE UPON YOUR LAW! THERE IS NO FORCE IN THE DECREES OF VENICE.
I STAND FOR JUDGEMENT. ANSWER, SHALL I HAVE IT?

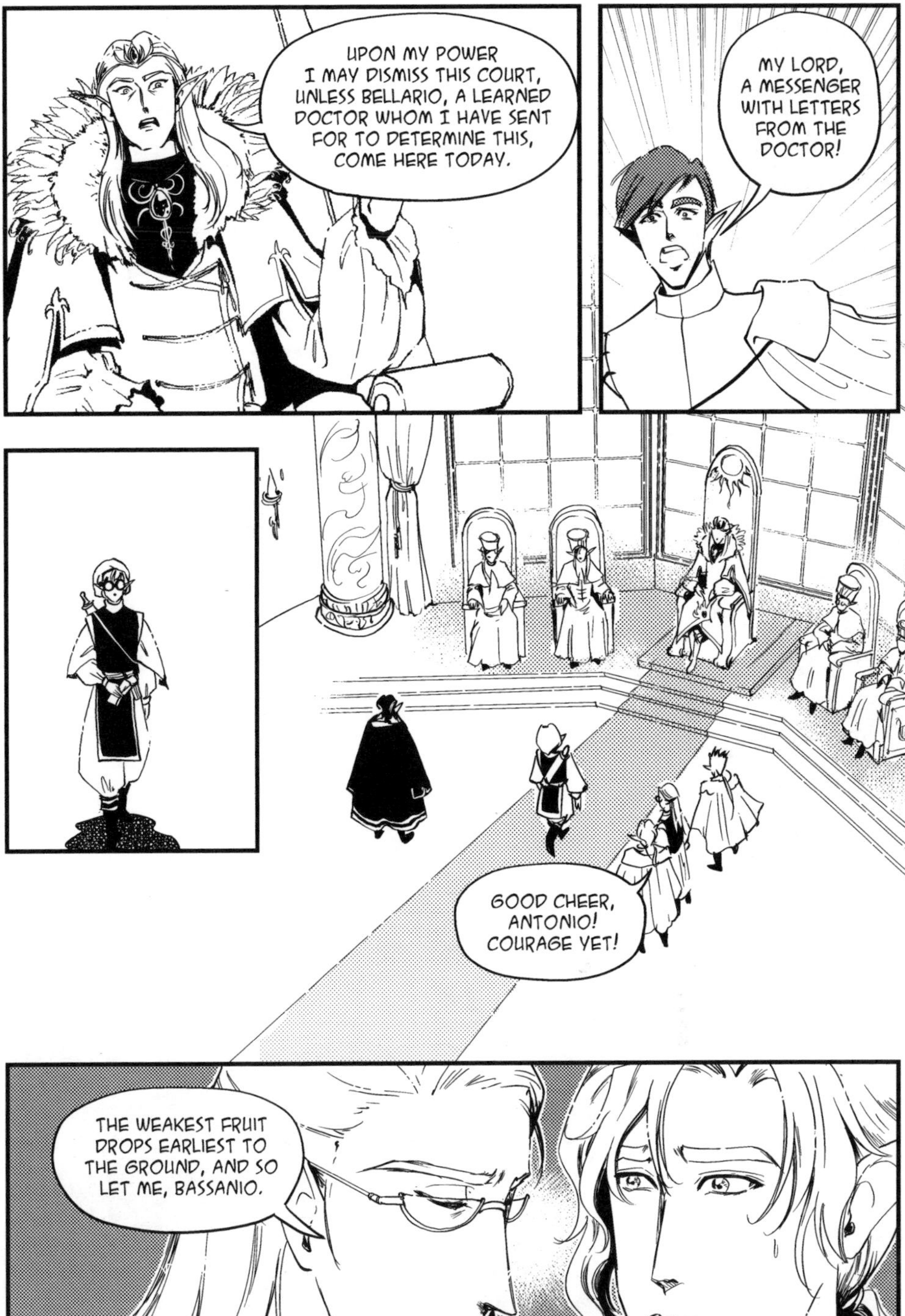
UPON MY POWER I MAY DISMISS THIS COURT, UNLESS BELLARIO, A LEARNED DOCTOR WHOM I HAVE SENT FOR TO DETERMINE THIS, COME HERE TODAY.
MY LORD, A MESSENGER WITH LETTERS FROM THE DOCTOR!
GOOD CHEER, ANTONIO! COURAGE YET!
THE WEAKEST FRUIT DROPS EARLIEST TO THE GROUND, AND SO LET ME, BASSANIO.

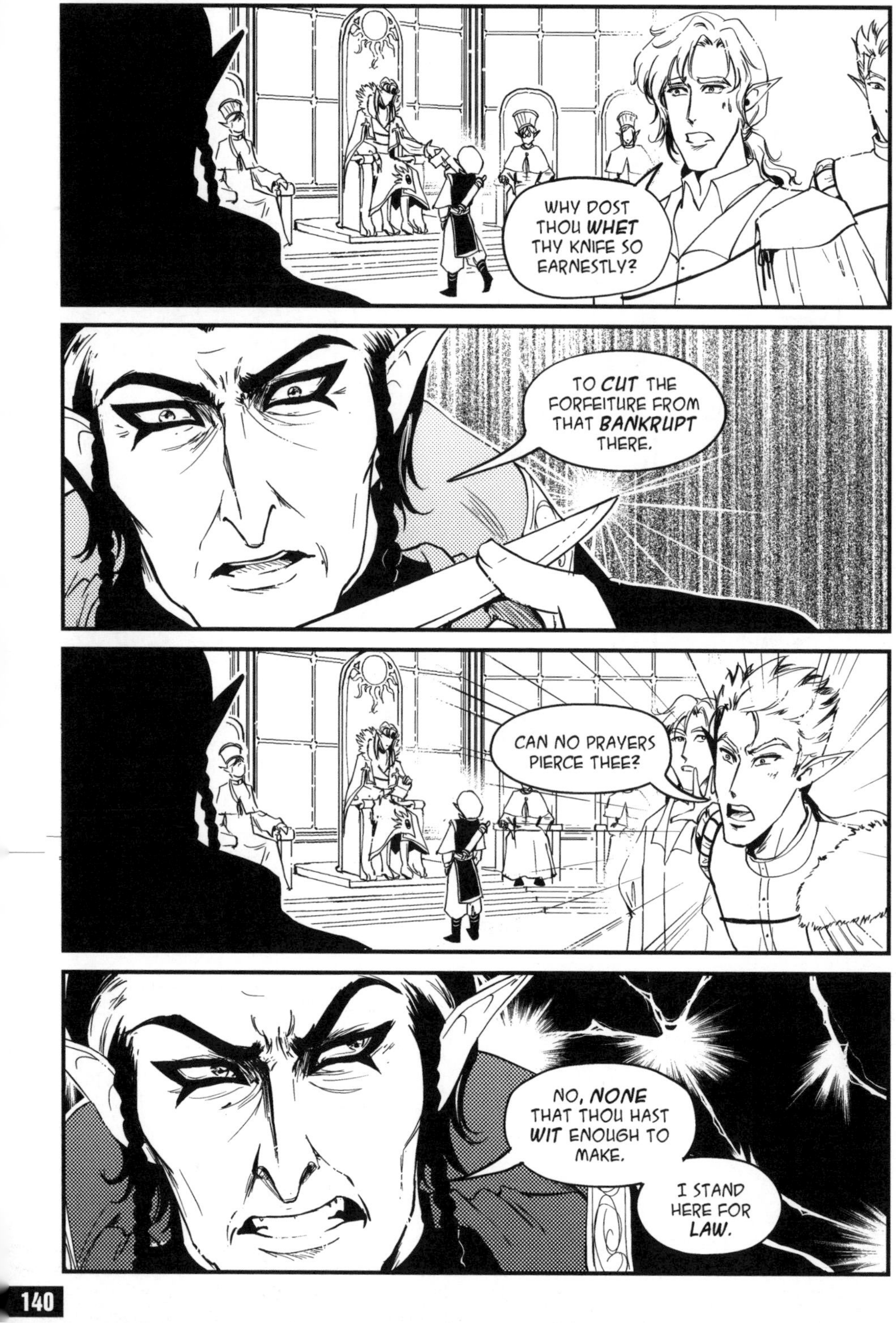
WHY DOST THOU WHET THY KNIFE SO EARNESTLY?
TO CUT THE FORFEITURE FROM THAT BANKRUPT THERE.
CAN NO PRAYERS PIERCE THEE?
NO, NONE THAT THOU HAST WIT ENOUGH TO MAKE.
I STAND HERE FOR LAW.

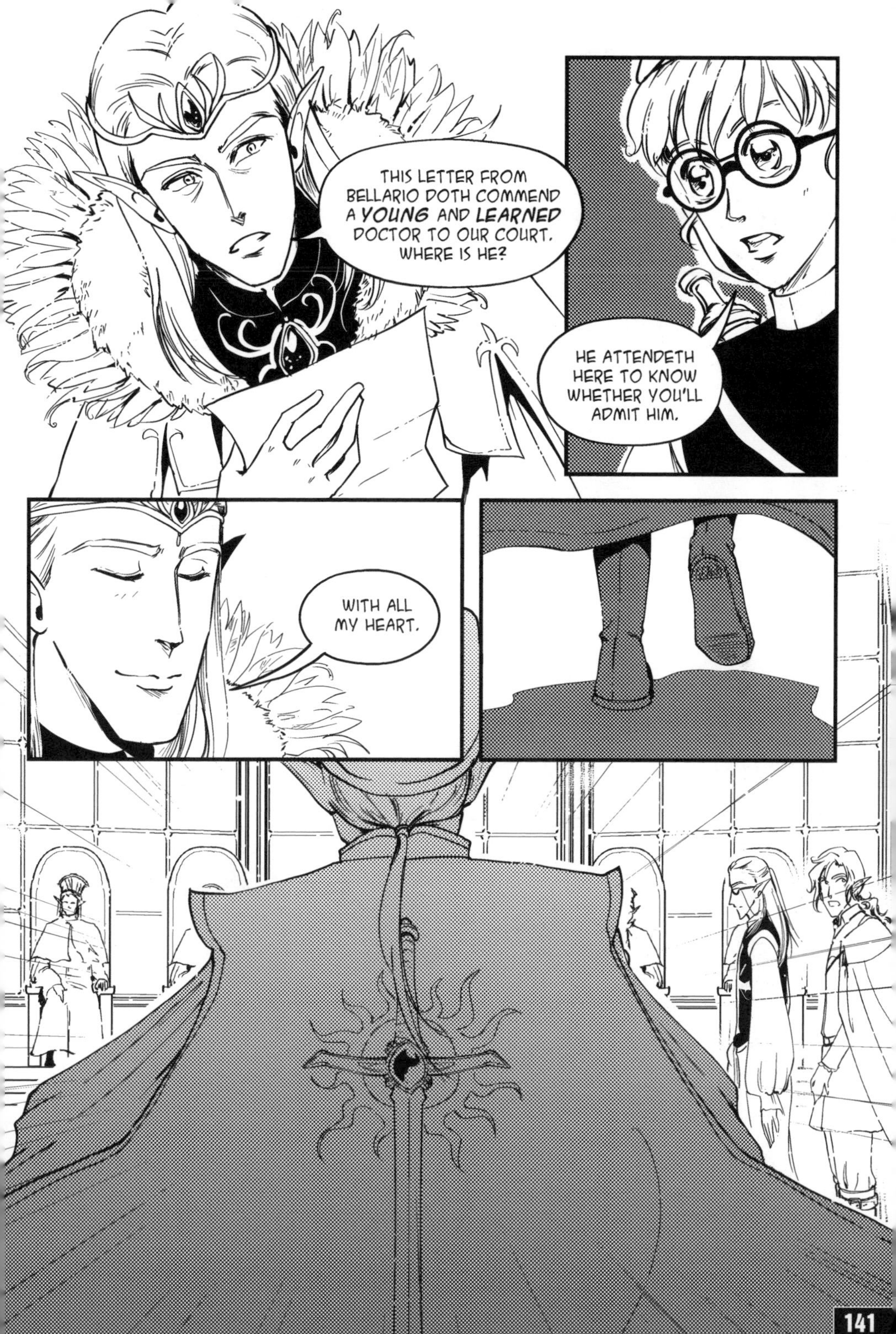
THIS LETTER FROM BELLARIO DOTH COMMEND A **YOUNG** AND **LEARNED** DOCTOR TO OUR COURT. WHERE IS HE?
HE ATTENDETH HERE TO KNOW WHETHER YOU'LL ADMIT HIM.
WITH ALL MY HEART.

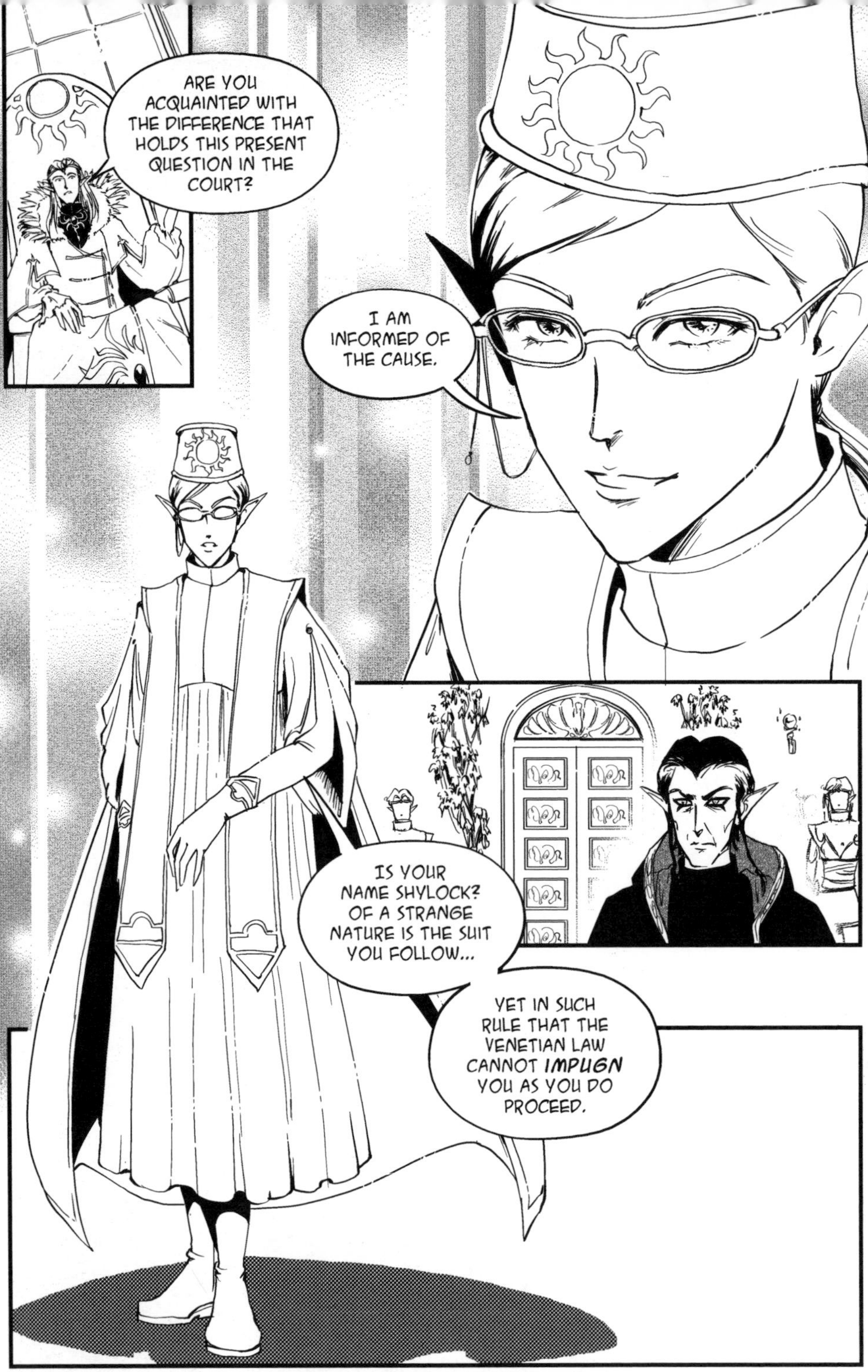
ARE YOU ACQUAINTED WITH THE DIFFERENCE THAT HOLDS THIS PRESENT QUESTION IN THE COURT?
I AM INFORMED OF THE CAUSE.
IS YOUR NAME SHYLOCK? OF A STRANGE NATURE IS THE SUIT YOU FOLLOW...
YET IN SUCH RULE THAT THE VENETIAN LAW CANNOT IMPUGN YOU AS YOU DO PROCEED.

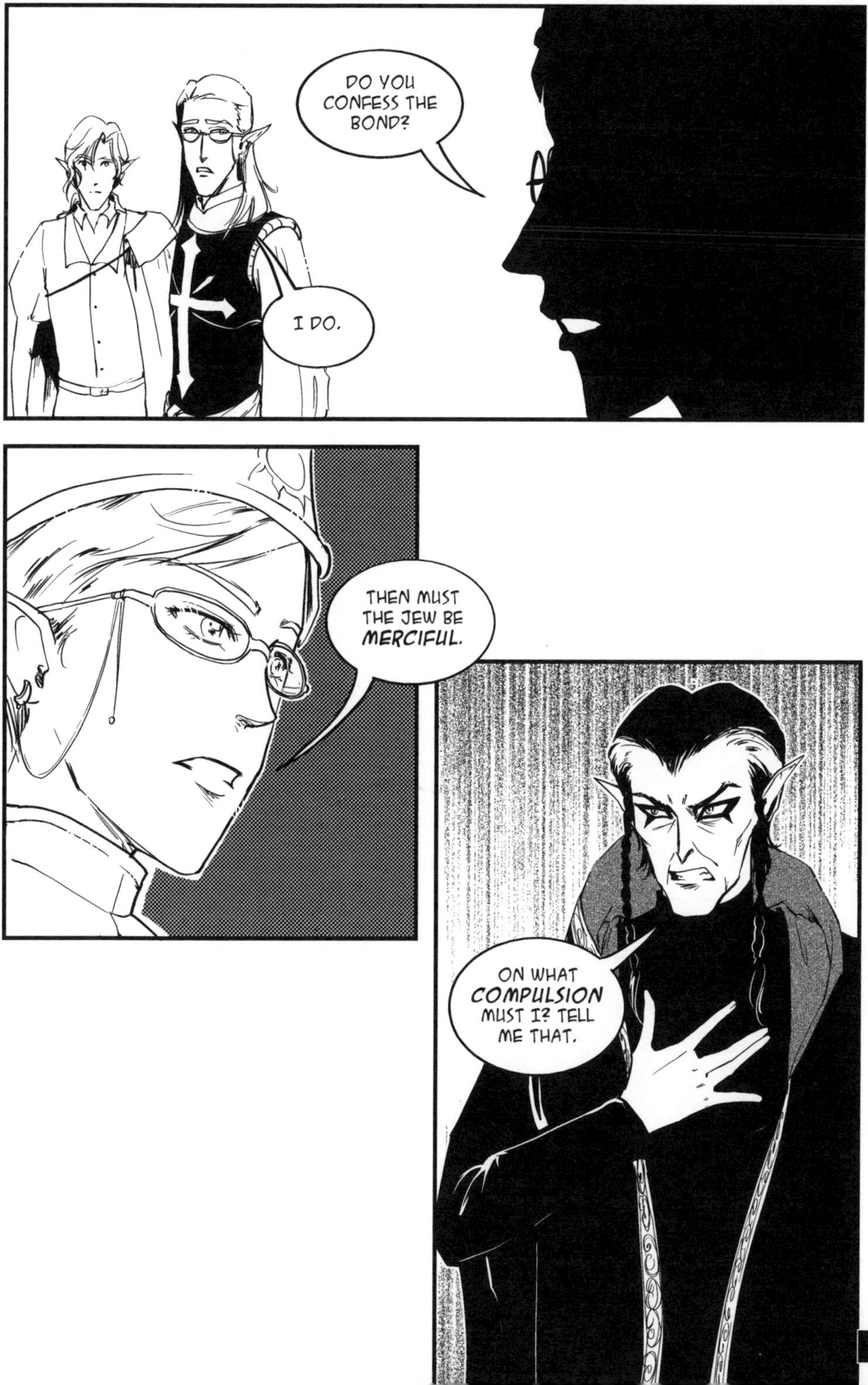
DO YOU CONFESS THE BOND?
I DO.
THEN MUST THE JEW BE *MERCIFUL*.
ON WHAT *COMPULSION* MUST I? TELL ME THAT.

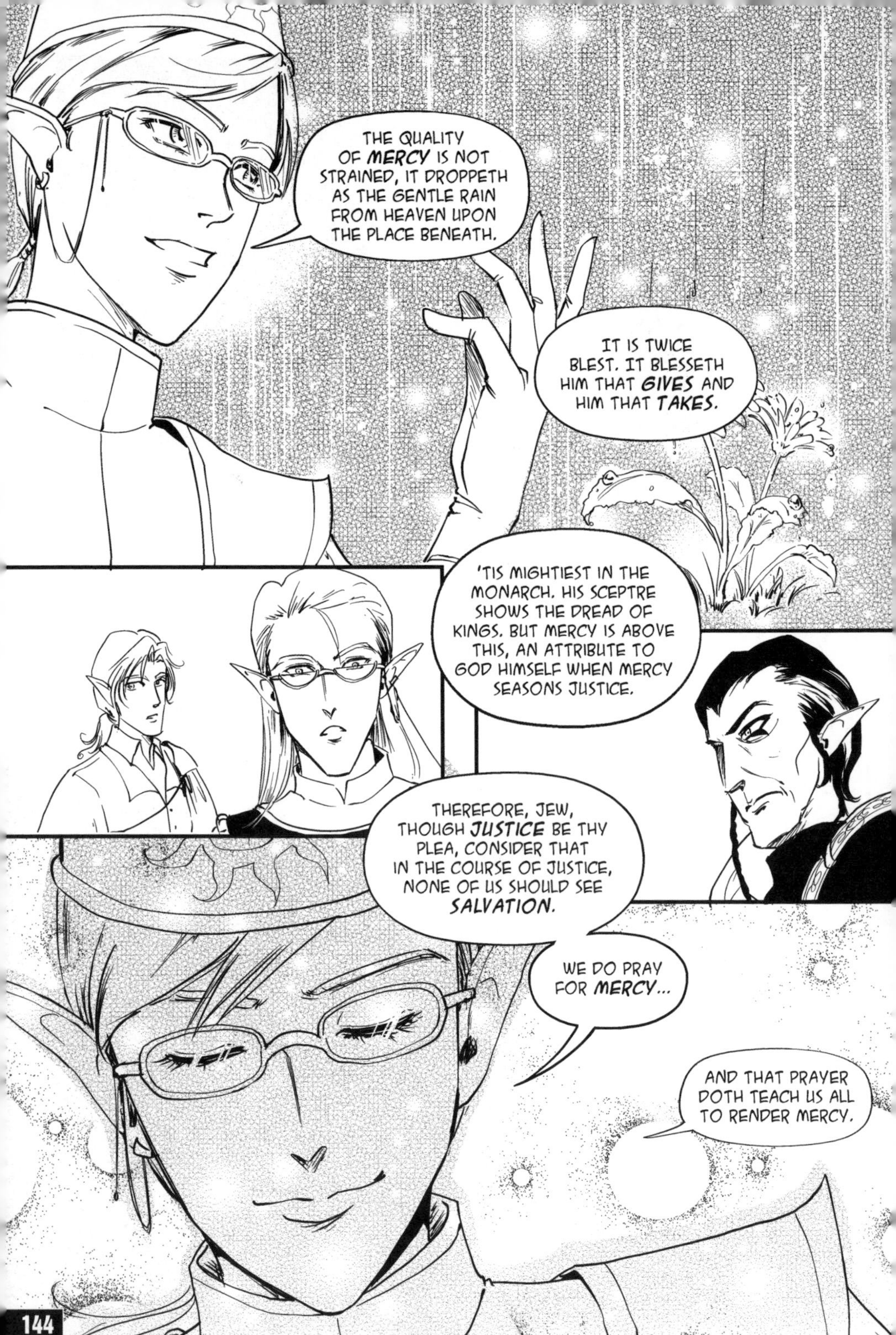
THE QUALITY OF MERCY IS NOT STRAINED, IT DROPPETH AS THE GENTLE RAIN FROM HEAVEN UPON THE PLACE BENEATH.
IT IS TWICE BLEST. IT BLESSETH HIM THAT GIVES AND HIM THAT TAKES.
'TIS MIGHTIEST IN THE MONARCH. HIS SCEPTRE SHOWS THE DREAD OF KINGS. BUT MERCY IS ABOVE THIS, AN ATTRIBUTE TO GOD HIMSELF WHEN MERCY SEASONS JUSTICE.
THEREFORE, JEW, THOUGH JUSTICE BE THY PLEA, CONSIDER THAT IN THE COURSE OF JUSTICE, NONE OF US SHOULD SEE SALVATION.
WE DO PRAY FOR MERCY...
AND THAT PRAYER DOTH TEACH US ALL TO RENDER MERCY.

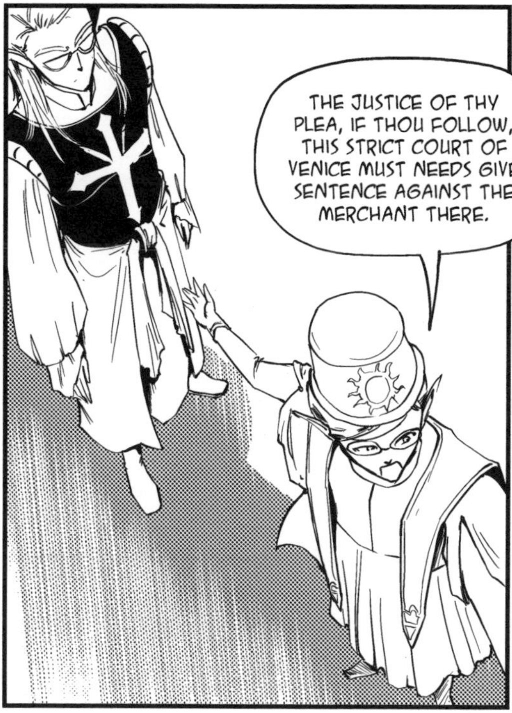
THE JUSTICE OF THY PLEA, IF THOU FOLLOW, THIS STRICT COURT OF VENICE MUST NEEDS GIVE SENTENCE AGAINST THE MERCHANT THERE.

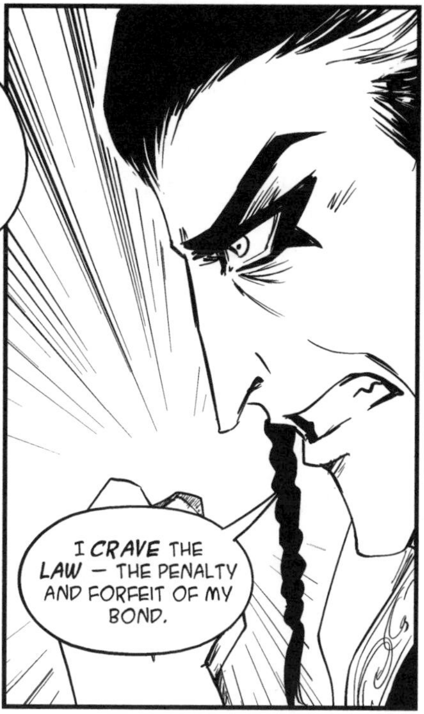
I **CRAVE** THE **LAW** — THE PENALTY AND FORFEIT OF MY BOND.

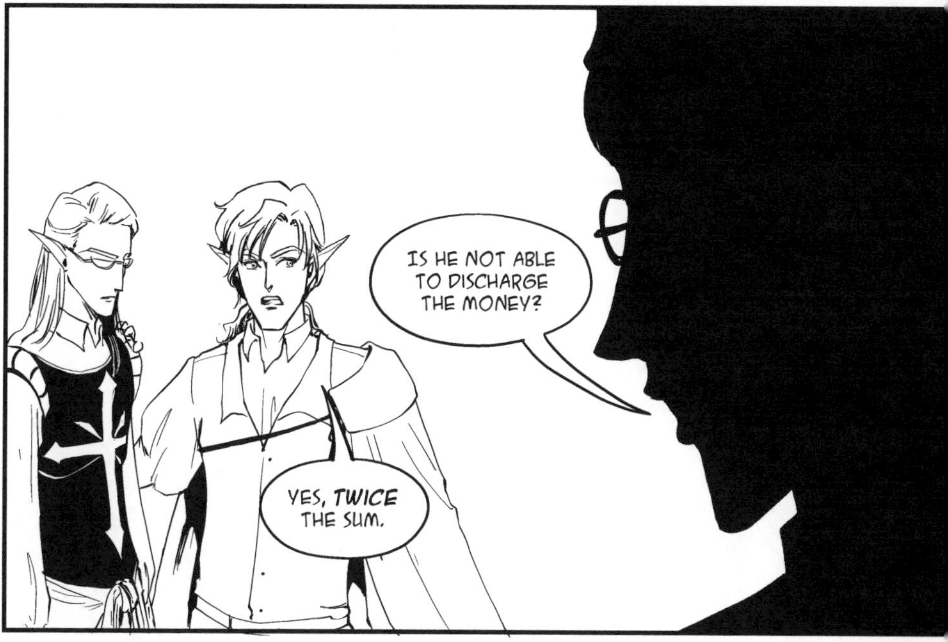
IS HE NOT ABLE TO DISCHARGE THE MONEY?
YES, **TWICE** THE SUM.

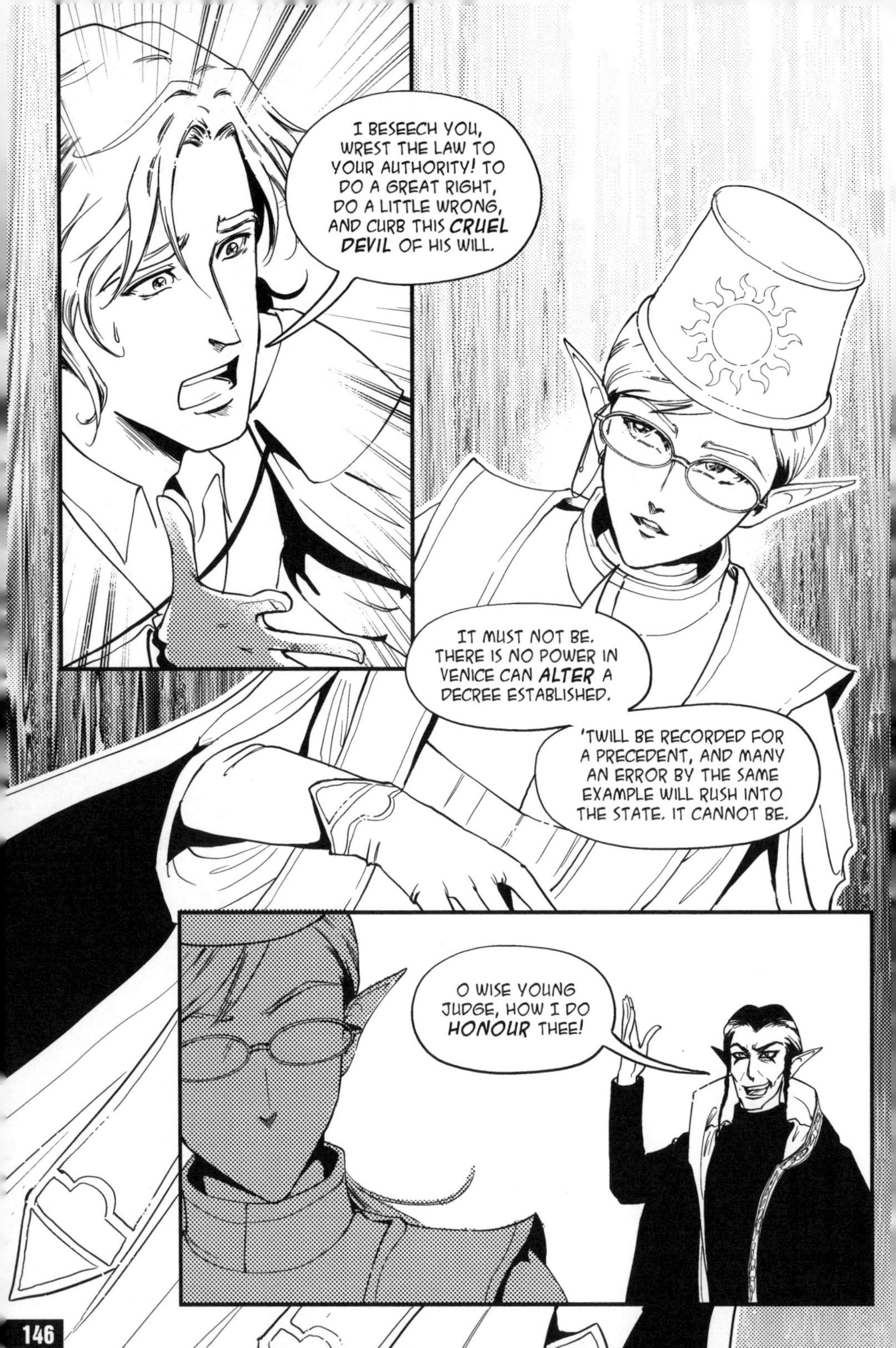
I BESEECH YOU, WREST THE LAW TO YOUR AUTHORITY! TO DO A GREAT RIGHT, DO A LITTLE WRONG, AND CURB THIS CRUEL DEVIL OF HIS WILL.
IT MUST NOT BE. THERE IS NO POWER IN VENICE CAN ALTER A DECREE ESTABLISHED.
'TWILL BE RECORDED FOR A PRECEDENT, AND MANY AN ERROR BY THE SAME EXAMPLE WILL RUSH INTO THE STATE. IT CANNOT BE.
O WISE YOUNG JUDGE, HOW I DO HONOUR THEE!

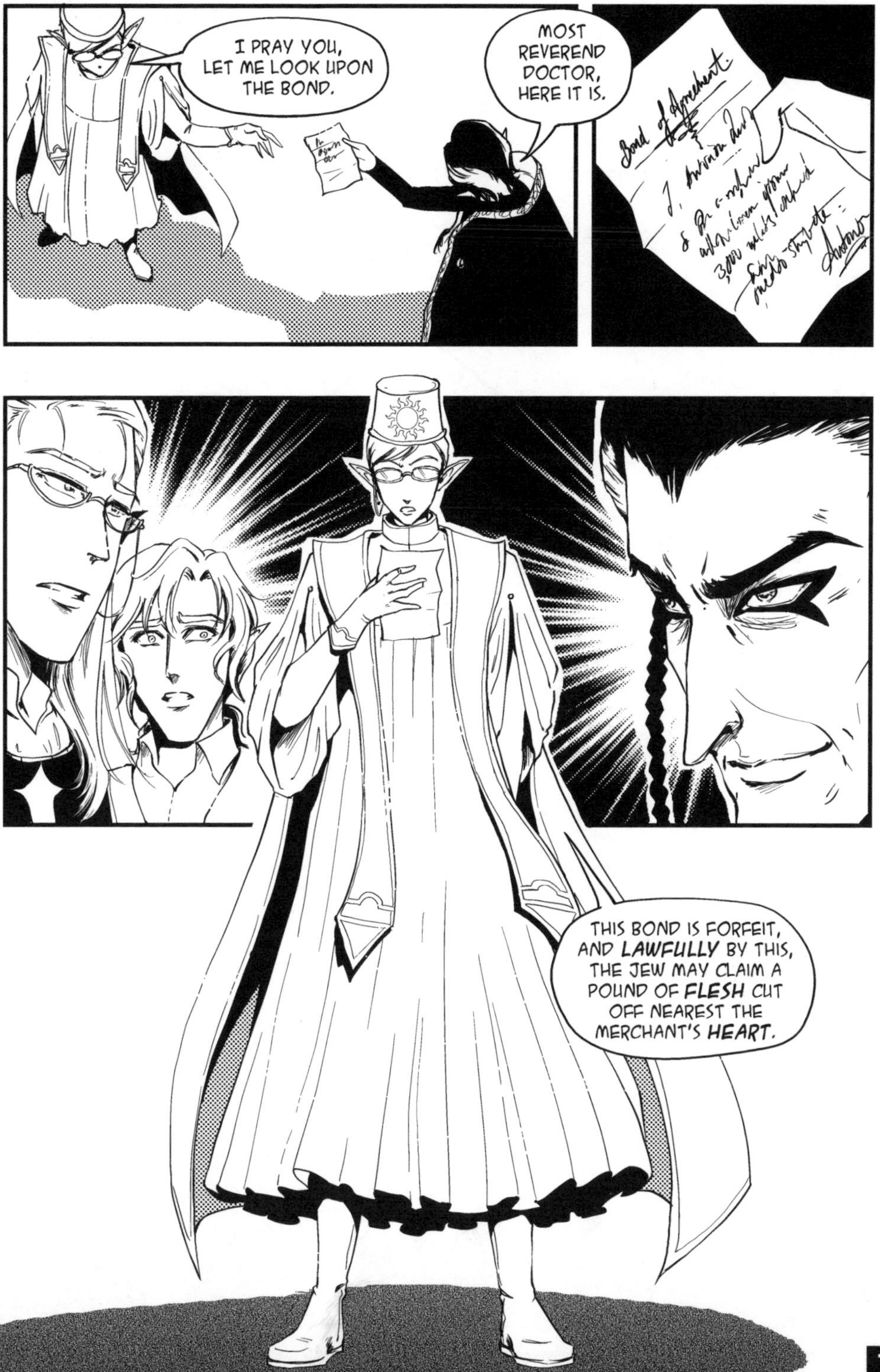
I PRAY YOU, LET ME LOOK UPON THE BOND.
MOST REVEREND DOCTOR, HERE IT IS.
Bond of Agreement
THIS BOND IS FORFEIT, AND **LAWFULLY** BY THIS, THE JEW MAY CLAIM A POUND OF **FLESH** CUT OFF NEAREST THE MERCHANT'S **HEART**.

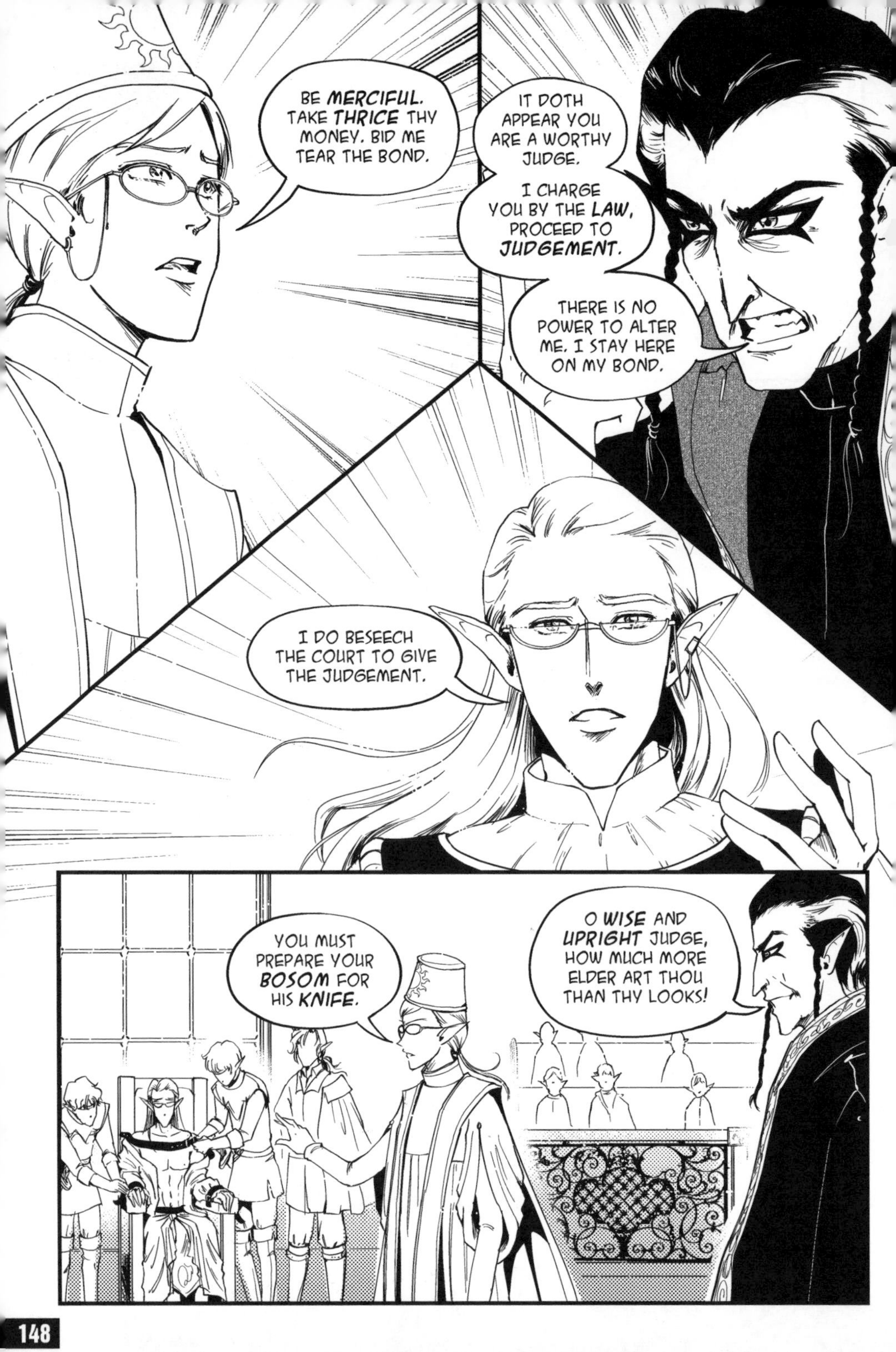
BE MERCIFUL. TAKE THRICE THY MONEY. BID ME TEAR THE BOND.
IT DOTH APPEAR YOU ARE A WORTHY JUDGE.
I CHARGE YOU BY THE LAW, PROCEED TO JUDGEMENT.
THERE IS NO POWER TO ALTER ME. I STAY HERE ON MY BOND.
I DO BESEECH THE COURT TO GIVE THE JUDGEMENT.
YOU MUST PREPARE YOUR BOSOM FOR HIS KNIFE.
O WISE AND UPRIGHT JUDGE, HOW MUCH MORE ELDER ART THOU THAN THY LOOKS!

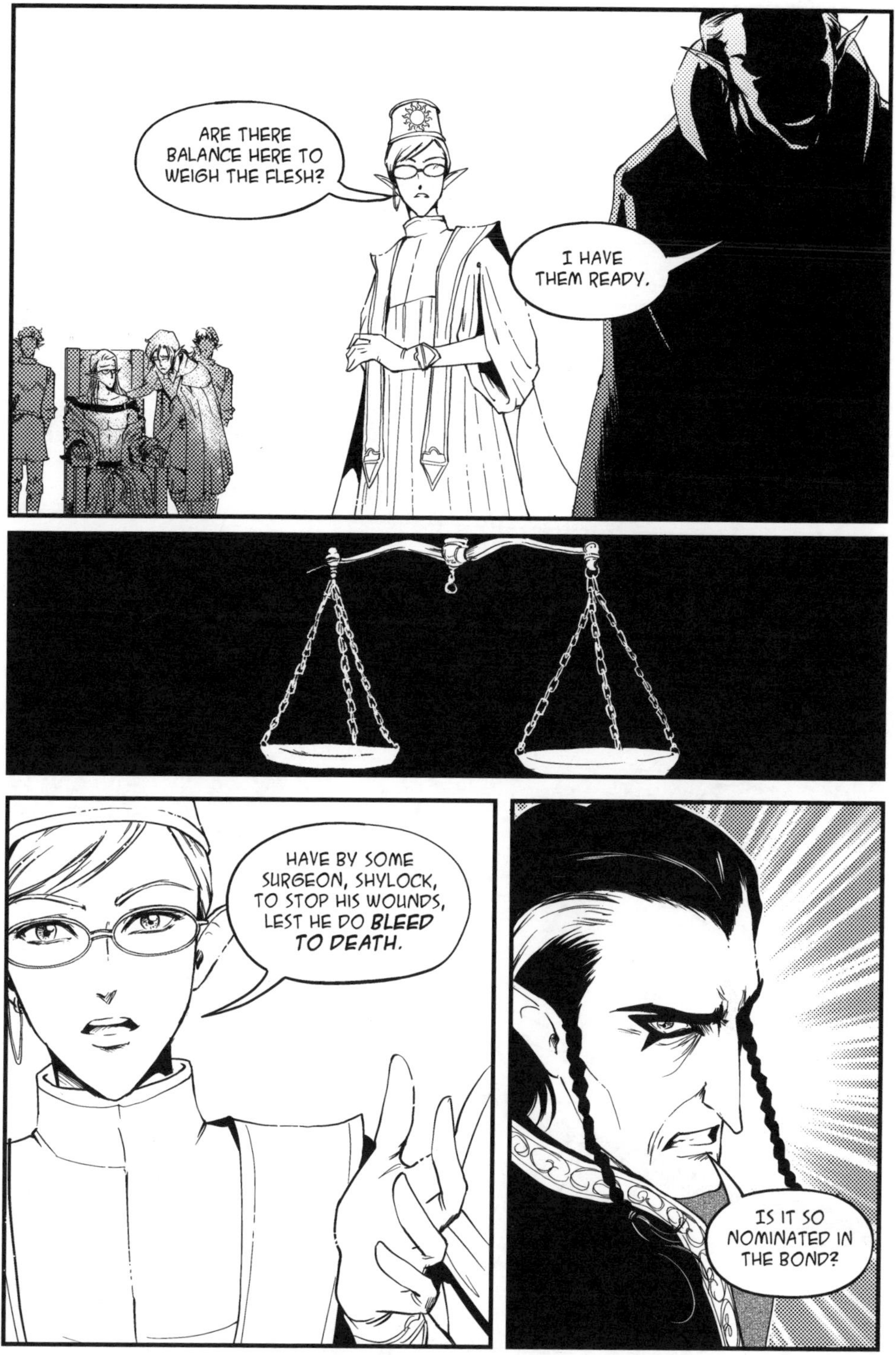
ARE THERE BALANCE HERE TO WEIGH THE FLESH?
I HAVE THEM READY.
HAVE BY SOME SURGEON, SHYLOCK, TO STOP HIS WOUNDS, LEST HE DO **BLEED TO DEATH**.
IS IT SO NOMINATED IN THE BOND?

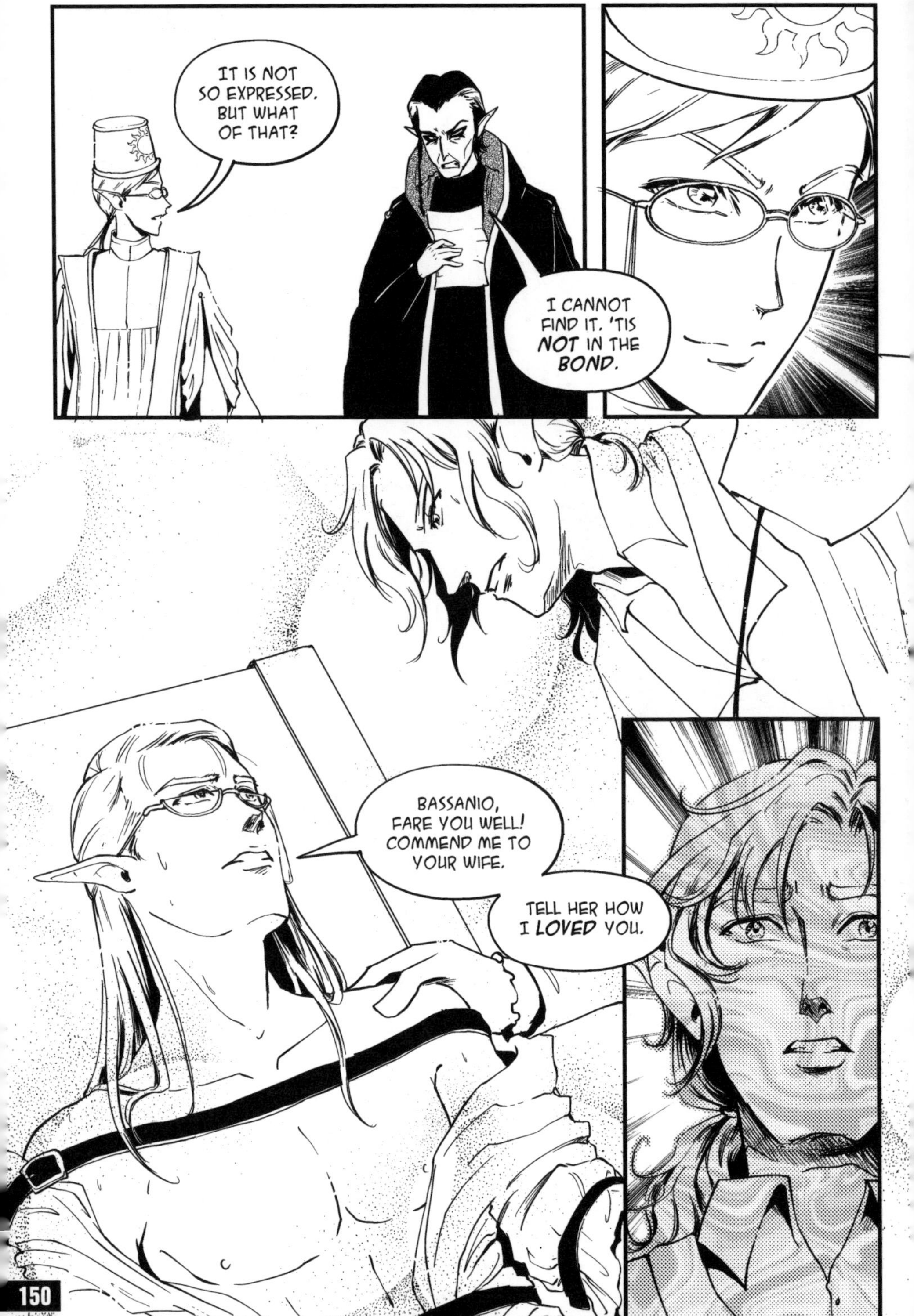
IT IS NOT SO EXPRESSED. BUT WHAT OF THAT?
I CANNOT FIND IT. 'TIS NOT IN THE BOND.
BASSANIO, FARE YOU WELL! COMMEND ME TO YOUR WIFE.
TELL HER HOW I LOVED YOU.

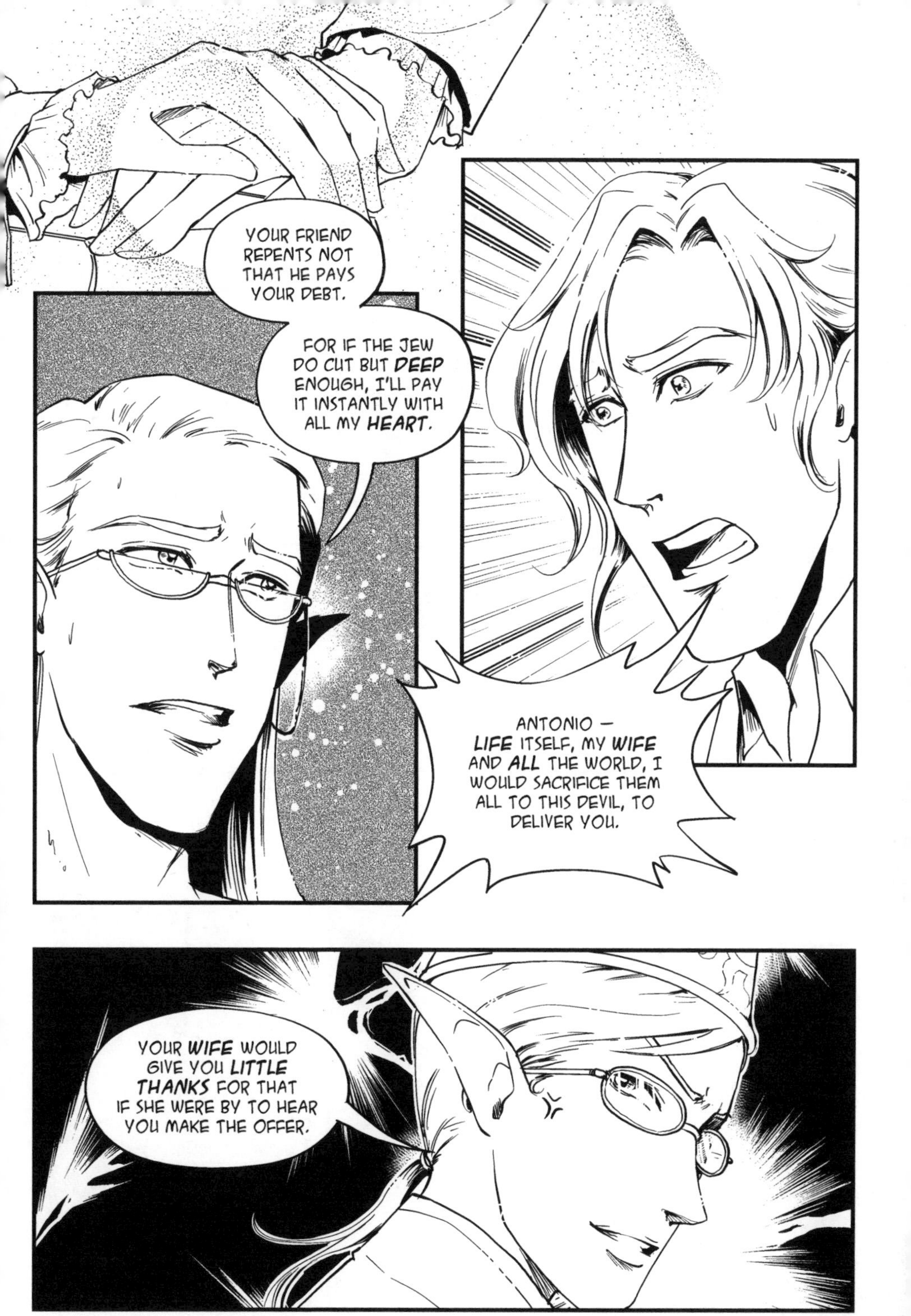
YOUR FRIEND REPENTS NOT THAT HE PAYS YOUR DEBT.
FOR IF THE JEW DO CUT BUT **DEEP** ENOUGH, I'LL PAY IT INSTANTLY WITH ALL MY **HEART**.
ANTONIO — **LIFE** ITSELF, MY **WIFE** AND **ALL** THE WORLD, I WOULD SACRIFICE THEM ALL TO THIS DEVIL, TO DELIVER YOU.
YOUR **WIFE** WOULD GIVE YOU **LITTLE THANKS** FOR THAT IF SHE WERE BY TO HEAR YOU MAKE THE OFFER.

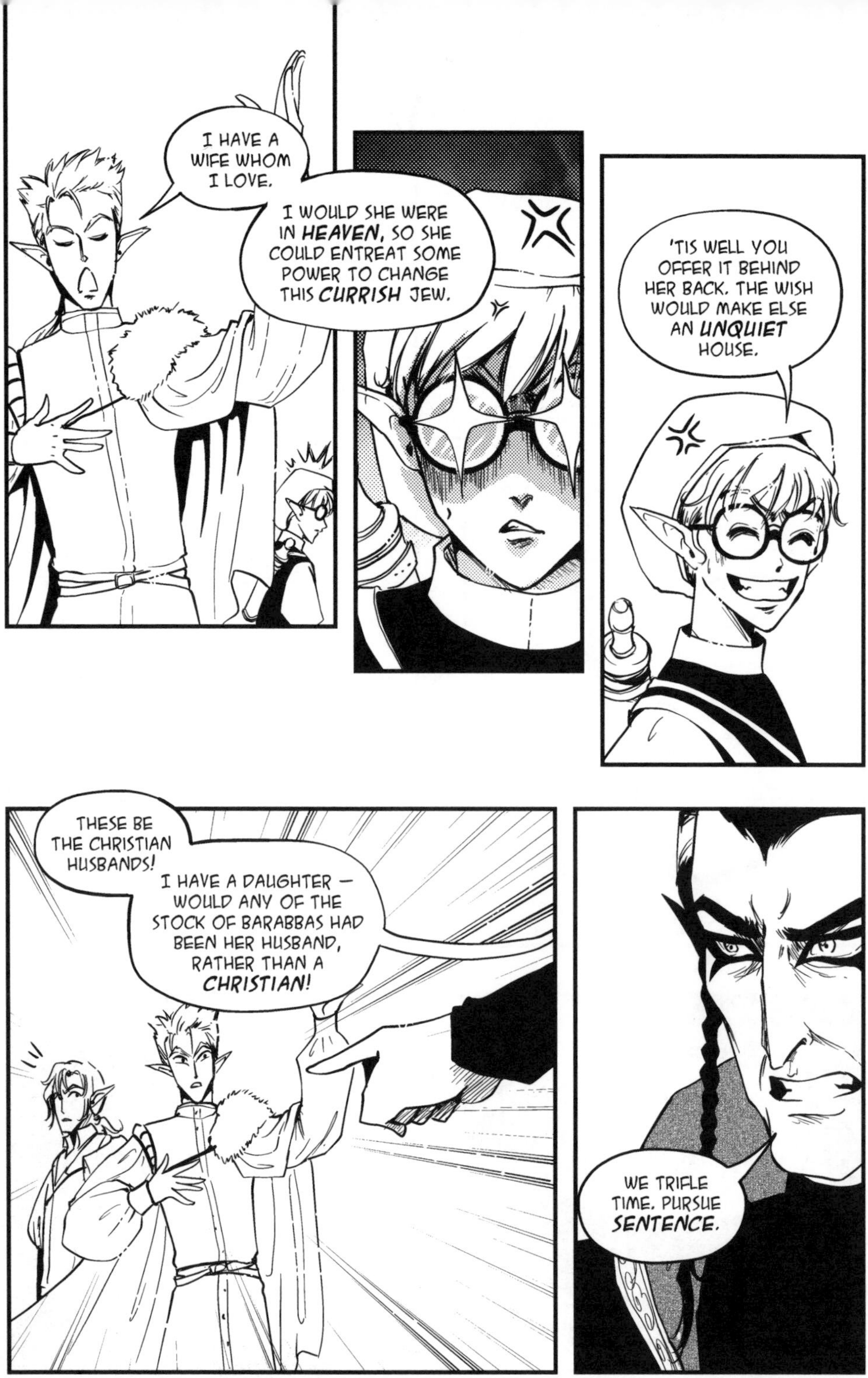
I HAVE A WIFE WHOM I LOVE.
I WOULD SHE WERE IN HEAVEN, SO SHE COULD ENTREAT SOME POWER TO CHANGE THIS CURRISH JEW.
'TIS WELL YOU OFFER IT BEHIND HER BACK. THE WISH WOULD MAKE ELSE AN UNQUIET HOUSE.
THESE BE THE CHRISTIAN HUSBANDS!
I HAVE A DAUGHTER — WOULD ANY OF THE STOCK OF BARABBAS HAD BEEN HER HUSBAND, RATHER THAN A CHRISTIAN!
WE TRIFLE TIME. PURSUE SENTENCE.

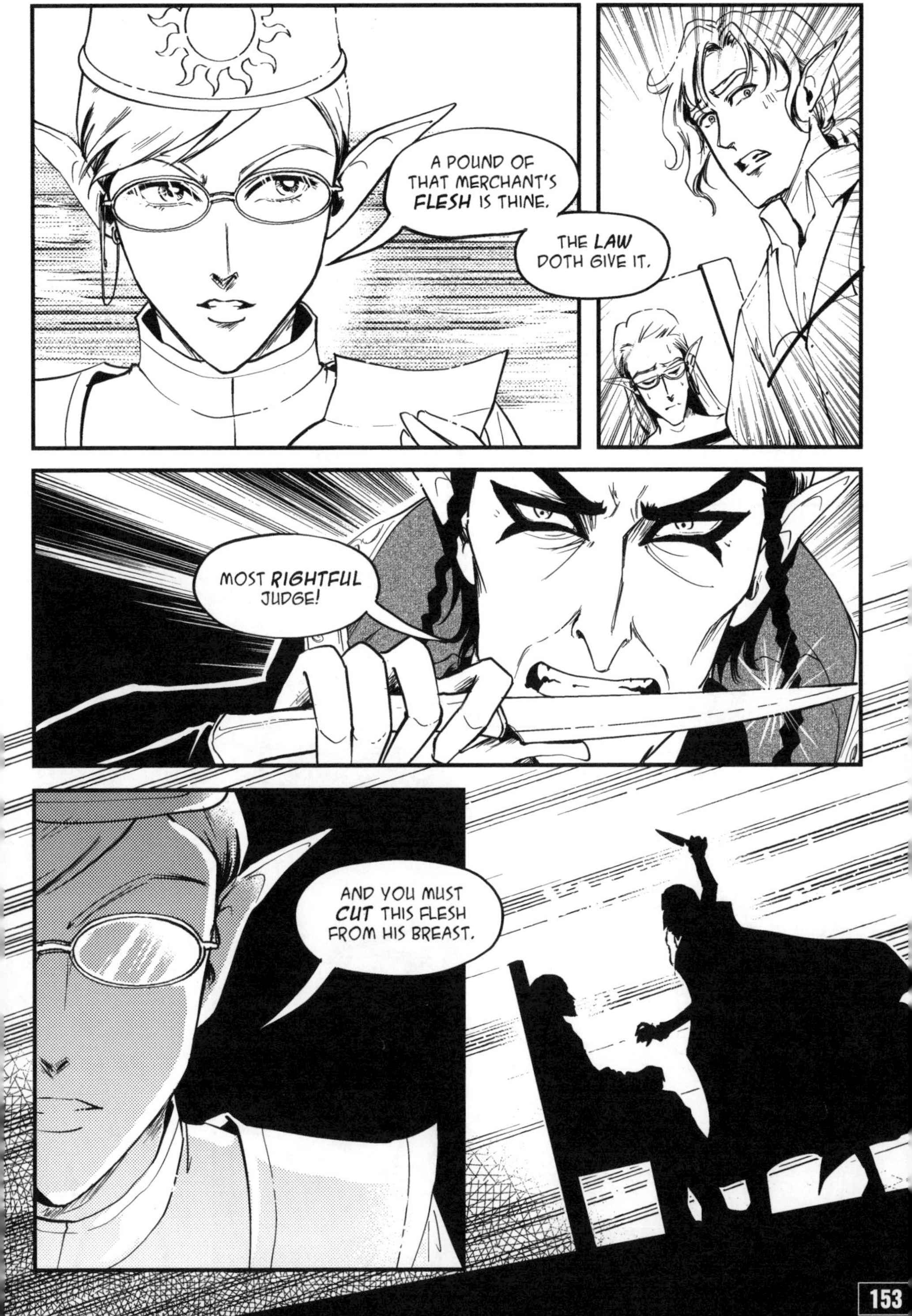
A POUND OF THAT MERCHANT'S **FLESH** IS THINE.
THE **LAW** DOTH GIVE IT.
MOST **RIGHTFUL** JUDGE!
AND YOU MUST **CUT** THIS FLESH FROM HIS BREAST.

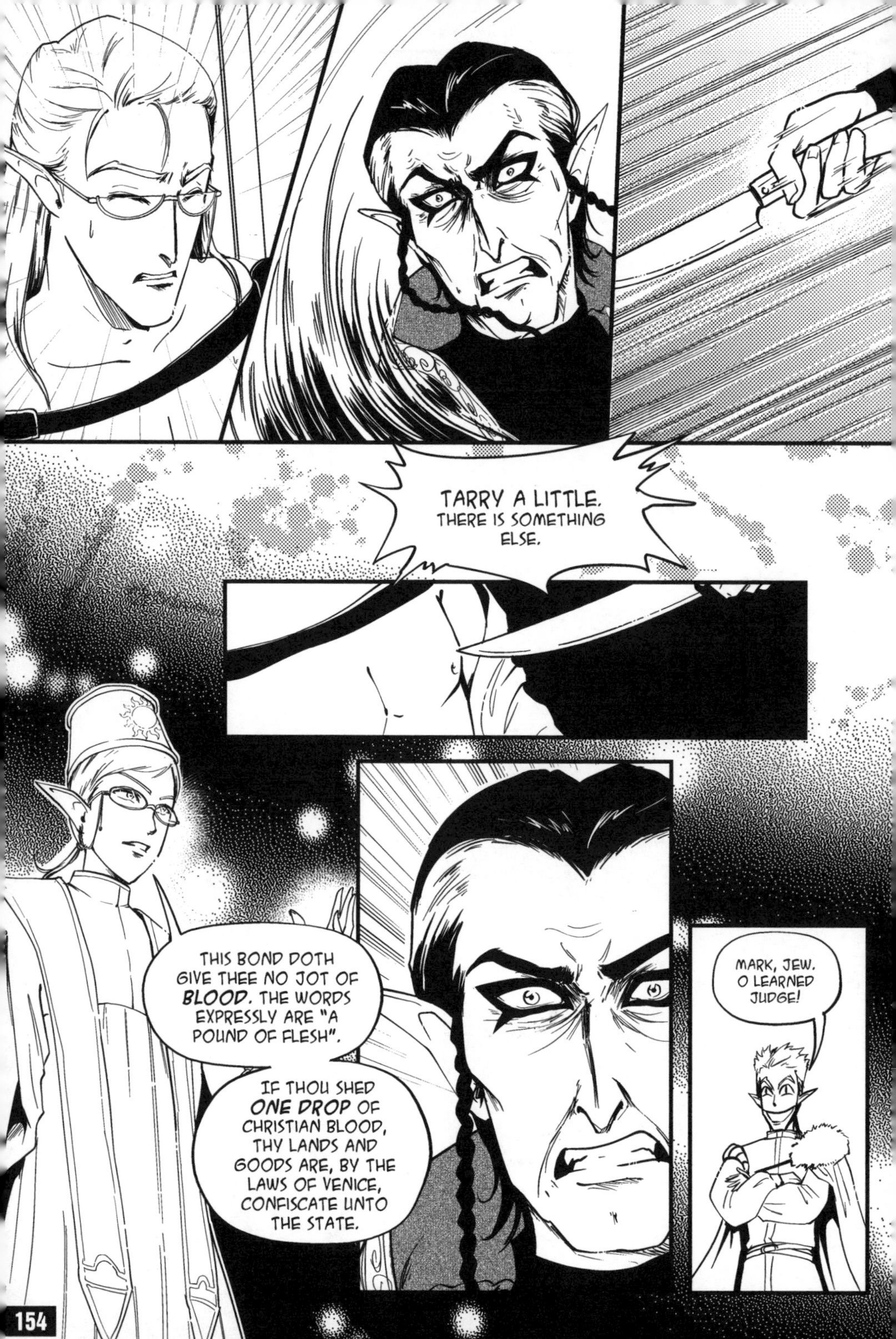
TARRY A LITTLE. THERE IS SOMETHING ELSE.
THIS BOND DOTH GIVE THEE NO JOT OF **BLOOD**. THE WORDS EXPRESSLY ARE "A POUND OF FLESH".
IF THOU SHED **ONE DROP** OF CHRISTIAN BLOOD, THY LANDS AND GOODS ARE, BY THE LAWS OF VENICE, CONFISCATE UNTO THE STATE.
MARK, JEW. O LEARNED JUDGE!

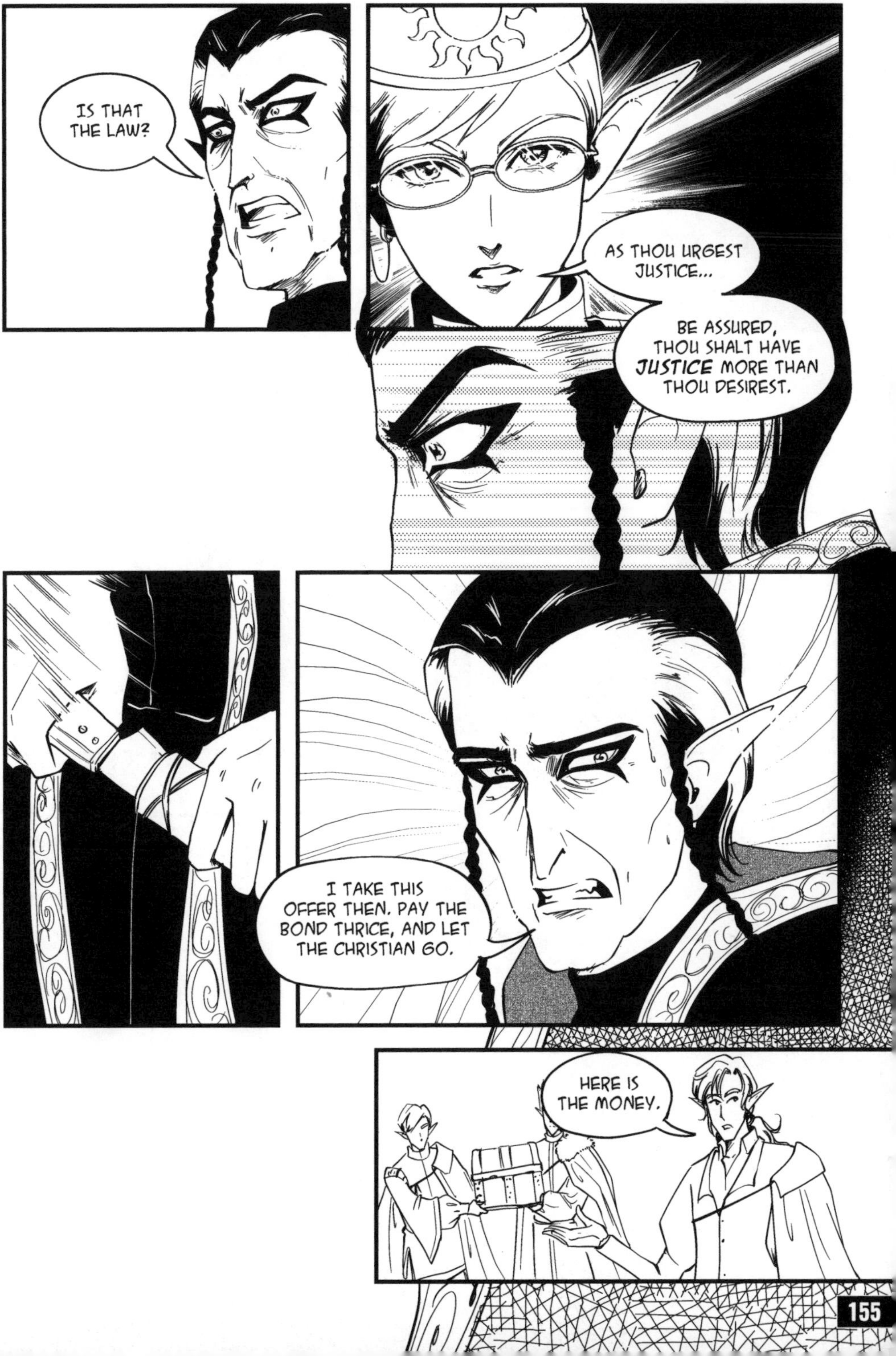
IS THAT THE LAW?
AS THOU URGEST JUSTICE...
BE ASSURED, THOU SHALT HAVE JUSTICE MORE THAN THOU DESIREST.
I TAKE THIS OFFER THEN. PAY THE BOND THRICE, AND LET THE CHRISTIAN GO.
HERE IS THE MONEY.

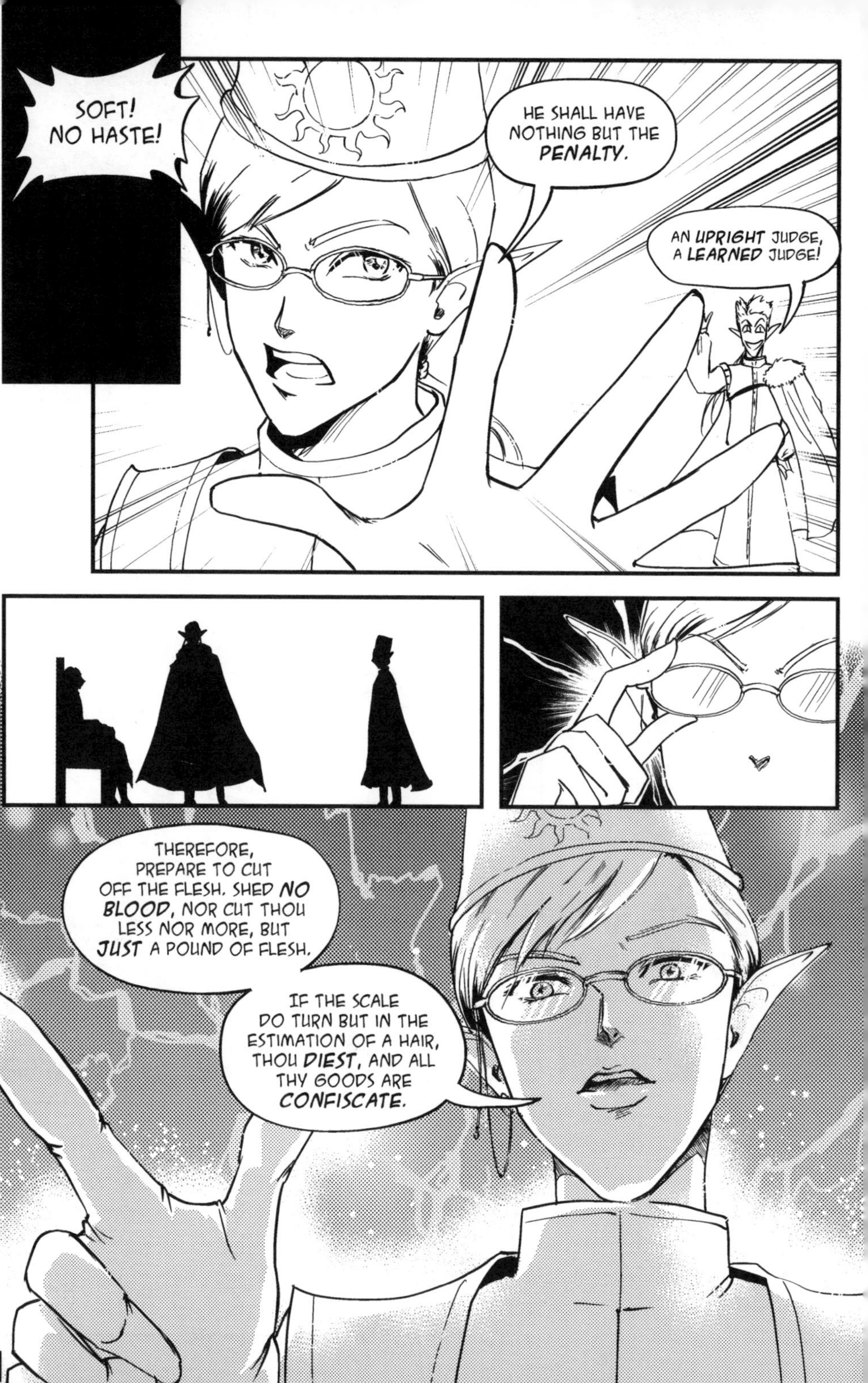
SOFT! NO HASTE!
HE SHALL HAVE NOTHING BUT THE PENALTY.
AN UPRIGHT JUDGE, A LEARNED JUDGE!
THEREFORE, PREPARE TO CUT OFF THE FLESH. SHED NO BLOOD, NOR CUT THOU LESS NOR MORE, BUT JUST A POUND OF FLESH.
IF THE SCALE DO TURN BUT IN THE ESTIMATION OF A HAIR, THOU DIEST, AND ALL THY GOODS ARE CONFISCATE.

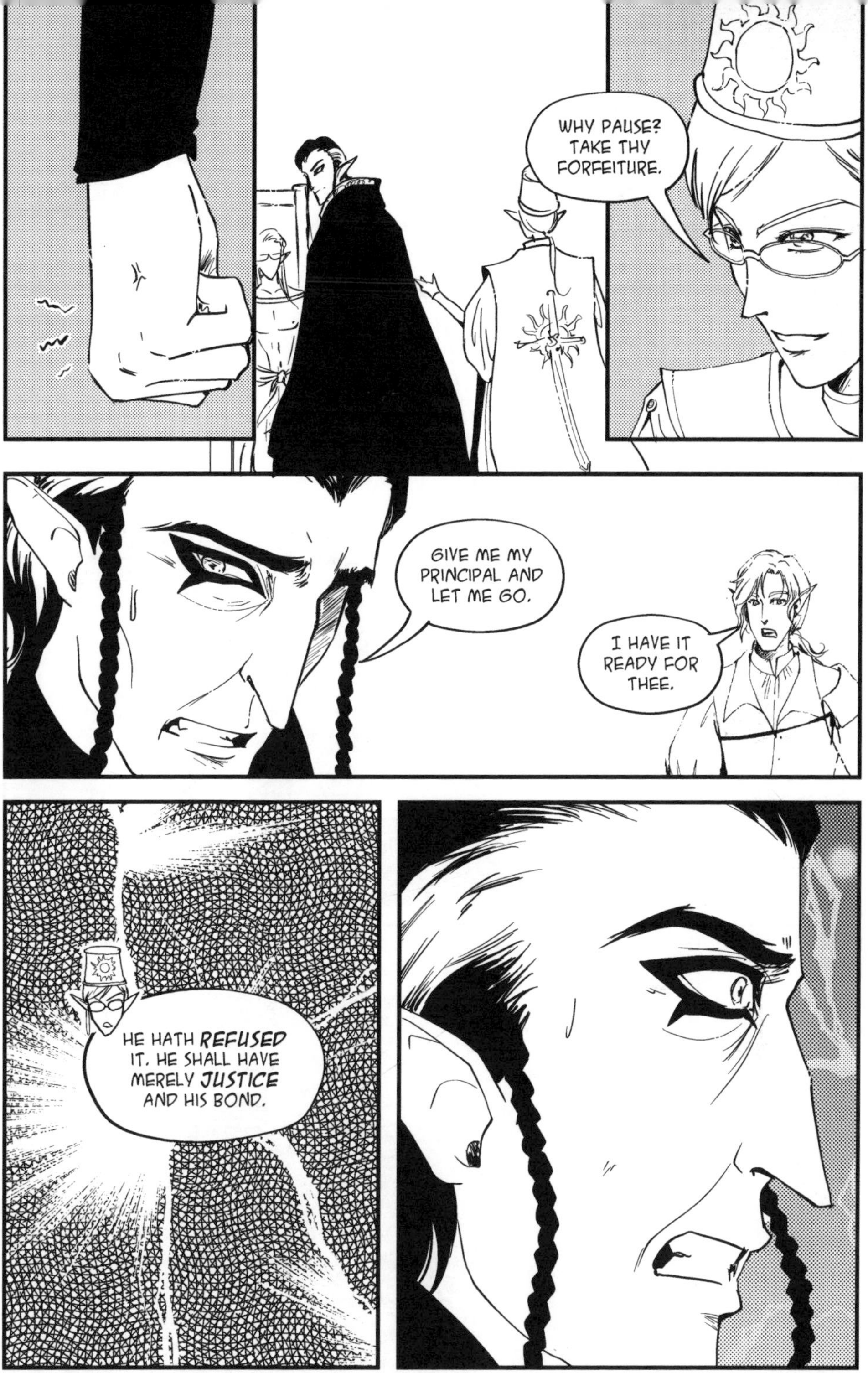

WHY PAUSE? TAKE THY FORFEITURE.
GIVE ME MY PRINCIPAL AND LET ME GO.
I HAVE IT READY FOR THEE.
HE HATH **REFUSED** IT. HE SHALL HAVE MERELY **JUSTICE** AND HIS BOND.

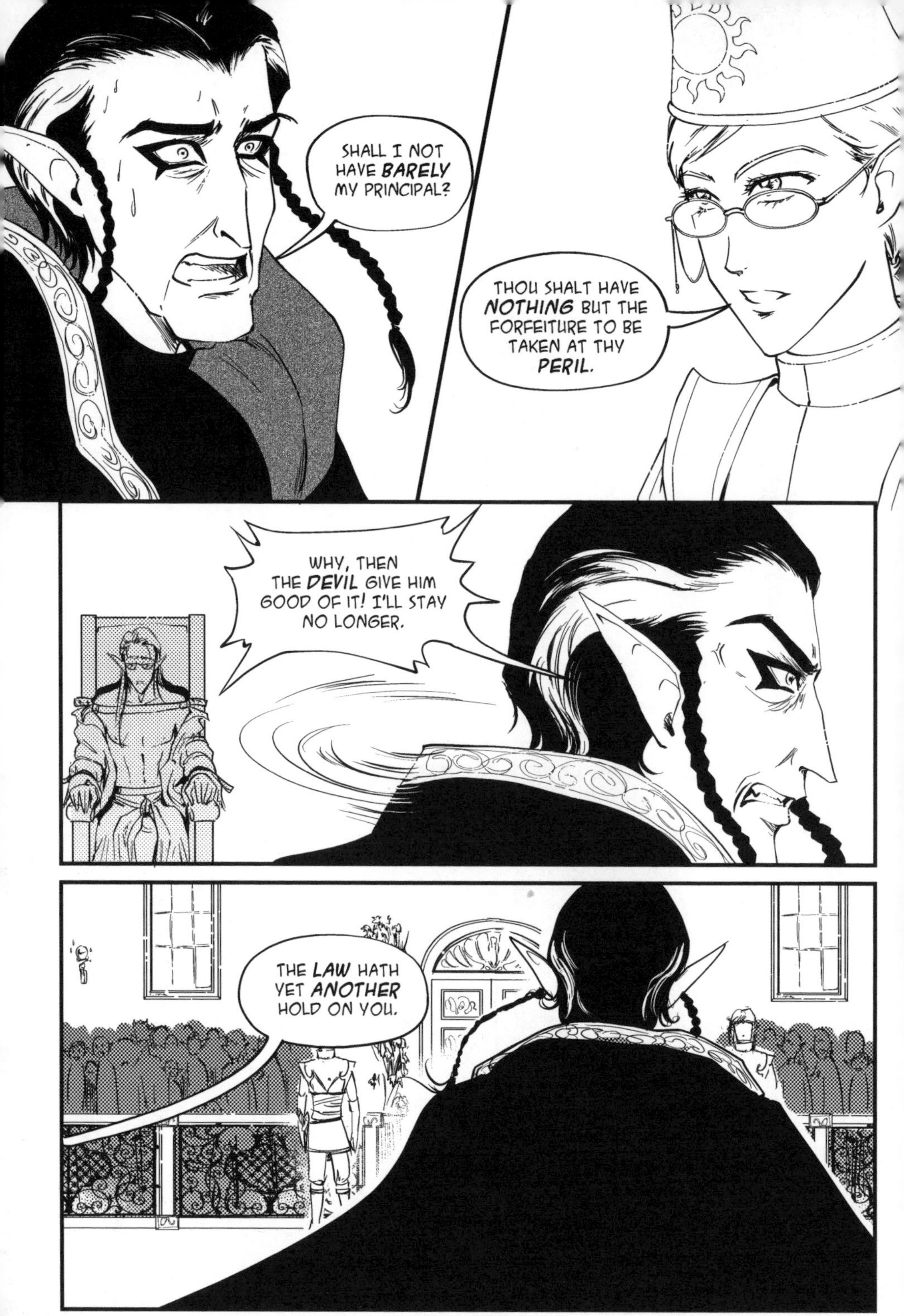
SHALL I NOT HAVE BARELY MY PRINCIPAL?
THOU SHALT HAVE NOTHING BUT THE FORFEITURE TO BE TAKEN AT THY PERIL.
WHY, THEN THE DEVIL GIVE HIM GOOD OF IT! I'LL STAY NO LONGER.
THE LAW HATH YET ANOTHER HOLD ON YOU.

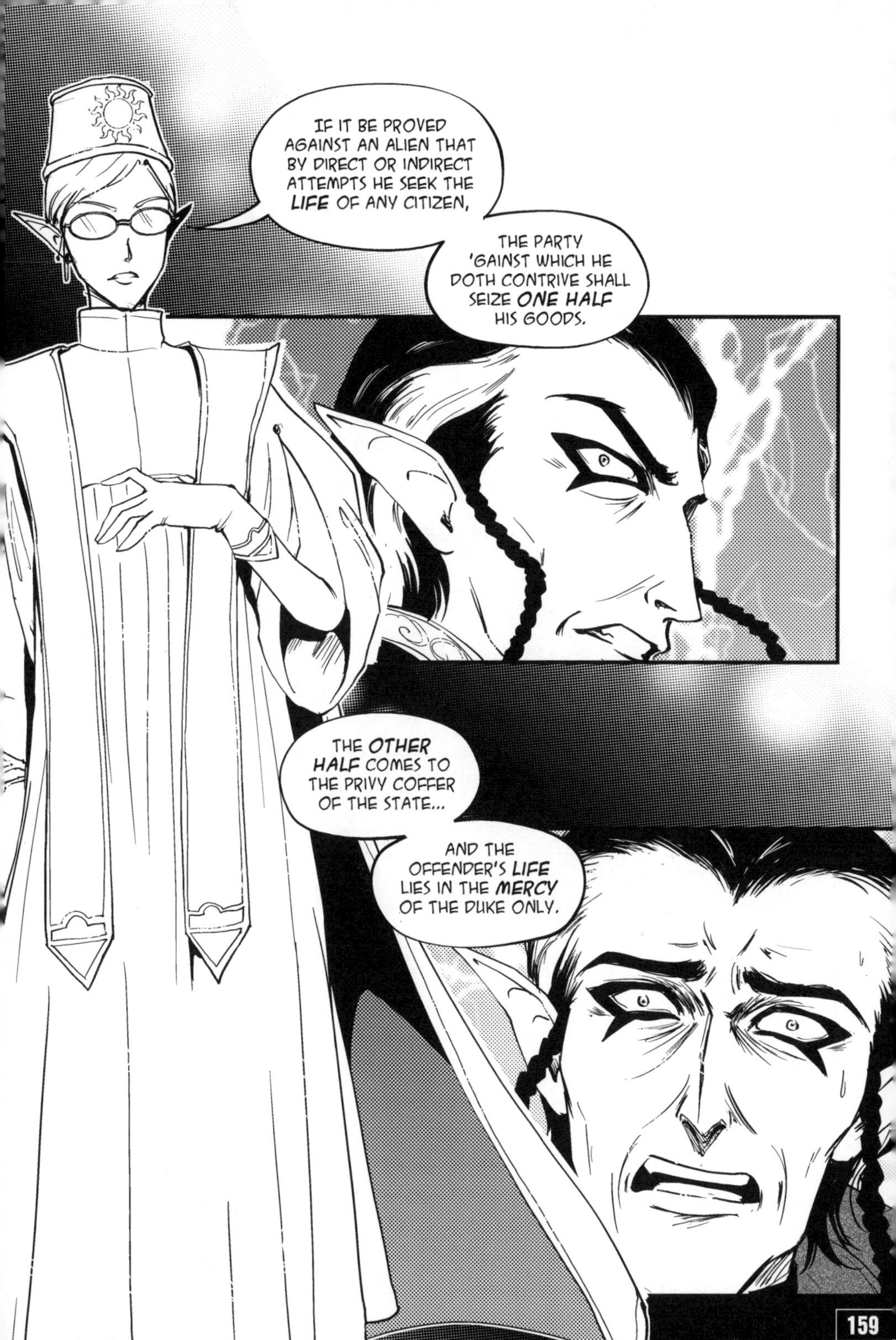
IF IT BE PROVED AGAINST AN ALIEN THAT BY DIRECT OR INDIRECT ATTEMPTS HE SEEK THE **LIFE** OF ANY CITIZEN,
THE PARTY 'GAINST WHICH HE DOTH CONTRIVE SHALL SEIZE **ONE HALF** HIS GOODS.
THE **OTHER HALF** COMES TO THE PRIVY COFFER OF THE STATE...
AND THE OFFENDER'S **LIFE** LIES IN THE **MERCY** OF THE DUKE ONLY.

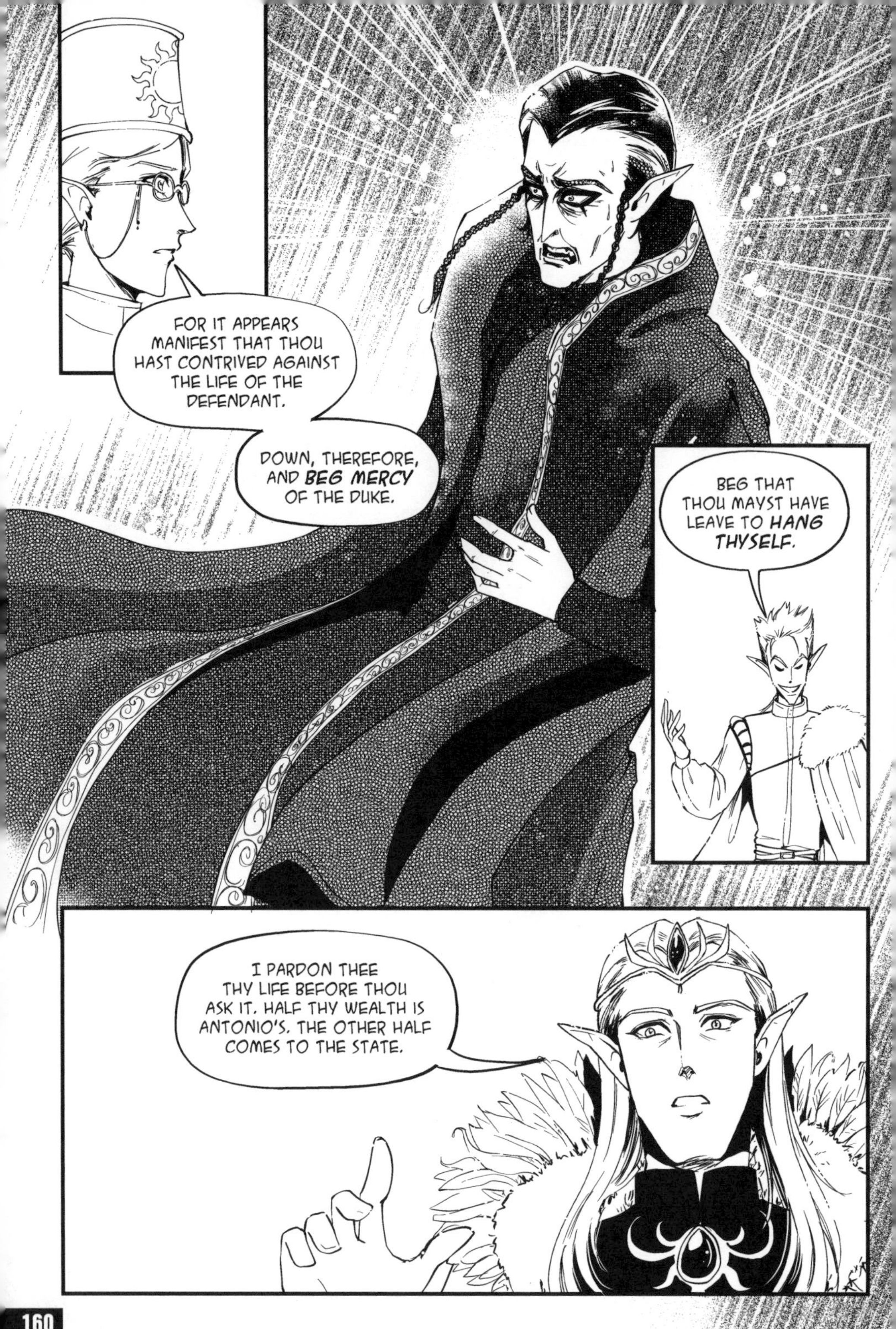
FOR IT APPEARS MANIFEST THAT THOU HAST CONTRIVED AGAINST THE LIFE OF THE DEFENDANT.
DOWN, THEREFORE, AND BEG MERCY OF THE DUKE.
BEG THAT THOU MAYST HAVE LEAVE TO HANG THYSELF.
I PARDON THEE THY LIFE BEFORE THOU ASK IT. HALF THY WEALTH IS ANTONIO'S. THE OTHER HALF COMES TO THE STATE.

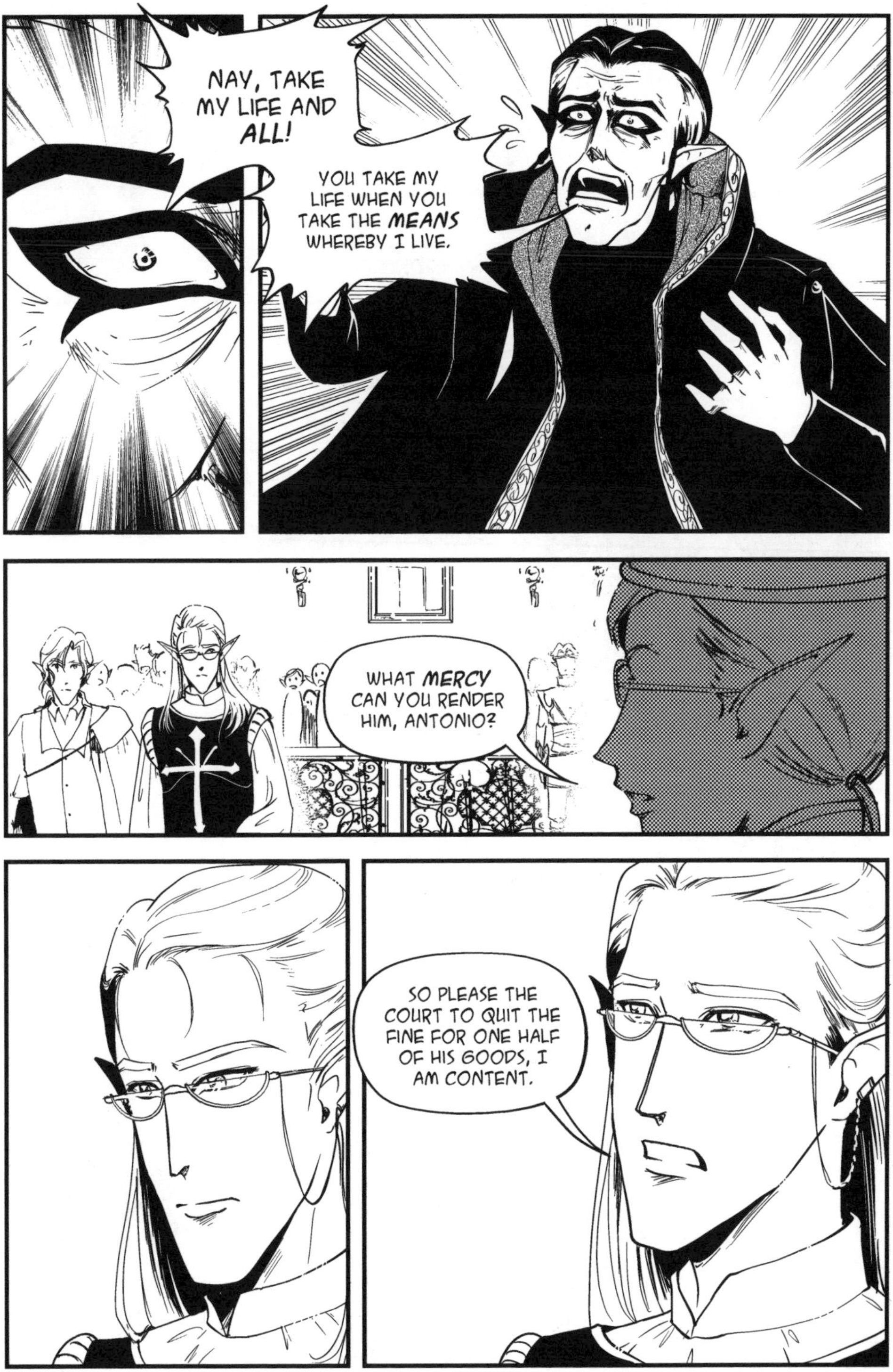
NAY, TAKE MY LIFE AND ALL!
YOU TAKE MY LIFE WHEN YOU TAKE THE MEANS WHEREBY I LIVE.
WHAT MERCY CAN YOU RENDER HIM, ANTONIO?
SO PLEASE THE COURT TO QUIT THE FINE FOR ONE HALF OF HIS GOODS, I AM CONTENT.

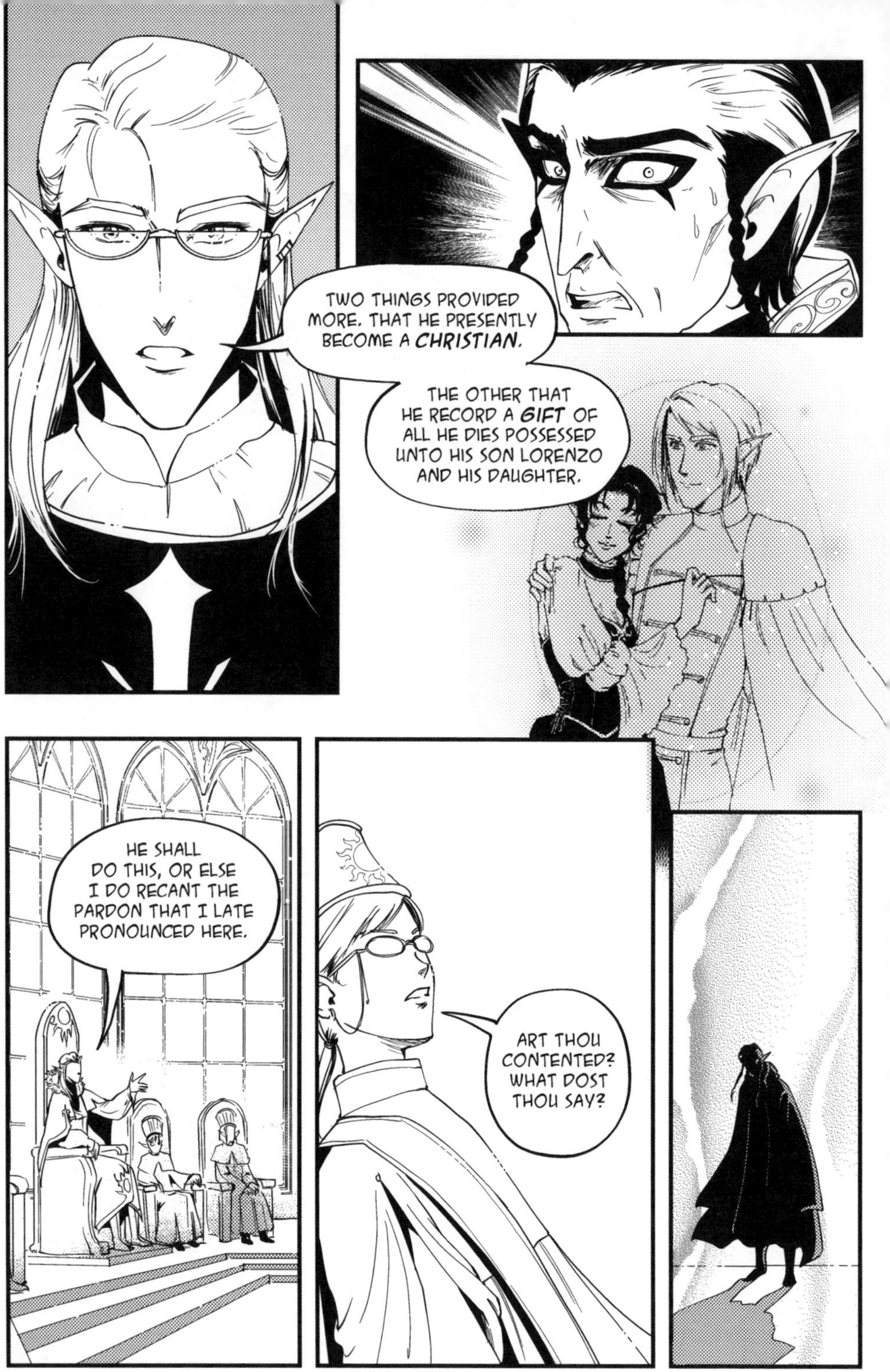
TWO THINGS PROVIDED MORE. THAT HE PRESENTLY BECOME A CHRISTIAN.
THE OTHER THAT HE RECORD A GIFT OF ALL HE DIES POSSESSED UNTO HIS SON LORENZO AND HIS DAUGHTER.
HE SHALL DO THIS, OR ELSE I DO RECANT THE PARDON THAT I LATE PRONOUNCED HERE.
ART THOU CONTENTED? WHAT DOST THOU SAY?

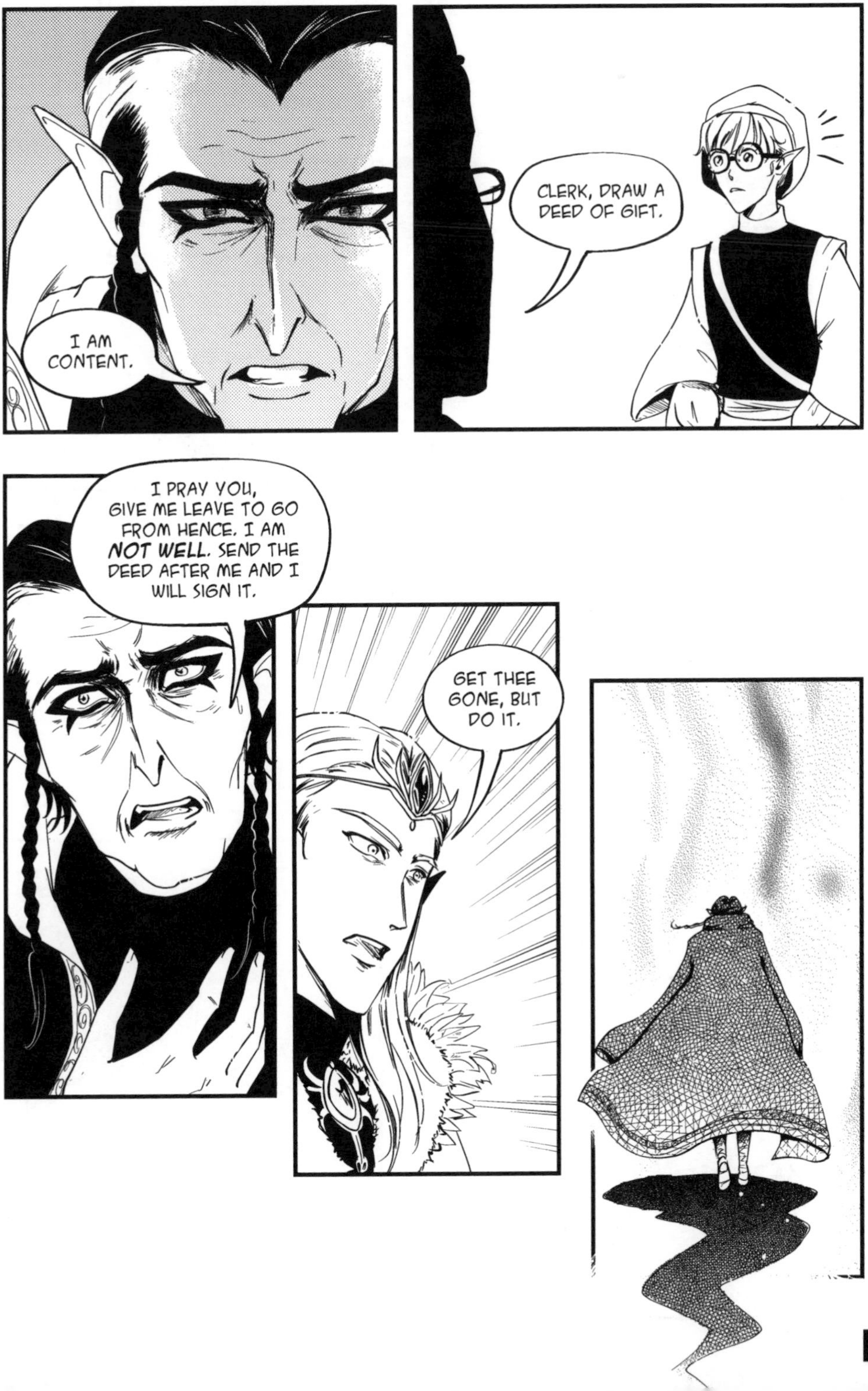

I AM CONTENT.
CLERK, DRAW A DEED OF GIFT.
I PRAY YOU, GIVE ME LEAVE TO GO FROM HENCE. I AM NOT WELL. SEND THE DEED AFTER ME AND I WILL SIGN IT.
GET THEE GONE, BUT DO IT.

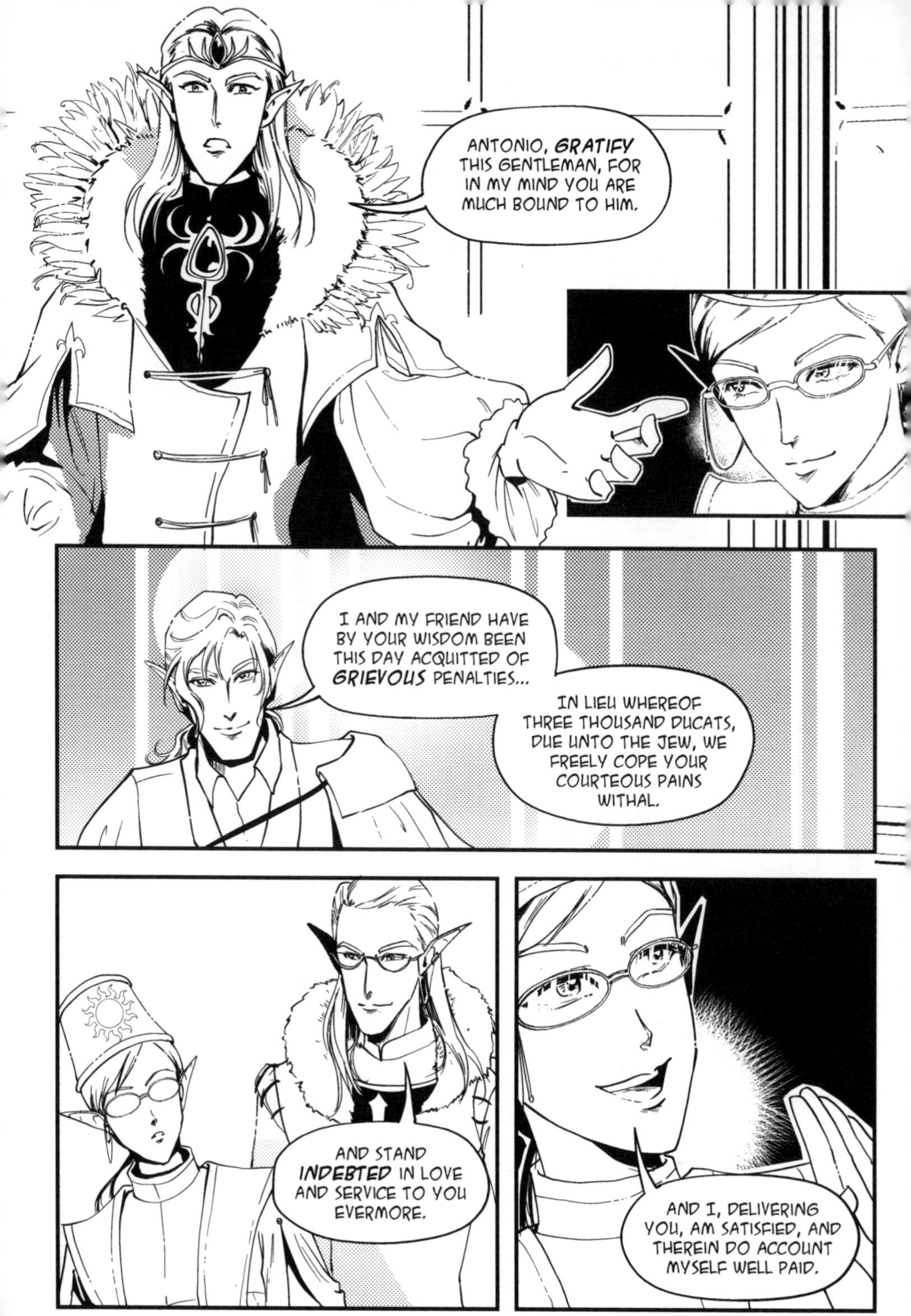
ANTONIO, GRATIFY THIS GENTLEMAN, FOR IN MY MIND YOU ARE MUCH BOUND TO HIM.
I AND MY FRIEND HAVE BY YOUR WISDOM BEEN THIS DAY ACQUITTED OF GRIEVOUS PENALTIES...
IN LIEU WHEREOF THREE THOUSAND DUCATS, DUE UNTO THE JEW, WE FREELY COPE YOUR COURTEOUS PAINS WITHAL.
AND STAND INDEBTED IN LOVE AND SERVICE TO YOU EVERMORE.
AND I, DELIVERING YOU, AM SATISFIED, AND THEREIN DO ACCOUNT MYSELF WELL PAID.

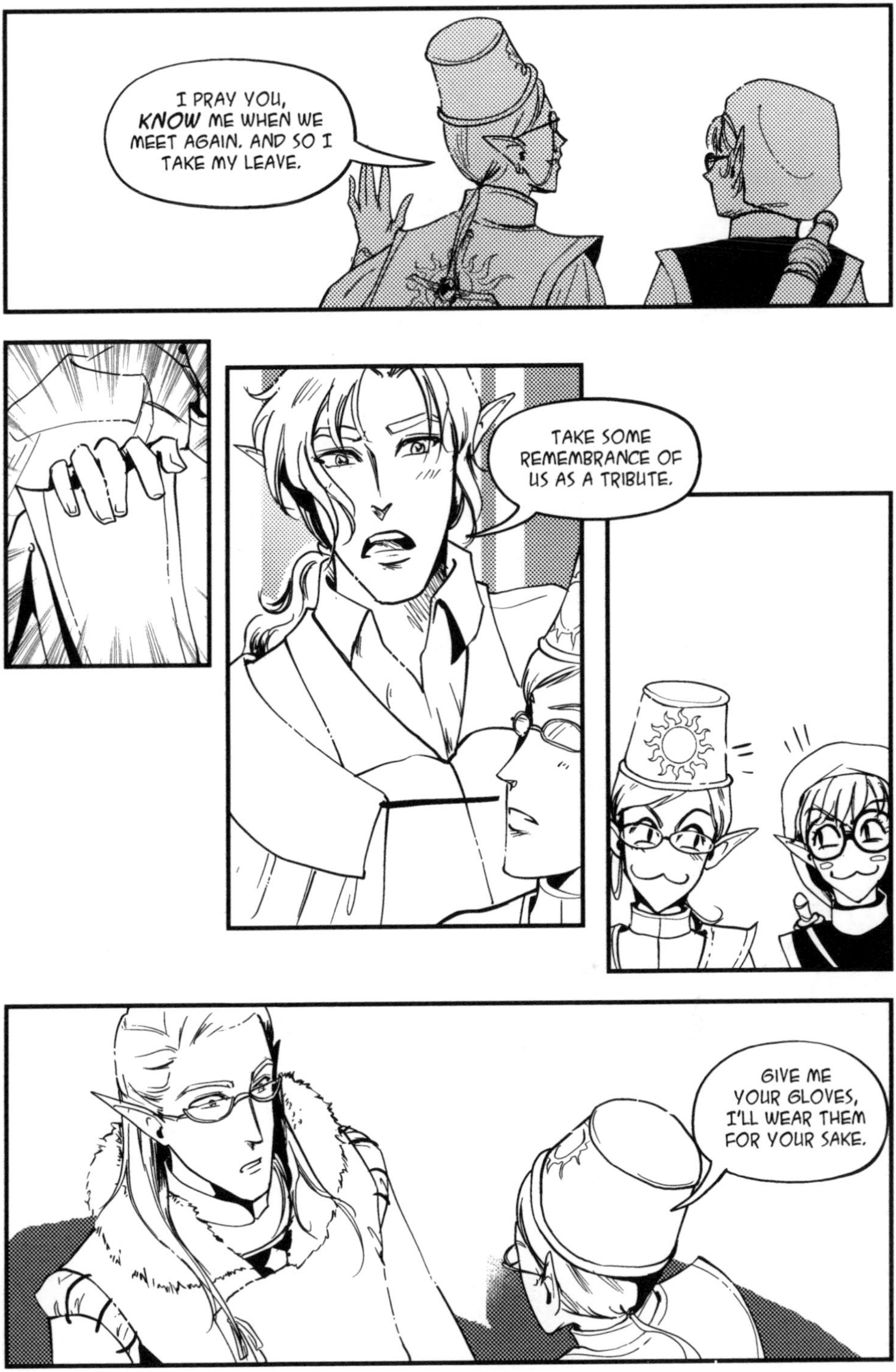

I PRAY YOU, KNOW ME WHEN WE MEET AGAIN. AND SO I TAKE MY LEAVE.
TAKE SOME REMEMBRANCE OF US AS A TRIBUTE.
GIVE ME YOUR GLOVES, I'LL WEAR THEM FOR YOUR SAKE.

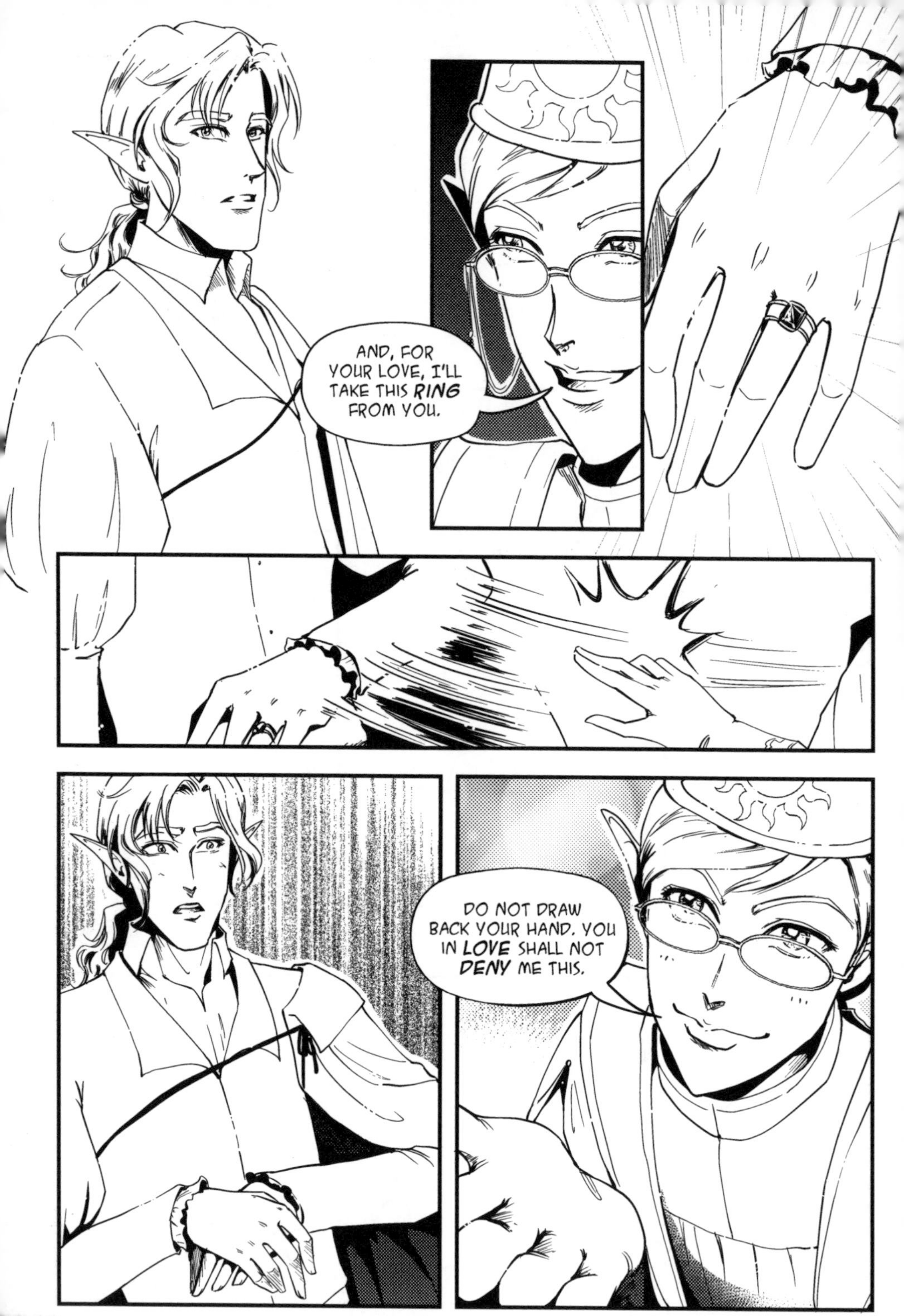
AND, FOR YOUR LOVE, I'LL TAKE THIS **RING** FROM YOU.
DO NOT DRAW BACK YOUR HAND. YOU IN **LOVE** SHALL NOT **DENY** ME THIS.

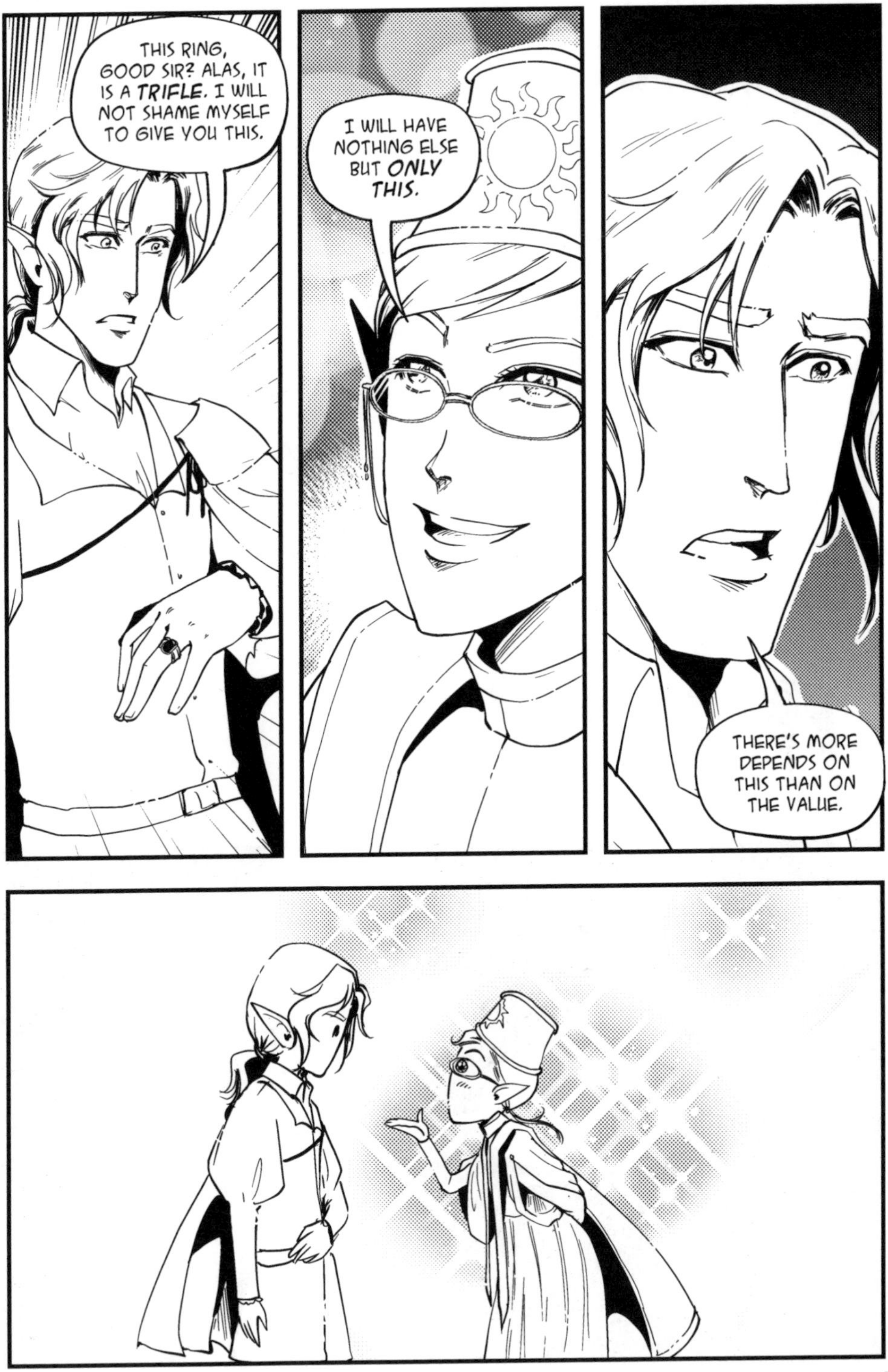
THIS RING, GOOD SIR? ALAS, IT IS A **TRIFLE**. I WILL NOT SHAME MYSELF TO GIVE YOU THIS.
I WILL HAVE NOTHING ELSE BUT **ONLY THIS**.
THERE'S MORE DEPENDS ON THIS THAN ON THE VALUE.

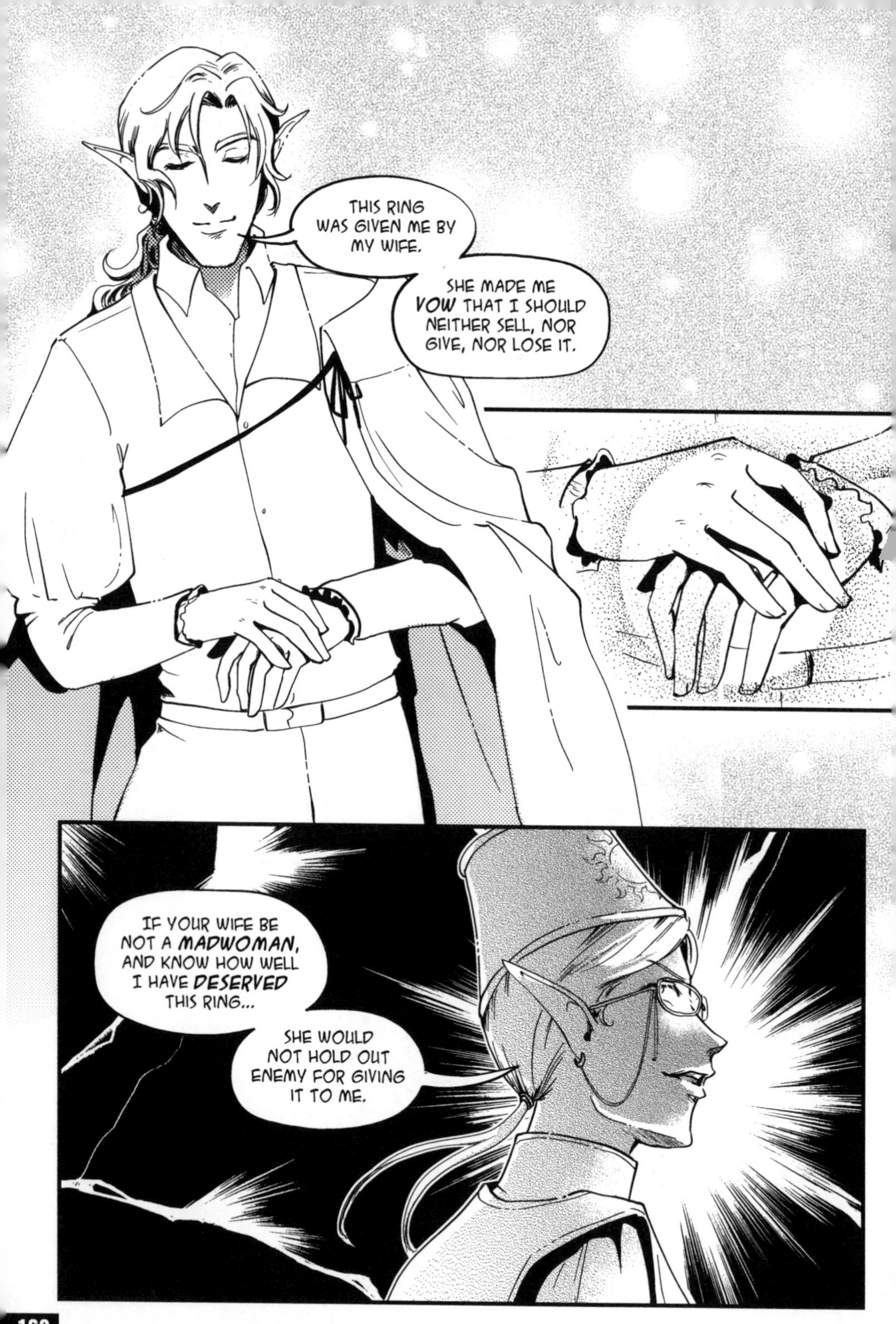
THIS RING WAS GIVEN ME BY MY WIFE.
SHE MADE ME VOW THAT I SHOULD NEITHER SELL, NOR GIVE, NOR LOSE IT.
IF YOUR WIFE BE NOT A MADWOMAN, AND KNOW HOW WELL I HAVE DESERVED THIS RING...
SHE WOULD NOT HOLD OUT ENEMY FOR GIVING IT TO ME.

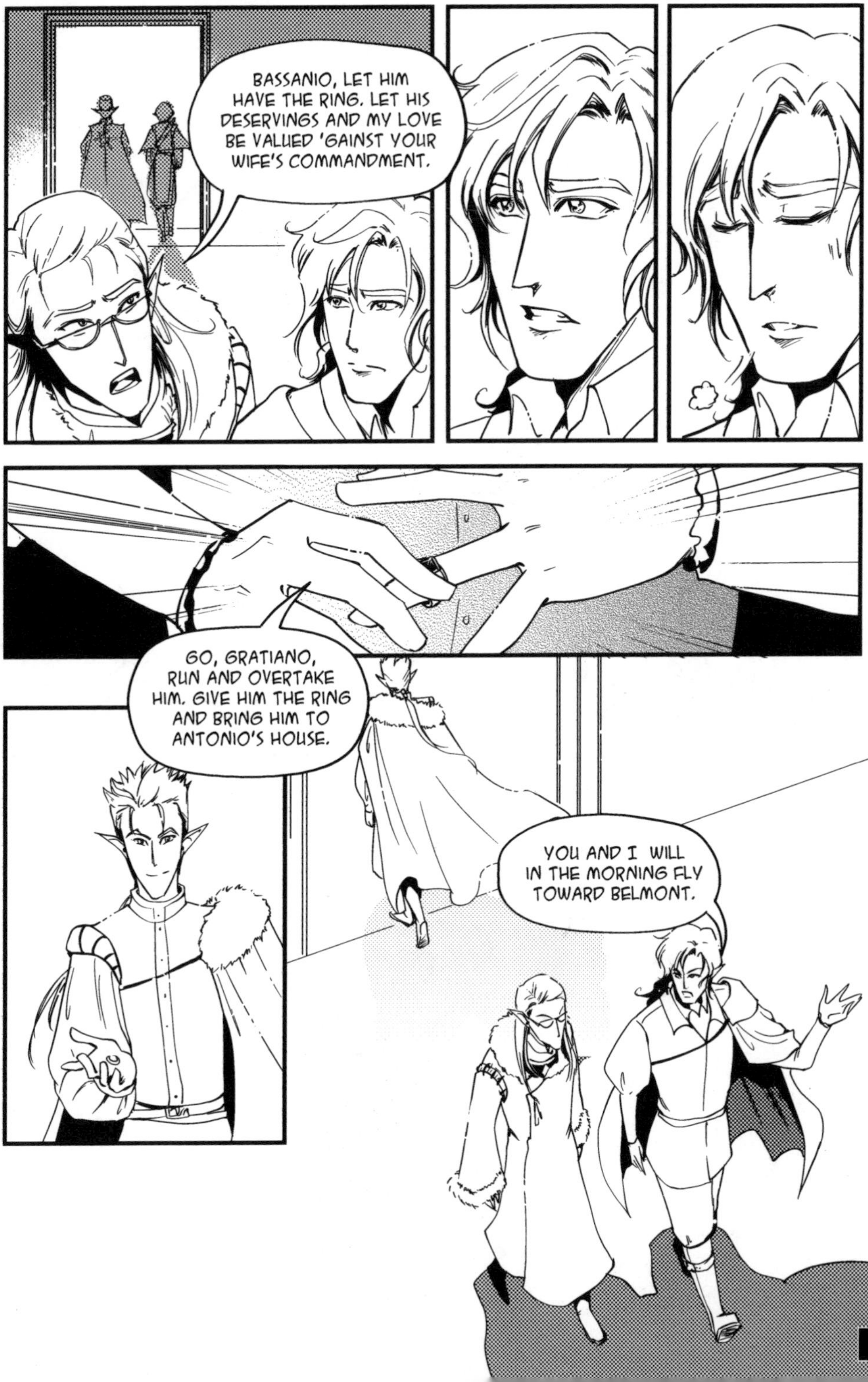
BASSANIO, LET HIM HAVE THE RING. LET HIS DESERVINGS AND MY LOVE BE VALUED 'GAINST YOUR WIFE'S COMMANDMENT.
GO, GRATIANO, RUN AND OVERTAKE HIM. GIVE HIM THE RING AND BRING HIM TO ANTONIO'S HOUSE.
YOU AND I WILL IN THE MORNING FLY TOWARD BELMONT.

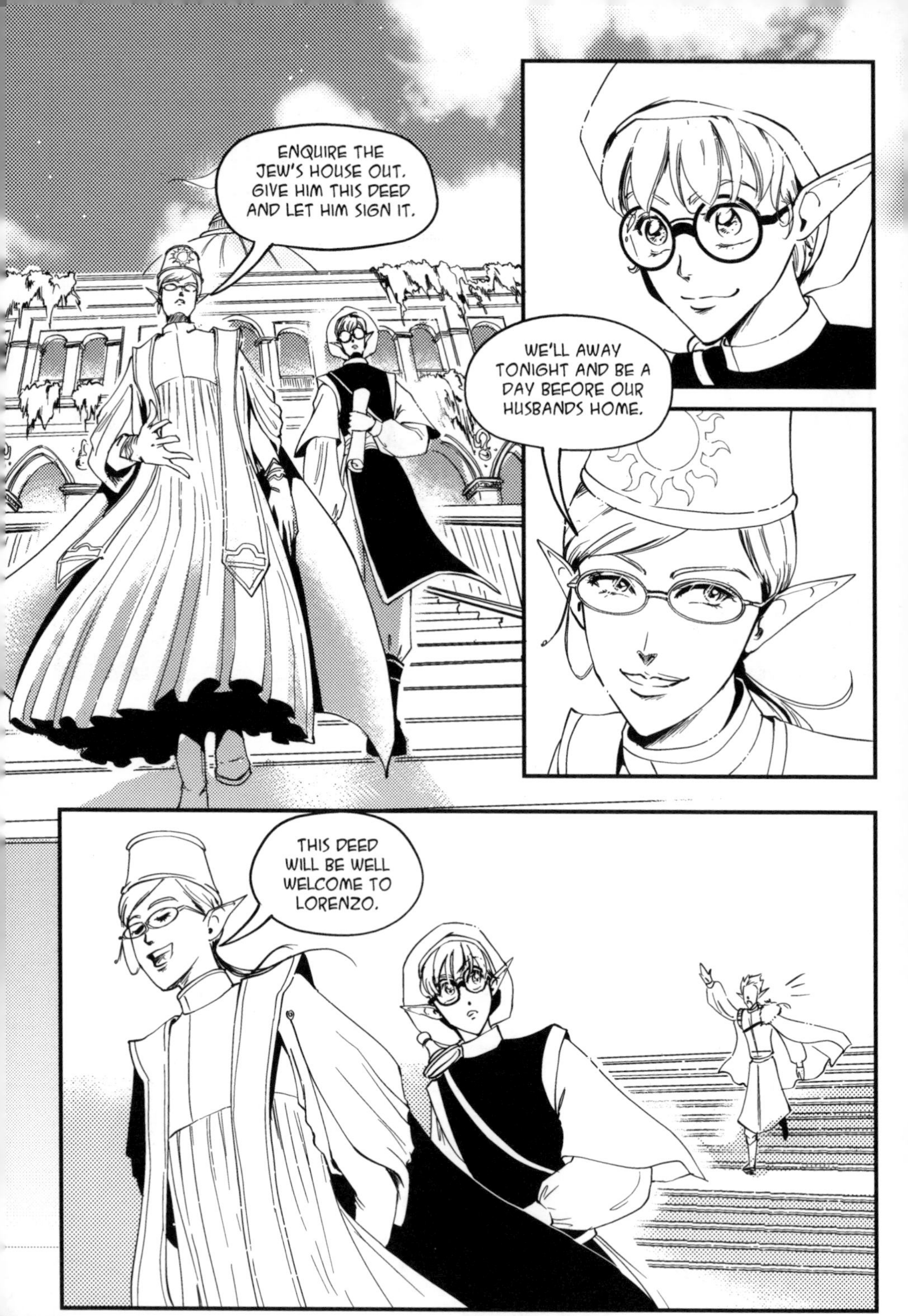
ENQUIRE THE JEW'S HOUSE OUT. GIVE HIM THIS DEED AND LET HIM SIGN IT.
WE'LL AWAY TONIGHT AND BE A DAY BEFORE OUR HUSBANDS HOME.
THIS DEED WILL BE WELL WELCOME TO LORENZO.

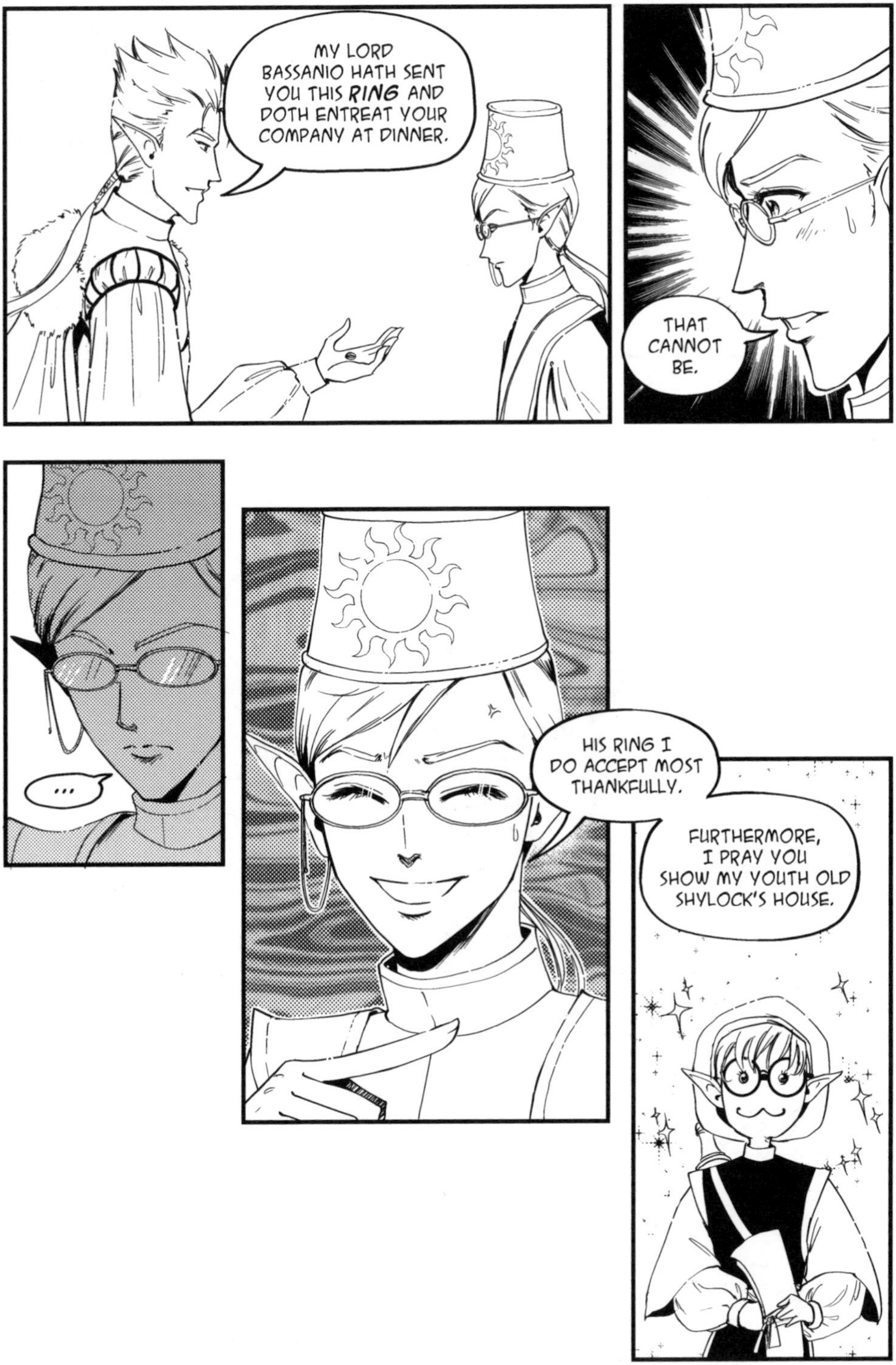
MY LORD BASSANIO HATH SENT YOU THIS RING AND DOTH ENTREAT YOUR COMPANY AT DINNER.
THAT CANNOT BE.
...
HIS RING I DO ACCEPT MOST THANKFULLY.
FURTHERMORE, I PRAY YOU SHOW MY YOUTH OLD SHYLOCK'S HOUSE.

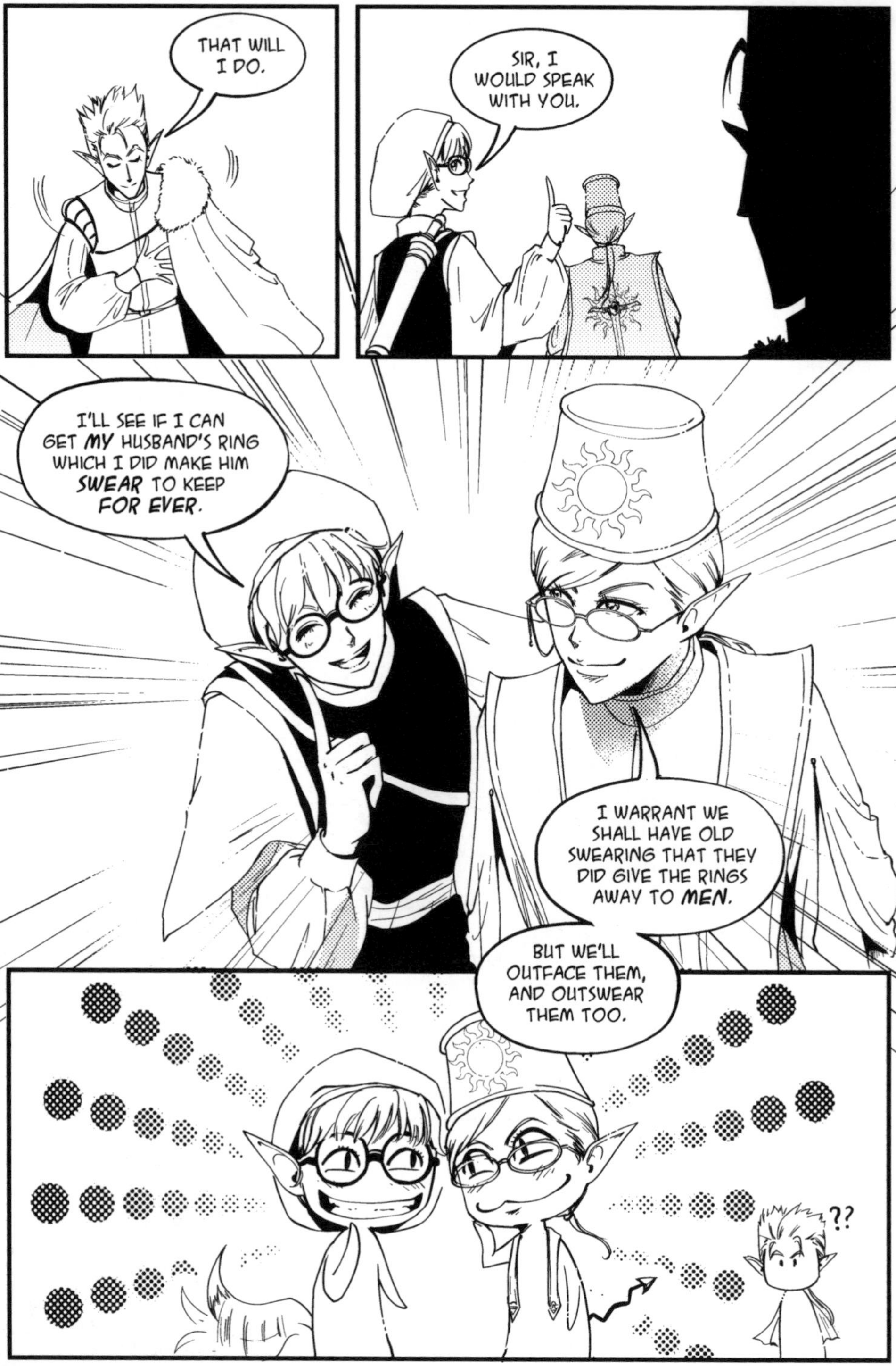
THAT WILL I DO.
SIR, I WOULD SPEAK WITH YOU.
I'LL SEE IF I CAN GET MY HUSBAND'S RING WHICH I DID MAKE HIM SWEAR TO KEEP FOR EVER.
I WARRANT WE SHALL HAVE OLD SWEARING THAT THEY DID GIVE THE RINGS AWAY TO MEN.
BUT WE'LL OUTFACE THEM, AND OUTSWEAR THEM TOO.
??

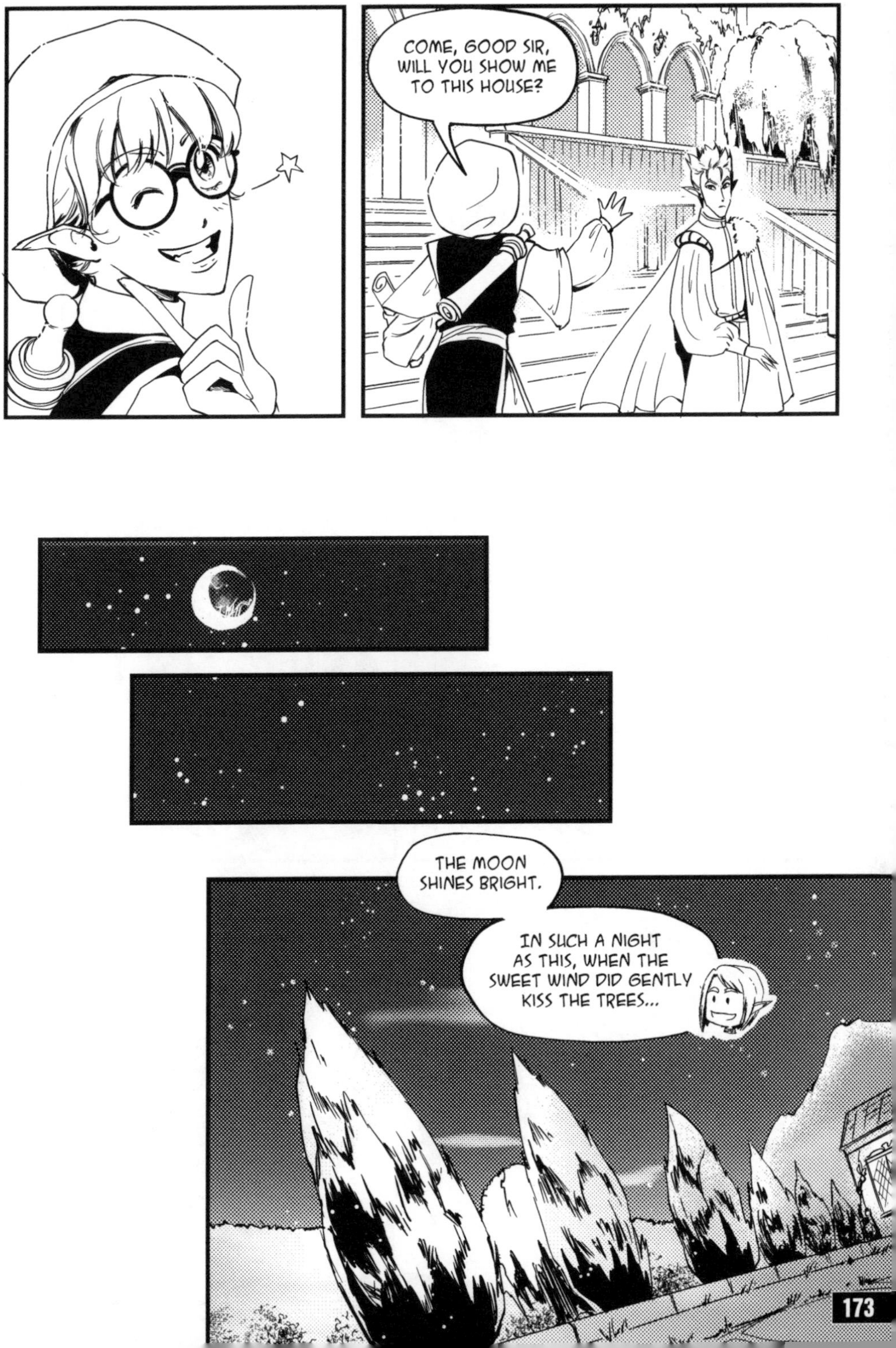
COME, GOOD SIR, WILL YOU SHOW ME TO THIS HOUSE?
THE MOON SHINES BRIGHT.
IN SUCH A NIGHT AS THIS, WHEN THE SWEET WIND DID GENTLY KISS THE TREES...

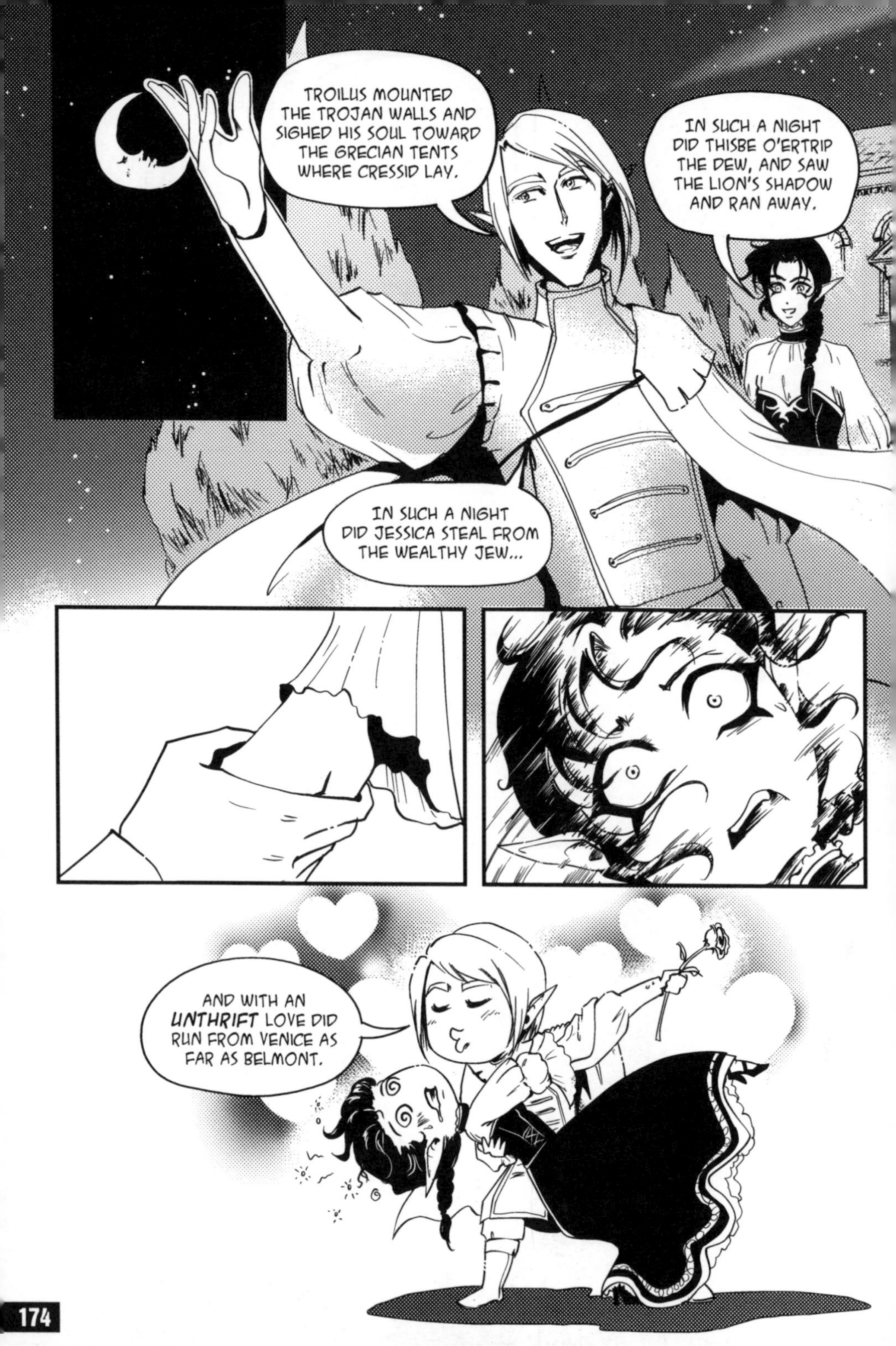
TROILUS MOUNTED THE TROJAN WALLS AND SIGHED HIS SOUL TOWARD THE GRECIAN TENTS WHERE CRESSID LAY.
IN SUCH A NIGHT DID THISBE O'ERTRIP THE DEW, AND SAW THE LION'S SHADOW AND RAN AWAY.
IN SUCH A NIGHT DID JESSICA STEAL FROM THE WEALTHY JEW...
AND WITH AN UNTHRIFT LOVE DID RUN FROM VENICE AS FAR AS BELMONT.

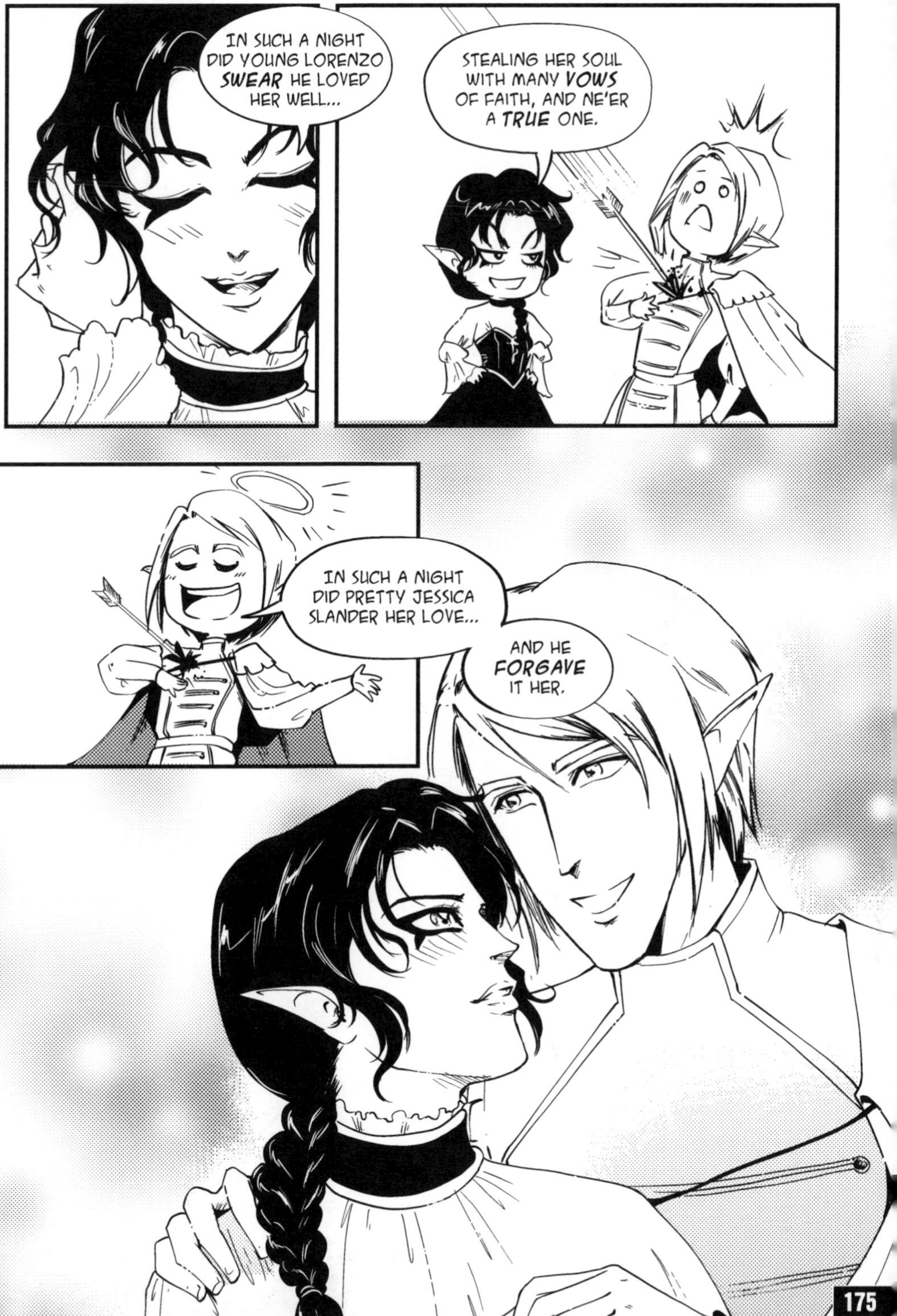
IN SUCH A NIGHT DID YOUNG LORENZO **SWEAR** HE LOVED HER WELL...
STEALING HER SOUL WITH MANY **VOWS** OF FAITH, AND NE'ER A **TRUE** ONE.
IN SUCH A NIGHT DID PRETTY JESSICA SLANDER HER LOVE...
AND HE **FORGAVE** IT HER.

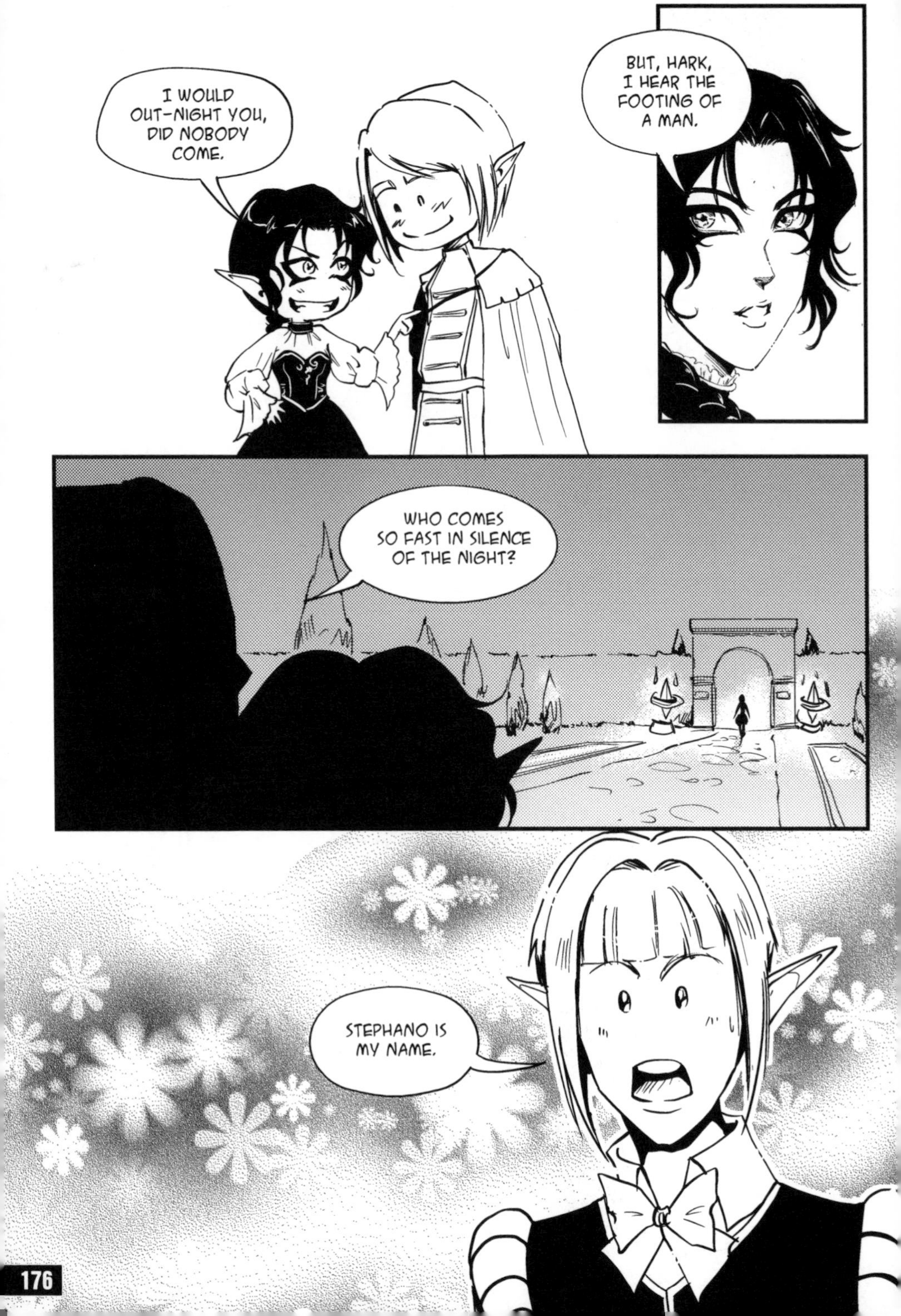
I WOULD OUT-NIGHT YOU, DID NOBODY COME.
BUT, HARK, I HEAR THE FOOTING OF A MAN.
WHO COMES SO FAST IN SILENCE OF THE NIGHT?
STEPHANO IS MY NAME.

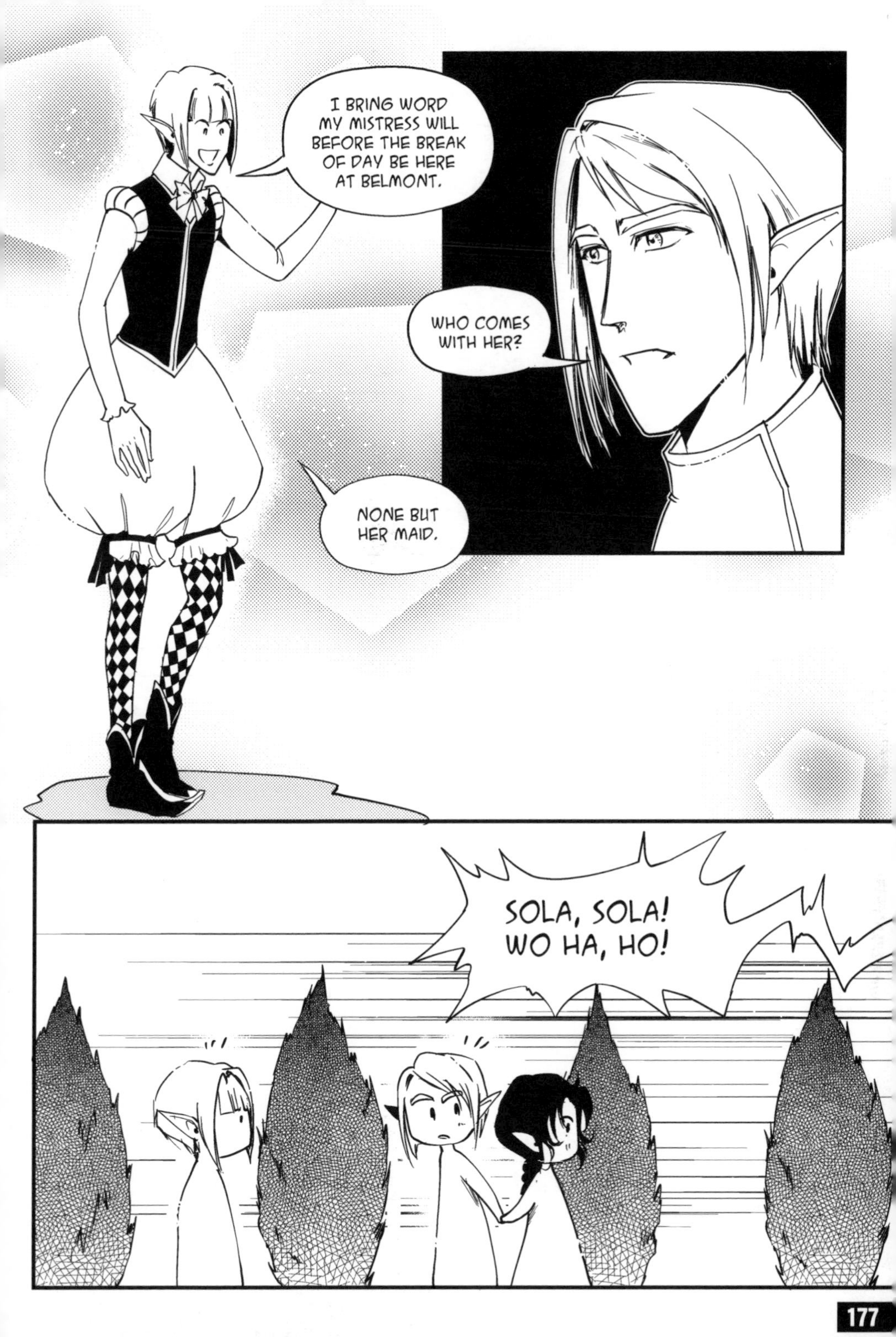
I BRING WORD MY MISTRESS WILL BEFORE THE BREAK OF DAY BE HERE AT BELMONT.
WHO COMES WITH HER?
NONE BUT HER MAID.
SOLA, SOLA! WO HA, HO!

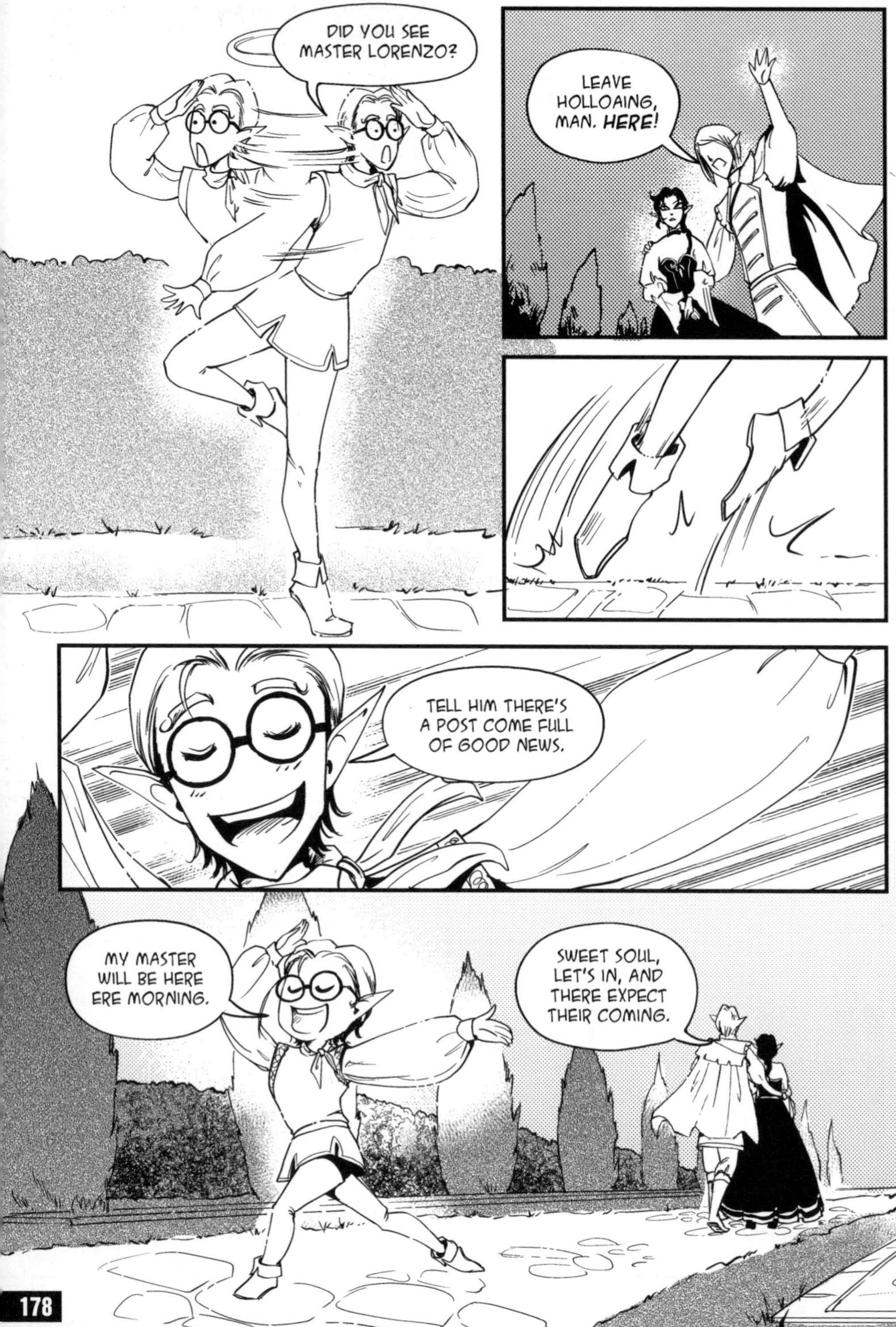
DID YOU SEE MASTER LORENZO?
LEAVE HOLLOAING, MAN. **HERE**!
TELL HIM THERE'S A POST COME FULL OF GOOD NEWS.
MY MASTER WILL BE HERE ERE MORNING.
SWEET SOUL, LET'S IN, AND THERE EXPECT THEIR COMING.

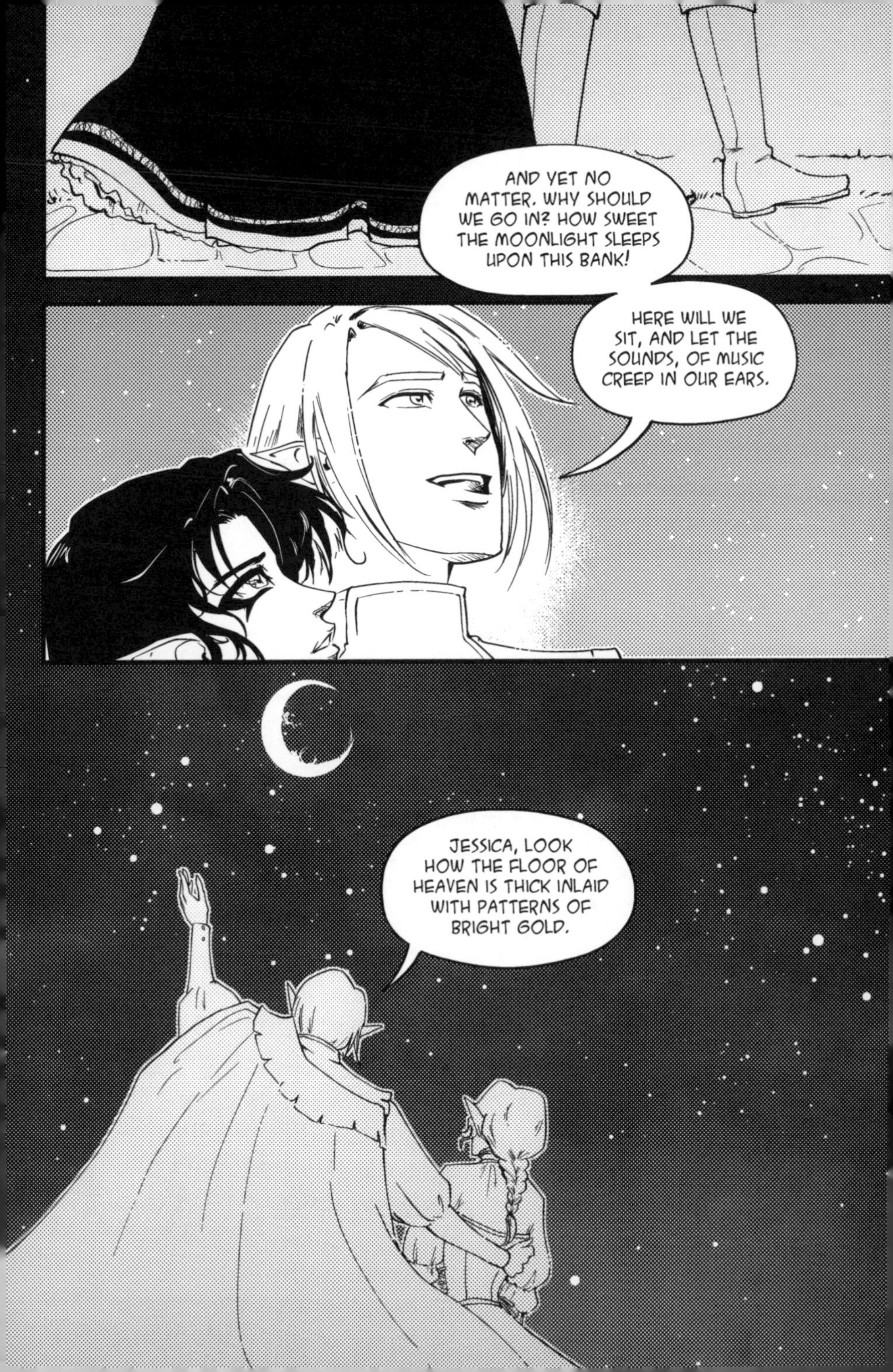
AND YET NO MATTER. WHY SHOULD WE GO IN? HOW SWEET THE MOONLIGHT SLEEPS UPON THIS BANK!
HERE WILL WE SIT, AND LET THE SOUNDS, OF MUSIC CREEP IN OUR EARS.
JESSICA, LOOK HOW THE FLOOR OF HEAVEN IS THICK INLAID WITH PATTERNS OF BRIGHT GOLD.

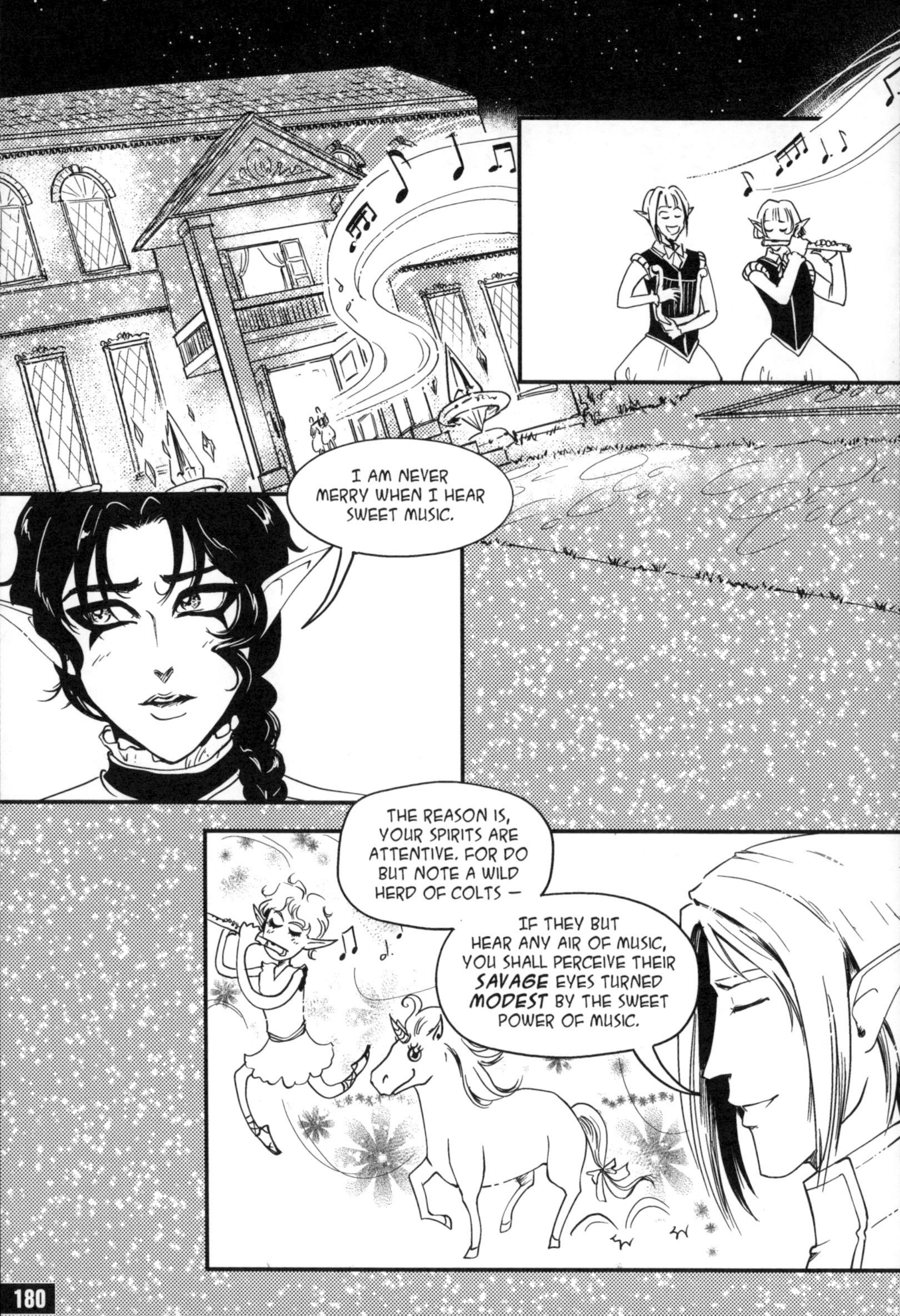
I AM NEVER MERRY WHEN I HEAR SWEET MUSIC.
THE REASON IS, YOUR SPIRITS ARE ATTENTIVE. FOR DO BUT NOTE A WILD HERD OF COLTS –
IF THEY BUT HEAR ANY AIR OF MUSIC, YOU SHALL PERCEIVE THEIR ***SAVAGE*** EYES TURNED ***MODEST*** BY THE SWEET POWER OF MUSIC.

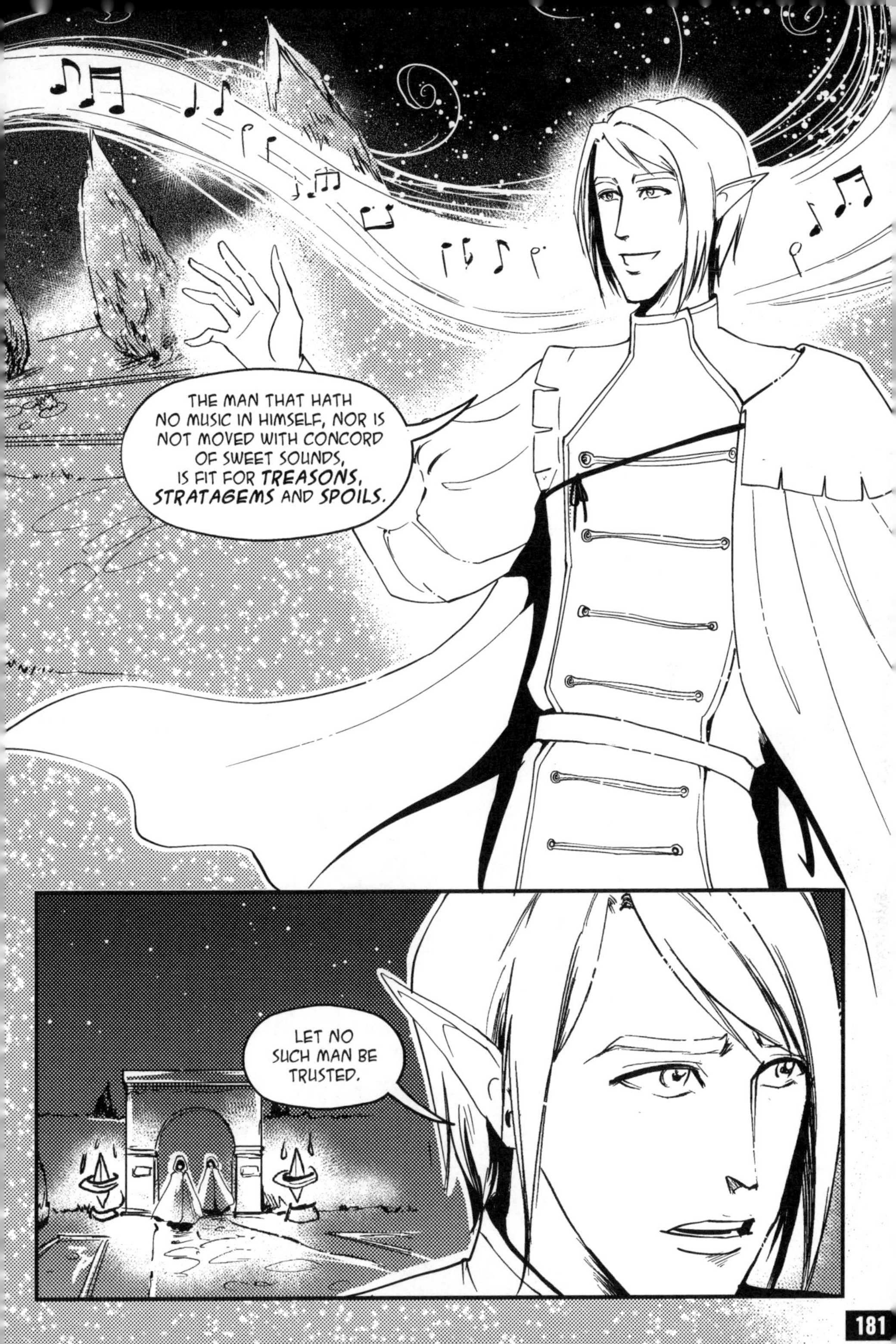
THE MAN THAT HATH NO MUSIC IN HIMSELF, NOR IS NOT MOVED WITH CONCORD OF SWEET SOUNDS, IS FIT FOR **TREASONS, STRATAGEMS** AND **SPOILS.**
LET NO SUCH MAN BE TRUSTED.

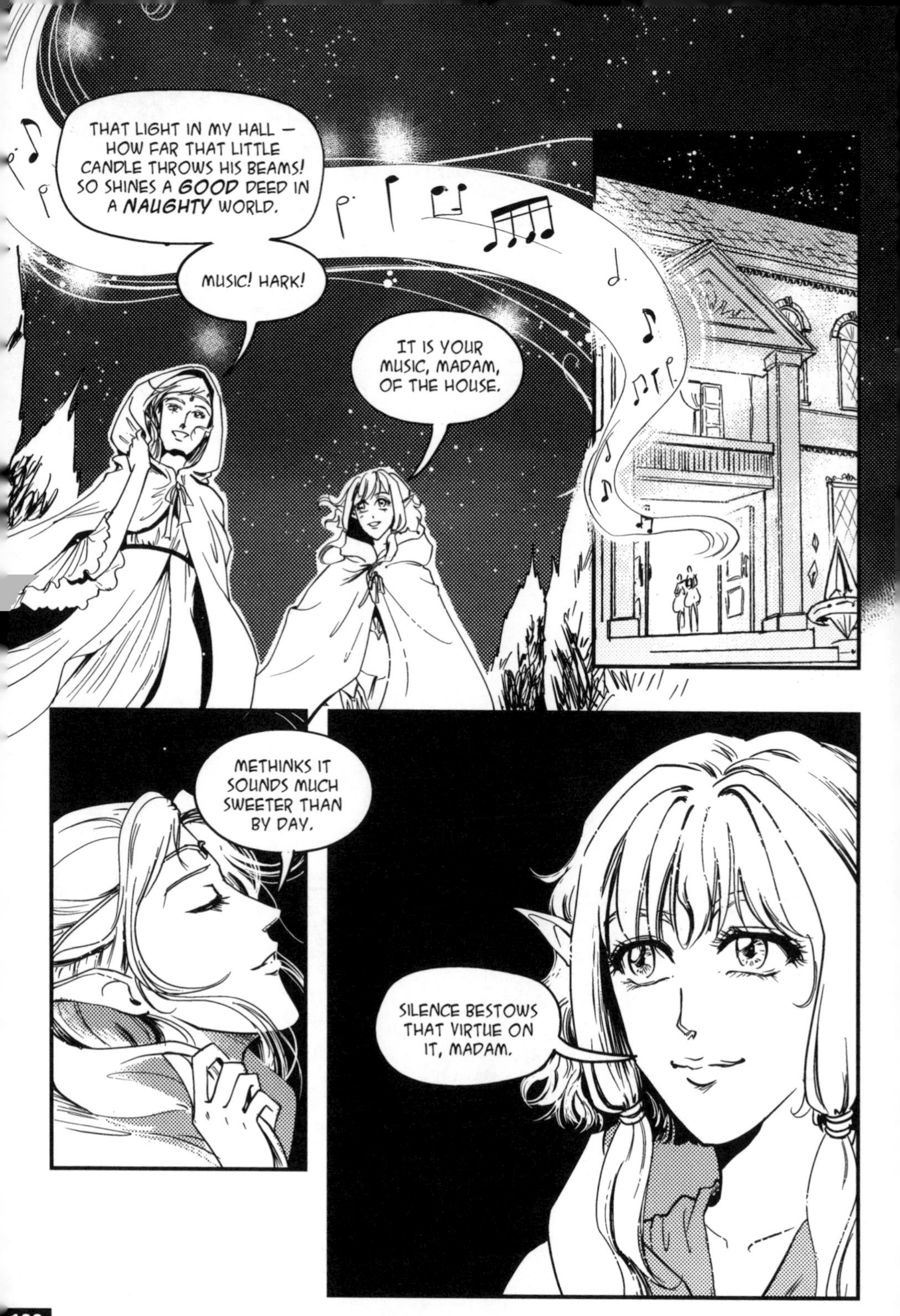
THAT LIGHT IN MY HALL — HOW FAR THAT LITTLE CANDLE THROWS HIS BEAMS! SO SHINES A GOOD DEED IN A NAUGHTY WORLD.
MUSIC! HARK!
IT IS YOUR MUSIC, MADAM, OF THE HOUSE.
METHINKS IT SOUNDS MUCH SWEETER THAN BY DAY.
SILENCE BESTOWS THAT VIRTUE ON IT, MADAM.

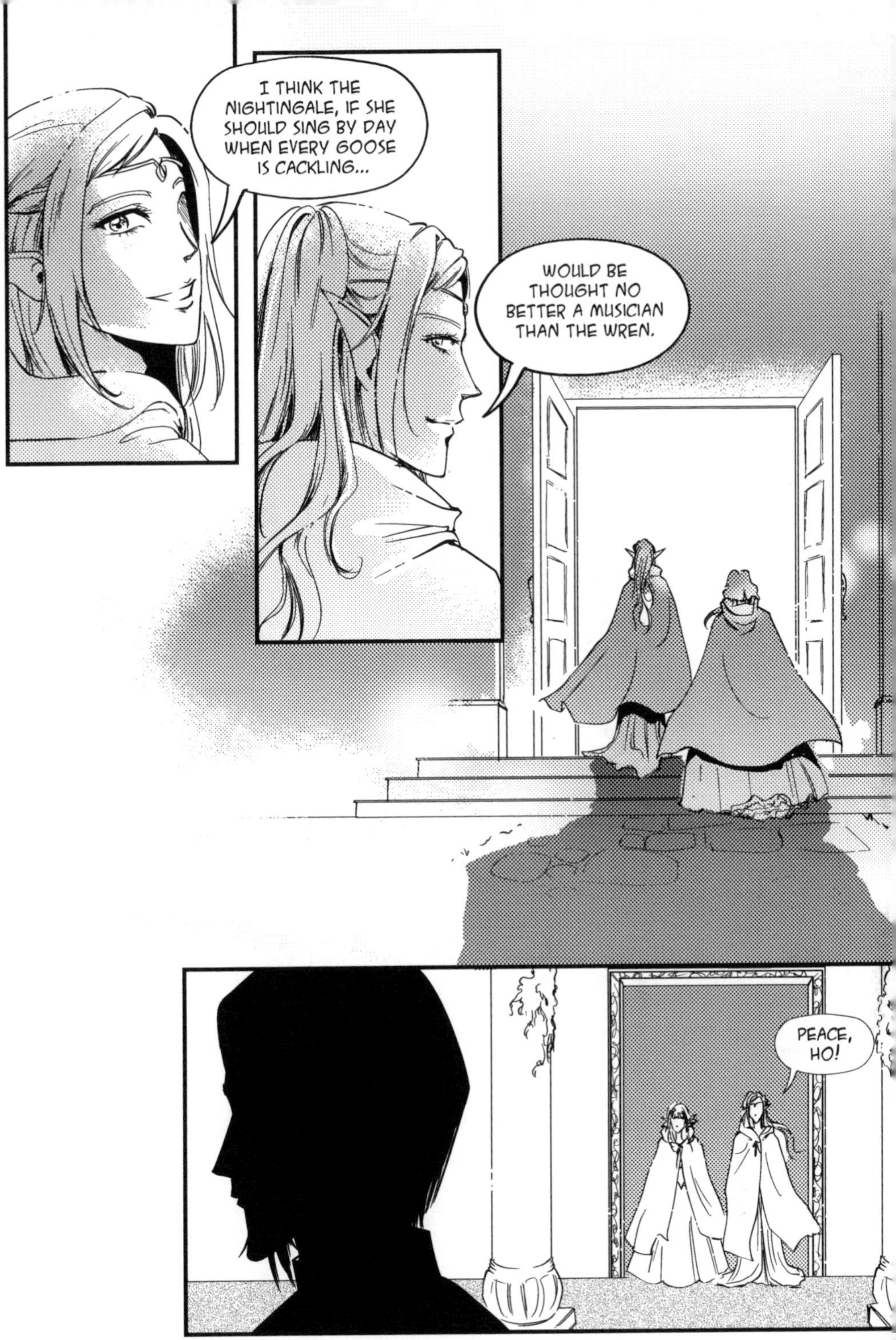
I THINK THE NIGHTINGALE, IF SHE SHOULD SING BY DAY WHEN EVERY GOOSE IS CACKLING...
WOULD BE THOUGHT NO BETTER A MUSICIAN THAN THE WREN.
PEACE, HO!

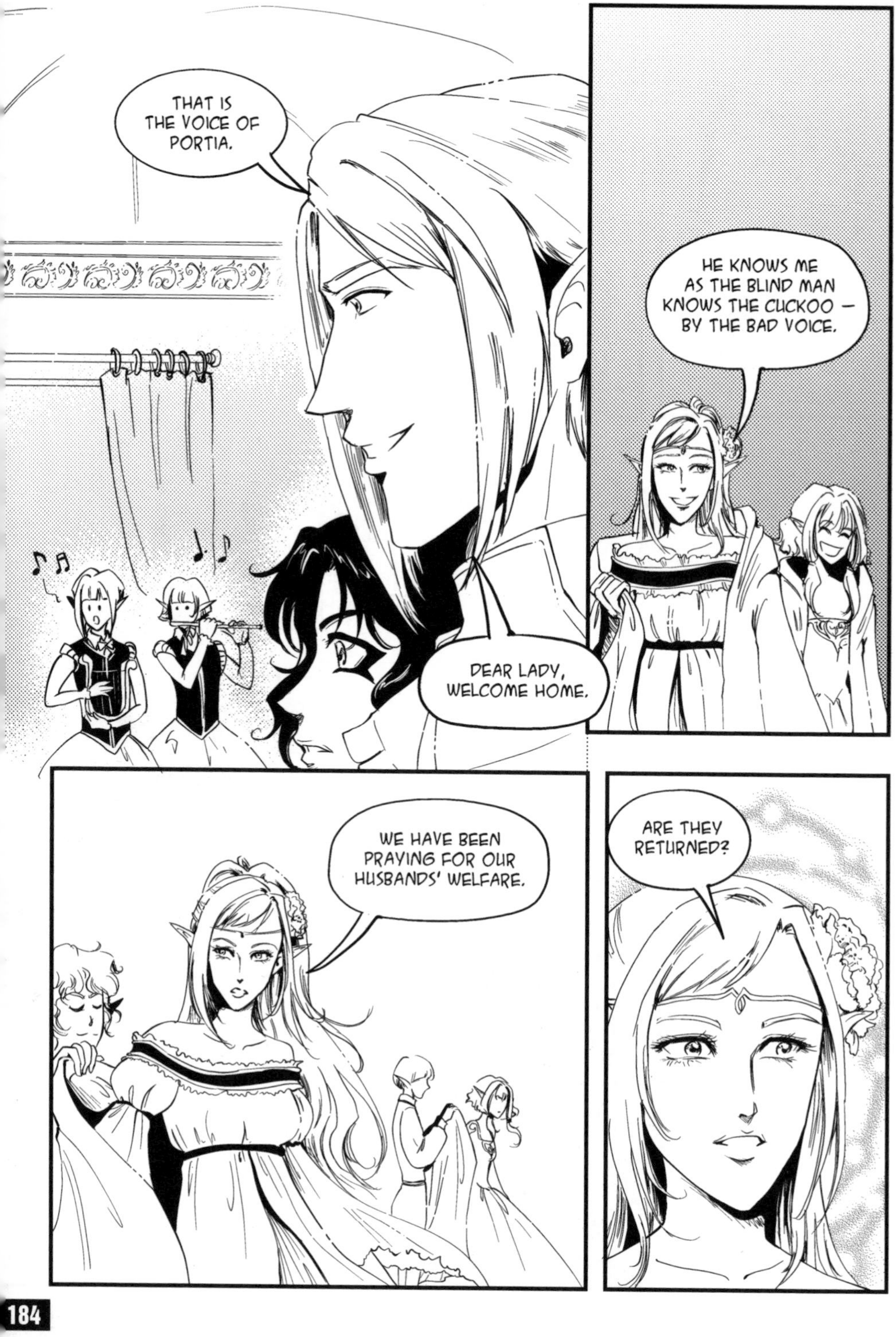
THAT IS THE VOICE OF PORTIA.
DEAR LADY, WELCOME HOME.
HE KNOWS ME AS THE BLIND MAN KNOWS THE CUCKOO — BY THE BAD VOICE.
WE HAVE BEEN PRAYING FOR OUR HUSBANDS' WELFARE.
ARE THEY RETURNED?

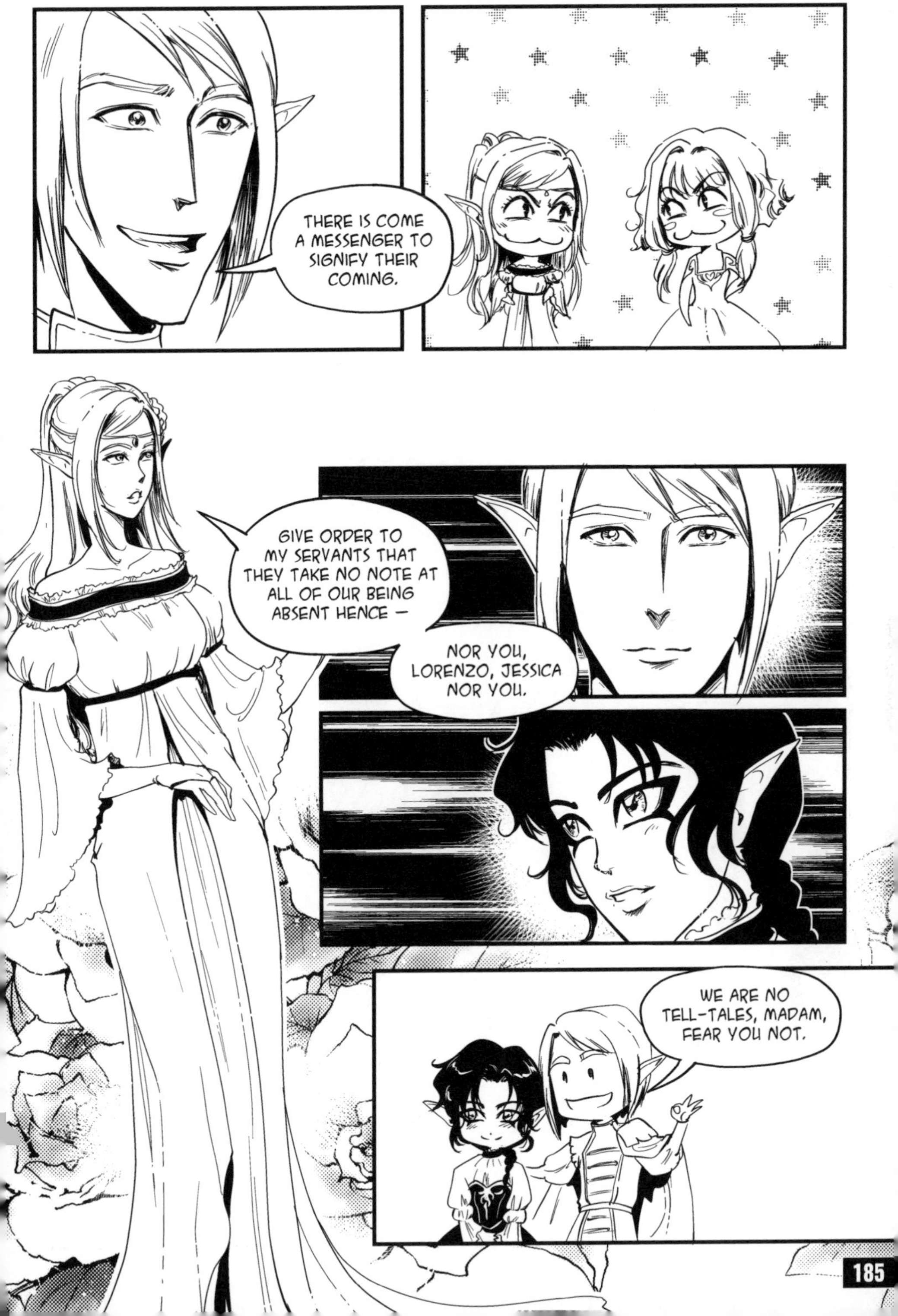
THERE IS COME A MESSENGER TO SIGNIFY THEIR COMING.
GIVE ORDER TO MY SERVANTS THAT THEY TAKE NO NOTE AT ALL OF OUR BEING ABSENT HENCE —
NOR YOU, LORENZO, JESSICA NOR YOU.
WE ARE NO TELL-TALES, MADAM, FEAR YOU NOT.

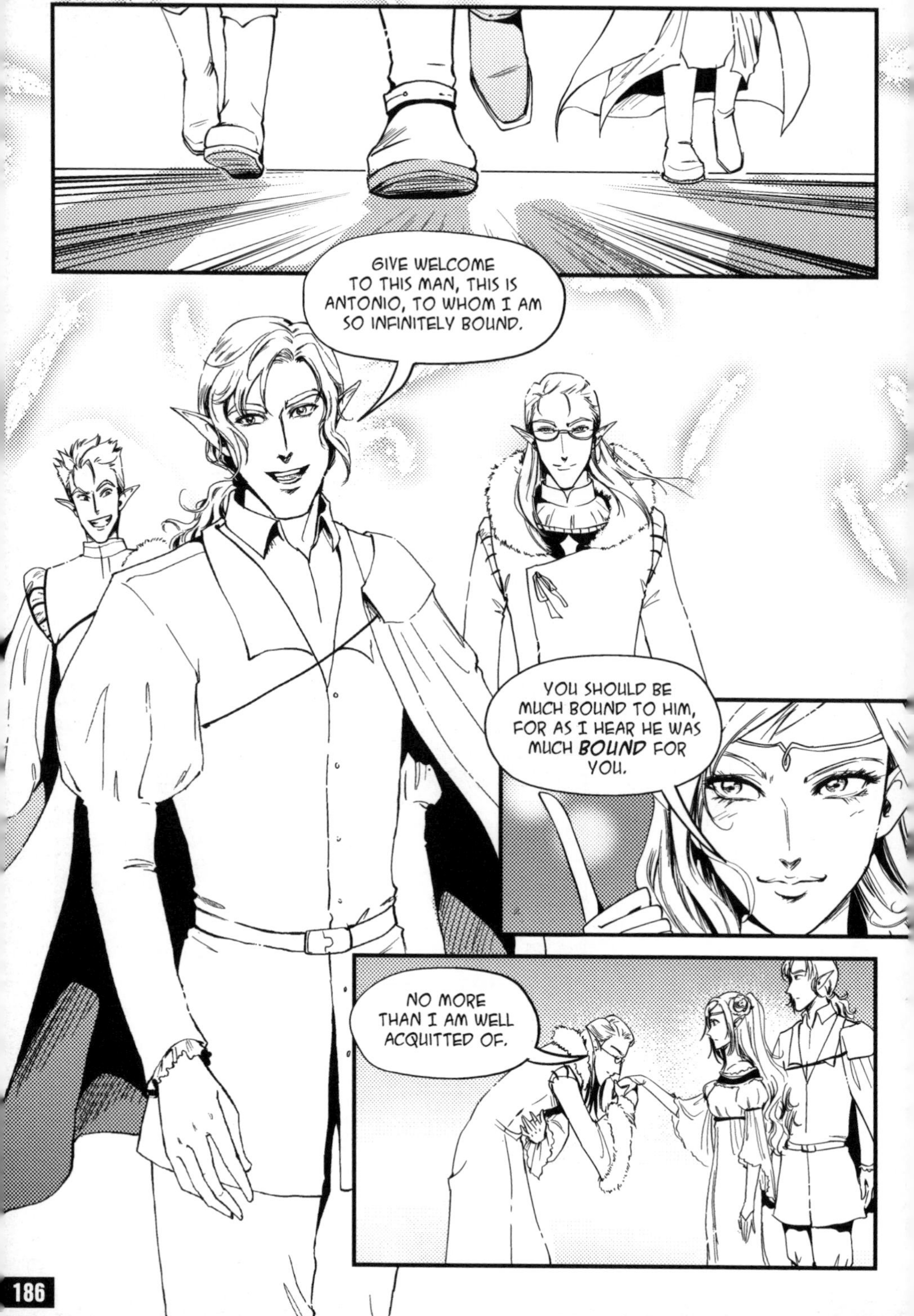
GIVE WELCOME TO THIS MAN, THIS IS ANTONIO, TO WHOM I AM SO INFINITELY BOUND.
YOU SHOULD BE MUCH BOUND TO HIM, FOR AS I HEAR HE WAS MUCH **BOUND** FOR YOU.
NO MORE THAN I AM WELL ACQUITTED OF.

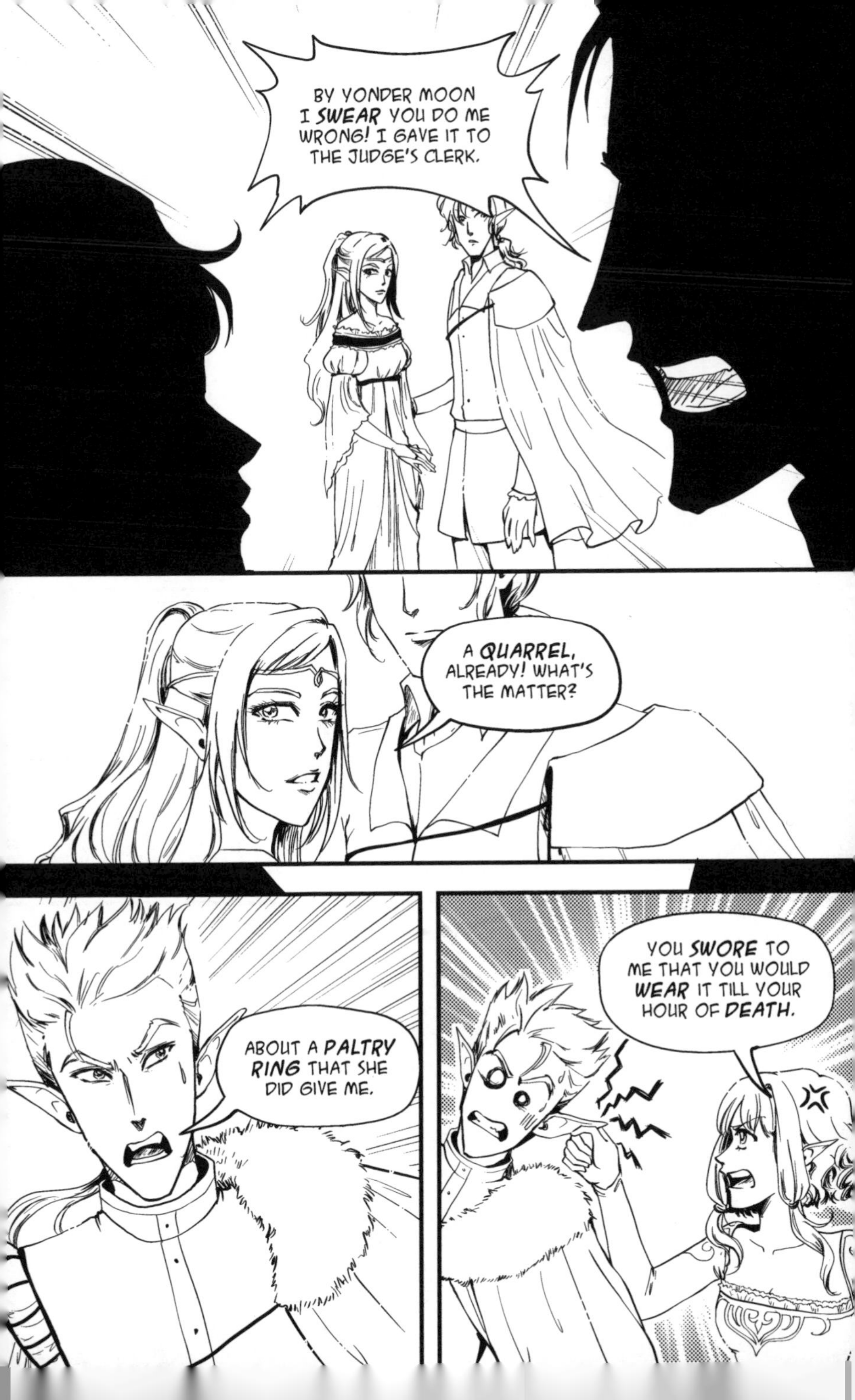
BY YONDER MOON I SWEAR YOU DO ME WRONG! I GAVE IT TO THE JUDGE'S CLERK.
A QUARREL, ALREADY! WHAT'S THE MATTER?
ABOUT A PALTRY RING THAT SHE DID GIVE ME.
YOU SWORE TO ME THAT YOU WOULD WEAR IT TILL YOUR HOUR OF DEATH.

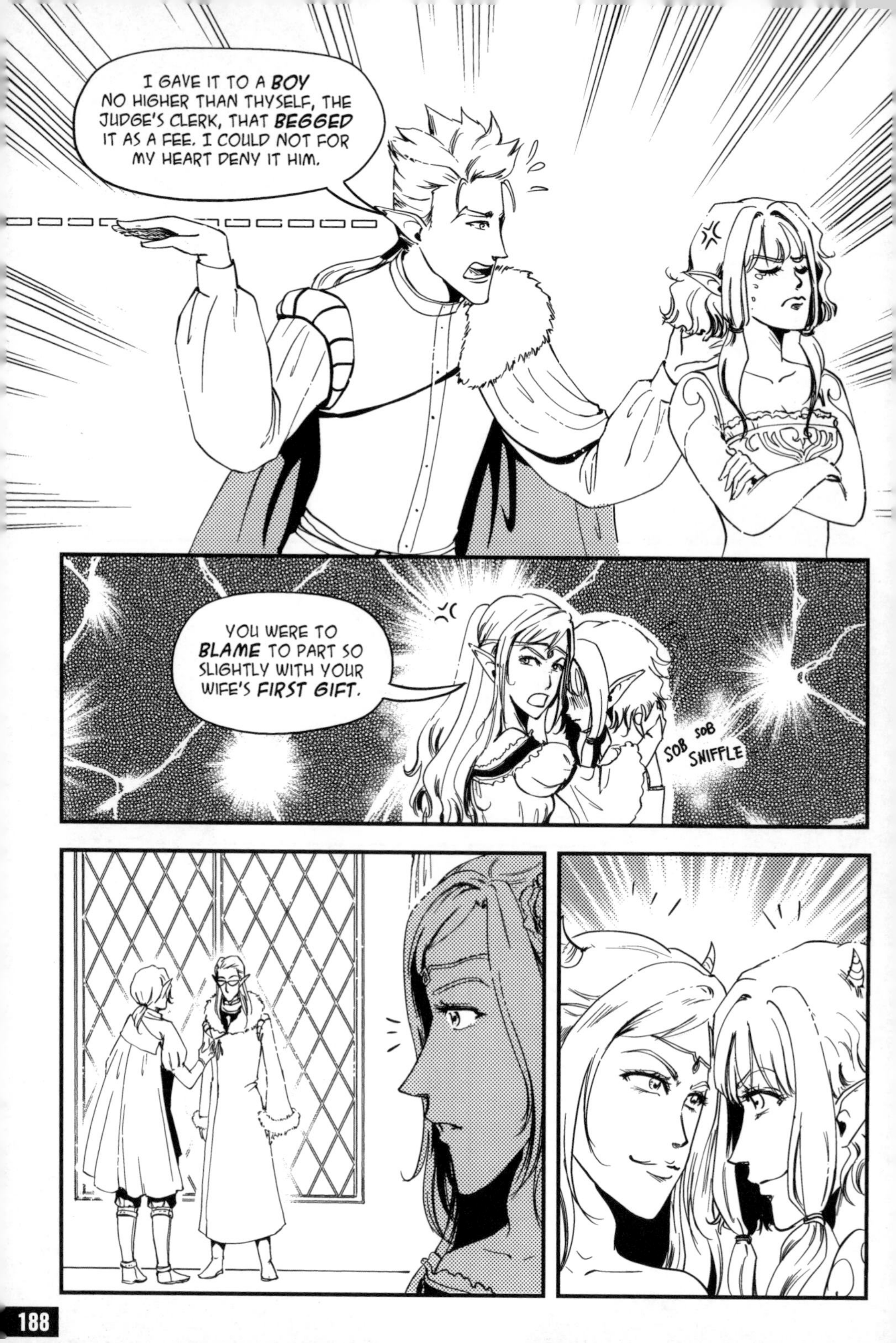
I GAVE IT TO A **BOY** NO HIGHER THAN THYSELF, THE JUDGE'S CLERK, THAT **BEGGED** IT AS A FEE. I COULD NOT FOR MY HEART DENY IT HIM.
YOU WERE TO **BLAME** TO PART SO SLIGHTLY WITH YOUR WIFE'S **FIRST GIFT**.
SOB SOB
SNIFFLE

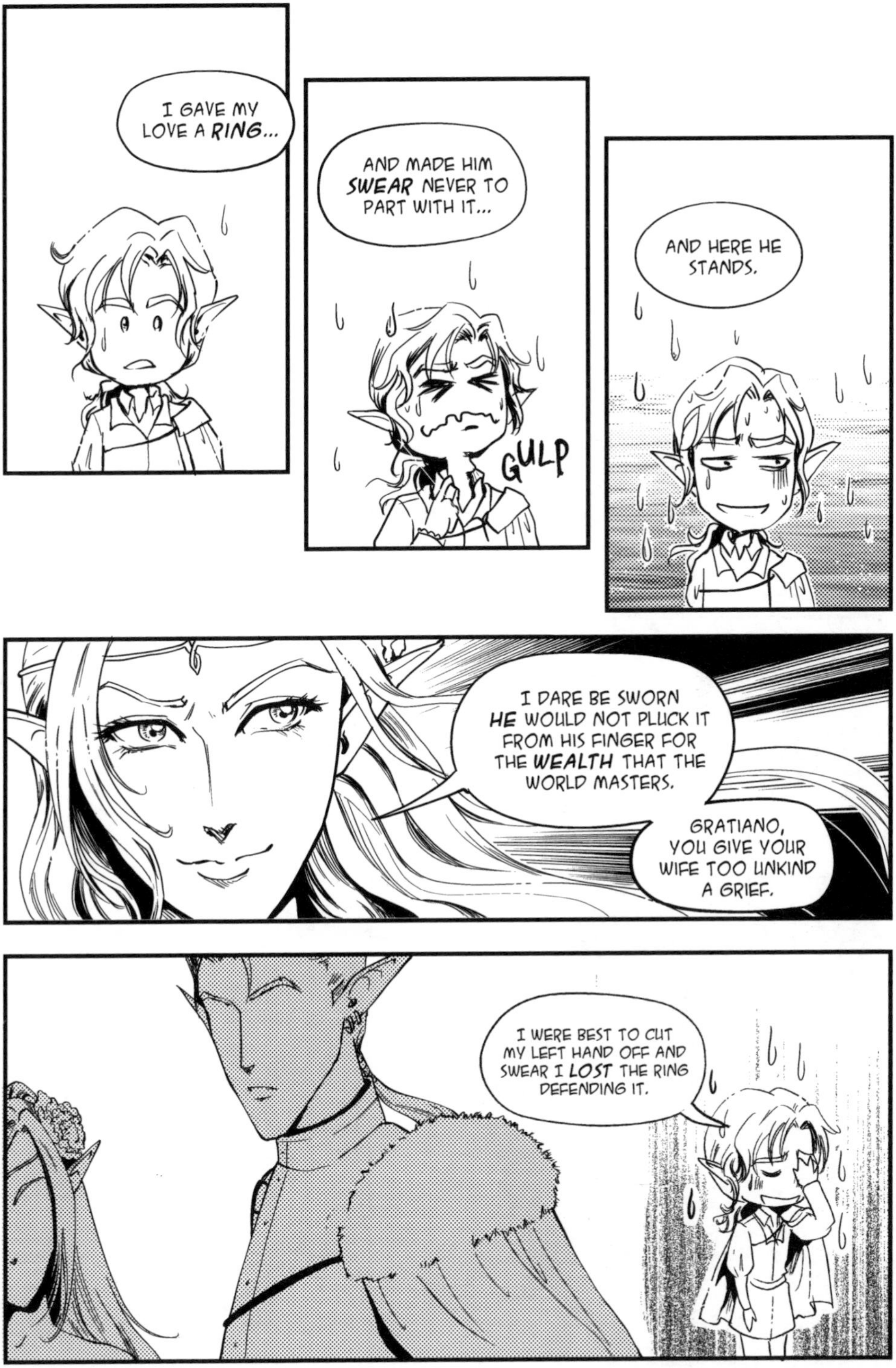
I GAVE MY LOVE A RING...
AND MADE HIM SWEAR NEVER TO PART WITH IT...
GULP
AND HERE HE STANDS.
I DARE BE SWORN HE WOULD NOT PLUCK IT FROM HIS FINGER FOR THE WEALTH THAT THE WORLD MASTERS.
GRATIANO, YOU GIVE YOUR WIFE TOO UNKIND A GRIEF.
I WERE BEST TO CUT MY LEFT HAND OFF AND SWEAR I LOST THE RING DEFENDING IT.

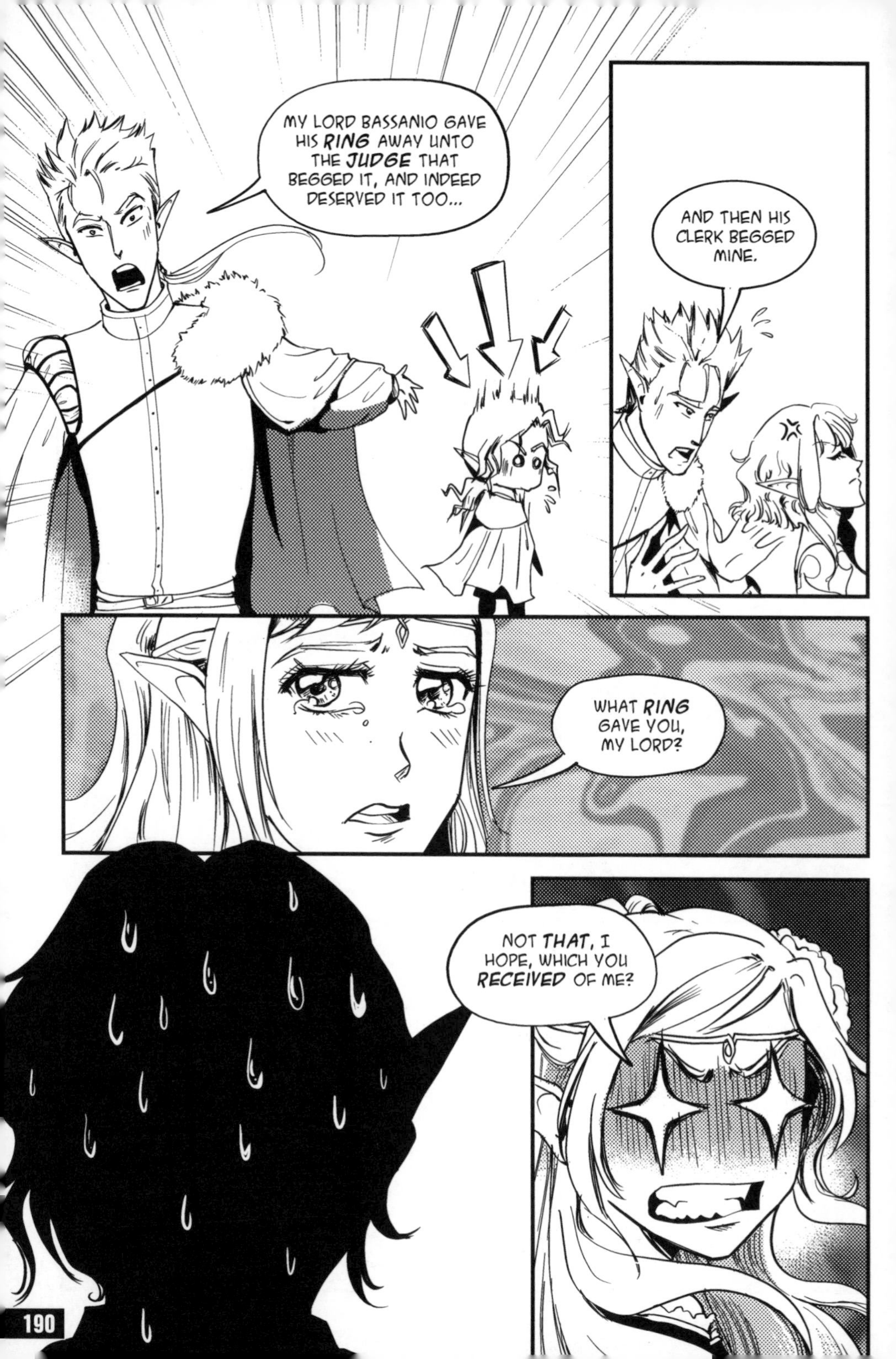
MY LORD BASSANIO GAVE HIS RING AWAY UNTO THE JUDGE THAT BEGGED IT, AND INDEED DESERVED IT TOO...
AND THEN HIS CLERK BEGGED MINE.
WHAT RING GAVE YOU, MY LORD?
NOT THAT, I HOPE, WHICH YOU RECEIVED OF ME?

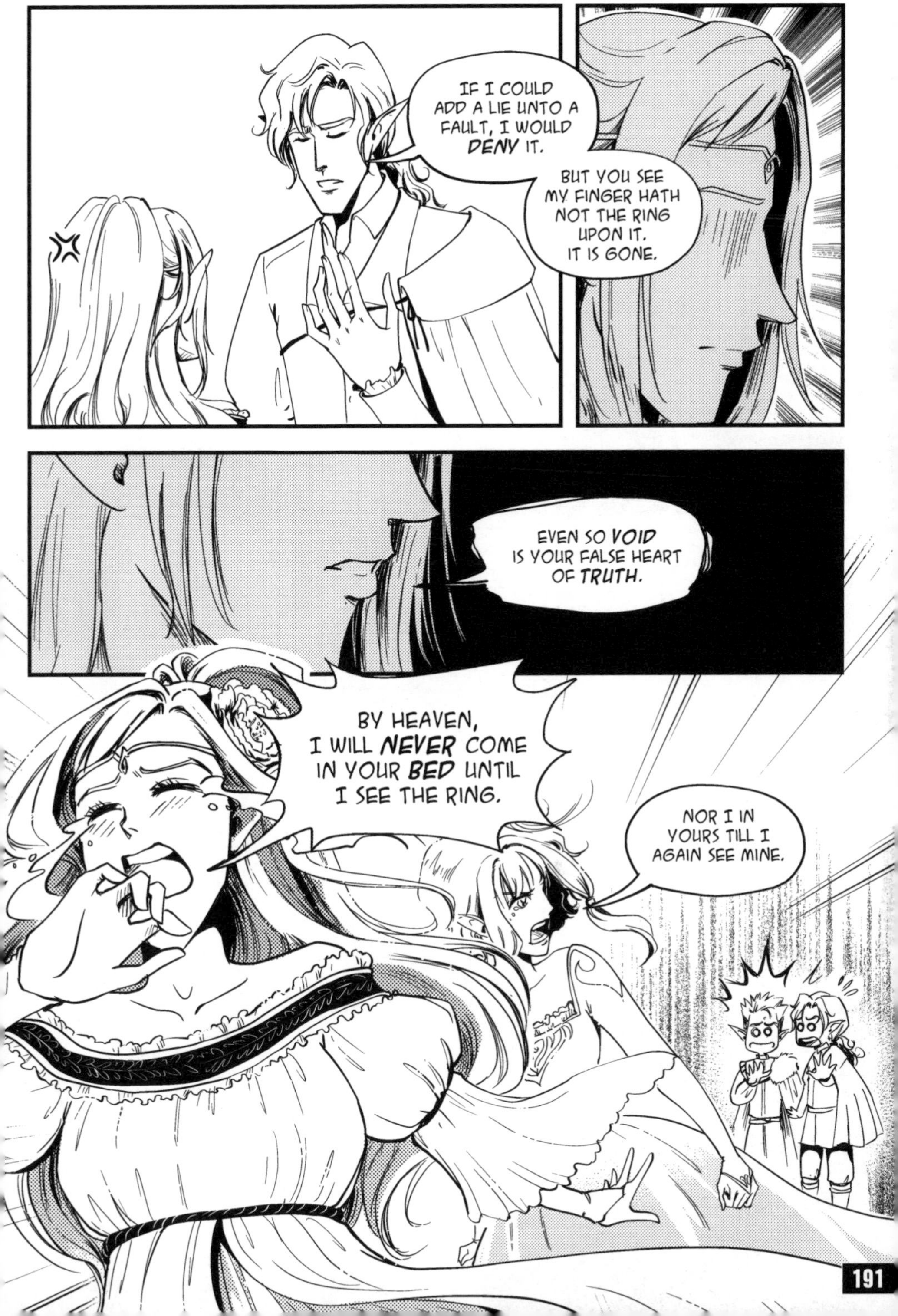
IF I COULD ADD A LIE UNTO A FAULT, I WOULD DENY IT.
BUT YOU SEE MY FINGER HATH NOT THE RING UPON IT. IT IS GONE.
EVEN SO VOID IS YOUR FALSE HEART OF TRUTH.
BY HEAVEN, I WILL NEVER COME IN YOUR BED UNTIL I SEE THE RING.
NOR I IN YOURS TILL I AGAIN SEE MINE.

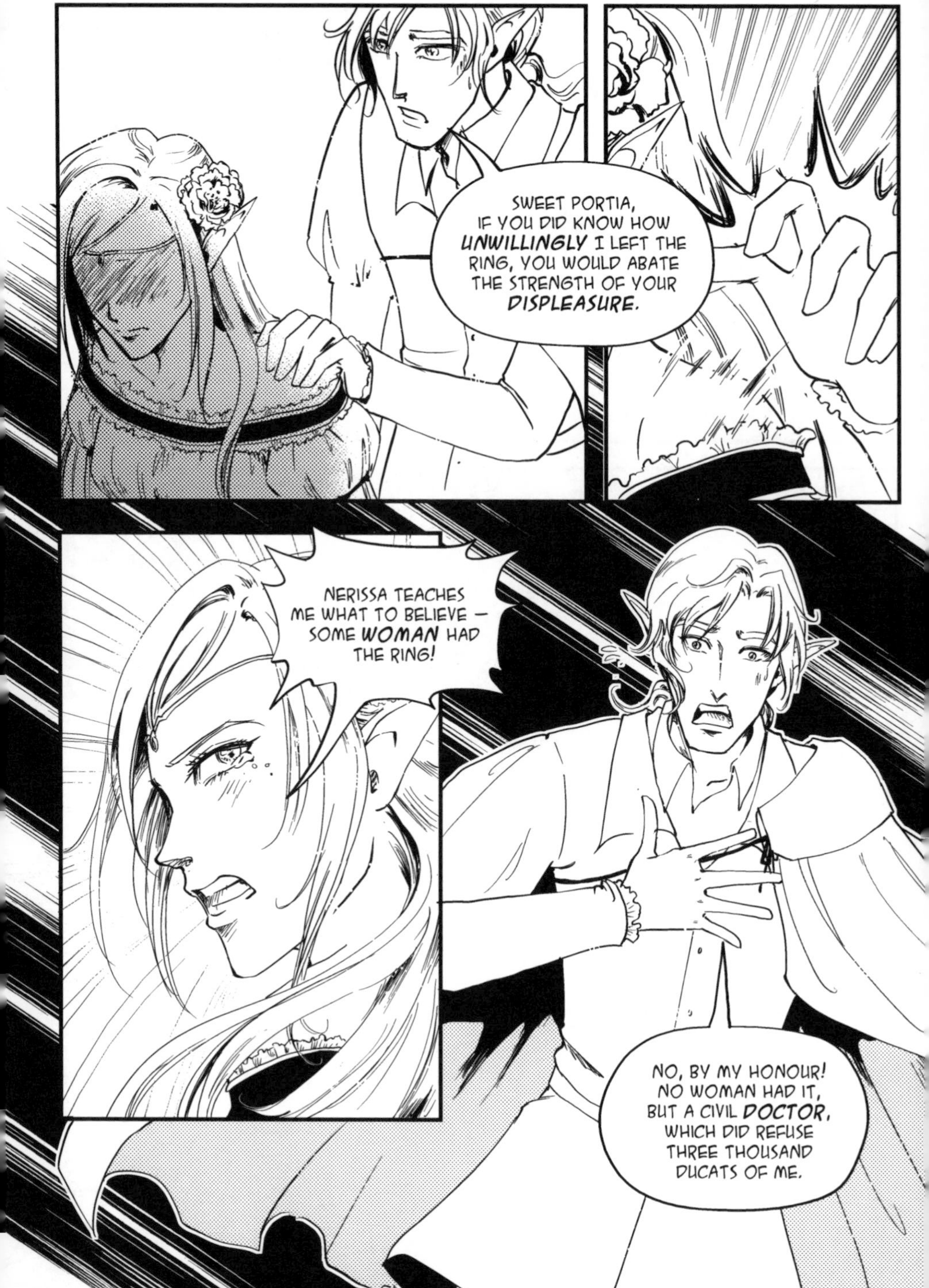
SWEET PORTIA, IF YOU DID KNOW HOW **UNWILLINGLY** I LEFT THE RING, YOU WOULD ABATE THE STRENGTH OF YOUR **DISPLEASURE.**
NERISSA TEACHES ME WHAT TO BELIEVE — SOME **WOMAN** HAD THE RING!
NO, BY MY HONOUR! NO WOMAN HAD IT, BUT A CIVIL **DOCTOR,** WHICH DID REFUSE THREE THOUSAND DUCATS OF ME.

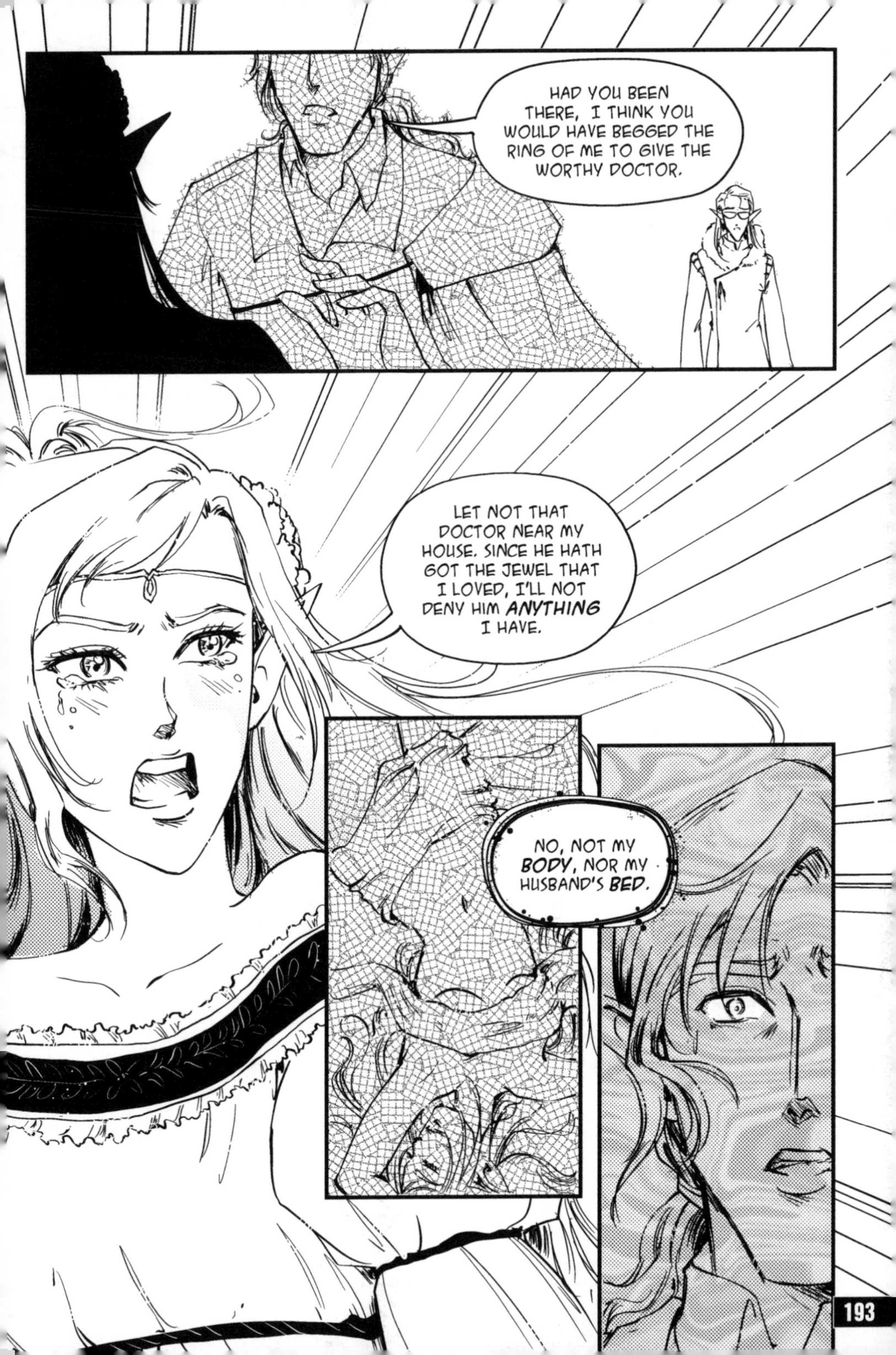
HAD YOU BEEN THERE, I THINK YOU WOULD HAVE BEGGED THE RING OF ME TO GIVE THE WORTHY DOCTOR.
LET NOT THAT DOCTOR NEAR MY HOUSE. SINCE HE HATH GOT THE JEWEL THAT I LOVED, I'LL NOT DENY HIM *ANYTHING* I HAVE.
NO, NOT MY *BODY*, NOR MY HUSBAND'S *BED*.

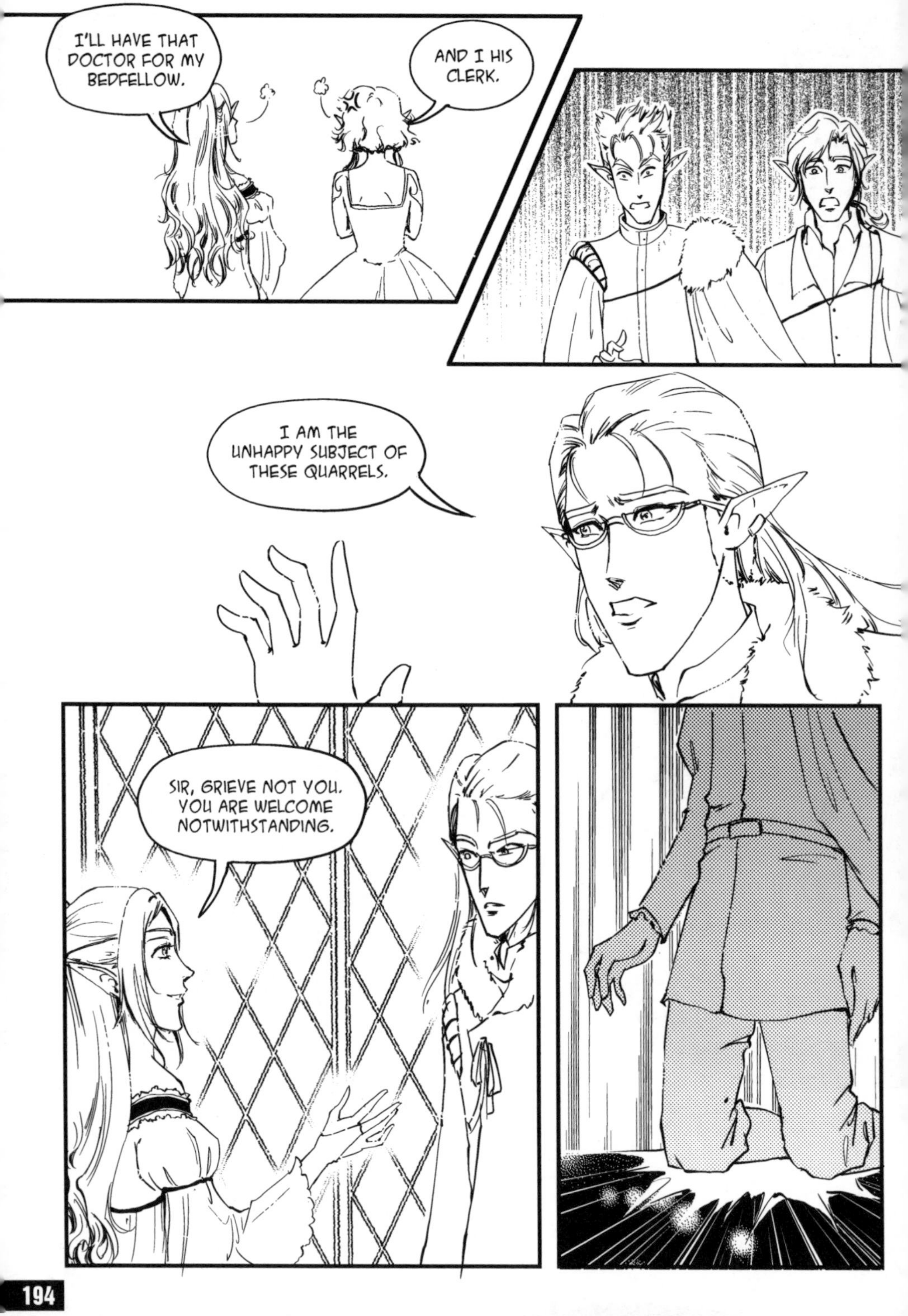
I'LL HAVE THAT DOCTOR FOR MY BEDFELLOW.
AND I HIS CLERK.
I AM THE UNHAPPY SUBJECT OF THESE QUARRELS.
SIR, GRIEVE NOT YOU. YOU ARE WELCOME NOTWITHSTANDING.

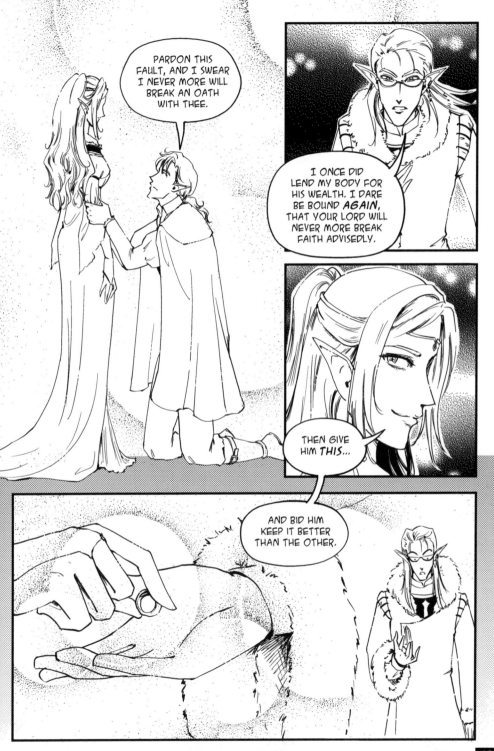

PARDON THIS FAULT, AND I SWEAR I NEVER MORE WILL BREAK AN OATH WITH THEE.

I ONCE DID LEND MY BODY FOR HIS WEALTH. I DARE BE BOUND *AGAIN*, THAT YOUR LORD WILL NEVER MORE BREAK FAITH ADVISEDLY.

THEN GIVE HIM *THIS*...

AND BID HIM KEEP IT BETTER THAN THE OTHER.

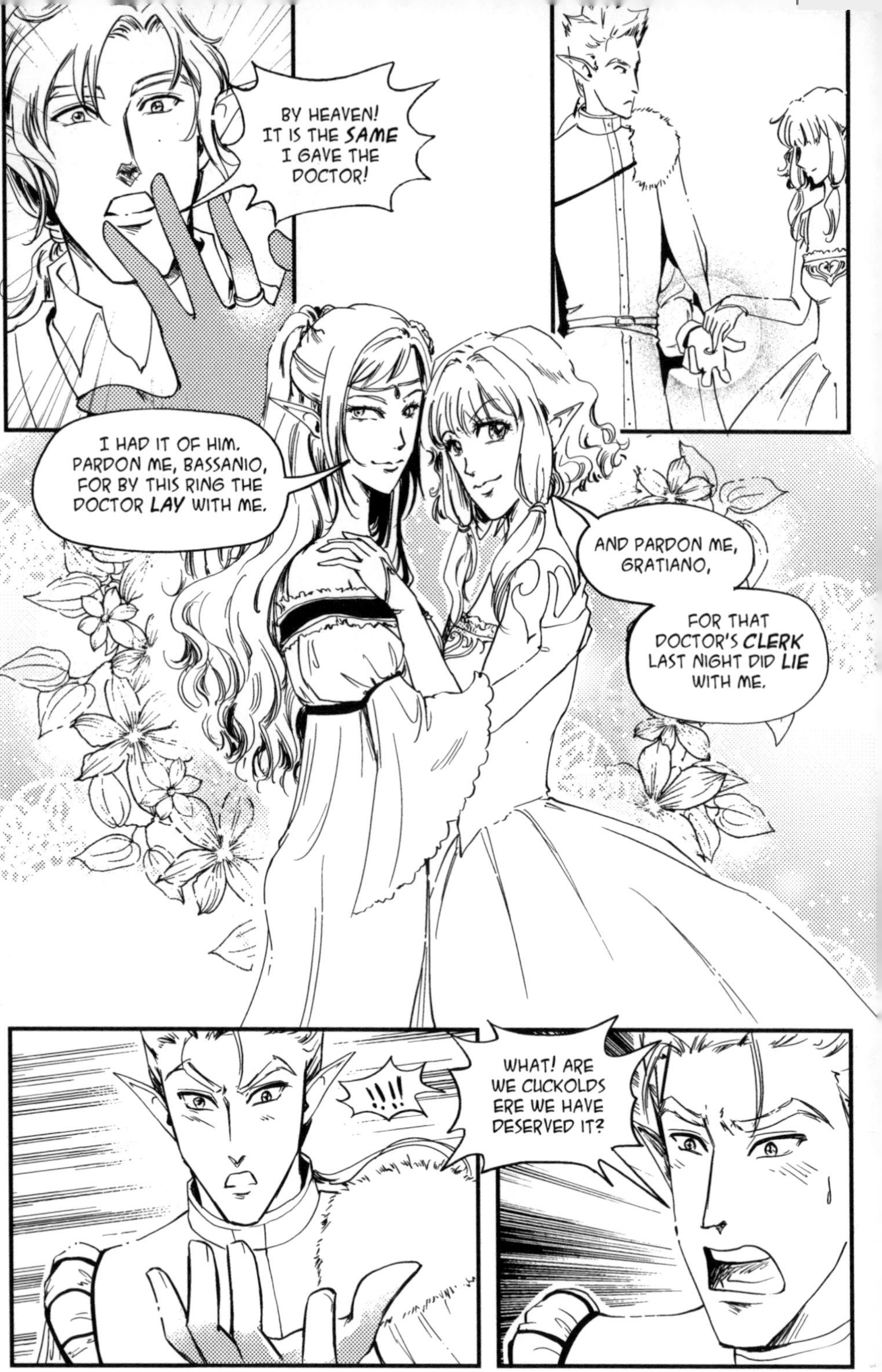
BY HEAVEN! IT IS THE SAME I GAVE THE DOCTOR!
I HAD IT OF HIM. PARDON ME, BASSANIO, FOR BY THIS RING THE DOCTOR LAY WITH ME.
AND PARDON ME, GRATIANO,
FOR THAT DOCTOR'S CLERK LAST NIGHT DID LIE WITH ME.
!!!!
WHAT! ARE WE CUCKOLDS ERE WE HAVE DESERVED IT?

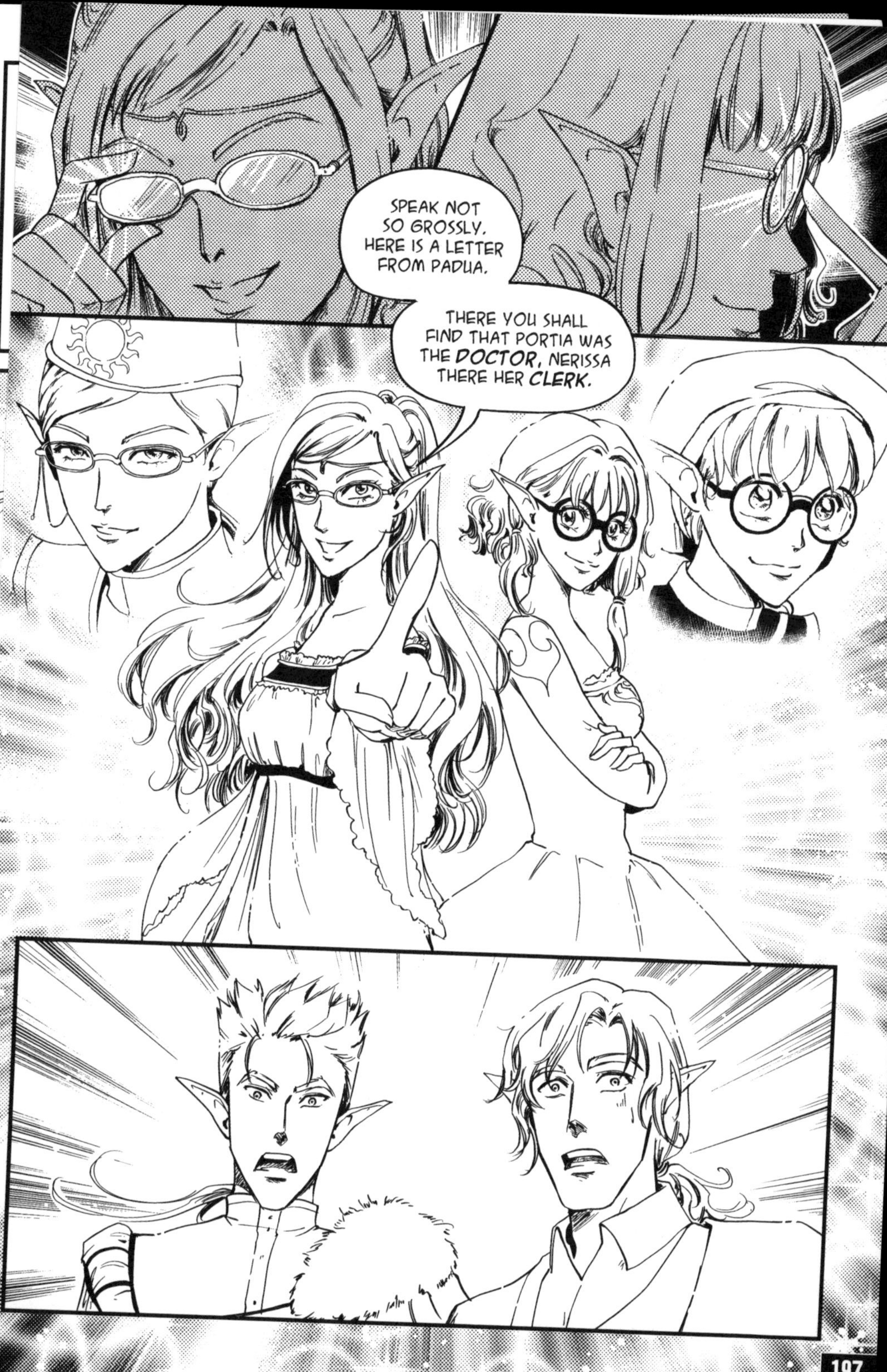
SPEAK NOT SO GROSSLY. HERE IS A LETTER FROM PADUA.
THERE YOU SHALL FIND THAT PORTIA WAS THE **DOCTOR**, NERISSA THERE HER **CLERK**.

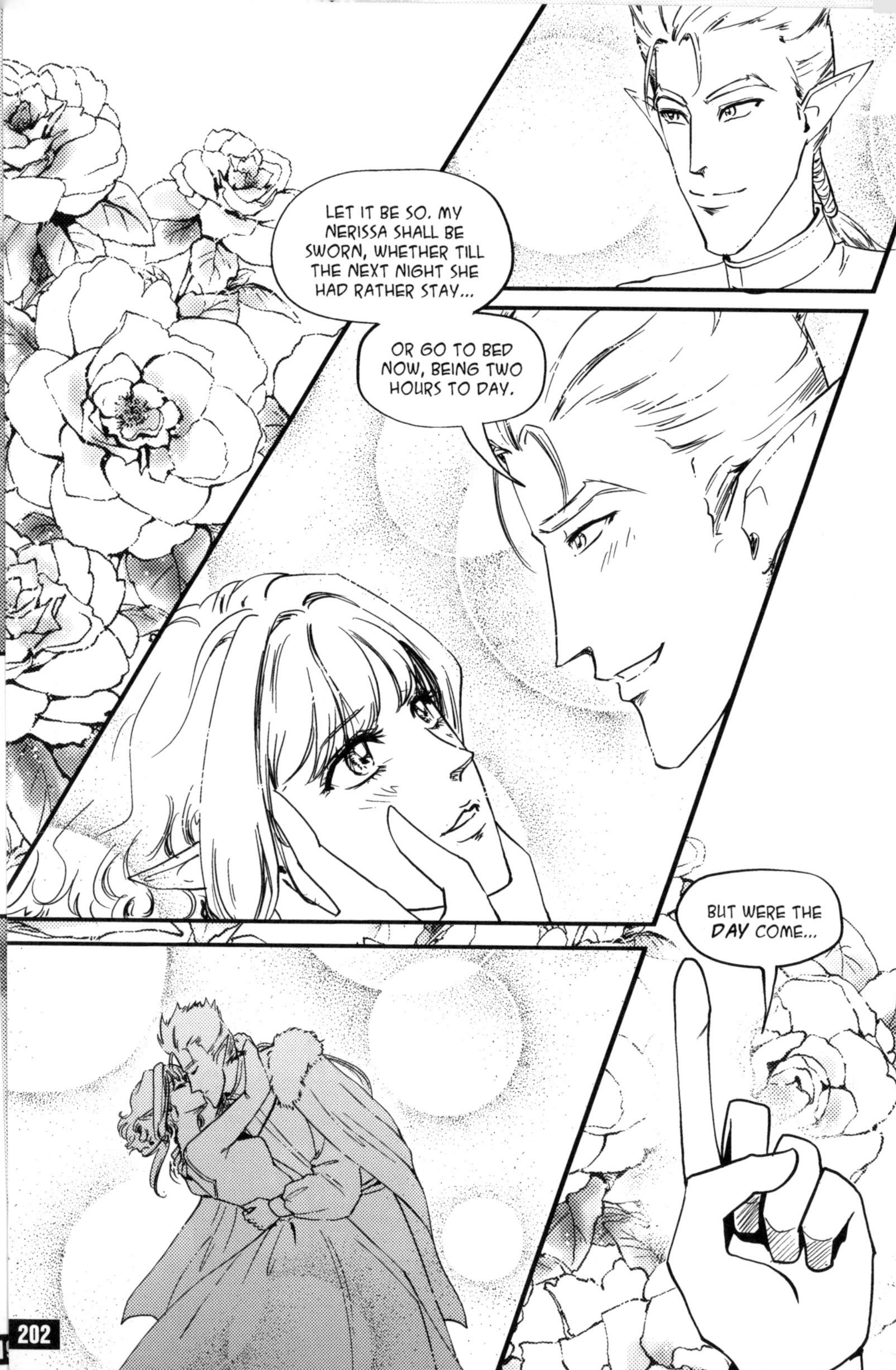
LET IT BE SO. MY NERISSA SHALL BE SWORN, WHETHER TILL THE NEXT NIGHT SHE HAD RATHER STAY...
OR GO TO BED NOW, BEING TWO HOURS TO DAY.
BUT WERE THE DAY COME...

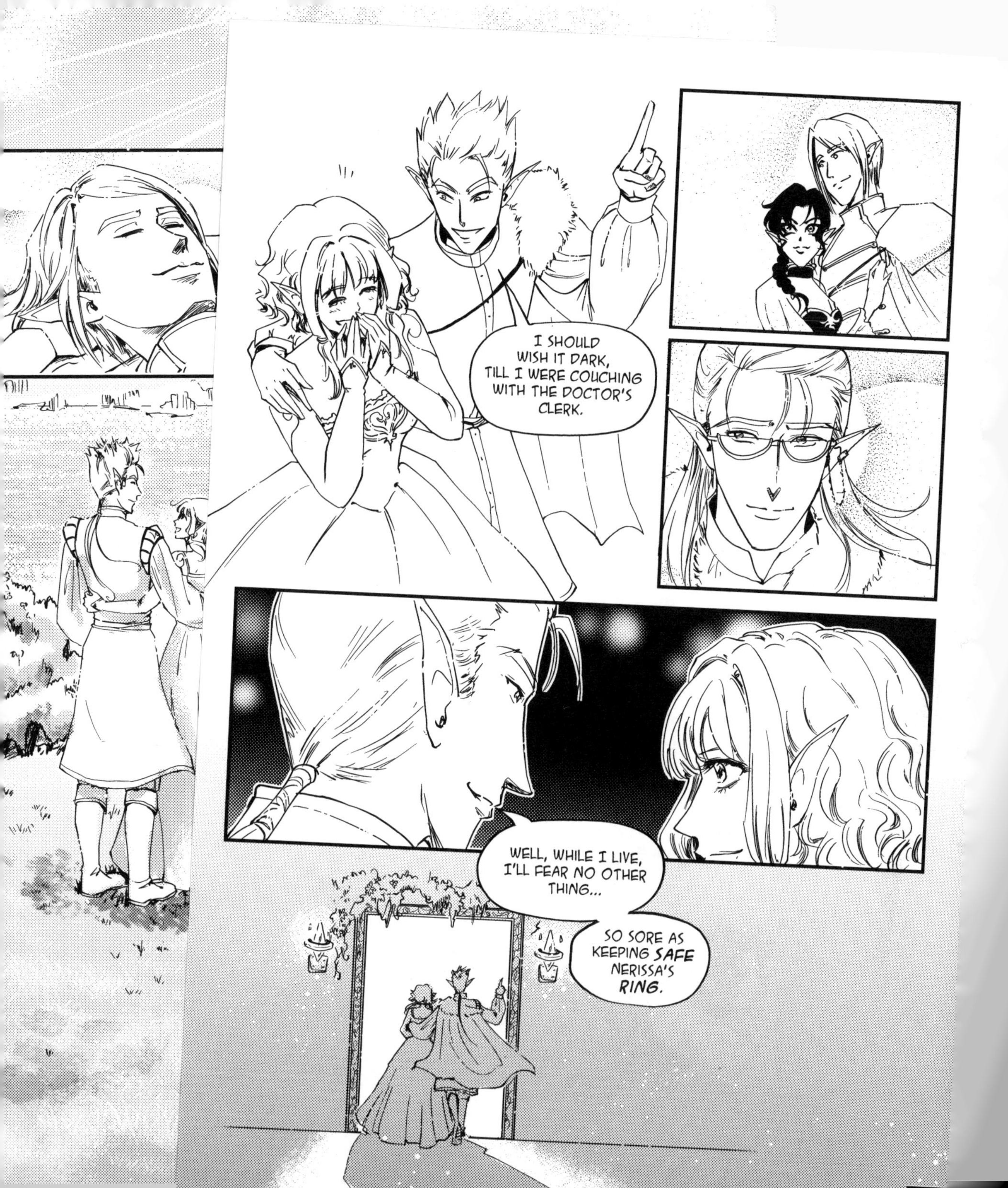
I SHOULD WISH IT DARK, TILL I WERE COUCHING WITH THE DOCTOR'S CLERK.
WELL, WHILE I LIVE, I'LL FEAR NO OTHER THING...
SO SORE AS KEEPING **SAFE** NERISSA'S **RING.**

PLOT SUMMARY OF THE MERCHANT OF VENICE

Bassanio, a virtuous but spendthrift gentleman of Venice, seeks to woo and marry Portia, a rich heiress living in nearby Belmont. But he needs money in order to compete with his rival suitors, and approaches his close friend, the merchant Antonio, for a loan. Since all his own wealth is tied up in a large cargo of goods at sea, expected home soon, Antonio agrees to borrow the sum himself from the Jewish moneylender Shylock. Resentful of the prejudice he has previously endured, Shylock nevertheless agrees to lend Antonio the money on the frivolous condition that if Antonio fails to pay it back after three months, he must permit Shylock to cut a pound of flesh from his body. Antonio signs a bond to that effect, and the deal is settled.

The terms of Portia's marriage have been determined by her late father's will: each of her suitors must choose between three symbolic caskets (made of gold, silver, and lead) — on pain of remaining single ever afterwards if they make the wrong choice, and this has deterred a series of worthless chancers, as Portia's maidservant Nerissa reminds her. To their relief, when the Prince of Morocco, and later the Prince of Aragon, take the test, they both fail, each rejecting the leaden casket in favour of, respectively, the showier gold and silver ones.

Meanwhile, Shylock's clownish servant Launcelot Gobbo has deserted his master to work instead for Bassanio; and Shylock's daughter Jessica, assisted by Bassanio and Gratiano before their departure for Belmont, successfully elopes with their friend Lorenzo during the Venice Carnival, along with a stolen casket of her father's gold and jewels. Shylock rails against his misfortune — but then news comes that all Antonio's ships have been lost at sea. Shylock vows to collect his pound of flesh in revenge.

News of Antonio's imprisonment reaches Belmont in the jubilant aftermath of Bassanio's successful choice of the lead casket, much to the relief of Portia (who has fallen in love with him) — and to Nerissa, who has fallen in love with Gratiano. The couples are betrothed, and both men sworn to wear their fiancées' rings forever. Bassanio and Gratiano hurry back to Venice — closely followed by Portia and Nerissa. Entrusting her home to the newly-arrived Lorenzo and Jessica, Portia disguises herself as a male lawyer from Padua (with Nerissa as her clerk), and appears for the defence at Antonio's trial. But what can Portia possibly say against the terms of Shylock's legally binding "pound of flesh"? And what can Bassanio say when the triumphant lawyer asks nothing for payment — except his engagement ring?

A BRIEF LIFE OF WILLIAM SHAKESPEARE

Shakespeare's birthday is traditionally said to be the 23rd of April – St George's Day, patron saint of England. A good start for England's greatest writer. But that date and even his name are uncertain. He signed his own name in different ways. "Shakespeare" is now the accepted one out of dozens of different versions.

He was born at Stratford-upon-Avon in 1564, and baptized on 26th April. His mother, Mary Arden, was the daughter of a prosperous farmer. His father, John Shakespeare, a glove-maker, was a respected civic figure – and probably also a Catholic. In 1570, just as Will began school, his father was accused of illegal dealings. The family fell into debt and disrepute.

Will attended a local school for eight years. He did not go to university. The next ten years are a blank filled by suppositions. Was he briefly a Latin teacher, a soldier, a sea-faring explorer? Was he prosecuted and whipped for poaching deer?

We do know that in 1582 he married Anne Hathaway, eight years his senior, and three months pregnant. Two more children – twins – were born three years later but, by around 1590, Will had left Stratford to pursue a theatre career in London. Shakespeare's apprenticeship began as an actor and "pen for hire".

He learned his craft the hard way. He soon won fame as a playwright with often-staged popular hits.

He and his colleagues formed a stage company, the Lord Chamberlain's Men, which built the famous Globe Theatre. It opened in 1599 but was destroyed by fire in 1613 during a performance of *Henry VIII* which used gunpowder special effects. It was rebuilt in brick the following year.

Shakespeare was a financially successful writer who invested his money wisely in property. In 1597, he bought an enormous house in Stratford, and in 1608 became a shareholder in London's Blackfriars Theatre. He also redeemed the family's honour by acquiring a personal coat of arms.

Shakespeare wrote over 40 works, including poems, "lost" plays and collaborations, in a career spanning nearly 25 years. He retired to Stratford in 1613, where he died on 23rd April 1616, aged 52, apparently of a fever after a "merry meeting" of drinks with friends. Shakespeare did in fact die on St George's Day! He was buried "full 17 foot deep" in Holy Trinity Church, Stratford, and left an epitaph cursing anyone who dared disturb his bones.

There have been preposterous theories disputing Shakespeare's authorship. Some claim that Sir Francis Bacon (1561–1626), philosopher and Lord Chancellor, was the real author of Shakespeare's plays. Others propose Edward de Vere, Earl of Oxford (1550–1604), or, even more weirdly, Queen Elizabeth I. The implication is that the "real" Shakespeare had to be a university graduate or an aristocrat. Nothing less would do for the world's greatest writer.

Shakespeare is mysteriously hidden behind his work. His life will not tell us what inspired his genius.

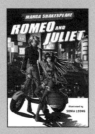